THE WITCHBOX

SANDRA RAMSEY

SANDRA RAMSEY

Paranormal Romance & Romantic Suspense

First edition. March 2023.
Copyright © 2023 Sandra Ramsey.
All rights reserved.
ISBN: 979-8-9874293-0-3
ISBN: 979-8-9874293-1-0

Developmental edit by:
athenacullenreads@gmail.com
Edited by:
emilynemchickediting.org
Cover design by Emcat Designs at:
https://www.facebook.com/EmCatDesigns

ACKNOWLEDGMENTS

With the completion my first novel, I have double digits of people to thank. To name them all would entail a novel in itself. The list begins with English teacher extraordinaire Traci Wiley, who told me to shut up and write. So, I joined Shut up and Write and the Central Pennsylvania Writers Workshop. Through their support and my misplaced commas, I managed to finish *The Witchbox*.

Equal in importance, my West Coast compadre Lauren (EL Roux, Author) who asked her husband dirty questions for me and made me change so many POV's. Love you. Not to leave out other important people, Don, Bobby, Mary (Elizabeth Reign, Author), Sarah, and my supportive family and friends. I wouldn't have done it without any of you.

CHAPTER 1

Cold Springs, PA 1742

Kenter Dewlight, High Priest of the MichAudha, rejoiced as the fingers of flame reached around the sides of the large iron cauldron and Verne dropped the Three Sisters into the vessel. She provided the seeds of corn, squash, and beans as a tribute to the Grand Master and payment for their use of magick. The offering swirled in the thick brew until the vortex pulled it into the hot, steamy depths.

Tonight marked the start of Ostara, the spring celebration. A time when day and night become equal and the light gains strength with the rising sun. In the new wild land of Pennsylvania, Kenter prayed the vision quest would project a prosperous future for their coven.

"I see many children sitting in learning circles, gaining skills in magick casting," Verne said. Her alto voice rose above the crackles of the fire. "We will have many years of fruitful harvests and joyous celebrations. A child is marked as our future leader and sees with your lavender eyes, High Priest."

Kenter contemplated the seer's words as she tossed valerian, mugwort, and dried lavender into the fire. The herbs ignited on contact and produced intense, bright flames. The tendrils of heat reached along the sides of the cauldron from the hickory-fueled fire. Burning embers escaped and snuffed out on the cool ground, returning the energy of the fire to the earth.

"Splendid work, seer," Kenter said. "I will impress upon the coven your success."

Verne pointed at the cauldron. "Stay yourself, High Priest. Our coire changes its vision."

Kenter considered the brew's behavior. Large bubbles broke on the surface, distorting the pictures and sending hot splatters across the altar. The evicted mixture released tendrils of steam into the cool spring air.

"I see a second future, but tis unfocused," Verne said.

"A second?" Kenter asked. He leaned over the cauldron. "In all my years, I have never seen a second version in the same vision quest."

Kenter closed his eyes and raised his hands. He whispered ancient Gaelic prayers in cadence with Verne. Their baritone murmur soothed the brew, and the surface melted smooth.

Darker images, frightening and violent, appeared. Metal wagons shaped like birds carrying people in the air, burning witches, and dying forests flashed from rim to rim across the vessel. A visage resembling Kenter fell to the ground. A final image flashed in the dying embers of the fire. It showed the cauldron broken and hard times for the MichAudha.

"Which vision shows the truth?" Verne asked.

"I think both. One for the near future and the other distant." Kenter pulled his priest's robe tighter around his shoulders. The thought of two futures troubled him. It could mean one small decision would change the future.

"We will perish if we lose the cauldron," Verne said. "Our coven will fracture over every decision made."

"Take care in making rash judgments, seer. It took much discussion and effort to convince the coven to move here. We dare not give them a reason to leave."

"You have great wisdom, High Priest. Tis why I see and you interpret." Verne pulled her shawl tighter.

"Before you leave, the vision showed a man with long black hair kneeling on the ground. Was it my son or myself?" Kenter asked. His fingers worried along the hem of his sleeve. "The Grand Master chose Gryphon. If something happens to him—"

"I must think about what I saw before giving you an answer. One should not know of their own death," Verne said.

"I will find a way to protect the boy after I pass. He is a seventh son on both sides, mine and Willa's," Kenter said.

"You fear someone in the coven means the young lad harm?" Verne asked. She placed a comforting hand on his arm. "All fawn over the boy. Who would dare?"

"You may have a different interpretation. I will join you later for our discussion of the visions and make plans for the future. And, Verne," Kenter paused to make sure she was listening, "I wish to discuss selecting a High Priestess as well."

"As you wish, High Priest." Verne waved her hand and using their magical method of travel, whisked away.

Kenter circled the sacred vessel. The High Altar crowned the summit of Sharp Mountain, overlooking the small town of Cold Springs. The spring breeze carried the sweet scent of honey locust and maple flowers as a raven chased the sun over the ridge. He filled his lungs with the deep woodsy scent of the hemlocks and expelled his stress with the air.

Ben, his familiar, padded across the altar stone with his tail flicking side to side in a casual rhythm. He came to rest by Kenter's foot and rubbed his cheek on the boot.

Kenter gazed at the black cat perched on his worn leather shoe. "Do you suppose we remain safe here in Penn's Woods? The vision showed much turmoil."

"One can hope," Ben said. "I would dislike escaping another set of witch hunts as we did back in Salem. It has been two hundred years and yet we still fear another set of trials."

"Are you daft? I would not wish witch trials here." Kenter

stepped back. The abrupt move dislodged the cat. "The vision did not suggest such horror."

"I said we would not want Salem to happen again." Ben stressed the word "not" as he jumped on top of a boulder to put him at eye level with Kenter. Blinking in slow motion, the cat's black eyelids revealed large green eyes. *The Moravians do not care for our activities at night. Their religious zeal could end us. We need to be cautious."*

"I agree. Their attention worries me. But what of our vision tonight? There were two versions, one of light, one of dark. Metal boxes that fly, buggies without horses…" Kenter's voice grew louder, his anxiety showing in the wrinkles streaking outward from each eye. "The bishop would condemn us."

"We should expect change in this new land, but it doesn't mean our destruction."

"You give wise counsel."

A little Towhee landed on a thin branch, distracting both of them. Kenter chuckled as Ben became enthralled with the fluttering wings.

"Take care, Ben. Willa would not want her familiar harmed."

"Willa's familiar can take care of herself. She sings of your favorite witch's arrival. I take my leave." The cat's focus never left the bird. Flicking his tail, he whisked away.

Kenter smiled as a blessed feeling of warmth enveloped him from behind. He sank into the feel of her arms as they reached around his broad chest. The weight of her head, prone against his back, afforded him comfort.

"Good morn, Willa."

"How do ye, High Priest Kenter. Were you discussing your vision with Ben again? I would think Verne becomes jealous of him." Willa circled to his front, keeping her hand against his torso. Her eyelids lowered to her smile.

Kenter lifted a strand of the long black hair draped over her shoulders. He rubbed the strands between his fingers and lifted it to sniff her fragrance. Notes of mint and sassafras drew into his mind. His heart thumped a double beat in the excitement of her presence.

"Willa, last night's preparations were perfect, as always. The hickory you added caused the fire to burn bright and hot. I saw into the future. It included your son." He stroked the back of her hand with his thumb. Her skin was so soft, he became distracted from their conversation.

"What of our son?" Willa stepped back to hear the news without distraction.

Kenter imparted a gentle kiss on the back of her hand. "You need not worry about Gryphon this day. Where does he play this morn?"

"Gryphon's at the creek to catch frogs. I believe he wishes to avoid Megaera Caroline and practice transformations for the promotion ceremony tonight. If a frog enters your lodge, tis I."

Her symphonic giggle pleasured his ears with ticklish vibrations.

"The boy accomplishes much for eight years, but his magick needs more discipline. I hope he leaves the coven elders intact," Kenter said.

They both chuckled as Willa looked to the other side of the Stony Creek. She pointed.

"There. On the far side of the valley you can spot Luna," Willa said. "Our son is never far from the beast. I worry her color draws too much attention. Worse yet, her paws track dirt into my cabin daily. Cats and birds are the preferred familiars. You should have counseled him better."

"I do agree. Luna's white coat makes spotting her easy even from this distance. Yet I do not influence familiars. They choose companions on their own. I never understood why some witches have them and others do not."

"I somehow thought you would know all, High Priest."

"Willa, you tease." Kenter stroked her cheek and brushed a kiss across her lips. "Why does Gryphon avoid the Caroline girl? I would think her a proper match for him. The family line needs more Fire Witches."

"Ever since Gryphon saved Megaera from drowning last summer, she won't leave him alone. And she practices only fire magick. Verne said the girl does not practice water skills. What kind of magick caster hates water? She is not a good match for our next High Priest."

"Or your new daughter." Kenter chuckled.

"I fear Megaera is an imp foundling. You know how nasty they become." Willa's voice became a whisper. "At least Gryphon seems wise enough to avoid her."

"You know imps do not live in our new world. I have never seen one here," Kenter said. He shook his head back and forth. He offered his hand. "Shall we walk?"

Willa took his offering, and they started down the trail. "Forget the imps. Megaera has all of Joan Caroline's undesirable traits, including her taste in the company she keeps."

"Now the truth will out." Kenter circled in front to stop Willa's next step. "I will not tolerate a battle between my Third Level witches nor the different sects of our coven. Not all witches can cast fire, and even fewer can cast all of the elements. Their dark magick aside, even warlocks lend a balance. My brother Wilmott is no threat, and Joan enjoys his company. Why do you wish otherwise?"

"I cast fire. You make as if I cannot." Willa crossed her arms, removing her hand from his grip.

Kenter lifted an eyebrow. With the inhale of a deep breath, he blew it out in a slow, deliberate manner. "I think the coven gains strength with both of you as Third Levels. Now I tire of this circular discussion. What plans do you have for such a spectacular morning?"

"I thought to visit the bower." Willa pointed at a copse of large hemlocks below the altar. "Perhaps I should rethink my decision."

Kenter lifted his hand and waited for her to take it. "I would prefer if you did not."

She paused.

He was thrilled when she took his hand. Inside the bower they found a familiar bed of soft moss and leaves. The branches of the old hemlock swung down like a pendulum and formed a curtain of privacy.

* * *

"Luna, over here, before she finds us." Gryphon ducked behind a boulder and called to the familiar. "Why does Megaera pester me?"

"You should have let her drown. She's a menace," Luna said.

"I thought she would stay away if we remained by the creek," Gryphon said. "I have no time for girls today. I must practice my magick before the coven meeting tonight."

"The elders seldom promote someone your age to First Level. Most remain neophytes for their first fifty years. But tell me, what will you turn your frog into?"

"I wish it to become a flying squirrel and leap into the trees." Gryphon's exuberance uncontained, a tendril of wind magick escaped his control. A pile of leaves tumbled along the ground. He frowned as they settled and returned the leftover wind energy to the soil.

"Spare me young witches." Luna gazed at the sky, pleading to the Grand Master. Turning her attention back to her boy, she said, *"Keep the frog on the level at which it lives in the earth. Water creature to water creature."*

"You give wise counsel." Gryphon stood from the hiding position and searched the forest in all directions. "I think we lost her."

"Ignore the girl. For tonight, young Wiseman, decide what you will demonstrate."

"Water to water?" Gryphon tapped his chin in hard

thought. He raised a finger and smiled. "I will turn a crayfish into a frog. I bet such a feat will impress the elders."

"I suggest you practice with your mother. I for one do not feel like hopping this night." Luna whisked away.

Harrisburg, PA 2019

Emmeline clicked print. She pulled the last page from the printer and tossed it on the pile with the others. The clock hit midnight as she headed for the kitchen. She leaned over and scratched Luna's head.

"Go pee so we can hit the sheets. It's past my bedtime." The flaps on the doggie door swooshed back and forth as she stretched her arms and arched her back to work out the kinks in her neck.

Emmeline glanced at the top page still in her hand. She pulled out Luna's bedtime treat as the flaps let both the dog and cold air in. With her eyes still focused on the top page, her hand lowered out of habit, and the treat disappeared. She wiped her palm on her sweats to remove the dog slime and looked at Luna.

"What the heck is this? I didn't print a poem." Emmeline held it up for the dog to see. Luna pawed her leg and gave a strangled yip. "Okay, I'll read it."

"Awake the druid. A Key lost in time. Release the magick for her to find. Words once read, release the power upon arrival of the Witching Hour." She glanced at the dog and raised an eyebrow. "Someone had trouble with their rhyme scheme."

Emmeline shivered and pulled the kitchen door closed. "Damn. It feels like the doggie door is stuck open again." Ignoring the chill, she complained, "This thing hurts my brain. Do I have to finish it?"

Luna nudged her again. "Alright. Uh, um. Seventh daughter and Seventh son, Grand Master's plan to be done."

Luna pranced around in a circle, whined, and pawed at Emmeline's leg.

"How does anyone decipher these obnoxious rhymes? The damn sonnet goes on for another four or five stanzas. I refuse to read any more."

Emmeline tossed back the last swallow of the bourbon, set the glass in the sink, and deposited the letterboxing clues on the table by her daypack. She frowned at the stack of student laboratory reports pushed up against the wall. Another set sat in the living room on the ottoman. "I'll grade all of them tomorrow night."

Luna stood next to her, head up. "If only you could talk."

Emmeline burrowed under the covers and slept in peace until the dreams started. She tossed and turned while dreaming about buildings that rose from the earth under a red moon. The deserted structures surrounded by empty streets absorbed falling words on sticky notes that lost their grip on a wall. Witch, key, seventh, and magick trickled into an old church with its bell tower alit with flame.

A gorgeous male figure appeared with Luna sitting at his feet. His broad shoulders, an eight pack, and sexy love handles made of muscle accentuated a perfect physique. The man wavered in and out of focus. She held her breath, identifying lavender eyes, long black hair, and an attentive penis that reached toward his winking belly button.

Emmeline moaned. His passion filled all her physical needs. Thrashing under the covers, she kicked her feet and arched her back under his touch. Each point of contact burned her with pleasure. He pulled them together, pressing slow, seductive kisses along her neck while he sought a home for his cock.

The moment he entered her, Principal Caroline and Marie Alley stepped into view and pointed their fingers. The principal's mouth formed silent words Emmeline couldn't hear.

"No." Emmeline kicked her feet again. A loud thump broke

through the haze of Emmeline's dream turned nightmare. She sat up, gasped for breath, and fought with the sheets tangled around her legs.

"Of all of the—" Luna popped up from the floor, her head the only part visible at the end of the bed. *"You kicked me off the bed, you insolent witch."*

Emmeline sucked in huge breaths, clasping the blankets in her fisted hands. She glanced at the alarm. The eerie green glow revealed the time as 3 AM. She fell back onto the mattress and tried to slow her throbbing libido. She licked her lips and swallowed.

She tossed the soaking pajamas on the floor and pulled the covers over her shoulders. Emmeline patted the bed and encouraged Luna to return. "Talk about a wet dream. Damn."

"You need to get laid," Luna said.

Emmeline curled up around her boyfriend pillow. The mattress dipped with Luna's weight as she completed her routine. She always walked in three circles before settling. She asked, "Why do dogs do that?"

"Three is important to all witches. You will learn."

Emmeline fell back into a restless sleep and awoke to the smell of a dark roast. Her eyes popped open. "Thank God for automatic coffee makers."

Throwing on jeans, a t-shirt, and hiking boots, she brushed her hair and teeth. The first cup of the day was so damn good, someone should figure out how to bottle the feeling. This particular bag was a gift from her neighbor, Edemay. Something in the brew settled her nerves and created an invincible feeling of power. The old lady said it was her imagination.

While she ate her yogurt and sipped the coffee, Emmeline read the clues for each letterbox identified for the day. The poem lay on top of the pile. She sneered at the two-page poem and stuck it at the back of the pile. The activity of letterboxing, similar to geocaching, required an analytical mind. But unlike caching, it allowed for creativity, and the answers were easier to find.

Luna sat at her feet, tail thumping on the floor. Her tongue hung out as she panted with contained excitement.

"Let's go. I want to find my boy today."

Emmeline stilled, the spoon halfway in her mouth. Her eyes widened. "Did you—"

"I did." Luna sat up and tilted her head. *"You released some of your magick last night reading the poem. Now you can hear me. I expect we're finished with the baby talk."*

Rising so quickly the chair fell over, Emmeline stared at her dog. "It's official. The kids have driven me insane. I knew I shouldn't have eaten those brownies in the teachers' lounge. I bet some kid doped it with something."

"You're not stoned or psychotic. You're a witch," Luna said. *"An ancient druid capable of immense magick. Today you'll find my boy and release him from the Witchbox."*

"I need a drink." Emmeline reached for the bottle of Jack.

"Emmeline. It's eight in the morning. You had too much last night. Put on your big girl panties and let's go."

Emmeline flipped her gaze back and forth between the bottle and the dog. She took a deep, reinforcing breath and made a decision. "I must have consumed more bourbon than I thought last night. I'll ignore the voice, breathe in a calm pattern, and leave the bourbon alone."

She tossed the yogurt container in the trash and headed out the door with her daypack over her shoulder. Once in the truck, Emmeline shifted into gear and drove. Luna sat on the passenger seat, looking out the side window. She rolled it down for Luna so she didn't get carsick.

"I'm glad we learned letterboxing in Dog Scouts." Emmeline's mood improved when her one-sided discussion did not meet with any canine verbiage. "I brought one box for planting today, but it needs a special place. The stamp sucks. I should make a new one, but I didn't have time. Damn formal lab reports suck hours from my life."

"You bitch about grading them all the time. Why assign them if you hate them so much?" Luna said. *"And I didn't think your stamp ugly. Your skill in carving glyphs of me improves."*

Emmeline's fingers tightened on the steering wheel, knuckles going white. Allowing her thoughts to drift in the direction of carving the stamps, she distracted herself from the talking dog issue. Maybe she'd had a stroke.

Emmeline took a deep, fortifying breath, and her fingers relaxed around the wheel. "One of the box clues today was written as a poem. You know I can't figure those out. We'll give it a go, but I'm not spending all day on it."

She blew out a breath when the truck hit the small frost cracks in the pavement. *Thump, ka-thump, ka-thump.* "Pennsylvania roads suck."

"This truck is a piece of junk. Why did you let Brad talk you into buying it?"

Still ignoring the dog's voice, Emmeline continued talking.

"Stress usually makes me dream about running Dr. Caroline over with a bus and perhaps taking Marie Alley with her, the little snitch. But last night, I got something better—well, almost." She glanced at Luna, now laying across the bench seat, her warm furry head against Emmeline's thigh. "I dreamed of a sexy guy with long black hair and lavender eyes. Who has lavender eyes?"

"Gryphon."

Emmeline blew out a deep breath. "I have gone insane. Wait. Oh my God. I imagined him naked!" She gripped the wheel, and the color faded from her knuckles again. "You were right. I need to get laid."

"Who's naked? Dr. Caroline? Horror for sure." Luna perked her ears.

"God, no. Not Dr. Caroline. The hunk in my dreams. He had a huge—" Emmeline hesitated. She was having a conversation with her dog. In the big scheme of things, who would she tell? Chuckling, she revealed the rest of the dream. "He took me in an old church. My every need was fulfilled until Caroline, the old bitch, showed up."

Luna put her head on Emmeline's arm. *"Why did you kick me off the bed?"*

"I think I had an orgasm."

"Gryphon has that effect on women. I do hope you're not disappointed in reality."

Emmeline entered Ft. Indiantown Gap and slowed. The speed limit dropped to twenty-five in the military zone. Brad's absence didn't bother her as much as it should. Finding and adopting Luna had filled her days after the breakup. Emmeline only spared Brad a passing thought when something broke on the truck. He'd never filled her heart. But last night—

Luna pushed her nose under Emmeline's arm. *"By the way, sex relieves stress."*

"Leave me alone. I'm driving." Shaking both hands in the air and flicking off the strange vibes, Emmeline grabbed the steering wheel again before the truck drifted off the highway. "I mean, I see auras. Why not a talking dog?"

She turned on the first gravel road past the decommissioned tanks. Emmeline's thoughts drifted back to her tragic childhood. When she was only two, her parents died in a car accident, and she ended up in foster care. Her life sucked once she was in the system.

Emmeline seldom got a home visit with potential adopters after she told them what color auras circled their heads. Once she was old enough, she educated herself on the meaning of each color and wanted parents with purple auras. They thought her a bit peculiar. She spent the rest of her time in group homes with all the other children no one wanted.

Now she uses the knowledge to ward herself from untrustworthy people. To this day, her gut instinct always matched their aura.

Luna leaned forward and licked Emmeline's cheek, breaking her trip down memory lane.

"Yuck. What did you eat today? Doggie toothbrushing for you tonight." Tapping the steering wheel, she switched on the radio. Perhaps she was deflecting. A talking dog, sexy hot dreams where her boss popped in—it was all too much. She rolled down the window, hoping the crisp fall air would clear her head and dry the tear forming in the corner of her eye.

She sang along with the music filling the cab. "John Cougar, John Deere, John 3:16, la la la. Gotta love some Urban, right, girl?" Emmeline ruffled the dog's fur while bouncing her head and shoulders in tandem with the music.

"Still deflecting. And please, no more singing. It hurts my ears."

"Not only do I imagine my dog talking, but she insults me as well. Are you sure you're not related to Dr. Caroline?"

"We've a long day ahead, I fear."

The truck tires crunched along the old gravel road. Cold Springs lay on the mountain behind the missile range for Fort Indiantown Gap. Emmeline downshifted and pulled the '54 Chevy 3100 into a shady spot.

"The weather should stay in the '60s all day, so no sweating." Emmeline shivered at the thought of exercise. "Should I carry today?"

"You won't need your pistol. My boy will protect you." Luna growled at the squirrel on a fencepost. Her tail wagged, and the bark demonstrated her excitement for the day.

"Now you're acting like a dog."

"I do so love a squirrel chase," Luna barked and pawed the window.

Emmeline's smile faded into a frown.

CHAPTER 2

Cold Springs, PA 1742

Eight-year-old Megaera Caroline pulled back the willow and pushed through a thicket of raspberry bushes. Unable to find Gryphon, she climbed toward the High Altar for a better view of the valley. Hushed voices from the bower drew her off the trail. A couple lay on a black robe, naked and entwined.

Megaera slapped a hand over her mouth to prevent an audible gasp. She whispered to herself, "Willa tries to gain his favor. I must tell Mother."

As she headed toward her cabin, a black cat stepped out of the undergrowth and hissed. Megaera lost her balance and fell to the ground. She threw a flame from her index finger, but it lost form and fell to the ground. Small tendrils of smoke rose from the dried pine needles and snuffed out.

"Well done, neophyte." Ben's tail flicked back and forth in quick motion. *"Do you present this trick for the coven tonight? I do not think they will promote you with a weak flame."*

"I am not a neophyte. You are a worthless bag of bones." Heat warmed her neck and cheeks in her embarrassment. "I will place your black corpse in an eagle's nest with your entrails lying about for the chicks to pick at."

"As if you have the power." Ben lifted and licked a paw. He twitched his tail and whisked away.

"Someday I will have my revenge."

Megaera got to her feet, and with heavy steps against the packed earth of the trail, she made her way to the Caroline cabin. Goosebumps along her arms warned of a darkness nearby. The forest grew silent when a caped figure stepped out, blocking the path. With lifted chin, Megaera stared at the imposing figure.

"What do you want, Warlock?"

"What troubles you this day, young Caroline?" Wilmott asked.

"Nothing of your concern. Be gone." Megaera pushed by and kept her eyes to her feet, unwilling to meet his gaze. "I am plagued by familiars and warlocks of no use to me. What else could go wrong today?"

His deep chuckle accompanied her as she plodded toward the cabin.

"Mother," Megaera shouted, walking into the backyard. "You will not believe what has plagued me this day."

The brush of fire magick blew across Megaera's cheek. She swallowed. Joan Caroline's irritation was evident from her mother's pinched lips and the force with which she shoved the pins over the clothes and line.

"Where did you go? Hanging the laundry fell to you this morn," Joan said.

"I have to tell you what I saw up by the High Altar," Megaera said. She reached for a twisted bundle, shook it out, and pinned it to the line.

"I suspect you saw Kenter talking to Ben," Joan said. "Last night's vision quest and preparations for the celebration tonight will keep the High Priest busy all day. As his Third Level, I too have duties that I should be doing. Yet here I stand completing yours."

"I saw Willa and the High Priest under the hemlock

bower," Megaera said. She shivered at her excitement and disgust. "They were rutting like pigs."

Joan placed her hands on her hips. "Why would you stop to watch? Have you lost all manners?"

"Willa does not deserve to become High Priestess. To join with the High Priest outside of a ceremony." Megaera reached for another piece of clothing. "Time has come for you to become the High Priestess, Mother."

"You try to reason beyond your years. Do we need to have another discussion?" Joan pinned a shirt to the line by its shoulders. "Have you practiced your magick for the promotion ceremony? Do you have the Three Sisters ready?"

Megaera held her breath, tired of her mother's nagging. Nothing she ever did was good enough for Joan. "They plot against you. Open your eyes."

"Kenter works hard to maintain balance." Joan handed her daughter a clothespin. "We should acknowledge our he remains strong for all of us and not worry with whom he trysts."

"It is time a Fire Witch took charge of the coven." Megaera grabbed more clothing, still twisted from wringing. She shook the fabric, and her ceremonial dress unfolded. "Every time we have a coven meeting, the old ones tell tales of the power available when we have both Priest and Priestess."

Megaera jabbed the clothespin onto the line so hard, it split in half. The dress fell to the ground.

"Take care, young witch, or you will rewash the lot," Joan said.

"I would use magick and redo them." Megaera crossed her arms in defiance.

"And what magick will you use? Fire will burn the clothing and you refuse to practice any other." Joan inhaled and shook her head. "And don't forget the teachings. Do not use magick to benefit yourself. The Returns of Three do not forgive, regardless of intent."

"I only need fire. Warlock Wilmott said his fire requires no offerings. I will make everyone else do my bidding when I am High Priestess."

Megaera stared at the line of dull, worn cotton dresses. Someday her clothing lines would hang colorful lace and pearl dresses with no patches or worn spots. Magick could bring wealth if cast in an acceptable manner.

Joan picked up the empty laundry basket. "I do not want you learning from Wilmott. You will not stir whispers of revolt within the coven. I forbid it."

"Mother," Megaera said.

"What now?"

"Did you fornicate with Kenter before my birth?"

Megaera noted a twinge of hesitation in her mother. Most witches in the coven never talked about who had sired their children, although most knew. Mothers tried to steer their children away from relations which would produce undesirable results. Did she have a blood connection with Kenter? If not, Gryphon seemed an excellent choice for her partner when the time came.

"I have never lain with Kenter." Joan walked with Megaera toward the house. "Does my answer meet with your wish?"

"Yes, Mother. I believe it did."

* * *

Verne pulled the door open to admit the High Priest into her cabin. Kenter's height prevented him from standing upright, and the dried herbs hanging from the ceiling dropped white and yellow petals on his head as he passed. She stifled a laugh and hid her amusement.

He sat on a bench before the fire and sneezed. "Why do you have ragweed, woman?"

"The keep is to my liking, High Priest." Verne poured a cup of tea for him. "I am anxious to discuss the vision. We should not tarry. I need to give the neophytes a lesson before the celebration."

"I have decided not to promote a High Priestess." Kenter held a hand in the air to stave off her response. "I have my reasons and will share them with you, but you alone."

"I will hear your reasons, but expect me to argue," Verne said.

"I would promote Willa, but the Fire Witches will take it as an insult and claim she has cast a spell on me. We do spend some time in the bower, as you may have heard."

"Witches know better than to judge who lies with whom. Your other choice, Joan Caroline, sleeps with a warlock. He made his deposit and left us with Megaera, the horrid child. I don't know what possessed Joan to take up with your brother."

Kenter's lips quirked.

"Wilmott comes and goes. I don't think he has a place in our discussion."

"Your brother's unfortunate practice of dark magick has bought him no good will within the coven. I could see the coven rejecting Joan based on her taste in pricks," Verne said.

"Shall I continue?" Kenter tapped the table with a finger.

"By all means, High Priest." Verne shook her head back and forth. "Tell me why the coven cannot have a High Priestess."

Kenter blew out a deep breath. "Aside from the Fire Witch issue, I cannot promote Willa. Her duties as High Priestess would take time away from Gryphon. The boy mastered the magick of wind and water at five and can perform some earth magick. But he lacks control with the earth and the ability to make fire."

"You deny the coven a High Priestess for the sake of the boy?" Verne shook her head. "The vision did not say he would perish."

"The boy will need his mother for training until he reaches Third Level. Willa wields the four powers. She needs to remain his teacher." Kenter rose and moved toward the door. "It is my decision."

"Third Level? It will take hundreds of years." Verne pulled open the door. A warm breeze blew into the opening. "The coven should not have to wait so long."

"I ask, did you see either Joan or Willa in the vision?" Kenter asked.

"I did not." Verne shrugged and took a fortifying breath. The vision held no image of the High Priest either. "What will the coven hear tonight?"

"The first one. I feel flying wagons would frighten them. My decision is final." Kenter whisked away.

Verne pursed her lips to consider his words. Was he making a mistake, putting Gryphon's needs above the coven? Did Kenter see something in the brew she did not?

The afternoon found Verne in a circle of neophytes. The whole lot of them could not sit still, regardless of their age. Standing, kneeling, or lying lazily against a tree, the neophytes ranged from toddler to fifty, although most were near or just past ten years. Gryphon had seen eight summers.

She paid particular attention to Gryphon this time. Until last night's quest, he was one of the many. Gryphon sat in the middle of his friends, although he was always the brighter star by his nature and not privilege. Sitting in front of the boys, the girls giggled and cast glances over their shoulders. Even at his young age, Gryphon drew others to him as spring apple blossoms drew bees.

The chatter filled her ears as she placed a bundle of herbs on a tanned deer hide and untied the string that held them together. Verne addressed the group. "Young witches. Still yourselves. The sooner we cover the purpose of these plants, the sooner you can return to your practice. How many of you will try for First Level this eve?"

Counting the hands waving, her heart skipped a beat. So many young ones eager to grow and advance in power within the coven. Most would try and fail. Some would cry, and others would put forth greater effort the next time.

"Let us begin." Verne reached for the first of the three plants and held up the stalk. "Who can tell me about this plant?"

"Corn." A red-haired girl no older than five shouted, "Everyone knows corn."

"Excellent." Verne heaped praise on the young witch. She held up a second plant laden with long green pods.

The boys were focused on some trinket, paying little attention to the lesson.

"Gryphon, do you know?" Verne asked.

"Huh?" His head popped up.

"What plant am I holding, young Wiseman."

"A bean stalk, and those long pods are beans," Gryphon said. "We all know your direction of thought. Tonight we celebrate the spring equinox. We will plant our fields with the blessing of the Grand Master and the fates. The men will plant their seeds so your lessons will continue to bore neophytes for years to come."

The children laughed.

Verne flashed a single narrowed eye at him, her "evil" eye. The glare gained the desired result, and the gathering quieted. Never having seen her own face, she couldn't begin to describe it. However, Gryphon didn't flinch. In fact, he stared back. Mayhap Kenter was right in his decision.

"You left out one important bit of information, young Wiseman," Verne said.

"I know, I know." A little brunette hopped up and down. She placed her hand on Gryphon's shoulder. "He didn't tell you why we study corn, beans, and squash. They represent the Three Sisters."

A blond girl with long braids along each side of her face added, "And you should always offer the Three Sisters when you cast big magick or magick that could benefit the caster."

"How do the Three Sisters work and exact revenge?" Verne asked.

"The essence of the seed returns spent energy to the earth so she may remain strong," the red-haired witch shouted.

Why the youngest shouted their answers loud, Verne could only guess. In her mind, she laughed. It was not like they sat half a meadow away. Perhaps it was because adults never seemed to hear them until they did something requiring discipline.

"You are all so smart. Anything else?" Verne asked.

"Energy should always remain in balance," Gryphon said. "The life within the plants will return the energy back into the earth. And magick without direction may become mischievous and seek a place to rest. Hence, the Returns of Three."

Thomas, a friend of Gryphon's, spoke up. "Remember when Norman tried casting his love spell without the Three Sisters? The errant magick struck his ass and caused a huge boil."

The entire group broke out in laughter.

Verne stifled her own laugh remembering how painful the boil was for the boy. Wishing a Return on no one, sympathy fell to poor Norman, whose face burned beet red.

"You all know your witches' lore. Only the fates know if you will become a First Level. Perhaps at the ceremony tonight your hard work will gain reward." Verne climbed up from the ground. "Make sure you have whole seeds for the Three Sisters, as you will use magick to benefit yourselves. You will want to avoid the Returns of Three."

"Fire Witches do not need the Three Sisters for protection," Megaera said.

Everyone quieted. All eyes fell on the girl.

"Oh, dear girl. Everyone should offer the Three Sisters. Do you want the Returns of Three to visit you?" Verne asked.

"Fire Witches protect themselves. We have no need of seeds and offerings."

"Who teaches you this?" Verne asked.

"Wouldn't you like to know?" Megaera narrowed her eyes.

Verne sensed all waited for a reaction. Instead, she dismissed the class. Clapping her hands in quick succession, she said, "Off to your mothers for chores before the celebration."

As the children dispersed, Megaera walked past everyone in a huff and pushed the little red-haired witch to the ground. Never turning to gloat over her cruelty, she disappeared into the forest.

"Why does she choose to harm?" the little girl asked.

She looked up to Gryphon, who came to assist her after she was pushed.

Gryphon leaned over, offering both of his hands. She smiled and accepted his assistance. He brushed off her dress, picked the leaves from her hair, and gave her chin a little caress with his thumb. "Better?"

Verne saw the child gaze at him like he had worked a miracle. Beyond them, the other children waited for him. Somehow, they knew he was their future leader. She expelled a deep breath.

"Now to attend to an urgent matter." Whisking away, Verne found Joan Caroline sitting by the stream.

"Joan. I wish a word with you."

"I watched from a distance and have no words." Joan offered the spot beside her. "I did not teach Megaera to shun the Three Sisters."

"You realize unless tribute to the Three Sisters burns in the flames, she cannot rise to First Level," Verne said.

Joan nodded. "I fear it becomes my mistake, to encourage Wilmott. He left me with a dark seed I cannot control. It does not play well for the coven."

"She'll turn around when she sees the others promoted. Perhaps not this time, but the next she will advance," Verne said.

"One can only hope." Joan stood and raised her hand to whisk. She smiled at Verne. "I must leave to finish preparing for the ceremony."

Verne became pensive when Joan's smile didn't reach her eyes. She wanted to help, but at times life must be left to its own path. A glance at the sun's position low in the sky indicated it was time for the celebration. She whisked to the meadow, where the pile of wood was set ready to blaze.

Verne smiled when Kenter whisked into the clearing. He took his place between Joan and Willa, his Third Levels. The younger children ran between the adults vying for the spots closest to the High Priest's seat. Their excitement fed power to the elders and the entire coven. The air thrummed with energy.

Once Gryphon appeared, everyone shifted so he could sit in the coveted spot closest to Kenter. Verne saw they did so without Gryphon asking. He walked to the seat as if it belonged to him. Kenter and Willa smiled while Joan frowned. Megaera sat off to the end of the neophyte line, away from the other children.

Verne stood, raised her hands, and addressed the coven. "May the blessings of Ostara feed power to the rising sun. With dawn on the morrow, light gains strength and the renewal begins. Hear now, our High Priest."

The thump of palms against thighs rose from the coven, welcoming Kenter to the circle.

"MichAudah," Kenter said. "We gather this night to offer blessings to mother earth and pray for a productive harvest in the fall. The vision of last eve showed a year of plentitude with the promise of hard work. We cannot ask for more in our new land. First-time fields will produce a harvest great enough to weather the long dark winter. Praise the Grand Master."

Kenter tossed the offerings of corn, beans, and squash into the fire. Returning to his seat, he wished the coven the seven druid blessings. "Mo sheact mbeannacht ort!"

The coven chanted in response. "May you accept life as

sacred. May you become one with nature. May your magick promote healing and rejuvenation. May you understand and respect the otherworld of the Grand Master. May you foster spiritual growth to its full potential. May you accept the sentient nature of magick and seek immersion in it. May life's journey guide you to live in and exit the world enlightened."

After the opening traditions, the young ones approached Kenter and asked permission to demonstrate the magick they had prepared. Kenter smiled and nodded at each neophyte as they approached, described what magick they would cast, and offered the Three Sisters to the fire.

"You set lofty goals this night," Kenter said. "I wish you success."

Gryphon took his turn. Remaining stoic, the boy lifted a crayfish from a bucket. With the wave of a hand, he called a gentle wind around the coven. It lifted a ruffle on the shirts and hems of the elders. Several females giggled and brushed their hems back into place.

He recited a Gaelic spell from the Book of Shadows. A crack rose above the sound of the ceremonial fire. The little frog leapt from his palm toward the flames.

Someone from the crowd shouted, "The frog. Save the frog."

Gryphon dove toward the fire and captured the frog, stood up, and presented it to Crone Verne with a bow. The elders chuckled at the sloppy magick as they discussed among themselves. With all heads nodding yes, Verne stood.

"Young Wiseman, approach," Verne said. "The elders promote you to First Level by their will. Take care in the use of your magick. May life's journey guide you to enter and exit this world enlightened."

Ten more neophytes attempted promotion before it was Megaera's turn. Four were able to achieve their purpose.

Megaera stood and walked to Kenter. "I will control fire."

Kenter nodded permission.

She arranged a small pile of sticks in front of the elders. Verne watched the elders' expressions as fire burst from her fingertips. Smiles, head nods, and raised eyebrows indicated they were impressed. Until she threw the flame.

Instead of hitting her target, the flame got loose and landed on the hem of an elder's dress. Megaera froze until someone shouted from the audience, "Put out the fire, stupid girl."

Jumping to do as told, Megaera ran to the elder and stomped the old lady's hem into the ground. Stepping in front of Verne, she bowed. "I give the gift of fire for the coven. May it remain strong and balanced."

The elders talked among themselves and shook their heads side to side at Verne.

"The elders ask you to try again at the next ceremony," Verne said.

Megaera's face showed anger rather than disappointment. A deep frown, furrowed brow, and reddened cheeks were directed at the elders and then at Joan. As if they were to blame for her lack of success.

An elder spoke up. "You should have offered the Three Sisters, young Caroline. Disregard of the offerings angers the Grand Master. There are consequences."

It took the rest of the evening to test all the witches hoping for a promotion. In the end, five neophytes earned First Level, three reached Second Level, and none advanced to Third. The elders expected big, well-controlled magick for Third Level. Many never reached it in their lifetimes.

"MichAudah. The tests have concluded," Verne said.

Cheering, singing, and dancing could not overshadow a lingering presence of evil Verne felt as she glanced at the forest. It seemed darker than usual for their first ceremony in the new land.

"Something wicked comes with tonight's lack of promotions," Verne said. She glanced at Kenter and tipped her head in the direction Joan traveled.

Kenter remained silent.

Harrisburg, PA 2019

"You can chase squirrels in a sec," Emmeline said. Luna barked and jumped out of the open door.

With the daypack slung over a shoulder, Emmeline smirked as the dog chased a squirrel under a log. She shoved her pistol under the seat and locked the door.

"Hurry, Emmeline. We need to find my boy." Luna ran back and forth, tail wagging and tongue hanging to the side. *"Forgive my indiscretion regarding the squirrel. Sometimes I forget I'm not a dog."*

Talking dog aside, Emmeline gazed at the mountain they were hiking. Brilliant pastel blue sky filled the horizon over the top of Sharp Mountain. Shimmering in reds and golds, the fall trees filled the air with a crisp, earthy scent. Autumn was her favorite season. The earth cleansed herself and prepared for renewal in the spring. The caw of a crow and a slight shimmy of the trees serenaded them in a morning symphony.

Emmeline rechecked the door locks and turned to find Luna sitting at her feet. "When I win the lottery, glossy black fenders will replace the rusty patina, and a flat black-cherry body will turn this truck into something sexy."

"There's something wrong with you. Sexy awaits in the forest. Besides, if you win the lottery, you can buy a new truck."

"If I had a new one, the boys from Iron Resurrection would be unnecessary. I want an LS 5.0 or better. You wouldn't put one of those in a new truck. Men working on metal. Let me dream."

"What would you do with so much power or a real man? And Brad wasn't, so you can't count him."

"You're not nice." Emmeline stared down at the dog. "I'm… Shit. I'm imagining my dog insulting me." Stomping her way up the trail, she moved past Luna.

"I'm not a dog. We can deal with your negativity later."

The five-mile hike melted away Emmeline's stress and negative thoughts from work. The crisp, clean air was the best medicine in the world.

"I need this today. It washes away my hate-filled thoughts about Dr. Caroline. Doctor? Bitch is more like it. I refuse to grant her the honor. And Marie Alley, the kiss-ass, must have printed her diploma off the internet."

"Betsy told me as much."

"Great. Now you're talking to Betsy. What's next? My dream man from last night coming to life?"

The warming day and continuous cardio did its job as she arrived at the historic Cold Springs ruins with nothing but the poem and finding the letterbox on her mind. She pulled the clue out of the pack. "I hate poem clues, but we'll give it a try."

"You started it last night. You have to finish it today," Luna said. *"It will activate more of your magick."*

"My magick. Sure. Here we go." Standing on a game trail, Emmeline reoriented herself to the ruins.

"I remember from the tour we took last year. The train station sat there." She pointed up the slope. "And the Grand Hotel was south and to the west." She followed her finger with her eyes. "So, the town square sits here." She tapped her foot.

Emmeline read the poem out loud. "The Key will find the Witchbox in an ancient place. A place where magick has left a trace. Seventeen twenty-four marks the opening door, where Moravians destroyed what was once life adored. It became a Cold Place to rest, where pioneers became guests. They gutted coal and cut the trees, and soaked in springs of mineral ease. To get there, take the train or horse and carriage to make the grade. From the station you will depart, to walk into the valley heart."

Emmeline pointed east to Stony Creek. "The mineral springs are to our east, and if I had arrived by train, I might walk through here." Emmeline tapped her foot in the same spot as earlier. "I would be standing between the second hotel and the stores on the main street, I think."

"You need to go to the church."

She ignored the dog and focused on the poem. "First find the steps of the Grand Hotel, twenty yards north, toward the building with bells. Do not take the trail but walk through the world, where spirits remain hidden in leaves that are curled. At twenty paces stop and turn to your east, the ghosts may haunt you like a furred beast. Travel forty more steps to the chapel altar, don't change direction or you will falter."

"I told you, go to the church." Luna trotted away, her voice fading. *"You're not listening."*

"When did you become a tenth grader? No skipping steps." Ignoring the canine's rambling, Emmeline read the final lines of the poem as she walked into the foundations of the old church.

"Under the stone that marks native life slaughter, lies the seventh son of a seventh daughter. Imprisoned within, the son is found. The Witchbox asks, take it from the ground.

Beware if you open it, you will find, a new life from the witch's mind. You may like it, you may not, but to open the box will take more thought."

A cool breeze skirted across the page, and the sun disappeared behind fluffy clouds. The clearing darkened with the loss of the sun.

"Creepy much?" Emmeline gave herself a hug.

A scraping sound drew her attention. Luna pawed at the ground, clawing the leaves and sticks off a stone.

"Holy shit." Emmeline knelt, brushing discarded leaves and dirt from an unusual stone embedded in the soil. "It has swirls like marble, but I think it's granite. Let's see, marble would be metamorphic and granite igneous. Right? It doesn't matter. It's cool."

"You're such a nerd."

The rock measured two feet long and a foot wide. Emmeline cleared the remaining debris from its surface. Greens, browns, and oranges swirled across the top as if it was painted. Closer inspection revealed not paint but natural layers of different colored rock.

"Move out of my way. I want to see my boy." Luna pushed Emmeline aside.

Emmeline's eyes widened as the stone rose from the ground, floated several feet, and dropped into the leaves. "What...the fuck?"

"Magick, my dear Emmeline." Luna sat. *"But mine only goes so far and will not work against Fire Witch magick. Now quit stalling and pull the box out of the ground."*

Staring at the dog, Emmeline stood up, waving her arms. "You can levitate shit?"

"It's magick, Emmeline."

Shaking her head back and forth, Emmeline peered into the hole. Grabbing a stick, she probed the darkness. The tip clunked against a solid object. Leaning over a two-foot-by-two-foot opening, she discovered the hole was lined with stone like a little tomb.

"I'm not sticking my hands in there. Rattlesnakes live in holes."

"You know they go into hibernation in the fall. No matter. Wish for the box to rise."

Emmeline glanced at the dog. "Okay. I wish the box would float out of the hole."

The box levitated and remained suspended in the air. She jumped back, tripped, and landed on her ass.

The box dropped by her hand.

"Holy shit!"

"You need a new expression. However, I am impressed. Your magick has great power." Luna walked over, sat in front of the box, and placed a paw on top. *"Gryphon, can you hear me?"*

"I warned you about the letterboxes with poems. There's always a catch." Emmeline rose and grabbed the box. It was a wooden box with symbols carved all over the surface. Her finger traced across some of the glyphs. "I think I saw these symbols on a Discovery program."

"It's Gaelic writing, from the time of the druids," Luna said. *"They were your people, Emmeline. Can you read the inscriptions?"*

"Sure. I'll just read ancient Gaelic. It says Emmeline has gone insane. Her dog talks and does magick. Beware of Bigfoot."

"You don't have to be so snide."

The sun remained behind clouds as the tree branches cast shadows across the site. A bit creeped out, Emmeline returned to the ground, sitting crossed-legged yoga style, and pulled out her cellphone. She called up the history of Cold Springs on Google.

"The lore suggests because so many died in the fires, spirits haunt the area even today. I guess ghosts explain the creep."

"Emmeline. Open the box. You wouldn't want the Grand Master to think he made a mistake in selecting you for my Gryphon?"

"Griffen? Do you mean the fire bird or my first dog?"

"Fates save me from young witches. G. R. Y. P. H. O. N." Luna got up. *"Open the box."*

"You're magical, you open the box." She tapped the box with a finger.

"If only it were so simple. You're the key of whom the poem speaks. I do not have the correct magick."

Emmeline snorted a laugh and picked up the box. Hearing something shifting inside, she turned it over and examined the ends but could find no obvious way to open it. Strange prickles and little tickles lifted the hair on her arms. The tiny nerve-like bursts continued across her breasts, down her abdomen, and straight to— "Holy shit!"

Emmeline dropped the box on the ground as if it burned. Power, intensity, and sexual energy oozed from the box. Her heart beat a rocker's tune as she toed the box away and pushed herself backwards. "What the hell is going on here?"

Luna pranced back and forth beside the box. "*Release my boy. Use your magick, hurry.*"

Kneeling, Emmeline eyeballed the dimensions. She used her scientific eye and estimated the dimensions as ten by five by four inches. "It's wood, not plastic, and looks homemade. This is bigger than a normal letterbox."

"*Of course it's homemade. It was carved over a thousand years ago. It's a Witchbox.*"

"Whatever." Emmeline grasped her chin in her palm to think, index finger tapping, "If I were a witch and wanted to open a Witchbox, I would wave my magic wand and say Hocus Pocus."

Nothing happened.

"*You watch too much TV.*" Luna rolled her eyes. "*Try again. Wish it open in your mind.*"

"Don't roll your eyes at me. I didn't even know dogs could do that." A slight cool breeze caressed the top of her hands. She raised the box and blew on it with a gentle rush of air.

"*Now there's a picture you can't unsee.*"

"Get over yourself." Emmeline frowned as the end of the box popped open. She pushed the piece back into its slot, and the lid lifted. "Holy shit. Did I do magick?"

"*Not well, but you did.*"

Sparkly purple dust escaped in a cloud.

"*Here he comes!*" Luna pranced and barked, did a few play bows, and lay down sphinx style while her muscles quivered, ready for action.

Emmeline dropped the box, stood up, and backed away from the cloud. The wind picked up and brushed across her skin. Clouds grayed the sky, and the branches creaked out an eerie song. The box vibrated in the dead leaves.

"What if I just released an evil Genie? Or unleashed a witch's spell that will screw up the rest of my life? Oh God, I could die teaching other people's children."

"*Alas, acceptance becomes insanity. Keep it up and they will lock you up."* Luna sat by the box. *"You do know Genies aren't real, right? They were just trapped witches like my Gryphon."*

Emmeline was frozen on the spot by an oppressive void of noise. No birds chattered, no leaves rustled, no branches squeaked. Turning in slow motion like a scene from a silent horror movie, she tried to make sense of her new reality.

A loud *whoosh* and *pop* penetrated the silence. The sounds of the world returned.

Emmeline took a deep breath, hoping the musky odor of leaves and decay would slow her rapid heartbeat. Instead, the clean brush of the ocean's salty breeze fired up little spasms in another part of her anatomy. Immersed in the scent, she clamped her thighs together.

"What. The heck. Is going on?"

Emmeline couldn't figure out why the smell made the hair on the back of her neck tingle and goosebumps spread along her arms. Each breath drew more attention to her unexplained arousal. As she turned at the sound of rustling leaves behind her, her breathing ceased. The image before her was breath-taking and unreal.

CHAPTER 3

Cold Springs, PA 1842

Megaera crept through the forest, climbing toward the High Altar along with the sun. Step after step, she pushed through the thickets to observe the end of last night's vision quest and listen to Kenter's discussion with his disgusting familiar. Her original plans to witness the entire process were delayed, as Joan made her stay in their cabin, crushing dried herbs.

Megaera made sure to close her mind to Ben's brain talk. She didn't want to alert them to her presence. Kenter and the cat stood on the altar and looked across Stony Valley. The one-sided conversation covered many subjects, but her interest rested with two.

By observing Kenter's body language, the tilt of a hand, the shift in tone, or the direction he set his head, she could decipher the times Ben talked. Kenter scratched a random part of his body. His stupid cat probably gave him fleas.

Megaera wasn't bothered by her lack of a familiar. They did nothing but give poor advice, track dirt into the cabins, and interfere with personal lives. Luna, for example. The horrid beast never left Gryphon alone. Did she watch when he humped?

"I think the discontent becomes my mistake to bear," Kenter said.

Now the conversation caught her interest.

Kenter looked down at the cat. "I wondered if not naming a High Priestess our first year here has encouraged the coven's discontent to grow these last hundred years. I spared Willa the position for Gryphon's sake. How sad she died before his advancement."

Megaera smiled. The malevolent sprite cast upon Willa had done an excellent job. The witch had lingered for weeks. Megaera had tried to console Gryphon so he could see her worth, but he'd rejected it. Such a shame she'd lost control of the sprite and it had taken Willa's life. Had Gryphon embraced her suggestions, Willa may have lived.

"The vision last eve repeated the prophecy," Kenter said. "The Key will come, and Gryphon will rise to power. But to what end? If the coven falls into discord—"

Kenter nodded and pulled his robe tighter across his shoulders. "I will work fire with him this day before the ceremony. I hope he does not burn down another barn. Crone MacDougal did not have a sense of humor about the incident."

Megaera thought on the times she'd messed up her fire practice. At least she hadn't burned down a barn. Poor Gryphon. Forced into manual labor to rebuild the barn. Kenter should have used magick to replace it. Although, she did enjoy from afar as his bare chest glistened in the sun while he pounded nails and sawed lumber.

Of course, the Key the priest spoke of would need to be eliminated. Nothing would block her pursuit of running the coven as High Priestess with Gryphon at her side. However, she would have to prevent him from gaining his full power.

Kenter sat down on a boulder, and the cat jumped onto his lap. Kenter said, "I did not watch Gryphon's victory during last eve's vision."

Megaera backed out of the shrubs. Her next step was to

place her mother on the High Seat. She picked up her bow and arrows and found a spot for the ambush. Spelled earlier using a verse from the Book of Fire, the arrows would fly straight. Megaera had dusted one point with crushed elder for its narcotic effect and arum lilies for the advancement of death.

The snap of a twig and rustle of leaves alerted her to someone on the trail. The morning song of the forest quieted as she drew the bowstring and released her arrow.

Kenter's eyes widened as the arrow pierced his back. He fell to his knees, unable to move.

Megaera stepped onto the trail, her bow nocked with another arrow.

Kenter pointed a finger at her. "Your actions condemn our coven. The Returns—"

Ben leapt into the space between his witch and Megaera. Losing focus and the mind block gone, she heard the cat speak in her head.

"What have you done?" Ben asked.

"Now is my time. Those of us with the power of fire will rule." Megaera pulled the string. In mid-draw, the arrow and bow disappeared. She shouted at Ben, "Give it back."

The cat vanished from sight before the fire lit her fingertips. Staring at the empty space, Megaera scolded herself for forgetting familiars had power. Lesson learned and not soon forgotten.

Focusing on Kenter's corpse, Megaera raised her arms and chanted a spell. His body flashed with flames and blew apart. Ash fell on the earth like a dirty winter's snow.

Months passed. Each week the coven held a meeting to discuss the High Seat. Each speech was more grating than the next, and Megaera tired of the rhetoric. With a quick shot of flame, she lit the central fire and stood.

The elders quit talking and stared at the brazen young witch.

"Are you out of your mind, Megaera?" Verne asked. "You

do not have standing to light the fire or speak on matters of leadership. You have yet to reach Second Level."

"You sit here and argue at each coven meeting, yet you never make a decision. You waste everyone's time, and the coven suffers. Joan Caroline sits next in line. As Kenter's Third Level, she casts fire better than any other witch here. Vote tonight. Make her our new High Priestess."

"You speak the truth, Megaera Caroline," one of the elders said. "But the decision will have long-reaching consequences. We take care so the right decision is made. You need more patience."

Megaera searched each face for a nod. Finding none, she stomped away. "They ignore me and see me as nothing."

A voice from deep in the forest startled her.

"They see only your youth, not the power you amass," Wilmott said. "Keep to your purpose, but do not use magick against them. They will not tolerate such disrespect."

"You press your will to my cause." Megaera's back remained to the warlock. "I know of your plan. You will not become Joan Caroline's High Priest. She will not sit in the position long enough to name one."

"You, child, have too much ambition." Wilmott whisked away.

Several weeks later, Megaera remained stoic as the elders promoted Joan Caroline to High Priestess. The coven would celebrate at Litha, the summer solstice, only a week away. Her plan was working as it should.

In four days, her mother would seek her first vision. Megaera planned on tapping into her blood connection and gaining a preview of the quest in her scrying bowl.

The preview view didn't come the morning after the quest as Megaera thought. She slammed the casting bowl down on the table. As daughter of the High Priestess, wasn't she entitled to know of the future before the rest of the coven? She stared at the bowl.

"You continue to hide the meaning of last night's vision quest from me." Megaera sneered at the bowl. She reached for the dark magick herbs and froze. A dull pressure pushed against her back, and the air drummed in her ears.

"What do you want, Mother?"

"Casting bowls are used for setting spells, not peeking at a vision from the cauldron," Joan said.

"I have found visions in my bowls before." Megaera's fingers curled into her palms. She squeezed so hard, blood filled the depressions and misshapen yellow nails on her hand.

"Verne and I will report our vision to the coven. Try patience." Joan held up her hand to stave off a retort from her daughter. "I will not argue with you. Why do you not yet comprehend the value of political alliances?"

Megaera huffed and faced her mother. "I wanted to know if I advanced to Second Level this eve."

"The elders judge you, not I," Joan said. "And the vision quest does not reveal the daily business of a coven member."

"You still bow under the power of Earth Witches. Why have you not named Wilmott as your High Priest? He has a blood claim to the seat as Kenter's brother."

"I cannot promote a warlock, Megaera Caroline. What messes with your thinking? You spend too much time with him. You have a lesson this moment with Verne, do you not?"

Joan whisked away.

"You're fooling yourself," Megaera shouted at her mother's departing.

A cool puff of air caressed the table, ruffling the piles of herbs. She tried to locate the source of the little breeze but, sensing no other witch, attributed it to nature. A brilliant red leaf discarded by the overhanging maple fell into her bowl.

"Blessed day, young witch." Wilmott stepped from behind the trees.

"You seem to pop up at the strangest of times," Megaera said. "The coven will not welcome you to the celebration."

Wilmott floated above the ground, his cloak so dark it made you think he left a hole in the world. The warlock's power was the only magick she feared.

In spite of her fear, Megaera reveled in the dark power that came from casting fire. It became an addiction and made her feel invincible. The more she gained, the more she wanted. It was unfortunate her practice slowed her from developing skills in wind and soil and kept her at First Level. As for water, she hated and avoided it at all costs.

"Mother would never dance with you at such an important event. She's High Priestess and must keep up appearances. You should wait for another time to dip your wick."

"I hoped to find your mother and dance with her this eve. Tis time you had a sibling." Wilmott surveyed the table. He lifted a brow. "Your insolence grows with your years, Megaera. Do not reach beyond your skills at this time."

"What do you know of what I do?"

"I recognize the potion you prepare. You do not have enough power for such a spell. The Wisemans have always cast strong magick and use it for protection."

"I don't—" The heat of embarrassment crept across her face. Megaera pursed her lips and took a deep breath. People who showed disrespect would one day learn what a mistake they made. Even Willmott. "You should go."

"After this eve, I leave for the old country. Our lessons are suspended until my return. Remember what I taught you. Practice all forms of magic. Grow your power in a balanced way."

He was gone. Megaera didn't even feel the brush of wind as he whisked away. Back at work, she punished her selected herbs in a crucible. "What do I care if I you leave?"

Left alone, she lost herself in the preparation. Her fingers traveled over the Book of Fire in a reverent manner. Her head stretched to crack her neck, and she noticed the seer as she pounded down the hill toward the cabin. She exhaled a long breath.

"Now what?"

"You remain a careless witch, Megaera." Verne waved a finger in the air as if Megaera were a petulant child. "You lost control of your dark magick. It flew by, on its way to cause some kind of mischief. You better hope it does no real harm."

"I cast no magick. You age past reason."

"I seek the High Priestess," Verne said. "You're needed at the coven circle for your lessons. Mirielda will be teaching today."

Verne whisked away. The wind blew her herbs from the table, where they were lost in the forest.

No longer able to cast her spell, Megaera went to the coven circle for the magick lesson. Mirielda, Verne's sister and apprentice, stood in front of the other witches.

Megaera had never cared for Mirielda. The witch seemed to have an air of superiority and wielded it over the others whenever the old witch taught. It seemed like she went out of her way to spotlight someone when they made a mistake.

"First Level witches," Mirielda said. "I will take Verne's place today so she may prepare for our ceremony tonight."

"Did our new High Priestess find a vision last night?" a red-haired witch asked.

"She did. A blessing for our coven," Mirielda said. "Tonight, some of you will see elevation to Second Level. You will be expected to demonstrate your skills in three of the four types of magick. How well you do determines promotion. Take care to make decisions for MichAudah and not yourself."

"And then Crone Betsy will teach us how to whisk and write spells," a freckled-faced witch said.

"Why can we not whisk now?" a bosom-rich redhead asked, twirling her hair, flexing her shoulders, and smiling at Gryphon.

"Have you learned nothing in the last hundred years? Do

you want to end up in a tree, or worse, the privy?" Megaera shook her head at the witch's stupidity. She sneered at the girl. "You have little power to work with. You may never whisk."

"You should not disparage others, Megaera," Gryphon said. He smiled at the girl as his lavender eyes twinkled in the late afternoon sun. "Some take longer than others to develop their skills. This is my third time trying for Second Level."

Mirielda interrupted. "Let's not forget, young witches, today's lesson revolves around manners."

Megaera listened as the class mumbled its discourse. At times they acted like spoiled neophytes, but these witches were over a hundred now. Some even older. She glanced at Gryphon, now occupied by the redhead.

"I remember my turn in your place," Mirielda said. "I too wanted to whisk away to places. But there was a First Level witch who could not wait, and he is no longer with us," Mirielda enticed the students. They quieted when she sat down with them to be at eye level.

"A young man, foolish enough to gather a large amount of power before he should, snuck off into a clearing instead of learning his lessons. So hot was the day, he wanted to soak in the springs, but too lazy to walk, he tried to whisk."

Every pair of eyes widened as they leaned forward, eager to hear of the witch's mistake.

"He forgot. The veil between this world and the afterlife thins during Samhain. His magick took him to the springs, but as he materialized..." Mirielda slowed her words, "a spirit pulled him into a whirlpool. He sank into the depths and drowned."

All the heads fell together, discussing the reality of the story.

"The springs rise knee high," Megaera said. "You cannot drown if you can stand up."

"You forget he had all of his magick with him," Mirielda said. "He was not strong enough to stand because the power weighed him down. The lesson is to make sure you're strong enough to wield the power you gather."

The group nodded at each other, absorbing the lesson. All except Megaera. She didn't buy the story for a second. Although, it was possible to drown in shallow water. She shivered at the incident long ago, when Gryphon had come to her rescue and pulled her from the swollen creek.

"We will go over the Witches' Creed one last time before the celebration tonight," Mirielda said. "The first question: What is the intent of magick?"

Hands waved in the air. She selected an energetic witch with blond hair.

"Magick should bend nature to a desired outcome, not alter it to your will," the blonde said.

"Excellent." Mirielda gazed around the circle. "New question. When is our magick at its strongest?"

A plump witch with brown hair shouted out, "During the Witching Hour of a solstice or equinox. All big spells need to be cast on the Witching Hour to gain use of the ancestors."

"Correct. Megaera, what is important to consider when casting magick?" Mirielda asked.

Megaera lay on her stomach, head propped on her hands and eyes narrowed on Gryphon, who at the moment had three female witches trying to sit on his lap. A pebble dropped in front of her head, and the group chuckled.

"Megaera. The answer, please."

"Huh?" Megaera's face reddened under the others' scrutiny.

"What must one consider when casting magick?" Mirielda repeated.

Megaera narrowed her eyes. "How much power the caster has available to them. Like if they were the only one who could shoot fire." She smirked and brought flame to her fingertip.

"No, Megaera," the red-headed witch said. "The answer should be: For a Second Level Witch, you must consider the consequences of one's actions, because it is impossible to do magick without taking the energy from somewhere."

"Correct," Mirielda said. "Now to finish. We will repeat the Witches' Rede."

The students rose from the ground and joined hands. In unison, they chanted, "And if it harms none, do what thou wilt, stay wary the Returns of Three."

Jealousy and anger rocked Megaera when Mirielda whisked away.

Harrisburg, PA 2019

Emmeline's eyes almost exploded in her head. The six-and-a-half-foot hunk from last night's dream stood in front of her, but fully clothed this time. His long black hair was pulled into a ponytail, the locks reaching past his shoulders and highlighting the luscious eyelashes surrounding those mesmerizing lavender eyes and plush, kissable lips.

A wide, expansive chest and well-muscled arms were encased in clothing from an old western movie. Not leather chaps and a big Stetson, but a thin string bowtie with white ruffled sleeves, a brocade vest, and a day coat. His long legs went on forever, surrounded by woolen trousers sporting a houndstooth pattern and flowing into well-worn calf-high riding boots.

"It's about bloody time. I have waited an eternity," the man said.

"I guess remaining dust in a box for over a hundred years did nothing to improve your manners," Luna said.

The stranger's frown flattened his plush, full lips. He brushed some dust from his coat, ignored the dog, and straightened to his full height. "Well, lass. Is your tongue stuck?"

The faint, sexy Irish brogue distracted her. Snapping out of it, she stepped back and put a hand on the knife strapped to her belt.

"Who are you?" Emmeline tightened her grip on the knife. She stooped down and picked up the Witchbox. "I know it's a historical site. I removed a letterbox so it's not desecrating the space."

"Emmeline. This is my boy, Gryphon."

"Holy hell. I assumed I hallucinated all this weird shit today." She shook her head and took a step backwards, her calves touching a downed tree. She sat, eyes wide. "This is a historical reenactment. That's it. You're here for a historical reenactment."

"Madam, I have no reference to your words." He searched for Luna. "Why does she require a weapon?"

"The old Crones didn't prepare her for your coming."

Emmeline swung her legs over the log. She grabbed her backpack, walked, and tried to put distance between them.

"My sugar's low," she mumbled to herself. "I need a cookie."

With a glance over her shoulder, she called, "Let's go, Luna. Bigfoot became some wackjob from a Playgirl fantasy. I'm out of here."

"Emmeline, give him a break. He remained in the box for a long time." Luna whisked in front of her to prevent her escape.

"What the—" She frowned at the dog. "Today of all days, I leave my gun in the truck."

Luna pranced from paw to paw. *"I will make a formal introduction."*

The hunky hallucination popped up next to Luna. Emmeline pouted and furrowed her brows. She remained silent, her mind racing to figure out where he had come from.

"Miss Emmeline Callen, may I present to you Viscount Gryphon Wiseman, Second Level Apprentice of the MichAudha." Luna nudged Gryphon's hand with her nose.

"I can introduce myself, you flea-bitten mystical

foundling." Gryphon tugged on his vest. He bowed to Emmeline. "Viscount Wiseman here. I am indebted to you for releasing me."

"I'm so happy you're free." Luna leaned against Gryphon's legs.

"Luna, stop. You spend too much time with Ben." Gryphon took a step back and brushed the dog hair from a pant leg. His attention fell back on Emmeline. He frowned. "Why do you dress in men's clothing?"

Emmeline flashed a glance down her body to assess her outfit. Nothing out of the ordinary. She wore distressed jeans, an orange T-shirt with a Browning symbol on it, hiking boots, and a Wolf Sanctuary ball hat. Normal for her weekends.

"I'm not a part of your troupe, if you're expecting a costume." She readjusted her hat and summoned a bit of bravery. "Where are the other actors?"

"Other actors?" Gryphon searched behind him. "Luna, what does she prattle about?"

"She thinks you're part of a play of sorts."

Luna padded over to Emmeline. *"He isn't in a play. A witch, your boss Megaera Caroline, imprisoned him in the box."*

"Witch—" Emmeline rolled her eyes. She waved her thumb over her shoulder. "I think I'll go now. You have fun."

"She's the Key," Luna said. *"You have to convince her to take the box. You're still attached."*

"I can feel my tether. Whether to her or the box, I am unsure." Gryphon stood up. "Madam, wait. Before you go, would you tell me what year we find ourselves in?"

"Great idea. Give her something to focus on. Emmeline excels at deflection."

Emmeline spun on her heel, fingers white from the tight grip on the knife handle. "What year? You're fucked up."

Her heartbeat accelerated. His presence was overpowering. It was crazy, but an unseen force, some deep, soul-wrenching attraction, kept her from leaving. And the smell. Her mouth watered at the touch of sea salt in the air.

"I asked you a question, woman. As my Key, you must answer me." He crossed his arms.

Emmeline's head rotated back and forth between the dog and the man, but she remained silent and narrowed her eyes. Sunlight cleared the clouds, and a beam of light brushed the stranger's head, making his aura twinkle. Her grip tightened on the knife.

"His aura's purple. And he's an ass. My jerk radar must be broken." She started walking.

"Of course it's purple. He's the future leader of MichAudha." Luna shifted her head to look at Gryphon while keeping pace with Emmeline.

"I'm not his fucking anything," Emmeline said. "If he follows me, I will stab him."

He popped up five feet in front of her, hands lifted and palms up. "We seem to be getting off on the wrong foot."

Chin in the air, Emmeline shifted her weight onto her back leg and waved a hand as a distraction like she'd learned in self-defense class. The fighting stance made her feel strong and in control.

"What is this position? A fighting stance?" Gryphon asked.

"I believe she thinks to gut you. I'd back up a step if I were you," Luna said.

Lavender eyes darkened to amethyst as he lowered his arms and made eye contact with her.

Emmeline swallowed, licked her dry lips, and reached for a water bottle. While she drank, she tried to decide what to do when the ridiculously sexy scent hit again. Her eyes widened at the unexpected twinge in her clit.

Her foot wouldn't move. Emmeline focused on the dog paw pressing on her boot. Unable to feel the weight of the dog through her hiking boot yet unable to lift the foot, she cried out, "Let me go."

Luna soared several feet into the air and crashed to the ground.

"Oh my God. Luna baby, are you okay? What happened?" Emmeline ran to kneel by the dog.

"I'll have to remember." Luna shook off the residual magick and some leaves. *"You released your magic, and it appears to be linked to emotion."*

"It is strong magick to cast without spells. The Grand Master chose well," Gryphon said. He leaned over the pair on the ground.

Emmeline returned to her feet and left them both as she headed down the trail. Luna would catch up, the dog never left her side. Her mind raced with questions. *Why didn't I run from the weirdo right away? Why was he so blasted good looking? I should quit drinking.* She closed the conversation with herself and kept walking.

"Why does she leave?" Gryphon asked. "Luna, stop her."

"Nope. Not me. Emmeline threw me across the clearing. It's your turn. Keep in mind, women in this time won't put up with your misogynist ways."

"Should I know the meaning of your term? You speak strangely in the here and now," Gryphon said. "Miss Callen, wait."

Emmeline kept walking.

"Madam, you have forgotten your box."

Emmeline stopped. Her shoulders rose and fell with a deep breath. People died in horror movies for making stupid decisions. They went into the barn, opened the closet door, or didn't leave when they found a working car. She swallowed and turned around.

He held the box out.

She glanced back at the church ruins and noted the top stone next to the tomb. It tore at her moral compass. She couldn't leave a historical site disturbed. Against her better judgment, she walked toward him, took the box, and returned to the open tomb.

Leaning over, she stuffed the box into her day pack and tried to figure out how to put the stone back. Emmeline detected his presence behind her, not from sound, but from the delicious salty breeze skirting across her tongue. She squeezed her eyes shut and rubbed them.

"You can put the stone back. It's heavy, I think." Emmeline stood and pointed. Her brain hurt trying to figure out how the stone had moved before. She gasped. The rock levitated, floated across the ground, and seated itself back over the hole. "Did I—"

"Great job, Emmeline." Luna trotted up to her and sat.

"I didn't— Never mind. I don't want to know." She pulled her knife from its sheath and waved it at him. "I don't know what game you're playing here, but it seems a damn stupid spot to play it. Leave me alone or you might find yourself lacking an important part of your anatomy."

"Games? No games. I have remained locked in my family's Witchbox since the fall of 1900. I have no knowledge of what has happened to my coven. This place seems familiar, but not. Where is Cold Springs?"

Emmeline stared, the words frozen in her mouth.

"You tell him, I'm still too sad about it."

Emmeline cast a glance at the dog. Lifting her head, she said, "Cold Springs burned in September of 1900. No one will buy your fantasy about someone incarcerating you in a box. I suppose you think you're a warlock!"

His eyes bulged. His mouth dropped open. Would he drool?

Gryphon tugged his vest down and stood taller. He lifted his chin. "I will have you know, I have never, nor will I ever, fall as low as a warlock. It's disconcerting you would have such a low opinion of me. Why would you think such?"

He actually looked offended. His lips were pouty, lashes

lowered, eyes soft. Quite the actor. Was this some sort of improv, Emmeline wondered. She perched her hand on her hips and answered his question. "Girls are witches, boys are warlocks. It's in all the books."

"Who teaches such false atrocities and puts them into books?" Gryphon asked. "I, a proud Earth Witch, practice in all four forms of magick. Wind is my birth power." He started to say something but paused and cocked his head. "The town burned?"

Emmeline lifted her brows. He seemed genuine. The angst in his voice caused pain in her heart. "In the fall of 1900."

"What has happened to my coven?" He sat down on a log and covered his face with his hands. "Why does my Key treat me with such impudence?"

"You're stuck. I have both of you to deal with now. Think about me." Luna stepped on his boot to keep him from moving. *"She doesn't know how to use her magick."*

"Not quite Broadway quality. More like high school. Thanks for the show. I'm out of here." A cloud of lavender dust followed Emmeline like a summer swarm of blackflies.

CHAPTER 4

Cold Springs, PA 1900

Megaera stepped with care through the early spring forest as she searched for the spring arrivals of mugwort, high john, meadowsweet, and the elusive valerian. The cold, snowless winter and warm, rainless spring continued to dry the land. After hours of searching, the slight trickle of water identified a spring struggling in the drought-stricken land.

It would take weeks for the plants to dry. Some of the ingredients would not rise from the soil until later in the summer if they did at all. If all her plans fell into place, she would cast the spell on the full moon of the autumn equinox and pull power from the ancestors. Gryphon would be hers.

Megaera noted smoke rising from a nearby dwelling and recognized the outskirts of Yellow Spring, the next town downriver. She hadn't realized she'd walked so far, and the two-mile hike home seemed daunting. She crouched to pull her final sprig and root of young valerian. After adding it to the collection bag, she wiped the sweat from her forehead.

Each step faded to thoughts about the magick she planned for the promotion ceremony this evening. If she didn't make Second Level tonight, she wouldn't have the power to cast the spell on Gryphon this fall. She hardly noticed the walk home.

Megaera was greeted by her mother's voice as she entered the cabin.

"Where have you been all day?" Joan stepped up and plucked an offending twig from her shapeless dirty-blond hair. "Why do you cut your hair so short? It gives you a mannish appearance."

Megaera's hands made fists, and she pinched her lips closed to refrain from speaking her first thought. She set the collecting basket on a nearby table and glanced a touch across the Book of Fire.

"I sought out herbs. If the drought continues, they will disappear from the valley."

Megaera continued stroking the book. Sparks of energy jumped into her hand. Admiring the tingling sensation, she rubbed her fingertips together. Her internal energy well hoarded power as if it were a bottomless pit. The continuous need to fill it drove Megaera to seek more.

Joan frowned.

"You become too attached to our grimoire. You should write your own spells," Joan said. She waved her hand toward the book, and the front cover lifted and closed. "What have you collected this day?"

"Anything I could find. The drought has no mercy." She nodded to the pouch and tried to assess her mother's current disposition.

"Take care while preparing the ingredients, and label them with the correct symbols on the pouches. Also, you have a magick lesson on whisking today. Meet Minerva at the forge when the sun seeks the earth."

"I have other activities planned."

"Do you want to advance to Second Level or not?" Joan asked. "I read the spell you had open in the grimoire. You do not have enough power."

"Mind your own business." Megaera closed the distance between them. Her voice was so low only Joan could hear, "My fire magick gives me more power than you can imagine."

"I fear you will end us all." Joan flicked her hand and whisked away.

"I thought she would never leave. Now, what else do I need?" As she pointed at the book, the pages flipped open to the spell. "I have all the herbs, but it appears I need two more items." Megaera tapped a finger on her bottom lip.

The Witchbox and grimoire she needed to finish the spell sat in Gryphon's cabin. She'd made other trips there in the past to snoop around and gather his essence. The careless boy left it lying about for anyone to gather. Megaera smiled at the thought of returning. The last visit had gone without discovery. His scent and magick essence lingered in the linens. She had lain on the bed and masturbated, imagining his strong hand doing the work.

Snapping out of the daydream, she made a plan. Removing the box now would give notice. But collecting both on the day she cast the spell would avoid discovery. Fall was only a few months away. She could wait.

Megaera earned her promotion to Second Level during the spring celebration. She barely passed, but with the drought, water magick was limited to what could be conducted in a bucket. It played to her advantage. The summer heat beat the land dry into September. Everyone remained vigilant when using magick. Even the Fire Witches vowed to cast only near the springs.

With enough power to cast her dark spell, Megaera crept around the back wall of Gryphon's cabin and listened for signs of his presence. No matter how carefully she stepped, dried leaves and grass crunched under her weight. As she reached for the front door, the wind magick set to protect the cabin yielded to her threat of flame and allowed her entrance.

Gryphon's morning coffee cup sat empty on the table along with his breakfast tin and fork. Megaera picked up the cup and placed her lips on the rim, she found no magick in the touch. A glance across the one-room cabin revealed the Book of Shadows atop the dresser. It slammed shut at her approach.

"Clever book."

Megaera studied the tome's cover. The word "Shadows" was pressed into the leather across the top and "Wiseman" along the bottom. The leather binding, faded and scratched, appeared in good shape for a book reported to be over a thousand years old. Even the Book of Fire couldn't boast of such history. She could feel its power as she leveled her hand above the surface. It repelled her touch.

The Witchbox sat next to the book. Megaera tried to pick it up. It wouldn't budge.

Megaera brought forth her fire. She traced the flame around the base of the box, releasing a faint spiral of dark smoke. A quiet *click* sounded, and the box gave up its grip on the bureau. Megaera levitated it from the surface, floated it across the room, and dropped it inside the collecting satchel she'd left on the table.

The grimoire was more difficult. Each time Megaera reached for the book, it slid across the dresser, out of reach. For such an old, bulky tome, it was fast.

"Come now. I only wish for a small corner of one page." Understanding the power the book contained, Megaera called her own magick. She cast translucent gloves over her hands with a cloaking spell and reached for the spell keeper.

Wind whipped through the cabin, turning the pages. A spell written in Gaelic appeared. Megaera narrowed her eyebrows, waiting to defend herself. Instead, the tome waited for her to make the next move.

Megaera lifted her scissors with slow, deliberate moves. As she lifted a page with her magick, she wiggled her fingers on the other hand and directed the scissors to the corner. The book vibrated.

The second she snipped a corner, the book slammed shut. The piece floated to the dresser like a discarded feather. As Megaera reached for the fragment, it fluttered and tried to move back to the book.

"Not so fast." Megaera slammed her palm over the piece. She dragged her hand to her, pulling the unwilling bit from the surface. After tucking the prize into her collecting bag, she returned to the book. "After Gryphon becomes imprisoned in the Witchbox, I will return for you."

On the way out the door, she paused by the bed. The Wiseman family quilt lay rolled at the foot of the bed. Megaera sat beside it. Lifting it in both hands, she took a deep breath and inhaled Gryphon's distinctive scent. Pulling the material through her fingers and savoring the slide against her palm, she was thrown off by the musk of sex and other females.

Megaera tossed the quilt away as if it were on fire. "When I return for the Book of Shadows, I will take you as well. After a washing, you will warm my bed. And someday so will Gryphon."

Barks and laughter from outside filtered into the cabin. Megaera peeked out the window and discovered Gryphon's familiar along with three female witches arriving at the cabin.

"Gryphon," a busty blonde shouted as the laughter and giggles from the others continued.

Megaera detested such frivolity. She stepped onto Gryphon's porch with her fists clenched. Her jaw tightened at the sight of them. Her entire childhood, these witches had laughed at her lack of female attributes.

"You ply yourself with drink so early in the day?"

"What are you doing here, you ugly old hag?" The red-haired witch snorted.

"We have an appointment with the Viscount. Gryphon

promised to act as our tutor in wind magick before the ceremony tonight," the brunette said. She giggled and fondled her
own breasts, rubbing across them and down to her crotch.

The redhead approached with her hands on her hips. "You
should go. Gryphon would never stoop so low as to lie with
your shriveled, bony mass. He prefers a much softer mattress.
Not to worry, we will tell him of your visit."

Faded laughter marked the trio's departure as they left
down the trail. Megaera finally took a breath. She told herself it
was not because she was jealous. It was because her magick
was superior to theirs.

The familiar's growl startled her. Megaera jumped off the
porch and turned. She shot a bolt of flame at the dog, but her
magick lost speed and froze in front of the canine.

Luna flicked her muzzle. The flame fell on the porch and
sizzled out.

"Your magick loses its purpose." Luna lifted a hind leg,
scratched behind her ear, and yawned. *"What is your purpose
here?"*

Megaera's hand grasped the lumpy satchel slung over her
shoulder. A confrontation with the familiar could lose her the
prizes she'd waited so long to acquire. It went against her
personality to yield, but it was necessary. She raised her hand
and whisked home.

"You're whisking quite well, Daughter," Joan said. She sat
at the table shelling beans from their pods for the celebration.

"Did you worry I would never serve as your Third Level?"
Megaera narrowed her eyes, waiting for her mother's
comment.

"I take pride in your success. When you have it. Will you
try for Third Level this eve?"

Megaera remained silent.

"We must discuss another matter." Joan stood and walked
to the work bench. "I become concerned about the spell you

marked in the Book of Fire. Only powerful witches and warlocks can cast it. Did Wilmott return?"

"I have not seen him. It's none of your business what spells I practice."

"As High Priestess, my duty is to the coven. Your imprisonment spell negates my mission." Joan crossed her arms.

"It has nothing to do with you," Megaera said.

"It does if you plan to imprison Gryphon. He may become a Third Level advisor this eve. What will you accomplish by denying the coven his power?"

"My plans remain my own. And Gryphon's mine, not the coven's." Megaera flicked her hand, and the Book of Fire soared across the room and into her arms.

"Consider the consequences of your actions, Megaera. Who will you rule when everyone dies?"

"You talk out of your ass, Mother. The spell does not kill anyone," Megaera said.

"Consider the Return of Threes," Joan said.

"Once I have my full power, I will run this coven, this town, and everything else." She sat on her bed in a flounce. "You can help me or stay out of my way."

Harrisburg, PA 2019

"Why does the weirdo keep following me?" Emmeline asked after a fast-paced twenty minutes. Catching her breath and sipping some water, she took a seat on a log near the trail.

"He must have planted the letterbox and made the tomb. I should tell someone, but who?"

"You need to accept what's happening."

"I think I hear you talking to me, but in truth I'm talking to myself." Emmeline grabbed several dog cookies from a pocket. "At some point, they will lock me up. Let's hope I don't turn into some mass murderer beforehand."

She tossed the dog a treat. "You won't whisper 'murder them' in my ear, will you?"

"Of course not. How disturbing." Luna placed her paw on Emmeline's thigh. *"I will always take care of you."*

"Aww. How sweet." Emmeline gave the dog a hug and a kiss on the head. "Want another cookie?"

The wind whipped around her feet, rustling some leaves.

"It's my fault. I did wish for a knight in shining armor. I should have asked for a never-ending supply of bourbon instead." Popping a salted caramel into her mouth, she continued, "Why are the sexy ones always weirdos or gay? I wish I had a—"

A quiet *whoosh* sounded, and a bottle of Jim Beam materialized between her boots, which were now covered in sparkling lavender dust.

"Oh, I do hope you didn't transform him into a bottle of bourbon."

"Did I?"

Emmeline leaned over and poked at the bottle with a stick. There was a loud snap and crackle, followed by a wall of muscle that knocked her backwards over the log. Her eyes closed in response to the impact. The breath was knocked out of her, and she gasped for air, pushing at the heavy weight holding her down.

"Son of a bitch." Her eyes popped open to find long black lashes around glistening purple eyes, and kissable lips lifted at one corner. The stranger's arms framed her chest and kept him suspended over her. The sleeve of his coat brushed along her sides, tickling her breasts with each rise and fall of breath. A shiver skated straight to her sex.

Emmeline lifted her head. A tantalizing breeze blew the scent of a warm and salty breeze across her face. It mingled with the caramel still on her tongue. She dropped her head to the ground as her girl parts twitched. Why was his smile so devastating?

"Fuck me."

"I would, but it seems a rather strange position to work from," Gryphon said.

"You had to open your mouth."

"Stop," Emmeline yelled as he leaned forward for a kiss. His movement stopped, even the fluttering of those long eyelashes.

Her hands pushed against his chest. He didn't budge.

Emmeline's heart beat a heavy rhythm while she levered her boots against the log and pressed. It took effort, but she managed to slide out from under him. He was suspended, his ass in the air over the log. Even when Emmeline poked him in the arm with the sharp tip of her knife, he didn't move.

"Well, that's embarrassing." Luna sniffed. *"I think you froze him, Emmeline."*

Emmeline got up and walked around the log, shaking her head, and mumbled, "Is he going to stay there all day?"

"I believe it becomes your choice." Luna stepped forward and sniffed him. *"Unfreeze him this instant."*

"Let's say for one second I buy into this whole magick scenario. Even if I did, I don't know what I did or how to undo it," Emmeline said.

"What were you thinking when you yelled 'stop'?"

"I don't know." Emmeline lifted her shoulders, expelled a long breath, and stared at the ground. "I wanted him to stop."

Luna pawed at Gryphon's arm. *"So tell him to unfreeze."*

"What? Should I say 'unfreeze' and wave my hand?"

Gryphon instantly collapsed around the log.

Emmeline stumbled backwards. "Holy shit."

Luna padded over and gave Gryphon's cheek a lick. *"Stand up. It's undignified."*

"What did you do?" Gryphon asked.

"I. Don't. Know." Emmeline's eyes flared, and she set her hands on her hips. The pounding in her chest continued as she lifted her chin. "Like it's my fault."

He brushed dirt from a sleeve, pulled a twig from his hair, and tugged the vest over his waist. Every move was mesmerizing, graceful, and sexy.

"Luna, do you see her eyes? Emeralds with bits of gold. I would say she has a bit of mischievous Fae in her." He reached out, lifted her hand, and brushed a soft kiss on the palm.

Out of nowhere, a loud grumble shifted all eyes to his stomach. "I believe I require sustenance. I'm not sure how, as this is not my corporeal form. In any event, would you have a bite to share?"

"What are you talking about?" Emmeline yanked her hand away. It still tingled where his plush lips had touched it. She raised the knife and stepped back.

"Give the man a cookie."

Gryphon smiled. "You were giving Luna a cookie only moments ago. Mayhap there's a spare for me? You should have prepared better for my coming."

"Uh-oh," Luna said. She backed away from Gryphon.

Emmeline smirked. "Sure. Have a cookie." She reached into her pouch, pulled out a dog treat, and tossed him a Milkbone.

"Gryphon, don't—" Luna snorted and walked away. *"Brought it on himself. Not my fault."*

Gryphon gave Emmeline a quick bow. "Thank you, madam. It appears a biscuit. You call them cookies in this time?" Biting into the tooth-breaking biscuit, Gryphon chewed and swallowed. He flashed her a smile, and the rest of the treat went into his pocket. "Biscuits have changed over time. I shall save the rest for later."

"Maybe you should give it to Luna," Emmeline retorted while emitting an unladylike snort. She picked up her backpack and stepped onto the trail. "Let's go, Luna."

"You have a role to fulfill," Gryphon said. "We must find the Book of Shadows and cast the spell to release my true form from the box."

"I don't want a part in his play," Emmeline said to Luna.

"What does he mean, true form?" Shaking her hands, she continued before her dog could reply. "Never mind, I don't want to know."

"You must accept the magick."

"No sane person would. It's crazy. Only one crazy a day. I've reached my limit."

Putting a bit of determination into her stride, Emmeline rounded a curve and arrived in the parking lot twenty minutes later.

"You're the key to returning Gryphon to his corporeal form. It's part of the prophecy."

"Is it? Does this so-called prophecy say, 'Step one, release Gryphon from the box' and 'Step two, return Gryphon to his corporeal form'?" She stopped at the truck, unlocked the door, and grabbed for her pistol.

Emmeline waited for Luna to say something. "No smartass answer? Who uses the word corporeal anyways?"

She tried climbing into the truck after the dog, but the wind blew around her feet, anchoring her in place. The drop in air temperature made Emmeline shiver as she unholstered the weapon, pulled the slide back, and loaded the first round into the chamber. A whirlwind of lavender dust appeared in front of her. As the cloud struck the ground, Gryphon materialized.

Reacting out of instinct, she lifted the gun and pointed it at his broad chest. She backed into the open door of the truck, the pad of her finger lingering over the trigger. A feeling of warmth and the smell of a salty sea breeze overtook her senses.

"I do not think a pistol necessary," Gryphon said. He crossed his arms.

"Step back, asshole, or I'll shoot." Emmeline readjusted her hand on the grip and pushed the safety off.

"Madam. Why do you refuse to address me by my title and offer respect?" He stepped forward, hand extended.

A loud crack echoed against the mountains.

In slow motion, Emmeline's world spun. Images wobbled,

enlarged, and shrunk. Dizzy and deaf to the world, she followed his hand in slow motion to a spot on the brocade vest. Red spread over the mute earth tones, obscuring the pattern.

"You shot me! Look at the mess you have made of my clothes," Gryphon complained.

Reality broke when he burst into a cloud of dust.

"Holy fuck. What did I do?"

"You need a new expletive other than 'holy fuck' or 'holy shit.'" Luna snickered. *"Bet he didn't expect you to shoot him."*

Luna jumped out of the cab and sniffed the ground. She sneezed, blowing the dust back into the air. A bit remained on her nose.

"I'll lose my job, go to prison, and give up my truck...and you!" Emmeline started hyperventilating. She grasped the door with one hand, the other covering her mouth as the dust swirled in the air. "We have to tell someone. Who the hell would believe it?"

Motioning for the dog to hop in, she sat in her seat and shut the door. Hands shaking on the steering wheel, she peered through the front window. "I need to call the cops. Oh my God, I'm losing it. Self-defense, right?"

"No body, no crime." Luna sat there beside her, tongue hanging out, unfazed.

"Oh my God. There's no body. I'm never doing a letterbox with a poem again." Emmeline pushed the clutch, twisted the key, and slammed the gears into reverse. The tires spun, throwing up gravel and dust as she tore out of the parking area.

"That's your take on this whole situation? No more poems."

"The poems are problematic. I've told you this before," Emmeline said.

The ride home remained quiet while she focused on the drive. Her hands continued to shake as she gripped the wheel and leaned forward as if it would give her a better view of the road. Not bothering with the radio, Emmeline listened to the crunch of stone and the thump of the tires.

Before she pulled onto the main highway, a flash of purple and the rich smell of sea salt caused Emmeline to slam on the brakes. The back end of the truck swung to the left before it stalled. From the corner of her right eye, she caught the violet-eyed waking nightmare sitting in the passenger seat with his arm around her dog.

CHAPTER 5

Cold Springs, PA 1900

Megaera whisked to the human church. Most witches had an aversion to the building and all it represented. The religious icon, the Holy Bible, sat atop something she needed for her spell. The pulpit would have to be moved, as it gave her access to the coven's sacred tomb.

A scratching sound from deep in one corner of the church gave her the shivers. The wooden walls creaked and moaned as if haunted by some aberration. Deciding it was best to ignore the spirits of humans, Megaera made room for her work.

A push of her magick knocked the pulpit over. The human book of lies clunked onto the floor, raising small whorls of dust. Fingers aflame, Megaera cast sparks of dark magick on the floor where the pulpit had stood and melted away the boards. Beneath them, the druid stone sat waiting.

Made from Connemara marble, the stone was placed there when the coven first arrived in the valley for their ceremonial fires. Swirls of gray and brown floated in the greenish stone as moonlight recharged its energy.

Calling for power, Megaera levitated the stone and shifted

it several feet away. Once filled with ancient artifacts from the homeland, the small tomb now sat empty. The elders had removed the items when the Moravians declared the clearing theirs and built the creaky old church. Who wanted to worship inside?

Noise still emanated from the dark corner.

She returned to the casting bowl to focus on the remaining ingredients of the spell, but a clunk and scrape made her lift her head.

Joan Caroline glided into the church. The long High Priest robe dragged across the boards, leaving a trail in the dust.

"You hide Gryphon's essence in the coven tomb. Clever. Even the seer could not see past the marble."

"It remains a safe place regardless of time," Megaera said. She placed the Witchbox beside the opening. "You cannot stop me. Do you intend to help?"

"Perhaps it is the least I can do to provide for Gryphon's safety while he is trapped. I owe the coven this much until the Key arrives to open the box. The next time you are both corporeal, the Key will have arrived."

"I will release Gryphon, and he will sit at my side." Megaera removed a hankie and blew her nose. "To much dust settles in these walls."

"I doubt this will help." Joan leaned over and dropped the Three Sisters into the open box. "I will pay the price for the deaths of Kenter and Willa, as I allowed you to practice your dark magick. I should have taught and watched you better and given you more guidance. But you will pay the price for denying the coven their High Priest."

"How did you know I was here, in this place?" Megaera asked.

"I saw an errant spell of dark magick and all it destroys in the vision quest last night. I offer the Three Sisters not to prevent but to mitigate the damage. The cauldron rejected the offering."

"I do not understand your insistence on making the offerings," Megaera said.

"Remember the Witches' Creed. A witch must carefully consider the consequences of one's actions. Have you considered what fate will fall on the coven when you cast this spell?"

"You make your offerings if it makes you feel better." Megaera returned to the herb table and began casting.

"What will you accomplish with such a hateful spell?" Joan gripped the edge of the table, fingers whitening. "Gryphon will suffer in the box. You issue punishment?"

"You worry too much. I wish only for time to gain my full power. When I take my seat as High Priestess, I will open the box, and Gryphon will join with me as my Third Level. When he is promoted."

Megaera levitated the open box to the bottom of the tomb. She threw a flash of magick to hush the source. Rubbing her hands together to remove residual dust, she returned to the work.

"Hemlock to paralyze, valerian for sleep." Megaera's high-pitched cackle lifted more dust from the pews; it remained aloft. Reading the Book of Fire to make sure the ingredients were added in the correct amounts and order, she continued, "Mugwort will amplify my magick and high john add strength. The meadowsweet and pumpkin seeds will aid my divination."

"I will need the extra boost of energy to imprison a seventh son. I always plan, Mother. You never gave me credit for my skill."

With the book in hand, she read the words after tossing the herbs into the box. She recited the spell: "Place of shadows, place of wind, I summon you to my will to bend. I seek to capture one of our own, before his power is fully grown. I give power from the Book of Shadows, Book of Fire now endowed. Capture the seventh son named Gryphon, my will be done."

The bit of page from Gryphon's grimoire floated into the

tomb. Wind whipped around the church, and ashes rose from the box. Screams shattered the peace within the church. The ghostly figures of Gryphon's long-ago relatives swirled about, seeking his corporeal form.

Megaera ducked twice as several shapeless gray clouds divebombed her. One pushed through her body, raising goosebumps and shivers. She clutched the Book of Fire while wind swept the room. Words whipped away once spoken, but she managed to finish the spell.

"Lock him in with family past, his power joined when the spell is cast. Directed by the fates, a prophecy, released by the sacred key. So mote it be."

Windows rattled, and the front door blew open with a slam against the wall. Megaera stared into the casting bowl, trying to read the surface. A malevolent force passed through the church, and a second later the candle flames blew out.

"What manner of magick? Mother, stop messing with my spell."

"This wind did not arise from your spell or mine. It blows without purpose. The caster did not control their magick." Joan kneeled to remove the box. "This errant wind does not bode well for your treachery. Stop before it becomes too late."

"I have already begun. I tire of your interference."

Megaera called flame and shot it at the High Priestess. Her power joined forces with the wind spinning around the pews and knocked Joan backwards, slamming her into the upended pulpit. The old witch slumped to the ground and remained still.

"Wilmott has shown me a few tricks these many years." Megaera stood with hands perched on her hips, waiting for a response.

Joan moaned and tried to sit.

Sneering, Megaera teased, "Surprised I have so much power?" She put a hand around her ear as if to listen. "I thought not." The high-pitched laugh bounced on the wind still blowing through the church.

Harrisburg, PA 2019

The dust settled around the truck tires. Emmeline fisted the steering wheel, took a deep breath, and raked Gryphon with a wide-eyed stare. Her hallucination having the audacity to reappear after she'd shot him didn't surprise her.

"Luna, didn't I shoot him?"

"You didn't shoot his corporeal form."

"Using that word again?" Emmeline stared at the dog.

"I have never before earned a bullet from a woman," Gryphon said. He leaned around Luna. "I have no difficulty pleasing females. Pray tell, what action deserved such a response?"

"Huh?"

"Gryphon wants to know why you shot him."

"Easy. He doesn't listen. I said step back." She met his eyes over Luna's head. "You came forward. I shot. Textbook self-defense."

"I hardly feel one step would warrant a hole in my favorite vest." Gryphon looked down at the intact vest. "Oh. My apologies. No hole. Excellent."

Air blew between her lips in a hiss. With her thumbs tapping on the steering wheel, the long pause provided a minute for reorganizing her thoughts. Nodding and turning the key, she drove toward home while her mind replayed the final moments of several horror movies. *Don't go in the closet. Don't turn on the light. Don't take a lunatic home with you after meeting them in the woods.*

"What is wrong with me?" Emmeline asked. Her hands slapped at the abused steering wheel.

Luna circled on the seat, smacking Emmeline's cheek with

her tail. Spitting out an errant dog hair, Emmeline said, "Sit. You're driving me nuts."

"I can't find a comfy seat." In a constant state of motion, she continued standing, turning in a circle, and sitting on Gryphon's lap.

"Luna, either sit down or turn around and sit, but quit sticking your blessed buttocks in my face," Gryphon snapped. "I should have done as Kenter said and thrown you back in the river. Cats or birds as familiars remain the standard for a reason."

"You loved having a dog as a familiar. It made more sense for the next High Priest to have a unique familiar." Luna preened. *"I think the black cat-witch is cliché, but don't tell Ben."*

"We did have some marvelous times, did we not?" Gryphon asked. "I am surprised the old Crones didn't turn us both into frogs on several occasions."

Emmeline remained quiet, absorbing the interaction. Their banter reminded her of arguments she'd had with her foster siblings. Of course, those fights were less intellectual, usually over a donated toy or newer-looking shirt. She didn't care for the fights then, and she didn't care for them now.

"Emmeline, I spent an entire day as a frog until he figured out the spell reversal. Don't think for one moment he had control of his magick."

"You should have stood away. I wanted the frog transformed as a bird." He rubbed her upright ears and laughed. Leaning around the dog, Gryphon asked Emmeline, "What do you call this conveyance?"

"You mean my truck?" Emmeline asked.

"It has less room than a stagecoach. Could Luna not ride in the wagon bed? She crowds this space."

"You're in her seat!" Not about to let some long-haired imaginary sexy brute evict her baby, Emmeline sneered, "You'll go back there before she does."

After being silent for twenty or thirty seconds, she continued rambling.

"She's a fine truck. The lines are sleek and sexy. She'll become a great truck once I have the money to fix her up. She's a gem." Emmeline stroked the recently refurbished dashboard leather, all the while ignoring the man sitting three feet away.

"Turn on your charm, Gryphon. Throw a small bit of wind magic at her. Let it blow across her face."

"I'm sitting right here," Emmeline said.

"A worthy idea." Gryphon chanted a Gaelic spell to make wind. Currents flowed around the cab, forming eddies.

"I meant open the window." Luna released a bit of magic and rolled the window down. *"The lever moves in a circular motion, rolling the window up or down."*

Gryphon played with the knob, opening and closing the window. "How splendid." He stroked the top of Luna's head.

"Based on his enthusiasm for a window handle, I can't wait to show him a television." Luna chuckled and rotated to face Emmeline. *"And you, my girl, have much to learn about magick."*

Emmeline burst out laughing. "Oh my God. I'm having entire conversations with myself while hallucinating. I'm talking and listening to my dog and...him. Albeit a sexy, wet-your- panties hallucination. I still don't understand why my psyche has made my dream man an ass."

"I do not understand. What are panties and why would they be wet?" Gryphon asked.

"It's a sexual expression. You make her, uh, I'm not going there. Figure it out."

"Women seem bold in this time." He tugged on the vest and cleared his throat. "It pleases me to know I make your panties wet. Perhaps an exhausting bedding before you release me from the box would settle your nerves?"

"You're doomed in this time. Stop talking."

"I must have inhaled some mold from the dust in the box," Emmeline said. "Yep, it's a drug-induced hallucination, like

King Tut's curse. The curse, a type of mold, along with super-stition had everyone in a panic. I hope it wears off by the time we arrive home. I still have papers to grade."

"I'm a bit surprised at your lack of a comeback on the bedding comment, Emmeline."

"I ignored it. Shit. What does it say about my psyche, inventing a sexy dream man who spouts sexist comments? Freud would have a heyday."

"Luna, can you translate what she said? I do not under-stand 'psyche,' 'Freud,' or 'heyday.'"

"She said you're not real and you're rude."

Sexual tension and fresh sea-breeze scent permeated the cab. Emmeline's skin heated, like the rise of a sunburn after a day in the sun. The kind that shows up hours later, with an itch and pain. She tightened her grip on the steering wheel and took a couple of deep breaths.

"Wow, the mold packs a whopper of an effect. I could sell it and retire." Emmeline rolled down her window. "Women would pay big bucks for a wet dream that follows them home. However, he'd be more desirable if his mouth stayed shut."

"I warned you, it takes a while for his charm to seep in," Luna said.

"Ladies. I sit within earshot of all you say," Gryphon said. "You act as though I do not exist."

"I'm going home and doing a double shot of bourbon."

The wind swirled around the cab, the temperature dropped, and the whole truck twirled in a circle. Grabbing the door handle and the wheel, she closed her eyes. Seconds later the spinning ended, shoving her back against the seat. Raising one eyelid, she saw the truck sat in her driveway. Emmeline looked around, taking in the familiar surroundings.

"What the fuck just happened?"

"Perhaps next time a little warning." Gryphon shook his head. His fingers remained curled around the armrest in a tight squeeze. "Did she whisk us here?"

"Emmeline. You give new meaning to the phrase 'going for a little spin.'" Luna stepped on Emmeline's leg. *"Your magick has quite a punch. Bravo. However, you need more control."*

"My mind has fractured." Emmeline couldn't figure out how they got home so fast. Exiting the truck, she called for Luna. "Let's go, girl."

"Yoohoo, Emmeline." A hand waved in the air from across the backyard.

"Does the woman sit and wait for my truck to pull in?" Emmeline asked.

The neighbor crossed the commons in between their houses.

"Mrs. Caststone. What's up?" Emmeline walked up to the fence. Luna trotted over and sniffed the cat through the chain link.

"Hey Ben, how's it hanging? We found my boy today," Luna said.

"Emmeline does not appear as happy as you," Ben said. The cat rubbed up against the fence, arching its back and purring loudly.

Emmeline frowned at the cat. Hearing the feline talk like Luna gave her pause.

"You should know," the neighbor said, "a group of church people came here today knocking on everyone's doors. I told them you weren't interested, but they left a pamphlet on the front door anyways. Oh, my. Hello there."

Emmeline looked over her shoulder at Gryphon three feet behind. She looked back at Mrs. Caststone, and her mouth dropped open in surprise. "You can see him?"

"You sure found yourself a spectacular specimen. I hope you keep him around for a while. He's yummy enough to eat. Well, except for the hair. Way too long for me."

"Mrs. Caststone!"

"I'm old, not dead, young lady," Edemay Caststone said. "Does he have a name?"

Emmeline stepped back. "Mrs. Caststone, my neighbor."

"Gryphon Wiseman." Extending his hand over the fence, he lifted her hand and pressed a kiss onto the knuckles. "It's a pleasure, Mrs. Caststone."

"Oh, call me Edemay. The other weighs on formality. I'm unable to convince Emmeline to use my first name. Always polite and proper, this one."

His beautiful lavender eyes sparkled, and Mrs. Caststone giggled. A slight breeze lifted the long black strands of his hair, almost as if it was caressing it. The locks wavered in the fading sunlight. He had a presence so big the backyard couldn't hold him. Emmeline's heart beat faster as she watched him with her neighbor.

A slight current carried the smell of sea breeze and mineral salt directly into her lungs and core. Her libido went into overdrive, and she noticed a tingle in a most sensitive spot. Her arm brushed across a nipple, causing a reaction. She gasped and clenched her fists. A cackle from Mrs. Caststone drew her attention.

"Mrs. Caststone, if you don't mind." Emmeline took hold of his sleeve and pulled him toward the house. "Gryphon and I have a few tasks to finish before tomorrow. We're tired, hungry, and stinky from our day. We'll talk again soon."

"Okay, dear. I assume Gryphon will become a permanent resident. You know, for the neighborhood watch and all. We wouldn't want the police called on your boyfriend."

"So glad you reminded me. Please, don't have him arrested." Emmeline glanced over her shoulder at the male specimen currently haunting her. "Who knows, maybe I will keep him. I have to find out if he has any skills in plumbing, mowing, and laundry. Have an enjoyable evening, Mrs. Caststone."

"Yes, it's imperative to have a plumber clean out your pipes now and again." She chuckled while walking away.

Gryphon followed Emmeline as she walked into the house. She opened a cupboard and removed a highball glass and a bottle of bourbon. Unscrewing the top, she poured two fingers into the glass. With one tip of her head, the liquor disappeared. She refilled her glass.

Clearing his throat, he broke the untenable silence. "Proper manners would suggest you offer your guest a libation as well. My last drink happened over a hundred years ago."

Emmeline downed the second drink like a pro, refilled her glass with more of the golden-brown elixir, and pushed the bottle down the counter toward him. Turning, she left the room without a word.

Emmeline dropped onto the couch and removed her hiking boots. She took a deep breath when big feet and long legs stepped into view. Lifting her head, she admired the twinkling amethyst orbs. No one had the right to possess eyes so crystalline. He stood there like a tall superhero figure with one hand on his hips and a tumbler of bourbon in the other.

"The whiskey in this century is excellent." He sipped the glass. "Did it clear up any doubts of my existence?"

"It's bourbon, not whiskey," Emmeline said.

"Excuse me?" Gryphon lifted his glass to study the amber liquid.

"Never mind. And to answer your question, I think I need another drink before making such a ridiculous decision." Back in the kitchen, Emmeline eyed her backpack sitting on the table. The Walther rested on top.

Removing the pistol from the holster and ejecting the magazine, Emmeline started counting bullets. "If I shot him, there will be one bullet short of a full load." As she pulled back the slide, a fully intact bullet popped out onto the kitchen table. "The magazine holds seven. If I fired once, and one's on the table, five would still be in the magazine."

She pushed the release and thumbed the remaining shells into her palm. Five. She lifted her head and stared at the spot on his chest. No hole or blood stain.

"*Ben's ridiculous,*" Luna said, bursting through the doggie door in a huff. She sat beside Gryphon. *"Good heavens, Emme-line. Don't shoot him again."*

"Convinced?" Gryphon leaned against the archway with his arms crossed.

"No." She reloaded the weapon, poured another drink, and walked into the dining room.

"You should slow down a bit," Gryphon said. "I don't think you will understand the rest of our conversation this eve if you keep downing your libation."

"Gryphon, be quiet and let her process. Magick will show her the truth."

Emmeline squeezed her eyelids shut and sucked down half of the amber liquid in the glass. "Nope, still there." She picked up the Walther and made her way down the hallway. She waved the gun. "I would suggest you don't follow me."

CHAPTER 6

Cold Springs, PA 1900

The floor shook, and Megaera saw the vision rise before her, playing out, translucent, in the air. The back wall of the church showed through, making some of the images unclear. She didn't know the spell would produce the visage, but it played in her favor. She could witness her magick working. The wood cross hanging on the back wall of the church darkened out some of the pictures, so she waved her hand and made the cross fall to the floor.

Gryphon sat playing cards with several humans. He tossed money into the pile and smiled until he gazed out the dusk-caked front window of the Grand Hotel. Pointed ears and a long muzzle showed up as a silhouette.

"The beast arrives to tell Gryphon of my visit." Megaera glanced at her mother and pointed at the vision. Her mother remained unconscious. With a shrug of her shoulders, she returned to the scenes playing out in the air.

Gryphon continued playing until his friend Thomas showed up. They exchanged words, and Gryphon deserted his game and left. They stood outside the privy and appeared to argue. But not for long, as he rewarded Thomas with a shoulder touch.

Megaera closed her eyes and pictured Gryphon touching her shoulder with such kindness and concern. Perhaps Thomas would have a use in the future, assuming he made Second Level. When she opened them, Gryphon was calling the wind in her vision.

"So Gryphon created the errant wind." Megaera looked at her mother. Small movements suggested she was coming around. Perhaps she would be awake to see her spell completed.

Thunder roared outside as the winds picked up. Megaera tilted her head to listen for rain, but none came. She returned her attention to the rest of the spell's vision.

The wind blew the hotel doors open and scattered cards, chips, and empty chairs. A gray cloud flowed into the gaming area. It circled Gryphon. Her spell spread its malevolence, pressing him to the earth and making him a prisoner where he sat.

Megaera smiled as Gryphon tried to escape with the others. The dark force she'd sent held him in place. The screams of the long dead shattered her eardrums as the ghosts flew around the church.

Gryphon disintegrated into small lavender particles. No longer corporeal, the dust formed a small tornadic funnel twirling around the room. Retaining only his conscience, the tornado swirled out the door and into the wind.

Megaera felt the power of Gryphon's earth magick as the spinning fury entered the church. The funnel found the box, and his ghostly ancestors pulled his essence into their realm. Little sparkles of wind energy tried to escape, but the power bearing down would not allow it.

Megaera called more fire, sending a streak of flame into the tomb. The ingredients snapped and crackled, catching fire as the funnel cloud emptied into the box. After the final wisp of

Gryphon's essence fell, the lid snapped shut. The wood seemed to creak in pain as the black magick penetrated the space and sealed the box.

The wind increased in intensity, blowing a distinct odor of brimstone through the shifting building. Megaera took a final glance at her mother as thunder and lightning struck outside. The wind bowed out the walls and rattled the shutters of the old church. More wind found its way through the cracks, sweeping through the building. Megaera heard distant screams and the crackle of fire before the church walls burst into flames.

Her joy dampened when a strong gust of wind blew hot embers out into the night. Before it was too late, Megaera raised both hands and called for the total well of energy. She commanded the druid stone to return home. The slow movement stirred her impatience, so she gave the block a push. It floated over the open tomb and fell into place.

"Close." Hands moving in circular patterns over the opening, she sealed the tomb and sank it deep into the earth. As a witch of the earth, Gryphon would remain safe.

Megaera cast a glance at Joan, still lying on the ground. At least her eyes were open and she could witness the emergence of her daughter's power. Megaera smirked and went to her mother. With a wave of her hand, she claimed the High Priestess robe as her own.

The wind quit. A dog howled.

Without warning, a large bolt of lightning struck the bell in the steeple with a loud crack. The garbled gong announced its discourse, and sparks flew in every direction. Curls of fire rode the renewed wind, spread, and fell on leaves and dried timbers.

The immense power released during the casting had drained Megaera's energy. A physical transformation took place. Her once useful fingers became withered and weak. The dress hung without definition on her bony joints before falling off and exposing the flesh. Her pantalettes slipped over flesh-less hips and hung on her knees, ready to drop at the first step.

Floorboards squeaked. In the doorway wavered a shad-owed figure resembling Kenter. It came forward with an arm extended and pointing a finger. She grabbed her bloomers and ran outside to find the entire town engulfed in flame. A crash behind her revealed the hottest flames, violet and blue, engulfing the church. Without remorse for her mother, she levi-tated across the commons with the High Priestess robe hanging on one arm.

Heat burned a blush across her cheeks and nose. Building after building lit on fire. Megaera ignored the humans and witches alike as they screamed and ran into the streets. Witches burned to ashes on the spot as the drought-stricken land fed the flames. Not one ounce of guilt rose when the three promiscuous witches ran from the woods aflame.

Megaera floated up the hillside as the tops of trees burst orange and yellow with the fire's heat. As she dodged several flaming limbs falling from trees, her fire magick carved a tunnel through the flames. She went to Gryphon's cabin and called her magick when she saw the Book of Shadows and the Wiseman family quilt levitate out of the burning building. She reached out and collected them in her arms.

Fighting the grimoire of shadows stole the rest of her energy, and she sank to the ground. Unable to muster enough strength to whisk, Megaera walked to her secret cave.

"The power surges within me. Soon I will have enough to do anything I want."

Luna stepped from the brush.

"Give him back."

Harrisburg, PA 2019

Emmeline sat on the bed, stroking Luna's warm muzzle. "I shot a guy today. He didn't die, and now I want to jump him.

It's a good thing my intense aversion to assholes keeps me right here with you."

"I don't understand your hesitation." Luna nuzzled an ear. *"You were chosen by the Grand Master for Gryphon. Go ahead. Jump him and get it over with."*

"I already opened the box. Why doesn't he go away? And who the hell is the Grand Master?" Emmeline asked.

"A tether still ties Gryphon to either you or the box. It's your job to release him. As for the Grand Master, consider him God." Luna licked Emmeline's cheek. *"I refuse to talk to you about sex. Ask one of your girlfriends."*

"I thought I told you not to follow me," Emmeline said. She narrowed her eyes at the man standing in the doorway.

"We have many tasks needing attention," Gryphon said.

"Magick keeps you attracted, Emmeline. But your head keeps you at a distance. Follow the magick. It comes from the heart."

"Your talking isn't making the problem any better," Emmeline snapped at Luna. She fell back on the bed, arm draped across her eyes. "Let's top off the day with a stack of laboratory reports to grade before tomorrow."

"I suggested you grade them on Wednesday, but you never listen."

Dropping the arm from her eyes, Emmeline focused on Gryphon. "You still here?"

"I wait for your magick to release me from my tether," Gryphon said.

The big hunk leaned against the door frame. No one had the right to exist in such a perfect state. A lock of hair had drifted down over his brow, making him look like a sexy model. Her eyes followed down the button line on his vest, and a gasp followed the burn creeping up her neck. The growing bulge in his crotch was unmistakable.

"Holy fucking God!" Emmeline sat upright.

"You have a foul mouth." Gryphon stood up straight and tugged his vest into place. He readjusted his casual stance by shifting his feet and plucking the trousers away from his thighs. He shrugged his shoulders, "But for an unknown reason, I find your manners enticing."

"Enticing? Well then, let me add," Emmeline sat up and pointed, "I can't believe I would dream up a white knight who sprouts a woody at the drop of a hat. How old are you, thirteen?"

Gryphon struggled to maintain a little dignity but failed. She found his embarrassment adorable. No. Wait. She admonished herself in her mind. How could she even consider him adorable? Cocky? Yes. Good-looking? You bet. Big asshole material? For sure. Her bottom line would have to read: Gryphon must go.

Gryphon rubbed his chin with an open hand. "I have not seen thirteen since—Luna, what year do we stand in?"

"2019. Do the math!"

"Ah, I passed thirteen two hundred and seventy-two years ago." Gryphon frowned at Luna. "I discern time has not dulled your sharp tongue, my friend."

"My sharp tongue kept you from many a disaster in your youth, Viscount."

"Uh, hate to break up your conversation, but you're two hundred and eighty-five years old? Fuck me. I fell down the rabbit hole." Emmeline put her feet over the edge of the bed and sat up.

"Gives new meaning to the term 'older man,' doesn't it?"

"When did you fall in a rabbit hole? Are you injured?" Gryphon walked over, knelt on the bed, and grabbed Emmeline's ankle. His large hands snaked up each leg, massaging the muscles and searching for an injury. "I do not feel any heat. Perhaps another part of your body is injured?"

"What are you doing?" Emmeline slapped his hands and kicked her feet. Another part of her body was feeling the heat, but now was not the time to deal with the problem. With a quick pull, she jerked her leg from his grasp.

"I merely render aid." Gryphon reclaimed a foot. He caressed her ankle and toes. "You do not appear harmed."

The room vibrated with tension.

"Emmeline, control your magick."

"Why are you telling me?" Emmeline asked.

"Because it's not Gryphon's magick. It's yours." Luna made her way across the mattress and rested her muzzle on Emmeline's shoulder.

Emmeline cast a quick glance at the dog, and the room calmed. She looked at Gryphon. "Why do you think I'm hurt?"

"You said you fell down a rabbit hole," Gryphon said.

Emmeline stared at him.

"Gryphon, it's a figure of speech. It's based on a story about a young girl who drank the wrong kind of tea." Luna switched her gaze to Emmeline. *"By the time Lewis Carroll published* Alice in Wonderland, *Gryphon no longer read the books of children."*

"I much preferred Whitman's *Leaves of Grass* at the time," Gryphon said. "'Now I will dismiss myself from impassive women, I will go stay with her who waits for me.' Whitman said what most people think. I admired his tenacity."

"I'm not surprised you enjoy Whitman. By the way, the expression 'fuck me' doesn't actually mean to, you know, do it."

Gryphon remained within arm's reach of Emmeline's feet. The temperature in the room increased by ten degrees. Her heart pumped a little faster, and her breathing slowed. If he continued to stay so close, she might spontaneously combust. She wanted to crawl inside his skin and live there. She pushed out a deep breath. "Oh hell no."

"Go sit in the living room and try to remember a memory spell," Luna said to Gryphon. *"I'll take care of our girl."*

Emmeline's houseguest retreated. She stared at the dog.

"I'm crazy."

"No." Luna laid her head on Emmeline's thigh and expelled

a long breath. *"Consider the possibility and go with it. What's the worst that can happen?"*

Emmeline remained quiet while she processed the question. Even if it were her subconscious talking instead of Luna, the question was pertinent. The worst? "I could get locked in a loony bin. I could wake up and find out this was all a bourbon-charged dream that went wrong. I could find out I was a witch."

"All of those, I suppose," Luna said. *"Consider the benefits of having magick. And Gryphon."*

Emmeline cocked her head. "He does have a purple aura."

"You think a little longer and stay out of the bourbon. I'll be out with Gryphon." Luna whisked.

The dog vanished without walking out of the bedroom. Emmeline swallowed back her fear and considered every word. She got out of bed and changed into some comfortable sweatshorts and an oversized flannel shirt. Her socks padded across the hardwood floor as she returned to the living room and leaned against the wall.

They were talking. Dog and man. The dog inside her head. Weird.

"I appreciate this room. It had a distinct earthy feel."

Emmeline looked around her living room and took in the décor. The plaster walls were the color of dry sand, and an area rug sporting geometric symbols in bold turquoise, orange, and green covered well-used hardwood floors. He was correct. It was earthy and comfortable.

"Your head must be spinning. What goes on in there?" Luna asked. She leveled her head on Gryphon's knee.

"I'm a hundred years in the future with a Key who refuses to accept her role in the Grand Master's plan," Gryphon said. "I also wonder what activities became history as time passed? How long will it take to catch up with the workings of the world? How does magick work in this time?"

"I felt the same way when I came through time," Luna said.

"My cabin, the Book of Shadows, everything I once knew burned with the rest of the town. All is lost." Gryphon lowered his head and rubbed his eyes with his hands.

"The book would have saved itself, but on the night of the fires I saw Megaera take it and your family quilt. They exist. However, I don't know where."

"I was a fool to ignore the signs and whispers about Megaera. I sensed her power growing at times but was foolish enough to think it a minor problem. I let the coven down."

"After Willa, I should have taken a more proactive approach to your training," Luna said. *"There's no one left in the coven with the strength to fight Megaera except you. And Emmeline."*

"My Key is still a neophyte. How do we use such undeveloped skills to fight a Fire Witch with such power?"

Emmeline stood up and padded across the room to sit in the recliner. "I guess since you're talking about me, I should be here. I don't understand what's going on."

Luna left Gryphon to sit between them. She said to Emmeline, *"The decision to wait on your training was decided by Verne, but the others agreed."*

"And the others are—"

"Betsy, Mirielda, and Edemay. They're the elders and make most of the decisions for the Earth Witches in the coven. Minerva, now in the House of Dawn as well," Luna said.

"Where is Verne?" Gryphon asked.

"She died after Emmeline arrived in town."

Emmeline's forehead furrowed. "All of my friends knew but didn't tell me?"

"They felt because of your tragic childhood, you would not accept anything they said about magick. You tend to deflect when a situation becomes difficult."

"It seems strange to fight one's nature. I was always in a hurry to advance my skills. I can't imagine not wanting to know." Gryphon glanced at Luna. "How many MichAudah survived the years?"

"The MichAudah boasted only twenty-seven witches after the fire. Their numbers increased but not their power. Megaera has most of them terrified, so they do as ordered," Luna said. *"We follow the prophecy, and your release marks the beginning."*

"Kenter told me of the prophecy after Mother died," Gryphon said. "Until I am free, I only have some of my power. I cannot fight Megaera in this weakened state."

"The prophecy's not as clear as once thought. You must let the fates drive this path." Luna walked over to Emmeline. *"Allow fate to guide you. You're more powerful than anyone in the coven imagines. You're a druid, not an Earth Witch."*

"Druid. Sure, I'll add ancient being to my...not going to fucking believe my weekend tale at school tomorrow," Emmeline said. "Luna baby. Let's see what we have to eat for dinner. I need some...space."

Gryphon cocked an eyebrow. "Luna baby? You do know she's a familiar, not a dog? I spent over two hundred years with her. She's far from a primitive beast, and you insult her with your baby talk, treats, and toys."

Luna nudged Emmeline's leg. *"It's true. I am not a dog. Although I enjoy the treats. I love you. With all my heart."*

Emmeline hushed out a deep breath. "Okay then. You stay here, and I'll go to the kitchen."

CHAPTER 7

Cold Springs, PA 1900

Verne stirred the cauldron. The smell of burned wood remained an oppressive reminder of the fires that had ravaged Cold Springs during Mabon, the autumn equinox. Life grew harder as they waited for Samhain. Multiple families were crowded into the cabins that hadn't burnt, and food supplies were running low.

But hope still remained in Verne's heart. Unable to use a ceremonial fire, they gathered at the High Altar to ask the Grand Master to send advice on this hallow eve. Thomas and Norman fed the fire with the only wood they could find on the charred hillsides surrounding Cold Springs. Much was already scorched by the flame of dark magick. She hoped it would not offend.

Megaera hung over her shoulder as the remaining coven gathered. Splatters of hot brew fell across Megaera's robes with each bubble and pop. Verne kept her face neutral, but each offense made her smile inside. Even the brew knew MichAudah's loss was Megaera's fault.

"Gach réidh, High Priestess," Verne said.

Through clenched teeth, Megaera restrained her voice. "You know I do not understand Gaelic. Speak clear."

Verne turned to the coven and raised her hands. "Our coire is gach réidh. What does it mean, children?"

A chorus of young voices shouted, "All ready."

Megaera stepped to the High Altar. With her chin held high, she resettled the bottom of the robe. "Continue, seer."

"It falls to you, High Priestess, to bring us the vision."

Megaera took a deep breath and cast a sideways glance at the simmering pot. She whispered to Verne, "The vessel does not care for me."

Verne felt safe with the coven surrounding them. Megaera wouldn't dare strike at her. She continued their quiet conversation. "Perhaps it feels you're a pretender."

"A Fire Witch should serve me, not one loyal to another line of magick," Megaera said. A glance found the eyes of the coven raising eyebrows and talking amongst themselves with occasional head nods thrown in her direction.

"None of the survivors can scry but I. You will have to deal with me," Verne said. "I tell you now. I remain loyal to Mich-Audah regardless of who sits on the High Seat."

"We have no time for this discussion. Ask the cauldron for guidance. I can create fire to keep us warm, but I cannot sprout food from my ass." Gnashing her yellowed teeth, Megaera adjusted the sacred robe and stepped toward the coven. She opened her arms with a false smile and said, "On this hallow eve, the Grand Master will listen for a familiar voice. Verne will conduct the quest."

Verne became lost in thought staring at the brew. With the approaching winter and no supply train stopping at the burned-out depot, the survival of the coven was in question. She dropped whole seeds of corn, squash, and beans into the brew.

"Spirit of the cauldron, I seek your wisdom this night. With our meager offering of the Three Sisters, we honor the Grand

Master. Show us what we must do." Verne waved her hands over the surface and chanted a Gaelic prayer. The coven echoed her words.

The boil settled, and the brew put forth a vision. Images wavered on the surface.

Verne stepped closer. The sounds of the night disappeared. The winds died. Only the crackling heat of the fire and the drone of chanting witches filled the night. The chanting became a baritone murmur as they danced in a circle around the cauldron.

She lifted her arms to the night sky and pleaded, "Cauldron of Wind, Earth, Water, and Fire. We ask for guidance. We seek to know the path MichAudah should take to honor the Grand Master."

The coven's chant thrummed in the quiet of the night. Step by step, their feet moved faster and faster to build power within the circle. The fire flared above the rim of the cauldron with white-hot flames, and a loud crack of lightning shot down from the sky and struck the altar stone.

A spark from the strike spat glowing licks of flame onto Megaera's robe and set it on fire. She tossed off the robe with irreverence and watched the flames consume the sacred fabric. In the final moment, Megaera remembered to use magick.

With skeletal hands lifted in front of her, she said, "By the power of Balor, I command you out."

The entire coven stared.

An elder pushed his way to the altar. "To call on the evil eye, you dishonor your role as High Priestess. I call for your removal as our coven leader."

Whispers soon became shouts. The coven grew riotous as Fire Witches argued with Earth Witches. As anger released uncontrolled magick, the overall power well of the coven drained its powers.

"Do something, Megaera," Verne said.

Megaera sent streamers of fire energy over their heads to

gather their attention. The crowd calmed and faced her. "Fools. You waste energy with your discontent. I claimed the High Seat with blood. It belongs to me as daughter of Joan Caroline."

The High Priestess stepped toward the fire and called one tendril of flame. It danced in the air like a cobra rising from its basket and struck at the elder under Megaera's command. It took only seconds for the blue flame to burn him to ashes.

"Twenty-eight now becomes twenty-seven. Seven is sacred and brings enlightenment to all," Megaera said. She levitated the burned robe, restored it, and settled it back on her shoulders. "You will soon learn of my power."

"How dare you, Megaera. You were taught better than—" Verne was interrupted.

The earth rumbled, and a plume of gray smoke rose from the cauldron. Everyone except Megaera dropped to their knees.

"The Grand Master speaks," Verne said.

"Read the cauldron before the vision fades," a coven member shouted.

Verne rose to her feet and leaned over the cauldron. "A battle will take place far in the future. A witch with black hair and lavender eyes will rise from an ancient Witchbox with the help of a Key. They will win control of the coven using power from our ancestral land. You will know when the trembling earth announces the loss of the sun."

Shouts of "praise be" and "blessed child" broke through.

"The Viscount died in the fires," Thomas said. "Who is this man?"

Verne searched the surface for the truth. "A dark magick imprisoned Gryphon in a Witchbox. It will be he who comes."

"Who dared to commit such offense?" another witch asked.

"The dark magick came from a warlock. Wilmott sought to take his brother's place," Megaera said. She waved her hands over the cauldron, pretending to see. Her vile words would add fuel to the fire in the coven's heart. None ever cared for

Wilmott once he started to practice dark magick. "I will sit in the High Seat until the earth magick of the Wiseman line and the fire magick of the Carolines lead together."

"Does the false Priestess speak the truth, Verne?" an elder asked.

Megaera raised her hand to strike again, but Verne pushed it down and through clenched teeth said, "You will not."

Verne waved both hands over the cauldron. "The vision has gone. We must wait for the Viscount to return. The truth will come out at the time of his rising."

Shouts rose from the coven. They chanted and danced around the fire, sending blessings to the Grand Master and asking Gryphon to return. No one celebrated Megaera's rise to power.

A young witch with a small child pushed to the front of the crowd. "We need food. How will we survive the cold?"

Verne palmed the child's cheek. "We move west, to where Stony Creek meets the big river. The Key will arrive when day becomes night and the earth trembles without reason. Return to your homes. Tomorrow we move toward our new destiny."

Megaera dug sharpened fingernails into the seer's arm as the coven retreated down the hill. Verne struggled to pull out of the witch's painful grip.

"What didn't you tell them?" Megaera narrowed her eyes.

"I saw two who arrive with Gryphon. One will have the power of the ancient druids, as I said. The second will resemble a ghost from the past. The future is not the way you have imagined."

"You hide information, old woman." Megaera pulled Verne close and spoke. "Tell me everything. I command it. Or face the fate of those who speak against me."

"High Priestess, you will not take another. Besides, I remain the last seer. Who would scry for you? I have told you all I have seen. The cauldron does not give specifics. But years will pass." Verne pushed the witch away with a burst of wind energy. "I saw a time of horseless carriages and fast-moving birds in the sky that carry people. That is all I know."

Megaera's jaw tightened. "If we leave on the morrow, you must secure the cauldron from the world. Use the coven's remaining well of magick. I shall save my energy for our protection on the journey. From here on, everyone must reserve what they can and work to build more."

After Megaera whisked away, Verne busied herself securing the altar site. She took a deep breath, knowing she had come close to death moments ago. Megaera was already out of control. What would she be like by the time Gryphon returned?

The whoosh of a whisk brough Mirielda to her side.

"Sister. Did you come to help prepare the cauldron?" Verne asked.

"As your apprentice, the task becomes mine," Mirielda said.

"Winter comes. Its harsh grip will test our strength. We can pool our funds and purchase supplies at the other settlements. We will survive by the Grand Master's mercy." Verne hugged the last remaining member of her immediate family. "Help me secure the altar."

Verne chanted the spell of invisibility and tossed her last whole kernels of the Three Sisters into the fire. It took most of the coven's collective energy to cast the spell and the coven would pay dearly to maintain it. Flames surged as the last crackle of fire went out, and the cauldron faded from sight.

"I wish we could take it with us," Mirielda said. She thumped her chest with an open palm. "My heart hurts to store our cauldron away from the coven."

"The coven needs the permission of the Grand Master. At the moment, we have little energy to do more than survive. After we regain out strength, we will petition for a relocation," Verne said.

"Do you need anything else?" Mirielda asked.

Verne took up her sister's hands. "We will push ahead in your training as a seer. You have an important part to play in our future." She held up a hand to stay Mirielda's question. "Do not ask of your future; only know you will have an important role."

"I dislike these riddles."

"You must know what I didn't tell the coven or Megaera tonight."

"You withheld part of the vision?" Mirielda's eyes widened.

"I tell you, and you alone. You cannot share this with the coven. Listen with open ears, even if you do not understand," Verne said. "On the day of a spring equinox, when the sun disappears and returns, the pull from the conjunction of the moon and Jupiter will deliver the Key, a druid of great power from the womb of someone she will never know. The true High Priest will come soon after."

Verne knew in keeping the secret, it would cost her life long before the eclipse.

Harrisburg, PA 2019

Emmeline opened the fridge, found nothing appetizing, and pushed the door closed. The bottle of bourbon sat on the counter beside her glass. She poured two fingers and returned to the living room, where she sat in the recliner.

"My neighbor saw you, so you're not a figment of my imagination. Even after several drinks, you're still here, in weird clothes, and talking to my dog...err, familiar." Emmeline shook her head at the final word.

"Weird clothes? I wear the finest available. In fact, I had these brought in from New York City." He tugged on the sleeve so the ruffle showed below the coat cuff and brushed imagined dust from the shoulder.

"Let's return to this witch thing."

"A witch is not a 'thing,'" Gryphon said with a tug on his

brocade vest and a chin lift. "We are sentient beings who draw the energy provided by the earth and the Grand Master to create magick. We live by the power we store in our energy wells and how we use our magick."

"Where does this energy come from?" Emmeline kept her eyes on the talking stud while she took another swallow.

"The earth holds energy in the soil, water, air, and living entities," Gryphon said. "We absorb this energy into our center, store it, and use it to cast spells. By manipulating the energy, it does our bidding. As children, we learned the rules and practiced. Druid or not, you too must follow the rules."

"It almost sounds like you're stating the Law of Conservation of Energy or the carbon cycle." Emmeline tilted her head to the ceiling and frowned as she pondered her last statement. Returning her attention to Gryphon, she said, "At least that's something I understand. By the way, you said you're a witch. How does it differ from a warlock? Isn't the classification gender-related?"

Gryphon's eyes bulged as he jumped up and paced the length of the room. Waving his hands while he talked, he said, "Warlocks cast dark magick from the bowels of the earth and spread evil. I suffered the unfortunate plight of having a warlock for an uncle. Why do you insult me?"

"Jeez. I'm sorry. Chill your jets."

"What is a jet?"

"This is going to be harder than I thought." Emmeline fell back against the recliner. She expelled a lungful of air and flopped a forearm over her eyes. "Never mind the jet."

"The boy's a quick learner. Let him watch television. He'll learn." Luna whisked away.

"Not sure I will ever become used to—" Emmeline pointed to an empty spot.

"Luna talking?" Gryphon asked.

"No. The poofing."

"Poofing?" Gryphon's head tilted, and he raised his brows.

"You speak of the whisk. A fine way to travel if you know your destination. You already whisked today when you returned your transport to your home. We will teach you how to use your magick."

Emmeline continued to stare at the space where the dog used to sit. A headache pounded her temples. She stood up and paced the living room, wringing her hands, now devoid of the glass. "This whole scenario is wacked. I wake up one morning with everything normal, well normal for me, and the next hour I have Mr. GQ and a talking dog. Everything's hard to accept."

In three long strides, he stood in front of her. His hands were strong and warm as he collected her hands. The large calluses on his fingers tickled her skin. A masculine scent, salty and wind-blown, washed over her senses. She could almost taste the salt on her tongue.

Everything about the man—witch—was overwhelming. The power to influence decisions he possessed was the kind a person is born with, not learned. Would she fall under his spell? Was he casting a spell on her right now?

"I sense your doubt. Let me cast a knowing spell to show you how I was imprisoned in the Witchbox. It will save us valuable time."

Emmeline frowned. At least he was asking.

Luna whisked in and dropped the mail on Emmeline's lap. *"Amazon came. The package is in the kitchen. I wish the driver would invest in treats other than Milkbone."*

"Grateful much?" Emmeline asked her.

"Let Gryphon cast his spell." Luna put a paw on Emmeline's knee. *"Once we figure out how druid magick works, you'll have full access to all of it."*

"We need to move forward in our purpose. May I cast the spell?" Gryphon's smile matched the twinkle in his eye.

"Alright. Go ahead. But if it hurts, I'm getting my pistol," Emmeline said.

"I would never hurt you, my sweet Emmeline. I will use a remembrance spell. Please." Gryphon waved one hand to the couch and motioned for her to sit.

Emmeline did as he asked. She remembered the pistol was in the bedroom.

Gryphon removed a bit of powder from the pocket of his vest and sprinkled it in the air. The purple dust sparkled like twinkling lights and danced on the fading rays of sun beaming through the window.

"From earth and air, I call to thee. Bring memories from the past to the Key. Show the life gone by, in minutes told, from my mind, my Key will hold. To pay the powers, I accept the Returns of Three. So mote it be."

"Doesn't rhyme very—" A breeze caressed Emmeline's cheeks, intensified, and whipped around the living room. Curtains lifted and pillows tumbled from the couch. A pile of papers resting on the ottoman dispersed across the floor. The lights flickered, and the temperature dropped.

"What should I do?" Emmeline could feel her heart pounding.

"You must accept the memories or they will blow away," Gryphon said. His deep voice caressed her like a piece of fine silk dragging across bare flesh, warm and sultry.

"I accept the memories."

A large masculine hand slid seductively down one of her arms. Tingles flowed through the limb and shot straight to her core. She tumbled down a dark tunnel. The light faded, as did the living room, Luna, and Gryphon.

Frame by frame, a slideshow of sorts moved past her eyes. Each picture reflected a different time, place, and activity. Native Americans danced around a campfire, covered wagons struggled up an incline, and mammoth hemlocks fell. A heavy heartbeat pulsed within her chest in rhythm with the changing slides.

A young boy ran across the hillside with a white dog. A

little girl with blond hair ran behind them, trying to keep up. The boy had urgency written in his wide lavender eyes. Gryphon was as handsome then as he was now. The image of the little girl made Emmeline shiver, but no clear view of her face appeared.

The scene of the children faded as the scent of tobacco filled the air. The clink of chips, laughter, and piano music did not distract her from the shouts in the distance.

A disembodied voice yelled, "Fire!" She smelled wood burning.

How could a dream have actual scent and sound? This was not a movie or slideshow. The scenes, the smells, and the sounds were actual memories from Gryphon's mind inside her head.

Emmeline made the connection to a line in the letterboxing poem she'd read this morning: 'Beware if you open it, you will find, a new life from the witch's mind. You may like it, you may not—' which took her to the little tomb and started this fantasy drop. Now she understood. Licking her lips, she allowed the rest of Gryphon's memories in.

Emmeline pulled back into the couch when flames flared. The heat warmed her cheeks but never rose to pain. Buildings ignited, and people screamed as they burned. Her fingers ached from the tight grip on a pillow as a tear rolled down her cheeks. Why didn't the history records mention the loss of life? It was devastating.

The past flicked by frame after frame. She saw Gryphon's eyes widen, and her hands grabbed the chair when he disintegrated into purple-colored dust and blew away like a tornado. The memories faded to what amounted to a static screen on the television, only in purple.

Emmeline's eyesight returned.

"Why's she crying, Gryphon?" Luna paced.

Gryphon raised one finger to rest on his lips.

The memory ended with the tall, dark-haired, sexy

Gryphon standing in front of her with another glass of bourbon and Luna beside him.

"A drink, perhaps?" Gryphon offered the glass with a sinful smile.

Emmeline grabbed the glass and downed the amber-colored nectar. She took a quick inhale of breath as the fire burned its way down. "Oh fuck. I'm in so much trouble."

"You did nothing wrong other than your atrocious language."

"I think Dr. Caroline played a part in the vision." Emmeline tried to extract a last drop from the glass.

"I do not recall a Caroline as a doctor," Gryphon said. "Does Megaera know of my Key?"

"Well, uh. She does but she doesn't."

"Dr. Megaera Caroline is my immediate supervisor at my job. She hates me." Emmeline's eyes widened. "Oh my God. She really is a witch. I was right?"

Emmeline glanced at Gryphon. His eyes changed color from a bright lavender to a dark gray. Wind whipped around the room, lifting curtains and chilling the air. Emmeline shivered, whether from the temperature change or the cold, piercing stare Gryphon gave her. Thinking back to earlier in the day, there were times when he'd tried to be charming. His eyes lit with little sparkles. Interesting.

"You work for Megaera?" Sparks of magick flickered in the darker corners of the room. "Megaera imprisoned me. Now she torments my Key? How is she still alive, Luna?"

"I do say, the last few years have been interesting." Luna jumped onto the couch with Emmeline. *"An ancient magick protects Emmeline. We don't know where it comes from."*

Emmeline wanted to retreat into the embracing sting of the bourbon, but reality would rise with the sun. Papers waited for grades, and too much alcohol suggested they wouldn't get done. She focused on those same papers, now spread across the living room floor with dog paw prints on them.

"I can't have another parent complain about me," Emmeline said. She crawled onto the floor and scooped up the papers.

Gryphon frowned. With the wave of a hand, they ended up stacked on top of the ottoman. "I have better purpose for your knees than picking up paper."

Emmeline stopped. Turned.

"Uh oh." Luna jumped down and ran to stand in front of Gryphon. "Before you fly off the handle at his comment, consider he is from 1900. Men were not advanced at the time."

Still on her knees, Emmeline crossed her arms. She took a deep breath and set her jaw. With narrowed eyes, she let her uncontrolled magick loose and pushed Gryphon onto the couch.

"You didn't happen to grade them, did you?" she asked.

"Do you wish for me to mark the papers with a score?" Gryphon made eye contact. His lips quirked on one side.

"Can you?"

"Child's play." Gryphon waved a hand again. The papers fluffed and settled. "I will warn against use of magick for one's own benefit. Returns of Three on personal gains can become quite brutal."

"Oh my, yes. The Returns of Three will have to be your first lesson."

Emmeline grabbed the stack of papers. Flipping through them, she noticed the lack of paw prints and scores in circles at the top. "Holy shit. You have a use after all."

His smile took a deep dive into Emmeline's psyche. She saw images of them naked and entwined. Apparently, he had a second use. She shook her head. "Stop doing that!"

"Stop doing what?" Gryphon asked.

"Feeding me images." Emmeline shot to her feet to relieve the pressure building between her legs and retreated to the kitchen.

"I create no images in your head. They are yours alone."

Gryphon followed, leaning against the archway. "If I may ask, images of what, sweet Emmeline?"

She narrowed her eyes at his cocky stance; he leaned against the archway with his arms and feet crossed. She set the empty glass in the sink and took two steps to the refrigerator. A pop sounded as she opened the door and stared at the contents. For the second time today, nothing inspired a quick and carb-loaded meal. She was deflecting. She needed comfort food to settle her mind and the bourbon buzz now ringing in her ears.

A presence settled along her back. Heat penetrated through the layers of her clothes, and the smell of a salty breeze over-powered the other odors from the fridge. The temperature differential between her front and back hardened her nipples and increased the throbbing of her clit.

A muscular arm held the door. Trying to exit, Emmeline turned to find her nose pressed against his broad, solid chest. Her lungs quit working, and an overwhelming attraction froze her in place. Gryphon's heavy heartbeat thrummed against her sensitized nipples while the heat from his erection seeped through her jeans.

"You will need to forgive me, but I must," Gryphon said. He leaned forward, took her cheeks between his two hands, and kissed her.

His lips pressed deep masculine flavors, a hint of smokey bourbon, and the salty sensation of the most amazing dessert you could dream of into her mouth. Rich, creamy, and warm, the flavors flowed over her tongue. She forgot to breathe, and her arms rose around his neck of their own volition and pulled his body closer without a thought.

The kiss was electric. In fact, lights flashed enough to break the kiss.

He pulled away. Emmeline felt the rush of breath across her face. Gryphon's lavender corneas darkened to a deep amethyst and glistened like gemstones with sparks of light jumping from them. Only the cold from the refrigerator remained.

The appliance beeped its open-door warning.

"I think I'll order a pizza." Emmeline escaped the hands still on her cheeks, afraid more electricity would zap her system. The tingling remained. Damn, the man could kiss. Grabbing the cell phone, her hands shook as she punched the quick-dial for the pizza shop.

Gryphon moved around the kitchen, touching, poking, and prodding several appliances, including the toaster, which clicked when he pushed the lever down. He pulled his head back and glanced at Emmeline.

"Luna. Why does she attach the box to her head?"

"She's ordering food. The box is a portable telegraph."

"Fascinating. I will have to try it."

Emmeline shoved the phone into her back pocket. "Pizza in about twenty minutes."

While Gryphon continued to explore the kitchen, Emmeline grabbed paper plates, napkins, and several pizza accoutrements. She tossed them on the dining room table.

The silence between them did not relieve the sexual need building lower in her belly as she followed his fingers on every twist of a knob and flip of a switch. Remaining close, Emmeline followed behind to turn off everything he turned on except her own libido.

A loud *ding-dong* sounded. Luna fired off a round of loud barks and ran for the door.

"What in the bloody hell is wrong with you?" Gryphon yelled at Luna.

"Stop yelling at my dog," Emmeline yelled back. "She's doing her job."

"Sorry, I forgot my dignity. Forgive me, Viscount." Trotting past them to the dining room to sit, Luna held her nose high in the air. *"By the way, the pizza's here."*

Emmeline dropped the pizza box on the table, flipped the

lid, and dropped a slice on a paper plate. She handed it to Gryphon and waved him toward one of the chairs.

"This is pizza. You can eat it as is or put on extra toppings. I have ranch dressing, garlic salt, honey, parmesan cheese, and pepper flakes. Oh, yeah. What would you like to drink?"

Gryphon frowned at the slice. He pulled out the chair and sat, poking the greasy pepperoni-topped object with his finger. He lifted his head to answer. "I will have any libation you have available."

"Why does every male in the world leave the choice of what they drink up to the women?" Emmeline grabbed two sodas and a beer and set them on the table near their plates. Picking up a can of Coke Zero, she popped the lid and set it in front of him. "This is soda. It's sugar and water with a fizz. No alcohol. The other is beer."

Gryphon sniffed the Coke and pulled his head back. He set the can down and picked up the beer bottle. "I shall try your beer."

Emmeline took the bottle from him, popped the lid with the bottle opener, and set it in front of him. She picked up the soda. "I've had too much alcohol. I'll stick with soda."

"Indeed." Gryphon read the label and took a big swallow of the beer. His smile drowned her in a flood of endorphins.

She was definitely in trouble spelled with a capital G.

"This is wonderful. I never thought to mix my whiskey with beer. In my time, beer was warm and rather tasteless. I will have to thank the brewer. Perhaps I will invest in his endeavors."

"It doesn't have—you can't—never mind." Taking a bite of her pizza, Emmeline pointed at Gryphon's plate. "Try it."

CHAPTER 8

Dauphin, PA 1988

Witches buzzed about, their excitement palpable in the bright spring sunlight. Ostara would be upon them with the rise of the moon tomorrow night. Verne shook off the negative memories that had plagued last night's sleep. The memories of flames consuming Cold Springs and the fading cauldron occurred only near the festivals.

Verne's stomach churned acid into her throat, and she shed a tear. The cauldron remained cloaked at the High Altar and was only unveiled for ceremonies and important vision quests. Most of Megaera's new recruits never wanted to make the trip or put forth the effort to travel to the altar site during the celebrations.

She glanced over her shoulder at Haven House. The manse, deserted after the 1885 Typhoid outbreaks, became their home in the winter of 1900. They had little to celebrate the first year, as every meal was a struggle for survival. Tonight's celebration marked their eighty-seventh Ostara and brought with it the hope of burgeoning crops, lots of babies, and the arrival of the prophesized Key. The last Verne kept hidden from all but Mirielda.

"Sister dear. Why the tears?" Mirielda said. "Ostara brings joy."

"The joy declines when the whole coven cannot join the vision quest." Verne frowned and took Mirielda's hands in her own. "Our voice remains weak around the cauldron with only those born to the coven. It must be set right soon."

"Do you suggest we move back to Cold Springs?"

"You know it's too late. The land was returned to the state of Pennsylvania. They leave it for the wildlife, which in itself is not a bad idea. We have a celebration to prepare. Gather the children."

Verne waved a hand, and the gathering chime sounded across the ceremonial meadow. Seven boisterous neophytes pushed and shoved each other for the best seat in front of the old seer. The older First Levels sauntered in as if the interference in their day was a big inconvenience. The Second Levels stood at the back.

"The coven will have its ceremonial dance at Haven House. Those who can whisk or have a ride will travel to the High Altar at Cold Springs for a vision quest." Verne flashed her evil eye at two boys not paying attention. After they settled, she continued, "When we return from the High Altar, the dance will begin. Some of you will fall to your dreams, and those who remain must remember your manners. Do not stare at couples during the planting song."

"Did you prepare for your tests?" Mirielda asked.

"I will call and control earth and wind," a young male witch said.

"We know all this. Can we go now?" A blond witch winked at the male.

"Seer." A third female flashed a sideways glance at the blonde's male. "Tonight will expose those who can and cannot. Is there punishment for those who cannot?"

"No one is punished. I feel like you have never had a lesson." Verne waved a hand toward the meadow and dismissed them. "Off to practice your magick and recite your Witches' Creed."

Mirielda grew quiet, and Verne glanced in the direction of her stare. She caught a flash of blue. "Quit hiding behind the tree, Thomas. Come out. What do you need?"

Thomas stepped from behind a large Sycamore. "Do you need help with anything?"

"I could use help with these banners," Mirielda said. A box brimming with strings of leaves and flowers sat at her feet. "The young were asked, but notice how fast they disappear whenever work arises."

"I'll help." Thomas picked up the box.

Verne noted the young witch's infatuation with her sister. "Do you miss serving Gryphon, young Thomas?"

"I do. But I have purpose serving as Second Level to the High Priestess. Norman and I work well together," Thomas said.

"Working for Megaera keeps you away from us," Mirielda said. "We spend too much energy keeping the cauldron hidden. It's not as if the High Priestess contributes energy to the coven's collective well."

"You should take care of what you say. You never know who can overhear." Tom smiled at Mirielda and slid the garland of woven flowers from her hand. "Perhaps we will dance during the planting song."

"I appreciate your kind offer, Thomas," Verne said. "Yet I feel too old to dance to the planting song. Perhaps Mirielda will grant the honor."

Mirielda giggled.

"I need to finish my chores for the High Priestess." Thomas smirked and whisked away.

"Verne. You chased away all of my help," Mirielda said.

Verne squeezed Mirielda's shoulder.

"I feel something on the rise. What, I do not know." Verne swung her attention to Megaera standing on the false altar. The old Crone had it poured earlier this year against the advice of the elders. Altars should form from the blessed stone of the earth, not cement.

Megaera directed from the raised platform, pointing at the ceremonial firewood pile and snarling at the new witches. Not born to the coven, these beings were recruited. They ran to do her bidding. A true MichAudah would never put up with the disrespect.

Leaning close to Mirielda's ear, Verne whispered, "The old hag emasculates the males with a flick of her crooked wrist. I doubt if any will stay long enough to produce children."

"What made Megaera so angry? It seems she fought against everything even as a child," Mirielda whispered. "We all grew up together and survived the same events. Megaera knows the Witches' Creed."

Verne embraced Mirielda. "Lack of sex can make a witch cranky."

They laughed at her joke.

Megaera stared at them as if she'd heard the comment. Verne sobered.

"Do you feel dark magick?" Mirielda asked.

"I do. I feel pushed against the earth by a great weight." Verne pulled Mirielda away from the trace of dark magick. The evil weighed the air down as if trying to trap them in place. It was cold and dark. Verne tossed a pinch of the Three Sisters into the air. "Bí Imithe."

"What did you do?" Mirielda asked. Her eyes widened in surprise.

"You need to practice your Gaelic. It means dark magick to go away." Verne laughed, throwing her arms around her sister. "Young witches spare me the trouble. Let us finish preparations. We need more yarrow for the fire."

As Mirielda whisked away to find more yarrow, Verne surveyed the activities taking place in the meadow. Flower garlands hung from the trees, the bonfire was piled high with dry wood, and Megaera struggled to hang the High Priestess robe near the altar.

Megaera's stick-thin body had no muscle, and her bony shoulders and elbows were noticeable under her blouse. Using black magick all the time consumed a witch's physical being.

"Now you pay the price, High Priestess," Verne whispered in her mind.

"Witches, I want your attention." Megaera addressed those in the clearing. Placing her hands on her hips, she stomped her boot. "I order you to give me your attention."

The coven continued to disregard her.

Megaera shot small strikes of fire at the closest witches and yelled, "Stop this incessant fluttering."

Mirielda whisked back to Verne's side with an armload of yarrow. Norman, the current Third-Level advisor, shuffled up and bowed to Megaera.

"Megaera surrounds herself with witches of lesser power," Verne said. "Norman will never gain enough strength for more than Third Level, and Tom will never achieve more than Second Level, I fear. Neither will have the strength to lead us if something happens to Megaera."

Megaera silenced the crowd. The coven pushed to stand within feet of the High Priestess. At least, the newcomers did. The MichAudah elders remained at the back of the crowd.

"I'm sure these new witches practice Fire Magick. At least the Water and Wind Witches still hold a numerical advantage in the coven. Votes at the coven meetings still fall in our favor," Verne said.

"True. But there are only two Wind Witches left. You and me," Mirielda said. "A few of the new ones have a small amount of power, and the others, pretenders with no magick. I'm not sure where they came from, but I would wager Megaera called to them."

"Witches!" Megaera waved her arms in the air. "I call you before me so I may impress upon you the importance of the upcoming celebration. The time to sow seeds begins and brings hope and prosperity to our coven."

"I have a dark feeling about this." Verne spoke in a whisper, holding Mirielda's arm tight and bracing for the news.

"I gather you all here this day before the Spring Equinox. As times change, so must we. It has become difficult to celebrate at the High Altar. Our fire must remain small, and the cauldron does not receive the flame it seeks."

Verne noticed the heads of the elders nodding in agreement.

"I direct us to bring the cauldron to this location and anoint this our new High Altar," Megaera said.

Strained murmurs wove through the crowd. Exchanges back and forth between the old coven members grew into shouts and revolt, stimulating cries.

"Silence." Megaera pushed fire over the gathering. The crowd quieted. "Today we go to the High Altar and bring our cauldron here." She struck the slab with Kenter's staff, and a loud thump sounded across the meadow. White smoke rose, revealing an image of the cauldron.

Verne wasn't fooled by the theatrical illusion as she read the faces of the coven elders. Lycopodium and gunpowder wouldn't fool the old witches. The chemistry of this new time allowed Megaera too much false magick. It was only chemistry with a flair. Many would be angry with this break in tradition. Perhaps Megaera's support would dissolve.

"We will consecrate the ground here," Megaera stomped the slab, "on this new altar stone, and celebrate the spring solstice where we live."

"The young fools buy into her illusion," Verne said.

"Verne will prepare a new cauldron brew for us," Megaera continued, "and tonight we will conduct a consecration ceremony. We will never have to climb the mountain again, and the cauldron will remain available for all of us."

"High Priestess. May I speak?" Verne asked.

Megaera gave a brief nod and yielded the floor.

"I caution. Do not do this," Verne said. "We had to prepare for weeks before we moved our cauldron to this new land. You were not yet born, but the old coven had petitioned the Grand Master for a new altar site. It's why our coire still sits on the mountain."

"Dear Verne." Megaera clasped her hands together and took a deep breath. "I will cast a fire spell to protect us while we move the cauldron. The Grand Master will accept our tribute, and the power of the Fire Witches will curtail any issues with the fates."

Verne began to disagree, but Megaera cut her off.

"Seven will go this day, under a cloaking spell. Norman and Thomas," she pointed at the two men in the front of the crowd, "will select the others."

The disgruntled crowd gained momentum.

"Silence!" A ball of fire shot from the new platform and landed in the bonfire pile, igniting it. The crowd quieted.

"I have the power to protect us," Megaera said. "As your High Priestess, you will do as I say."

Verne knew no one would challenge the High Priestess this day. The excitement of the day had crashed and burned into a black hole.

"I hope this blasphemous act will not affect the prophecy," Verne said. "Perhaps it will entice it to come sooner than projected."

Harrisburg, PA 2019

Emmeline squeezed a bear-shaped container over the top of her pizza. A golden, viscous substance fell on the surface and pooled in the crispy round meat. She folded the slice in half and bit a chunk off the end. The chewy cheese pulled off the edge and slung across the open expanse to her mouth.

Gryphon ceased breathing when Emmeline's tongue darted

out to grab the strings of cheese at the same time as her delicate finger twirled the remaining strings in a technique that must require years to master.

The cheese-wrapped finger rose to her mouth while plush pink lips closed around the digit. It was the sexiest move he'd ever seen a woman do, except for pleasuring herself or giving him a blow job.

He released a breath, his cock pushing against the trouser buttons.

"Dig in," Emmeline said. "Is something wrong?"

"I would have thought manners increased over time." Gryphon was still recovering from the earlier distraction. He raised an eyebrow. Focusing on her mouth, he licked his lips. "I never imagined having to eat with my fingers in this time."

"Before the two of you argue manners, I would appreciate a slice." Luna's ears perked. *"And Emmeline, before you say 'pizza's not for puppies,' remember I am a familiar, not a dog."*

"Have at it," Emmeline said. She dropped a slice on a plate and set it on the floor. "If you have gas tonight, you're sleeping on the couch."

"How can I eat this?" Luna asked. *"Can't you cut it up for me?"*

"I thought you were a familiar, not a dog. Use magick to cut it up."

"Not the point." Luna sat and took a deep breath. *"Grand Master save me from insolent witches."*

The corner of Gryphon's mouth quirked as he watched the interaction. It reminded him of their interactions in days past. Adjusting to a familiar was exhausting. It was like having a second mother who nagged about different tasks at the same time as the first mother. Luna always did have a smart mouth. He refocused on Emmeline's, his thoughts taking him to places other than daily tasks of long ago.

"It's how we eat pizza. But I can provide a fork and knife if you need one." Talking with her mouth full, Emmeline took a few seconds to finish chewing. She swallowed. "Pizza, wings, hamburgers, hot dogs, and ribs are exceptions. We tend to use silverware for our other meals."

"Indeed." Gryphon took a bite.

Twenty minutes later, he finished the last piece in the box and a third beer.

"I forgot how much guys eat," Emmeline said. Laughing, she raised her hands in the air and waved them about. "I wish we had another pizza."

A box appeared on the end of the table with a ripple of air and a quiet *pop*.

Emmeline widened her eyes. "Holy shit."

"You should not waste your magick on such frivolities."

"Do the Returns of Three affect druids?" Gryphon asked Luna.

"I have no idea."

"Excuse me. Sitting right here." Emmeline waved a hand.

"Do not!" both shouted in unison.

Gryphon grabbed her hand and pushed it back to the table. Blowing a deep breath of air, he stood and patted his midsection. "I enjoyed the pizza. Now I have need to take care of some personal business. Where may I find the privy?"

"Down the hall, first door on the left. The light's on the right," Emmeline said.

"Your privy sits in the house?" Gryphon asked.

"Yep. No more outhouses. Don't forget to put the seat back down when you're finished." Emmeline leaned over to Luna and asked, "Think he can handle the toilet?"

"Ten bucks says he won't figure out the flush."

Several minutes later, Emmeline joined Luna in the open doorway. She gasped.

Gryphon turned to face her. He stood in front of the toilet with pants to his knees and his hand on his cock.

"Where does the mess go?" Gryphon said.

"Push the handle down, Gryphon," Luna said. She lifted her

nose up and spoke to Emmeline. *"Close your mouth, dear. He does make you want to reference an old cliché."*

"Huh?" Emmeline looked at the dog.

"Well hung."

"What handle?" Gryphon asked.

"The silver one to your left."

The whoosh and gurgle of the flush returned his attention to the toilet. "Amazing."

When he lifted his head, he noted Emmeline's wide-eyed stare and flushed face. If she was embarrassed at his nakedness, why did she stare? He managed to stuff himself back into his pants, but her stare still affected him. The buttons were now more difficult to fasten.

Emmeline stepped back into the hallway. "Sorry, but the door was open."

"Does privacy in this time become as elusive as eating utensils?" Gryphon asked.

"Put the lid down as Emmeline asked and wash your hands."

"Wouldn't want it caught in between those," Gryphon said.

Emmeline's laughter filtered into the room.

"It seems unkind to poke fun at someone who grew up without indoor plumbing." He put the lid down as instructed.

"I don't think it's why she laughed. Are you finished?"

"All stowed away." Gryphon stepped out into the hall next to Emmeline. He tugged his vest back into place. "Did I use the privy in the correct manner?"

"You're supposed to close the door for privacy," Emmeline said.

"Luna did not inform me of the etiquette." Gryphon leaned down to whisper in her ear, "The privy door at home always closes on its own."

Emmeline shivered and took a step away. "Did you wash your hands?"

"I used the paper. It exceeds one's expectation."

"Washing has eliminated many diseases. Use soap and water at the sink and dry with the towel hanging by your head."

Gryphon returned to the bathroom. The water rushed into the sink. "These towels are of an exceptional quality."

He returned to walk beside Emmeline down the hallway. Their shoulders touched, and he felt his cock harden even more. "Bloody hell."

"Good thing you have buttons. I guess a zipper could create quite a hazard." Emmeline burst out laughing as she moved faster into the living room.

"I do say, I have never had a female laugh at the sight of me before. Do I lack something for a male in this time?"

"Blame it on the bourbon. She's had more than normal."

"Oh, no. As dicks go, yours is...nice." Emmeline snorted, her eyes wide, and she covered her open mouth with a hand. "My vibrator tends to keep me satisfied without complications, so you don't have to worry about me jumping your...nice dick tonight."

"What language does she speak? Explain vibrator."

"I tried to tell you on the mountain. Women in this time are different. I refuse to explain how a vibrator works. However, I do wish to observe your reaction when she does."

Back in the living room, Emmeline dropped to the couch and expelled a deep breath.

Gryphon chose the recliner. He lifted a beer to his lips.

"I thought you drank all the beer at dinner," Emmeline said.

Gryphon glanced at the bottle. "I wanted one, so I conjured one." He waved his finger in a circle, and a bottle appeared in her hand. "We will soon have to discuss the use of magick. When and when not to use it should become an important first lesson. I have just demonstrated both."

Gryphon pulled a long swallow of ale.

"Should and shouldn't? I don't think tonight's the best

time." Emmeline took a drink. "I don't think I can handle any more of this alternate universe right now."

"As you wish." Gryphon smiled. "Refrain from making wishes and waving your hands at the same time until we do."

"You can't order me around in my own house." Emmeline narrowed her eyes and pointed the beer bottle at him.

"He's saying for tonight," Luna said. *"You don't want to burn the house down or cause something just as tragic, do you?"*

"I can burn the house down?" Emmeline asked.

"Yes," Gryphon said. Silence remained between them while he observed Emmeline.

He followed the beer bottle to her lips. Watched her delicate swallow. The freckles on her nose danced every time she repeated the motion. She pouted when the bottle was empty and looked into the empty vessel as if more would appear. His cock throbbed when she licked the last drop from her lips.

He could smell her sweet, sultry caramel scent over the hops of his beer. It teased his nose. Her green eyes sparkled like emeralds. They drew Gryphon into a pool where the weight of them softened every muscle in his body. Almost.

Was he supposed to be attracted to his Key? No one told him what their relationship was to be. He'd always imagined the Key would be some dutiful apprentice who followed his every move and took his every direction. He was not expecting the foul-mouthed, green-eyed druid who disobeyed and talked back at every turn. Nor was he expecting an attraction to her that burned as hot as a cauldron fire.

Emmeline's mind was active, if the facial tics and her occasional glance in his direction were any indication. She furrowed her brows and then relaxed. Narrowed her eyes and relaxed. He concentrated on the pulsing need between his legs and the forthcoming tightness in his crotch. Why not throw caution to the wind and hump her?

She stared at him. Could she read his mind? Gryphon shifted in his seat.

"If you keep giving me the eye with such intent, you will need to help me out of an uncomfortable situation," Gryphon said. His hands remained on the arms of the recliner, but the erection tenting his stretchy trousers was obvious. "Shall we continue this conversation in a more appropriate location?"

"And then he speaks," Emmeline said. She grabbed the empty bottle, stood, and left the room while saying, "I knew it wouldn't take long."

"Excuse me?" Gryphon asked.

Emmeline returned with a shiny package. She dropped them on his crotch in a deliberate act, knowing his condition. He brought his legs up to protect himself while he grabbed for the item. The advertisement on the front said Vanilla Oreos.

"Have a cookie."

Gryphon was fascinated with the packaging. It crinkled with each attempt to find an opening. He ran a hand over the logo on the package and examined his fingers.

"It won't rub off," Emmeline said.

"Pardon?"

"The label. It won't rub off."

"Yes, I have come to the same conclusion." Gryphon raised the package to his teeth.

"No!" Leaping across the room, Emmeline grabbed the package from his hands and demonstrated the self-sticking flaps on the top.

"Did you conjure this magick?" Gryphon asked. "How splendid."

Gryphon popped a cookie into his mouth. Taking a second while still chewing, he swallowed some beer and waved the cookie in the air. "These taste much better than those you had earlier. Why did you not have these?"

"Yeah, um. I would forget about today's cookies. Enjoy the Oreos." Her eyes widened as she glanced at Luna.

"Someday we'll laugh and talk about the Milkbone incident."

Gryphon's strong jaw made quick work of the treats.

"Let me show you some twenty-first century magick." Emmeline located the remote on the side table next to the recliner. She pushed the power button. When the big screen flared up, *Iron Resurrection* began playing on MotorTrend.

The big screen grabbed Gryphon's attention. Pushing another cookie into his mouth, he leaned forward and pointed at the television. "What manner of magick do you perform?"

"It's called a television. You can watch the news, find out what's going on in the world, learn cooking or mechanical skills, and enjoy a fictional story." After a few minutes' demonstration with the remote and stopping on several channels, Emmeline dropped it into his hand.

"You, my little Key, cast powerful magick." He continued munching cookies as the channel changed every few seconds.

"Typical. You're already addicted to the remote." Emmeline stretched her neck and sighed. "You watch this while I grab a shower and fix up the spare bed for the night."

His lack of an answer was the only response.

CHAPTER 9

Dauphin, PA 1988

Verne whisked to the concrete altar as the cauldron floated across the empty meadow. Seven witches struggled under the weight of the ancient vessel. The acrid odor of brimstone from ceremonies long past seeped out and caught on the currents of air floating through Stony Creek Valley.

"Our coire!" Verne examined it, checking for damage. The worry lines etched around her dark green eyes revealed the wear and tear of a life long lived.

The day lost its light as the moon moved into position. The eclipse took many by surprise. Elders cried out, afraid they were being punished for offending the Grand Master. The earth trembled. Screams caught Verne's attention as the members of the coven fell to the ground. Many chanted sacred prayers against evil.

Verne leaned over the cauldron. Light shone through a fissure that ran across the bulbous portion of the old iron pot. Her mouth ajar, she searched for Megaera.

The coven continued their hysterics over the earthquake and eclipse. Megaera shot fire into the ground, creating an explosion and commanded them to stop as she floated to the altar. She met Verne's stare.

"Witches. Stop your prattle," Megaera said. She grabbed Verne's arm and squeezed. "You didn't tell me about today's eclipse. You make me appear foolish."

Verne pointed a finger at Megaera. "I asked you not to move the cauldron today, although I knew nothing of an eclipse. Now our corie has sustained damage."

Megaera bent to examine the cauldron. Tapping a yellowed nail under one of the handles, she glanced back up at Verne. "It could have cracked when they moved it from Salem. I've never seen the vessel empty. The fissure might have gone unseen for centuries."

"If the cauldron leaks, the brew will fall into the fire." Verne narrowed her eyes at Megaera, no longer worried about the High Priestess's wrath. "It will affect all spells cast now and in the future. No vision quests can take place. We may cease to exist!"

The crowd had quieted, focused on Verne and Megaera arguing on the altar.

Megaera held a hand up to stop any outburst. She told the coven, "I, High Priestess of this coven, will use fire magick to heal the cauldron."

The High Priestess weaved ancient Fire Witch symbols in the air and cast flames against the cauldron. A layer of magick settled around the pot. "From the forge's fire, iron hot, the cauldron formed, Grandmasters thought. Iron, copper, silver, gold, before our eyes, our future holds. Metals deep, find your wound, and heal thyself with current moon."

Megaera bathed the wounded cauldron in the fire. The cauldron glowed red as the metal cooled, and the fissure disappeared as the moon revealed the sun. The coven fell to their knees. "Rise, worthless simpletons. You need to have more faith in me. Return to work.

"Verne, walk with me to the manse. I'll have words with you," Megaera said.

They walked in silence for several minutes before reaching the outside entrance to Megaera's private rooms.

"I have need to work on my own for some time. You will prepare the brew for the cauldron and have everything ready for the consecration tonight."

Megaera didn't wait for a reply and shut the door in Verne's face.

Several hours later, Verne finished her chant over the brew as the remainder of the coven assembled.

Megaera whisked to stand beside Verne and raised her hands over the vessel. She dropped her offering into the brew, and the mixture slowly pulled the leaf-wrapped packet under its tumultuous surface.

Bubbles rose faster and faster across the surface as the iron heated. Green and gray flames curled around the sides as a drip smacked into the hot fire. Steam rose. Everyone's eyes were closed as they chanted prayers.

Verne narrowed her eyes at Megaera. She had seen the brew drip into the fire. The seer struggled with a dilemma: tell the coven the cauldron had leaked or allow this ceremony to take place. Different scenarios of each path played out in her mind. Now she understood how Kenter felt all those years ago. Either choice had consequences.

The eclipse and earth trembles suggested this was the beginning of the prophecy. She must make her decision. Verne tossed powder of the Three Sisters over her shoulder and prayed it was the right choice. She allowed the High Priestess to continue.

Megaera nodded to Verne. "Today we ask for the Grand Master to bless this fire-anointed vessel. During this solstice moon, we will reap the benefit of our sacrifice during this time of renewal." Megaera waved her hands over the cauldron and dropped her offering into the brew.

"Seer, scry for us this eve. Tell us of the vision," Megaera said.

Verne peered at the surface of the viscous liquid. The stench of death remained a trace in the air. Megaera's skin, normally pale and pasty in complexion, grew translucent, exposing the blue veins running through her cheeks. Verne caught the green flames of fire reflected in Megaera's eyes. She allowed the vision to come. She raised her hands.

"A power from the Fairy Kingdom on Isle Magee was born at the start of the Witching Hour." Verne paused and smiled at Megaera. "The power will join forces with a familiar and a blooded heir to restore the MichAudah."

"Not possible. I—" Megaera's mouth closed before she could release the truth. She leaned in to Verne's ear and said, "You try my patience, seer. What else did you witness?"

Verne's reply was covered by the crowd's cheers. With the tension broken, musicians cued the music, and the witches danced around the fire. Clothing was tossed about, and the majority of the coven became a writhing mass of flesh.

Megaera squeezed Verne's arm. "What of the rest of the vision?"

"The Key born this night will have to face evil alone. Without her twin." Verne tossed explosive powders into the fire. A burst of greens, reds, and oranges flared. "The Key comes. A druid who follows the path of our ancestors teaching the next generation. She brings with her the ancient magick and a stag coated in the green of the highlands and white of ice from Larne Lough to protect her."

"When does this witch arrive?"

Verne leaned forward and whispered, "Lorgaidh tu I deicheadan bho seo a-mach. Coimhead airson an damh ramming."

"Meaning?" Megaera raised her open hand in question.

"Two decades, more or less, High Priestess. She will live under the protection of a ramming stag." A slow smile slid across Verne's face. "Gryphon, I suppose."

Megaera whisked away, pulling the stench of death across the clearing.

Wilmott emerged from the forest behind the new altar. "Good evening, Verne."

"Wilmott. I thought you gone for good," Verne said. "Did you come to rid us of your wayward seed?"

His smile rose and fell. "I thought better of you, Verne. Such vicious words about your High Priestess."

"Your purpose, Warlock?"

"I went to the old country to visit with my sister Edemay. The family was devastated to learn of Kenter's passing," Wilmott said. "I don't suppose you ever found out what happened to him?"

"No, we didn't." Verne turned to walk away.

"Megaera pulls power from the world. We felt it across the waters, and the ancients sense it," Wilmott said.

Verne spun on a heel and pointed her finger at the warlock. "You must take some blame. You gave her a taste for dark power."

"I cannot control her greed." Wilmott brushed dust from a sleeve. He lifted his chin to meet Verne's eyes. "You must have felt the death spell she cast this night. It will have more consequences and less power than she thinks."

"Why tell me this?" Verne stared at the dark spot that was the warlock. The scent of death, cold and heavy, lingered in the air. It reminded Verne of the night Willa had drifted into the fade. When she opened her mouth to say more to Wilmott, he was gone.

Over the next twenty-nine years, Verne kept an eye out for signs of the druid's arrival. The cauldron dripped brew into the flames at each ceremony. Clear visions were rare, and she was ready to give up hope. How could the prophecy be wrong?

Mirielda suggested they start using the internet to find the Key, and several witches took jobs working at the most logical school in the area because of the prophecy. The home of the

Ramming Stags, Allegheny Superior School District served one-third of Dauphin County. Their school colors were green and white. Mirielda was sure the symbols and magick would draw the girl.

Behind Megaera's back, the Earth Witches were encouraged to store energy in their wells instead of casting spells. Their collective grew in power. Verne wanted everything ready when the next eclipse would announce the arrival of the Key. At least she hoped it would.

The news blasted the upcoming eclipse every hour as the day approached midsummer. Her heart beat faster in anticipation. As she raised her hand to whisk to Mirielda, a text beeped on her cell phone. Megaera wanted a meeting.

"High Priestess. I didn't mean to interrupt, but you texted for me to come."

"I want you to scry for me."

"Right now?" Verne lifted her eyebrows. "The coven has an impromptu celebration this day. I don't believe I will have the time."

"What celebration?"

"A total solar eclipse happens today. In fact," Verne glanced at her watch, "in one hour. They announced it on all the news channels."

Verne jumped with glee like a schoolgirl and clapped her hands. "This eclipse portends the arrival of fortuitous events. We will dance and make offerings under the meteor shower that will follow. Will you join us, Megaera? The coven would enjoy their High Priestess's presence."

"I don't have time for such frivolity." Megaera wrinkled her nose. Her hands closed into fists.

"Isn't it joyous? The prophecy continues, and Gryphon will rise soon," Verne said. "You've waited so long."

Harrisburg, PA 2019

"Let me show you where you will sleep tonight," Emmeline said.

Gryphon found one of the sports channels and remained focused on a soccer game. He pointed. "I played a similar game with the natives as a child. The Algonquin called it stickball. It resembles this soccer, but with sticks as well as feet."

"Sports, cars, and weapons. I think guys are born with or without the gene," Emmeline said. "You must have it. Soccer has matches, not games."

"It was harsher than your soccer. I assure you, blood flowed and tempers flared." Gryphon remained fixated on the big screen. "My friend broke a leg once. A young buck pushed Thomas off a small ravine. If it weren't for the healers, the lad may have died. Only the strong survive stickball with the People."

As a commercial came on, Gryphon's head tilted at an angle. "You were saying?"

Invisible energy blasted Emmeline's soul. Electricity sizzled in the recesses of her brain. She swore sparks jumped from his eyes when he talked to her. Her thoughts drifted back to the kiss from earlier, the warmth he'd created at the refrigerator, and the recent view of his large dick. This man was dangerous on so many levels.

A commercial touted the add-ons for the new Ford F-150. Her eyes swung to the television.

"Why does your truck appear so different than this one?" Gryphon asked.

"First of all, my truck's a Chevy and an antique. Secondly, an F-150 costs more than I make in two years. Besides, I prefer my old truck. It has character."

"I have missed out on so many adventures and inventions while I waited in the box." A hand swept the room, encompassing all of the new devices. "It bothers me that Megaera took their joy from me."

Emmeline swallowed. She absorbed his sadness and loss.

How would it feel to travel in time and fall into an advanced society? Everything he experienced for the first time was commonplace and normal to her. Did anything surprise her anymore?

She nodded to herself. Gryphon was the surprise of a lifetime. Somehow the man had wormed his way into her heart. She wouldn't admit it out loud, but the crazy witch did it for her in ways she couldn't describe. Still, her scientific mind remained unconvinced.

Emmeline slipped the remote from his hand and powered down the system. "You have lots to learn. I say we turn in for the night."

A wisp of silky hair fell over his forehead. Resisting the urge to smooth it back, she waved him down the hallway to an open door. A light brush of his fingers and an accidental touch on her arm sent waves of need straight to her clit. "Shit."

"What vexes you?" Gryphon asked.

"You're sleeping here." Emmeline cleared her throat and waved him in. "I laid out sweats and a T-shirt leftover from my last boyfriend. I'm not sure if they'll fit. You're a bit...bigger than Brad." Her eyes rolled south before she jerked them back to his face. Her cheeks warmed.

"Let's hit it, Luna." Emmeline left and walked into her bedroom.

"Luna. Where do you go?" Gryphon asked.

"I sleep with Emmeline. She lets me on the bed."

"I daresay I never thought you would betray me."

"Can I sleep beside you in the bed?"

"Heavens no. You track in too much dirt."

"It's decided."

Emmeline listened, their little spat endearing. Before crawling into the bed, she pulled out the drawer on the nightstand. The Walther lay ready to fire. Just in case.

October winds blew a few branches against the window when Emmeline recognized the familiar tilt of paws, the usual pattern of three circles, and the long, drawn-out moan as Luna settled at the foot of the bed.

"Luna."

"Yes, Emmeline."

"Since you can talk, tell me why you moan when you lie down."

"Well. I—uh. I don't know." Falling on her side, Luna took up the lower half of the bed and moaned. *"It feels good."*

Emmeline released a loud moan from deep in her lungs. "You're right. It feels good."

What seemed like five minutes to Emmeline was the entire night. She opened her eyes as exhausted as when she'd crawled under the covers last night. Morning light filtered through the curtains. After getting ready for work, she found the spare bedroom empty. Emmeline headed for the living room and discovered Gryphon sleeping in the recliner and the TV playing one of the sports channels.

"Well shit. I guess everything yesterday did happen."

As the coffee brewed, she leaned against the doorway and observed her house guest. He had changed into the clothing set out for him. The flannel shirt barely fit and hung open, showing an impressive, well-defined chest. The smooth, sun-kissed, skin, tight over muscular pecs, changed to a dusky rose around the nipples. And there she had it. She was staring at his nipples and following a line of black hair down to his waistband.

She stomped her foot and returned to the kitchen. "What's wrong with me?"

A scratching at the back door tore Emmeline away from the morning peep show. Luna sat at the door, waiting to go out. She reached for the knob and pulled the door open. "I got you, girl."

"Crap. I can use my magick now." Luna whisked out of the house instead of using the doggie door, leaving Emmeline standing in a quiet kitchen.

"I guess it can't get more real." Emmeline filled the dog bowl. Did Luna still eat dog food? Shrugging her shoulders, she dropped the bowl on the floor and poured a cup of coffee. A glance at the clock had her swearing. "Shit. I'm late again."

As she grabbed the briefcase, a solid wall of bone and muscle interfered with her movement toward the door. She slapped at his arm. "Would you quit doing that."

"When you free me from my box, I will have flesh and bone. At the moment, my form becomes somewhat hard for you, but not as hard as I will become," Gryphon said.

Emmeline snorted. How did he manage that with a straight face? "I have to say, your double entendre made my morning."

"I have no—"

Emmeline cut him off, swiveled to the counter, picked up a coffee travel mug, and stepped into the fleshy wall again. She eyed the tight fit of the sweats. The clothes that fit loose on Brad strained at the seams on Gryphon. Everywhere. "We're going shopping today after work. There's a DXL shop at the mall. You're going to need it."

Gryphon remained in her way. Emmeline melted when he tucked a stray hair behind her ear and played with the curl. His energy poured into her skin like creamy lotion. He leaned forward, and his lips grazed across her cheek.

The kiss was mind blowing, panty wetting, and toe curling. Holy hell. How was she supposed to teach today with those images floating around her mind? She'd stop and giggle after every sentence.

"I do not understand," Gryphon said.

"Huh?"

"Your words. Shopping. After work. What is your meaning?"

Emmeline shook her head to clear the fog created by her steaming libido. Her heart beat heavy against her breasts as she placed each hand over a flannel pocket and pushed. "You need to move. I have to go to work. After work, we will shop for clothes for you."

Taking a minute to reflect, Emmeline couldn't put together a reason why he couldn't just conjure up some new duds if she showed him a picture. Her mind went to the wrong places as it pictured a hot body, leather pants, and a motorcycle jacket with a patch portraying Death and his scythe on the back.

"Emmeline, try to conjure some clothes for him. He looks ridiculous."

"I don't have time to worry about this. I'm late."

"You need to try. I'll turn time back five minutes so you won't be late."

"You can change time?" Emmeline's eyes widened. "Never mind."

"I left a bowl of offering on the counter," Luna said. *"Raise your hand, close your eyes, and ask in your mind for something you want. Don't say it out loud. Reach into the bowl, take out a pinch, and throw the powder in the air."*

"You want me to throw this powder in the air?" Emmeline asked. "I guess magick comes with a cleaning price tag."

"You don't clean much anyway. Now, after you throw it in the air, say, I offer you Three Sisters in honor of your will."

"Sure. Okay. Here goes." Emmeline squeezed her eyelids tight, took a deep breath, and held it. A quick breeze flew through the kitchen. Reaching into the bowl and tossing the powder in the air, she recited, "I offer you Three Sisters in honor of your will."

A pop-hiss sound, like pulling the tab on a soda, echoed in the kitchen. When she opened her eyes, a naked Gryphon was pouring a cup of coffee. He paused mid-pour and glanced down. He looked up and raised his eyebrows.

"Oops." Luna snickered. *"I know it's been a while—"*

"This was your desire?" Gryphon asked. "It pleases me, but may I have my coffee first?"

Heat crept up Emmeline's neck and over her cheeks.

Gryphon's cock, already hard, rose along his abdomen. Its deep red head glistened with a pearl that pleaded to be licked. "Holy hell, what's wrong with me?"

"Well, we hardly need to ask the question, Emmeline. It was your magick." Gryphon crossed his arms and leaned back against the counter.

Emmeline gripped the counter tight enough to pale the skin on her knuckles. Eyes shut, she tried to block the last thought about the pearl from her brain. She lifted one eyelid. Gryphon was back in his original clothing.

"I will speak with Mirielda today," Luna said. *"We need to find out how to teach her to control her magick. Until I return, I suggest she doesn't use it. No telling what else might disappear."*

"I quite agree. We wouldn't want anything happening to my...trousers."

"Uh, hey. I'm still in the room," Emmeline interrupted. "Wait, Mirielda's a witch?"

"Our coven seer since Verne passed," Luna said. *"Go to work. Don't use any magick."*

"May I have another cup? Coffee has much improved this century." He held out a cup. "What flavors do I detect? Hazelnut and—"

"Caramel," Emmeline said.

Gryphon floated the cup under his nose and sniffed. How was it fair for the man to have lashes so long and luscious without using any enhancers? And how did he manage to make everything so sensual without trying? All the crap she'd read about love at first sight and fated love was bullshit. Right? She had to admit, he seemed the perfect man, except for the whole witch and talking thing. Damn it.

"The flavor is divine. Stimulating, even. Yet I sense something of a distinctly magical nature."

"I make it the same way every day. I don't even buy it. Edemay and Betsy always have a bag for me. It's gourmet or something. The bags seem to last...forever. Oh, shit." Another piece of the magical puzzle clicked into place. She set the cup on the counter and pushed it away. "All this time?"

"What troubles you?" Gryphon moved his thumb across her knuckles in a sweet caress.

Emmeline's pulse quickened, and she tried to pull loose. His presence was overwhelming. She was hurt by the idea her friends had lied to her. Neglected to tell her all the sordid details. For over five years. Her mind was in turmoil. She tried to reel in the crazy. The only place to regain sanity was work. Grabbing the briefcase, she headed for the door. "I need to go to work."

"Go?" Gryphon followed. "You cannot leave. We must practice your magick."

"You can take a shower once I'm out of here, so you'll have a little privacy. Watch TV or read while I'm gone. Help yourself to anything in the fridge." She stared at the stove and hesitated for a moment before tossing a credit card on the counter. "Order food to be delivered. Ask Luna. She can tell you where to call. Don't answer the phone."

Gryphon protested. "You can't go without me. You—"

"I have to go. The day will end before you know it." Closing the back door a little hard, Emmeline departed. She was halfway to work when she caught movement in the right-hand corner of the cab.

"I must say—"

Emmeline slammed on the brakes, sending Gryphon airborne.

His head struck the windshield before he bounced back into the seat, grabbing the Oh-Shit grip above the door. Rubbing the smashed spot on his head, he reproached, "Shite. Watch what you do with this conveyance."

"You're fucking crazy." Emmeline frowned. "I could wreck. What in the name of all that's holy are you doing here?"

"Emmeline, you do not listen," Gryphon said. "I go where my Key goes, without choice or will. Must you use such vulgar language?" He paused. "Do you have the box with you?"

"I was going to ask Betsy about it."

"We were not sure whether my tether was to you or the box." Gryphon shook his head. "Since you have it with you, we still don't know."

Emmeline pounded on the steering wheel. "You mean you have to go everywhere with me? You're insane. I can't take you into work with me. How would I explain...you? You don't even have clearance. Oh my God. I'm going to get fired."

Firing the engine, Emmeline drove to school and pulled into the school lot. "The cops will come. You'll set off a lockdown. I'll go to jail for letting you into the building!"

She glanced at him and then gripped the steering wheel. "What if I leave the box in the truck?"

Gryphon shrugged. "We can find out."

"We need a plan for if you follow me, box or not." Emmeline tapped a finger on the wheel. "I know. I'll say, hey kids. Meet Gryphon. He's a witch I found in a box over the weekend. Watch as he poofs in and out of places as lavender dust. Isn't this cool?"

She waved a hand in the air.

"Emmeline, no." Gryphon secured the hand.

The truck ticked as the engine cooled, but nothing else happened. Gryphon asked, "I wish for you to put your hands back on the wheel. We cannot have magick loose without a purpose."

The exhale of breath was audible throughout the truck cab. Scowling, she pointed an index finger. "Don't. Say. Another. Word."

CHAPTER 10

Harrisburg, PA 2017

Several days after the eclipse, Verne pulled up in front of 379 Hallowed Drive. Sitting in the little Civic, she checked the GPS on her cell phone and turned to the black cat sitting on the passenger seat. "I don't know how we ever functioned without the internet all those years ago. It's like cheating on a scry."

"Perhaps. But it does save time. And chanting," Ben said.

Verne switched off the car and ran a hand around the steering wheel. "I do so love my little car. And let's not forget you don't have to saddle it, brush it, feed it, and it never shits on your shoes while you're cleaning its hooves."

"I can see the appeal."

Verne exited the car and waved her hand. A large gift basket appeared at her feet. With an Alleghany Superior School District T-shirt on, she picked up the basket, knocked three times, and waited. The door pulled open, and a surge of untapped power rushed against her. It was pure, untouched, and…immense.

"Can I help you?" the young woman asked.

"Good morning. I do hope you're Emmeline Callen," Verne said.

"Yes."

"I'm Verne Hutchin, a member of the ASSD teachers' union. I have a gift basket to welcome you to our ranks." She lifted the basket filled with sticky pads, pens, tape, markers, and other school supplies that would make any teacher curl their toes. A bag of gourmet coffee and a new coffee mug with the ASSD logo rested on the treasures.

Emmeline's eyes widened, and she smiled. "How nice of you. Please come in."

Verne entered the condo. Bare walls and packing boxes indicated the girl had recently moved in. "I hope I'm not disturbing you. By all appearances you have a great deal of work to do. May I help with anything?"

Emmeline grabbed a box from the couch and motioned to Verne. "Thanks for the offer, but I got it. I didn't know the union had a welcoming committee. No one said anything about gift baskets at yesterday's orientation."

"We didn't say anything because we wanted to surprise you. The staff is excited to have you on board."

Emmeline pointed to the gift basket. "I found the coffeemaker ten minutes ago, but not the coffee. Would you care for a cup?"

"Ready the pot. I'll open it for you."

Verne chanted a Gaelic prayer to enrich the protection spell. While opening the bag, she searched the apartment for the source of the immense power thrumming through the living space. Unable to identify the source, Verne entered the kitchen and put her hand on Emmeline's shoulder. A tiny spark shocked her hand, and they both jumped.

"Shit, you scared me." Emmeline lifted a hand to her chest and stepped back from Verne. "Did you feel an electrical jolt?"

"I did. Static electricity in the air, I suppose. Here's the coffee."

Emmeline reached for the bag. "It smells terrific. By the way, did I hear you...chanting? It sounded Gaelic. My foster mother spoke it quite often. I didn't understand half of what she said."

"But you understood half?" Verne raised an eyebrow. She read a wariness in Emmeline's expression. The power strengthened around the girl, so she stepped back to give the magick its space.

"I suppose," Emmeline said.

"The old ways fade," Verne said. "And yes, it's Gaelic. I hope you don't mind a little Wiccan. I always give thanks to the Grand Master for his gifts."

"Wiccan." Emmeline nodded and moved to add space between them. "Great. I'll start the coffee."

"I'm so sorry," Verne said. She glanced at her watch and frowned. "I didn't realize the hour. I have other baskets to deliver today. Coffee another time?" She handed Emmeline the coffee mug.

Emmeline noted the logo on the cup and muffled a laugh. The acronym, ASSD, was paired with a huge elk impaling its antlers into a wolf-like creature's butt. She covered her mouth with a hand.

Verne smiled and pointed at her shirt. "I know, how perverse. The person who picked a ramming stag as a mascot must have eaten magick mushrooms, don't you think? We all make fun of the logo. Wait till you hear the kids."

"I can imagine." Emmeline walked her to the door and pulled it open.

"Don't forget, the union association would love to have you as a member. Applications are already in your school mailbox. Enjoy the rest of your day."

"Yes, thank the union for me." Emmeline closed the door.

Verne climbed into the car. "Oh, the power radiating from this girl is unfathomable. I must tell Betsy."

"*I'll do it.*" Ben whisked away.

* * *

Megaera stared at the computer screen. The image of an elk stag cloaked in a green-and-white blanket ramming its horns into the ass end of a wolf gave her pause. Norman walked into the room.

Her chair rotated to face her Third Level. "Have you found the girl's address yet?"

"I have not," Norman said. "The computer freezes every time I click the link."

"If we can't find the address and the busy coven witches won't provide the information without torture," she tapped her long, yellowed nails on the tabletop and wrinkled her nose"I'll have to dig out the data on my own. I will also work at ASSD."

"You want to work at the school?" Norman asked.

"It's in a witch's nature to teach, and we have so few young ones now. It satisfies an urge to pass on knowledge and helps us blend in with human society."

Megaera paced to the window and scanned the distance. "I don't care for children, but perhaps the teachers' supervisor. How hard can it be to keep a bunch of educators in line?"

"As you wish, High Priestess." Norman rolled his eyes. "You will cast the spell this evening?"

Thomas whisked in.

"Sorry to interrupt," Thomas said. "Several herbs arrived with your Amazon order this morning. I finished grinding those needed to refill your pharmacy. Have you any more tasks? I was called to work in the garage today."

"The coven's day jobs were not supposed to interrupt coven duties." Megaera returned to her desk and examined a notebook. "None for this day. However, I will become a supervisor of teachers at Betsy's school. I will need an appropriate wardrobe. Have it in my chambers by opening day."

"You're going to work with children?" Thomas laughed.

Unexpected fire grabbed for the dry fabric of his flannel shirt and ignited it. The shirt disintegrated into soot, and blisters rose. The witch fell to the floor, writhing and sobbing. The room smelled of melted plastic and burned meat.

"Take care who you mock next time." Megaera walked to the door and glanced at Norman. "Take this imbecile to the healer. And Norman—"

"Yes, High Priestess."

"Thomas's tasks are yours until he heals." Megaera returned to her private chambers, slamming the door as she entered.

She went to her casting table, pulled up a stool, and caressed the Book of Fire. "I can't find competent help these days. To think they're the best MichAudha has to offer."

Her hands passed over the tome. "I seek a spell for replacement and new purpose."

The book shuddered on the table, and its pages flipped open to a short spell.

Gathering the ingredients from the supply cupboard, she sprinkled the powders into the bowl and cast. "I wish to become the principal of ASSD." Seconds later, a black puff of dust rose from the tome and hovered. She opened the basement window. "And with the wind, I cast this spell."

With a flick of her wrist, the dust formed a white orb and escaped out the window.

"So mote it be."

Three days later, Megaera popped a grape into her mouth as the morning news came on the television. Norman walked in, pale and drawn.

"What has you all in a bundle this morning?"

With a shaking finger, Norman picked up the remote and raised the volume. He pointed at the screen.

A reporter stood on the sidewalk in front of the ASSD business office with two photos in the upper corner of the screen. He looked into the camera. "Frank Bora, the principal of Alleghany Superior High School, died in an automobile accident late last night. His car slid off one of the hairpin turns on the Blue Mountain Parkway and rammed the vehicle of a local resident, Verne Hutchins. Ms. Hutchins was a lifetime resident of Dauphin. Details for services will be available this afternoon on our website. Counselors remain available for both the school district and the families throughout the week, and the school board will have an executive meeting this evening to appoint a temporary principal. School will open next week as planned."

"Two for one. Splendid." Megaera stood and placed a hand on Norman's shoulder. "Did you pick out the suit for my first day? I want to make an impression."

"Yes, Priestess. You will definitely make an impression." Norman wiped at his eyes to clear the tears.

"Why do you cry? It's unbecoming."

"Our seer died last night with the touch of your magick." Tears rolled down his face. "Your spell had unintended consequences. You forget your Witches' Creed and the Three Sisters."

"You have no evidence I did anything. You push my tolerance for insolence." Walking to the window, Megaera gazed out to the altar. "Not to worry. Mirielda will take over for Verne this day. Call her."

"Yes, Your Highness." Norman handed her the official guidebook to ASHS with a sneer and whisked away.

Two days later, Megaera tugged on the heavy polyester business jacket, adjusted the pencil skirt around her knees, and stared out the window of her new office. Norman whisked in with a box in his hand.

"Should you whisk during the day? We have humans surrounding us on all sides," Megaera said.

"With the door closed, no one saw me. Your name plate came this morning; I thought you would want it." Norman opened the box and gave her the desk ornament to examine. "Also, the grief counselors have set up in the cafeteria and the gym."

"What in heavens for?" Megaera asked.

"For grief counseling. Many liked Mr. Bora and Mirielda. She will now take leave to replace Verne as seer."

Megaera examined the shiny black metallic bar. Engraved on the top line was Dr. Megaera Caroline, with Principal in smaller letters on the second. "This pleases me. Now—"

"Excuse me," a young woman said. "I'm Marie Alley Benedict. You wanted to see me?"

"Ah, Mirielda's replacement." Megaera tapped long fingernails on the arm of her chair and scrutinized the human. "Norman, leave us."

Megaera sniffed and leaned back in her chair. "You're a recent hire here at ASSD?"

"Yes, ma'am. I received the phone call yesterday." Marie Alley sat in the offered seat. "I thought I'd have to substitute all year. I still need to take my Praxis for Biology. I don't know much about science. I'm only certified in English."

"I'm sure you'll make the best of the situation. I want to talk to you about loyalty and rewards." Megaera smiled, chanting a small spell. The magick filtered through the air and embedded deep in the woman's psyche.

As Megaera's lap dog, her job would be to spy on the other witches and the girl. Of course, the spell only worked because of the low morals her little rat already embraced. She was tasked to hear, see, and find out details about the Key.

"You will leave now. Become friends with Emmeline Callen and tell me everything she does." Megaera snapped her fingers.

The new teacher shook her head as she stumbled out of the office.

Norman returned and handed Megaera a long list of duties for the principal and droned on about tasks to be done. Her head would explode if he continued to prattle. "Will you shut up."

"Of course. What do you wish, High Priestess?"

"I wish to examine the new teacher files."

"You'll find them in the file cabinet." Norman opened the file cabinet and pulled several files. "You store files in them."

The chair swung back around. Fire lit Megaera's fingertips as she pulled Norman across the office with longs strands of white-hot fire. Once he was in front of her, she released the fire's hold, and he dropped to the floor. "You need to watch your insolence. I believe Thomas could advance once he heals."

"Yes, High Priestess." Norman climbed from the floor and handed her the file she wanted.

Megaera removed a photo. Auburn hair and green eyes stared back. Handing Norman the file, she raised her hand to whisk. "I'll be in my chambers. Call only if necessary."

She picked up the phone and called Mirielda. "I need you at Haven House tonight."

"High Priestess, I have plans for this evening. I need to prepare Verne for the House of Dawn."

"I need it done this night." Megaera took a deep breath. "We all grieve for the loss of Verne. But the coven will need your strength."

"Fine. I'll be there on the Witching Hour."

Megaera read the time from her wristwatch. She paced the altar as the Witching Hour began. She could feel her energy strengthen as she closed her eyes and lifted her chin to the night sky. To her, the feeling was better than anything else. Footsteps brought her head up.

"It's about time. You're late."

"The clock has yet to strike a second time. What do you want?" Mirielda asked.

"Call the fates for me and ask them if this girl arrives as The Key." Megaera handed Mirielda a photo of Emmeline Callen.

"The new science teacher." Mirielda stared at the picture. "I feel no magick from her."

"Perhaps she doesn't know of her power yet. You should want to know if she's the one. You will scry."

Mirielda cast several herbs into the pot, including the Three Sisters. The cauldron came to life as the brew bubbled and swirled. "A circle of protection blocks my view. It comes from a belief in Awen. Druid magick."

"Druid magick? No druids exist." Megaera grabbed Mirielda by the collar and shook her. "Search again."

"I see no magick in this girl." Mirielda pushed Megaera's hands away with magick. She stepped back to put more space between them "I know druid magick comes from nature and gathers as energy while they seek enlightenment. It's created. Our magick is energy already in existence. We take it from one place and send it to another. It exists in a state of entropy."

"What do you see?"

"Three numbers. Three, seven, and nine. Sacred numbers." Mirielda crossed her arms, and a tear fell. "If this is all, I must attend my sister."

Megaera allowed Mirielda to leave and headed back into her chambers. She filtered through past memories of the ancient teachings. For millennia, the number three had held great significance to the coven. The Returns of Three, the Three Fates, and the Three Sisters all guaranteed well-being for the coven.

"But what of the other two? I need to read the ancient tomes to find more meaning in seven and nine."

Back in the scrying room, Megaera pulled an old tome from the shelf and sat down to page through it. The dust caused a sneeze, and a flame burst from the page. The unexpected loss of control gave her pause. A quick wave of her hand suppressed the flame with minor damage.

She searched the room for witnesses—a mouse or spider who could scurry away and tell enemies of her weakness. Finding none, she continued. Nothing she read would suggest the importance of the numbers in this time and place.

Tired, she checked the suit hanging on the back of the door. She would suffocate in the business suit. The woven fabric of pinks, lavenders, and purples would make her look like an Easter basket. Why had Norman selected it?

Disgusted with her Third's selection, she waved a hand and turned the atrocious fabric into a black business suit of the same style. The two-inch spiked heels required another wave and transformed into a low one-inch heel on all-black leather.

Harrisburg, PA 2019

Emmeline pulled the truck into her parking spot in the faculty lot. After turning the truck off, she sat in silence. Her hands remained on the steering wheel. The scent of a sea breeze drifting across the cab was like a quick-acting Xanax. Her shoulders relaxed enough to loosen her hands from the steering wheel.

"Why do you smell so good?" She took a deep breath and looked across the seat.

"Would you rather I smelled…not good?" Gryphon asked.

"We have to come up with a plan. What should I do with you today?"

"I do not understand the problem." Gryphon pointed to the other staff members walking inside. "No one stops them at the door."

"Can you stay dust the whole day?" She bent over, retrieving an empty water bottle from the floor. "I have an empty water bottle. You could poof into it."

Gryphon cringed and took a deep breath. "I have no idea. But I suspect I will follow as dust until you settle in one location, like yesterday."

"You can't go in. You don't have clearances."

"What does a clearance do?"

"They check the criminal records to make sure you don't molest children or want to kill people. I don't have time to go into details. Suffice to say if you're caught, it'll brings cops and your friend Megaera."

"Not a good idea." Gryphon tugged on his vest and gave a nod. "You could try a spell, but since you have little control over your powers, I would prefer to keep all of my bits and bobs."

Emmeline sighed. "I guess we have no other choice. You stay dust until I stop. Correct?"

"Assuming I follow you and not the box. You are correct."

"We're going to make a run for it. I will walk to my room as fast as I can with no stops, and you can materialize in my room. I hope." Emmeline puffed out a deep breath and grabbed her travel mug.

"How far must we go into this building? And once there, will there be a place to wait out the day?" Gryphon asked.

"I only have a short walk to my classroom." Emmeline tapped the steering wheel. "You could stay in the teachers' prep room. No students allowed. But at some point, I'll have to go to the office."

"How far away is this office? Farther than the distance from the log to your truck yesterday?"

"You mean the log you assaulted me on." Emmeline nibbled on her bottom lip. She remembered the log from yesterday. The weight of his hard body on top of hers, silky hair draping over her chest, and the scent of a sea-blown wind, salty and warm. Her cheeks heated.

Gryphon flashed her a coy look. "From the cherry of your blush, I assume you did not find the encounter as unpleasant as you make it sound. But still, how far?"

"It's not as far as the log was from the truck. I think. I don't know. I never measured it."

"We have a plan. I will follow you in, materialize, and spend the day in your prep room. You will need to find excuses and avoid going to your office if possible." Gryphon lifted a hand. "Will we find Crone Betsy nearby. She can help."

"Yeah, a couple of doors down the hall." Frowning, she rearranged her grip on the travel mug. "I don't understand why she didn't tell me about all of this. I thought she was my friend."

"They knew about the prophecy. I will wait to hear why they did not train you while I lingered in the box." Gryphon placed a hand on her arm. "MichAudha depends on you to free me so we may regain control of the coven and destroy Megaera. I will become the new High Priest. It was my destiny before the fires."

"And me?" Emmeline asked.

"You, my beautiful witch, will provide me with enough power to accomplish the task."

"I energize your power takeover and then what?" She inhaled a fortifying breath and popped open the truck door. To give up something she never knew she had in the first place shouldn't affect her. Did she expect to stay involved with Gryphon after his little coup?

"You know what? I don't want to know. Let's do this," Emmeline said.

The door closed, so Emmeline didn't hear his last statement. Scurrying across the parking lot to the back security door, she pulled out the scanning card and took a deep breath. She did want to know how she fit with the coven after Gryphon took over. God, how stupid? She was a pawn in this whole crazy scheme. At least she hadn't fucked him last night and didn't have to live with that act of stupidity.

As the door opened, a swirl of lavender dust circled overhead and paused in the air. It creeped as it hovered, waiting for her next move. It followed her all the way down the hall to the classroom, a stalker in fluffy purple form.

Emmeline turned the lock, pushed into the room, and flipped the light switch. A call from the hallway froze her.

"Emmeline." Betsy paused in the doorway. "Did you make the trip to the springs this weekend?"

The swirl of lavender dust became Gryphon.

"Oh Gryphon, you're a sight for these old eyes. We thought this little druid would never release you."

"Crone Betsy. I'm ecstatic you survived the fires." He bowed.

"How do you two know each other?" Emmeline asked.

"Betsy has many roles. She was my Second Level teacher in magick school, one of the coven elders, and my aunt. Or cousin?"

"We should have told you earlier. We tried, but you resisted every word," Betsy said.

Emmeline crossed her arms and tapped her foot on the floor. "Ya think?"

Betsy fussed with her sleeves for a moment. She addressed Gryphon. "We didn't know when she would come. And when she did, we had our hands full protecting her from Megaera. There were three or four attempts on her life. It's hard to tell; the girl is a dreadful driver."

"Excuse me-the fuck-anyways." Emmeline slapped a hand over her mouth after realizing where she stood. She lifted a hand to stave off Betsy's admonishment. "I'm living in this weird nightmare with some GQ model who turns to lavender dust, smells like mouthwatering sea salt, and kisses like sin. Why didn't you tell me?"

"Do you hear how poorly she speaks?" Gryphon asked Betsy. "People let her teach their children?"

"Women have changed in this century." Betsy clapped and giggled. "Our little druid needs a firm hand."

"Since the two of you know each other," Emmeline walked away from them, "figure out what to do with Houdini while I set up for the day."

Ignoring them, Emmeline fired up the computer and projector, fussed with papers on the desk, and wrote the day's agenda on the board. She followed the pair into the lab under the premise of making coffee.

"Betsy. We have quite a discussion waiting for us, but the

immediate problem sits in front of you." Emmeline pointed at Gryphon. "He's unapproved and an enemy of our boss. You know how snoopy Dr. Caroline can become. And what if Marie Alley stops in?"

"Well, bringing the man to work wasn't the smartest move you've made. You should have called off sick," Betsy said. "I understand you were not told. I blame myself. I'll cast a spell so only you and I can see the Viscount. After school we'll make the spell stronger, but you'll have to help."

"Me. Cast a spell. Why not?" Emmeline gave a short laugh. "It went so well yesterday and this morning."

Gryphon rolled his eyes to the ceiling as red rushed up the muscles in his neck.

"From the look on Gryphon's face, I don't want to know," Betsy said. "Or perhaps I do."

Betsy pulled a few items out of her satchel as she prepared the herbs and chanted a few words.

The first bell rang for homeroom, and the sound of kids in the classroom broke the moment. "Whatever you're going to do, do it quick. The invasion has commenced," Emmeline said.

"Oh dear, we're out of time. I will cloak the room with a hiding spell, but it will break if you step over the threshold." With a wave of her arms, the herbs she had set out caught on fire, and a light breeze stirred the paper towels sitting on the counter.

Emmeline walked out to begin the day with the scent of a sea breeze in her nostrils, a tasty cup of coffee in her hand, and a heavy weight in the bottom of her stomach. How would they ever pull this off? If Dr. Caroline was a witch, wouldn't she sense Gryphon and come snooping?

CHAPTER 11

Harrisburg, PA 2017

Emmeline thrummed her fingers on the armrest as she sat in Dr. Caroline's office after school on a Monday. The request for a meeting arrived late on Friday in an email. Counting today, it was the third time she'd been summoned to the office. Her stomach churned over the weekend trying to figure out what complaint the old bat had whipped up this time.

Betsy, Minerva, and Mirielda sympathized and made strawberry daiquiris after the football game on Saturday afternoon. Betsy and Minerva brought chocolate hazelnut cookies, and Mirielda brought the rum and strawberries. The alcohol, now long gone, did nothing to calm Emmeline's mind. The meeting couldn't start until her union representative arrived.

While they waited for Bill to show, Emmeline took note of the black aura hovering over Dr. Caroline's head. Not all black auras signified darkness, but this one was true black. The void suggested a missing soul or the presence of a dark entity.

The woman's overall appearance could win the Best Witch contest the student council sponsored. A black woven polyester business suit two sizes too big hung from bony shoulders. Teachers and students talked behind her back about the horrendous manicure on the inch-long, crooked fingernails painted with shiny red polish. If you tossed in the matching blood-red lipstick smeared in a haphazard manner across her thin lips, Megaera was the perfect poster model for a horror movie.

Emmeline had little fashion sense, but dang if the principal couldn't do better with her hair. It was stringy, dirty blond, and cut to shoulder length. It curled around her chin like some kind of cheap wig. The wrinkles around her mouth and eyes formed from her continuous frown.

Bill knocked on the door frame before taking a seat next to Emmeline. "Sorry, I had to deal with a student. What infraction has drawn your attention to Miss Callen this time, Dr. Caroline?"

"Two issues." Megaera laid a folder on the desk. "First, Miss Callen was not in the classroom when the bell rang on Friday morning. I called in and a student answered. Second, Mary Janes aren't professional. Your client needs to improve her wardrobe."

"I was outside my door on hall duty Friday morning. I didn't hear the call." Emmeline would have said more, but Bill grabbed an arm.

"We can find several teachers and students to verify her presence if needed," Bill said. "As for your concerns regarding the dress code, our contract does have one. If you lower Ms. Callen's rating because of shoes, a grievance will follow. Since this makes your third unfounded complaint about this teacher, you now border on a hostile work environment case."

"No need for a grievance." Megaera sat up in the chair, lips pinched to the point they paled under the lipstick, and wrote a note in the employee folder. "I'm trying to help Miss Callen become her best. Young teachers need guidance, as I'm sure you know. I have nothing else. Have a safe drive home."

Dismissed as if the issues were their fault, Emmeline followed Bill out the door. It didn't matter how this meeting had gone. In the end, she had an enemy sitting in the principal's office. It was a no-win situation.

"I'm tired of this—"

Bill put a finger over his lips and signaled Emmeline to follow. Once outside the building in the smokers' area, Bill fired up a cigarette and took a deep drag.

"What did you do or say?" Bill asked. "I've never met a new principal so eager to step on a teacher this early in the year."

"I don't know." Emmeline shrugged. "I think Dr. C needs to get laid. I mean, holy witch on a broom."

"If I had to guess, I would say Dr. Caroline wants rid of you." Bill raked his fingers through his hair. "Maybe a relative wants a job in the science department."

"We already have her little spy, Marie Alley. That twit doesn't know a somatic cell from a jail cell. No biology certification, and she took the Praxis in Biology after she was hired. Who else would hire her but a relative?"

"I'll let the Association know." Bill smothered his smoke in an overfull ashtray. "In the meantime, watch who you talk to, arrive early, leave late, and keep the parents happy. Write down anything Marie or Megaera says and keep it in a file."

"Did you know Megaera was one of the furies in Greek mythology?" Emmeline explained as they walked into the parking lot. "The name means jealous or spiteful. I Googled it. Thanks again, Bill. Catch you tomorrow."

On the way home, a tire blew on Emmeline's little Ranger along a curve on Old Jonestown Road. The bed swung to her left. She overcorrected it and came close to putting it in the ditch. Sitting at rest, she took a quiet moment. She took a deep breath and yelled at the steering wheel. "Could this day suck any more than it already does?"

Emmeline removed the spare and kicked it after discovering part of the jack was missing. "Well, fuck. I guess it can. Where did I...shit."

Tightening the tie holding her hair back, Emmeline grabbed her phone and searched for tow services. Terrific, only one bar of reception. Deciding it was faster to walk, she gazed down at her Mary Janes. At least these made better walking shoes than bitchy Caroline's pointy-toed monstrosities.

Before the first step, a truck slowed to a stop beside the Ranger. The driver rolled down the window. Damn, he was good-looking.

"Need some help?" the driver asked.

Nodding, Emmeline put on a sweet smile. "You wouldn't have a jack I could borrow?"

"How about I fix it for you and you can take me to dinner?"

"Deal, but no sushi." She smiled and pushed out a hand to shake. "I'm Emmeline."

"Brad."

Rolling the lugs in her hands, Emmeline leaned on the Ranger while Brad worked the jack. He had a well-proportioned physique, broad shoulders, and narrow hips. The cold didn't distract her from checking out the hero or his truck. "Your Ford. A '64?"

"A girl who knows trucks?" Brad frowned at the Ranger. He spun the lug wrench and gave a final jerk on the last nut.

"I always wanted a '54 Chevy. They have sexy front ends, like yours." Her eyes widened after she realized what she'd said.

He wore a half-smile and struggled not to respond. Brad tossed his lug wrench and jack into the bed of his truck. "Marry me."

Both laughed, and the evening got a whole lot better.

On Friday evening of the same week, Emmeline sat in a funeral home at Bill's viewing.

After going through the reception line, Emmeline sat in a pew replaying Monday's meeting with Dr. Caroline in her head. She had told Bill, 'Catch you tomorrow,' as they left the smoking area and headed home. It was all surreal. Her blown tire ended with Brad, and Bill's ended with death. Life's not fair.

The whole staff was in shock. Everyone except for Principal Caroline. Three staff members had already died this year. Memories focused on an accident from long ago. The loss of her parents, being raised by strangers, not getting adopted, and car crashed had put her life on a different track every time she planned. Emmeline swallowed her tears.

A strange man sat down in Emmeline's pew with only a foot of space between them. His aura shimmered with black specks in a dark gray cloud. She shivered and crossed her arms against the chill but didn't want to look rude by shifting further away. It was a funeral. Grief made people act strangely at times.

He leaned over and whispered, "It's sad, isn't it?"

Emmeline turned her head to acknowledge his statement and nodded.

"My name is Wilmott. We don't know each other, but I need to give you this." He slipped a folded square of paper into her hands.

The small square opened to beautiful handwritten script. She recognized the language to be old Gaelic. She was unable to decipher the message. Two plant sprigs were attached at the bottom with clear tape. Sage for sure, but the other might be rowan.

"What do you have there, Emmeline?" Betsy dropped into the seat formerly occupied by the man, who had disappeared.

Scanning the crowd to point the man out for Betsy, she found Dr. Caroline staring at her. The stare was dead and cold. Her aura was still totally black. Maybe darker than on Monday, if it was possible.

"I don't know. A man gave it to me and said I would need it someday."

"Emmeline. I watched you the entire time I stood in line. You were by yourself." Betsy glanced around the room and back to the paper. "Rowan next to sage? Strange to give you both. Sage purifies the air, but rowan protects against witches and fairies."

Emmeline giggled. "Fairies and witches? Well, maybe the guy was a witch and disappeared with the snap of a finger. His aura was a dark smoke gray."

"You shouldn't joke about magick." Betsy squeezed Emmeline's hand. "We're going for a drink. Want to join?"

"No. I promised to meet a friend at Applebee's."

"Do you have a date?"

Emmeline blushed as they walked. At the trashcan by the door, she found it impossible to toss the paper and stuck it in a pocket, focusing on a soothing glass of cold beer and Brad.

* * *

December rolled in with brisk winds and snow. Megaera stood on the witches' altar. The priestess cape flowed behind her, snapping in the wind. Norman stood ready as each gust pushed her deteriorating frame backwards.

"I feel power in this storm. It's the perfect opportunity to rid us of the Key," Megaera shouted into the wind as Norman stirred the cauldron. "Wintery roads will explain another accident. No one will know any different. Car accidents happen all the time."

"High Priestess," Norman said. "If a car accident takes the Key, the coven will become suspicious. Too many people close to the coven have fallen to the same tragedy, and they keep a close eye on Emmeline."

"You try my patience, Norman. The coven's too stupid to recognize a pattern. They spend their energies trying to fit in with the humans." Megaera leaned close to Norman's ear and whispered, "I feel you don't support my plans. If the winds blow me off this altar, would you seek to save me?"

"Yes, High Priestess." Norman continued stirring. "Thomas and I would put effort into the task."

"Indeed." Megaera wrapped the robe tighter around her shoulders.

"The wind challenges our fire." Thomas whisked to the altar and dropped an armload of firewood beside the cauldron. "Perhaps we should do this spell another time."

"I control the fire. Do not worry about the flame." Megaera's pale, wind-scoured face reddened. She shot a single flame across the altar and singed Thomas's shoes. He jumped. "Your burns, they healed well?"

Norman dropped seeds of corn, squash, and beans into the cauldron, chanting a Gaelic prayer. Each addition grated on Megaera's nerves. "Norman, do you add the Three Sisters to all of my spells?"

"Yes, High Priestess. Verne told me to."

Megaera swallowed as the brew accepted the offering and a bubble broke the surface with a puff of sulfur. The old seer still haunted her purpose. Perhaps the spells didn't work as expected because of the addition. The Book of Fire never listed the Three Sisters as an ingredient. Unwritten or unwanted, the fire roared around the cauldron, the hot blue and green arms of heat reaching for her. She stepped back.

"What did you do?" Megaera asked.

"I added the Three Sisters and stirred," Norman said. "The cauldron drips into the fire. Your repair did not hold."

"The cauldron warns you, High Priestess," Thomas shouted into the wind.

Scoffing, Megaera removed the vial of Dragon's Blood from her cloak and shook two drops into the seething mixture. Raising hands to the night sky, Megaera spoke the spell she'd modified from one already in the Book of Fire.

"Wheels that turn, will slip and slide. From this, the druid cannot hide. During the month of Yule, magick unfurled, to find our Key, a red-haired girl. Emmeline Callen dies this night in bitter cold, to prevent the coming as was told. So mote it be."

The wind picked up, the brew dripped into the fire, and the fire roared. The vessel screamed as the temperature grew. It became so hot that it glowed a brilliant deep orange as the handle melted over the spit. The vessel dropped into the fire with a thunk, tipped, and spilled the brew across the altar. The smell of brimstone burned everyone's noses.

With both hands extended to the sky, Megaera's cackle rose above the wind. "Go with the wind, my spell of dark fire. Do my bidding."

Harrisburg, PA 2019

Emmeline's blood pressure settled as she addressed her first class of the day. "Today we'll tackle homeostatic functions in hibernation. A video will show you several animals who hibernate and how their feedback loops work. Then we'll discuss the metabolic feedback loops, and you will draw them in your notebooks."

Within a minute of her clicking on the movie, half the students went to sleep, and the other half pulled out their phones. If only osmosis worked with knowledge as well as it did with salt water, Emmeline thought. But their lack of attention provided a moment to check on her guest.

Stepping into the prep room, she found Gryphon reading a book and drinking coffee. "What are you reading?"

Gryphon flashed the cover of *On the Origin of Species.* "Darwin made the famous voyage when I was learning to whisk about the forest as a Second Level. The poor writing is a bit of a bore, and I have no idea where witches would fit on his evolutionary tree. But it did retain my interest."

"I can't go there right now." Emmeline turned on the

computer and entered the school password. Demonstrating how to do a search, she said, "You can learn modern devices like the microwave or read up on the history you missed while...dust. Type your question here, hit enter, and pick one of these bold areas to open the document."

"A library at your fingertips. Marvelous." Discarding the old book, Gryphon moved the stool closer to the keyboard.

"I have to go back to class. Please stay in this room."

Emmeline pondered where Darwin would put witches on his tree. Perhaps in the same class as man but a different branch. The problem was reminiscent of the chicken question. Who came first, a witch or *Homo sapiens*? Her laugh woke the kids.

The end of fourth period came as a relief. Period five was lunch. Emmeline realized she hadn't packed one because Gryphon had distracted her with his salty scent, warm lips, and gentle touch. Running to the cafeteria was risky. As she was heading back to tell Gryphon of the problem, Betsy burst into the classroom with a picnic basket over one arm.

"I figured you didn't think this whole scenario through, so I called Edemay. She whisked in some lunch. Some of Gryphon's favorites are in here. I advise you to avoid anything to do with fish."

They went to the prep room to find it empty.

"Oh, shit. I thought you said—" Emmeline waved at the empty room.

"I thought he would listen to me," Betsy said.

"Where the hell's he at?" Emmeline panicked until she sawGryphon stepping out of the other prep room on the far side of the lab. She blew out a deep breath. "You were told not to leave the room."

"I was looking for the privy," Gryphon explained with a shoulder shrug. "Too much coffee."

Emmeline moved toward a cupboard, grabbed a large glass beaker, and shoved it in his hands. "Use this."

Gryphon walked past Emmeline, focused on Betsy, and removed the basket from Betsy's hands. "Lunch. Splendid. I'm famished."

"Was he ever spanked as a child?" Emmeline asked.

"Many times. His mother had to cut a new switch every week."

Holding an unwrapped sandwich toward Betsy, Gryphon asked, "What manner of fish do you feed me?"

"It doesn't matter. It's food. Eat, stay here, and use the jar as Emmeline has indicated."

Betsy grabbed a sandwich from the basket along with a bag of chips and a soda and handed it to Emmeline. They both returned to the classroom.

Emmeline set the food on the desk. "Betsy, you've been a friend since my first year of teaching. But right now, I feel deceived. All this time you knew, but you let me go on not knowing. Why?"

Silent at first, Betsy tugged on the fabric forming a ruffle on the button-down blouse. "We discussed it, Mirielda and I. Mirielda thought it too soon to tell you. After the mishap in New York and the loss of your dog, I wasn't sure of your capacity to deal with witchcraft."

"What did New York—?" Emmeline's eyes widened. "You should have told me."

"I'll stop by right after school. Enjoy your lunch." Betsy walked to the hall door and glanced around the room as if she were looking for something. "Not here. We'll talk tonight."

"Come at seven," Emmeline said. "I'll pick up take-out after we hit the mall. Maybe you can explain why Gryphon can't poof himself some new clothes."

"Rules exist for using magick." Betsy stepped out but returned with a small smile. "What kind of clothes will you buy? Keep in mind he was wealthy and always wore the finest clothes at the height of fashion. He's a Viscount by birth."

"I have no idea what a Viscount is, and I don't care." The

corners of her mouth tipped up as she thought. "I should take him to Goodwill, but my ex's sweats didn't fit him at all, so he'll be hard to find clothes for. The big galoot will have to deal with whatever's on sale at DXL."

"Finish strong," Betsy said as she left the room.

It was their teachers' motto. Emmeline could not muster the energy to match the older woman's enthusiasm. The bell rang. The "class from hell" filtered in the door, boys pushing and shoving and girls glued to their cell phones. *Christ, it's like herding cats*, she thought.

The moment the ninth period dismissal bell rang, Emmeline dropped into the teacher's chair. Her dry throat was soothed by a drink of water. Staring at the doorway into the lab and hoping he stayed put, she took more time to store her laptop and straighten the desk. With a final rush of breath, she walked into the lab.

Before Emmeline opened the prep room door, Betsy came barreling in at full speed.

"Let's cast this invisibility spell, and you can take Gryphon to the mall. We will need a few chemicals, a flame, and this piece of sage." She waved the twig in the air. "How did the Viscount enjoy the afternoon?"

"I'm not sure." Emmeline pulled open the door to the project room. Her eyes widened and her jaw dropped.

The mouse cord swung back and forth from the counter. Gryphon sat on the floor, still, silent, and covered in pale white dust. His hair curled at the ends.

"Is he dead?" Betsy asked.

The door to the chemical closet hung open from one hinge, and chemicals were spread across every surface. Small piles of unknown materials sat on little aluminum trays scattered across the prep bench, and nearby a Bunsen burner flickered its blueish-orange flame.

"Oh, broomsticks," Betsy said. "You left him unattended all afternoon?"

"What the hell did you do?" Emmeline yelled at Gryphon. "OMG! What if he set off the fire alarms? Betsy, help me here!"

Gryphon crossed his arms over his torso. "I tried to fix this device Emmeline gave me."

His comment brought on a round of laughter between the two women.

"Your attachment to the Witchbox limits your power." Betsy knelt in front of him. "Please tell me you didn't try to cast a spell?"

The computer sat cockeyed on the counter, the screen frozen on a porn site. Large font spelling out BLOCKED stretched across a muscular, naked man.

"What did you ask it to find?" Emmeline tried to hold back her laughter but didn't succeed. She unhooked the cable and electrical plug. "How did you override the school filter?"

"I entered, find undergarments for large men." Gryphon frowned and dusted some powder from his sleeve. "I searched for the best type to purchase for our shopping journey this evening. I do not wear such items, but it appears popular at this time."

Both women broke out in hysterical laughter.

"I fail to find this situation humorous," Gryphon said.

"It took our coven a long time to figure out technology. We found out by accident, magick and electronics don't mix." Betsy continued to snicker. She waved a hand. A light breeze blew through the small space. All of the powder disappeared, and the bottles capped themselves and floated through the air to put themselves back on the proper shelf. The door, now on both hinges, closed.

"Holy shit," Emmeline said.

"She says that a great deal," Gryphon said.

Betsy ignored them. "We need to cast the invisibility spell."

"Of course." Gryphon tapped a finger on his chin. "Invisibility spell. I have not cast one in quite some time. If you have some parchment and ink, I will write the spell first and Emmeline can chant it."

"I will lend some of my power, but Emmeline will have to cast the spell." Betsy smiled at her. "Try to restrain yourself. We wouldn't want Gryphon turning into a frog."

"Me? Do magick?" Emmeline paced the little room, shaking her hands to reduce her stress. "I'm a scientist. Magick is chemistry with a flair I can do this."

"Gryphon can write the spell down but can't cast it without the Book of Shadows. I suppose you could call it a lojack for spells of this nature."

"How would I have the skills to read it?" Emmeline began hyperventilating.

Gryphon took both her hands and squeezed them. "Emmeline. The language came from your people. You're of an ancient sect of druids from Isle Magee. You will know the ancient language when you encounter it. Trust me."

Gryphon's unique scent filled the room. Magick. Sure, no problem. Holy shit. He was doing the *thing* again.

"I keep telling you to stop that." Emmeline narrowed her eyes at Gryphon.

"Stop what, Emmeline?" Gryphon took the pen and paper from her.

"What's he doing?" Betsy asked.

"Never mind." Flashing a raised eyebrow at Gryphon, she sighed. "Let's have at it. I'll read ancient Gaelic. No problem." Emmeline paced the small space, shaking her hands and mumbling.

Gryphon closed his eyes and moved his hands in the air as if turning the pages of a rather large book. The pencil levitated and wrote Gaelic symbols on the tablet all by itself.

"While he writes, find some sulfur and copper. Also, do you have a clean Pyrex beaker? We need something heat resistant." Betsy claimed the beaker and chanted over the makeshift casting vessel, adding bits of sage and a pinch of powder from a brown leather satchel.

"Guess it's fortunate I teach science," Emmeline whispered.

"Fate determines everything. The ancients chose you. You never had a choice in your path or occupation." Betsy squeezed Emmeline's shoulder in sympathy.

Emmeline's mind floated with careful thought at Betsy's last statement. Nothing in her life had been an accident or choice. Even becoming a teacher and working here at ASSD. What evil prophecy would take parents from a child? Each moment, each decision, was nothing more than a predetermined path. It made her head spin.

Gryphon handed Emmeline the spell.

Emmeline swallowed a big lump in her throat. The paper rattled because of her shaking hands while she examined the symbols printed in neat lines. "I know these symbols."

"You must concentrate on the symbols, but don't try to figure them out," Gryphon said. He trailed a hand along her ponytail, one finger riding the ridge of an ear and continuing along her neck. "It will come to you when you clear your mind."

Emmeline shivered at his touch, flashed him a quick glance, and licked her lips. She stared at the page. The letters blurred at first and rose from the page, floating like a balloon. Dancing on the air, the words twirled and tumbled toward the beaker. She read the words in Gaelic but spoke them in English without trying.

"To be seen by few, not many. The witch will offer a penny. Into the fire, a visual pyre, Earth, Wind, Water, and Fire. Until the Witching Hour, the cloak will last, the day's tasks to pass. So mote it be."

One by one as they were read, the words fell into the beaker. Once the "e" in the last word was spoken, the ingredients in the beaker caught fire, and a little ball of blue smoke puffed into the air.

"Blow the ball to Gryphon," Betsy said.

Emmeline blew a gentle but steady breath. The words reappeared on the page, and the little blue puff exploded all over Gryphon. He twinkled as if someone had spilled glitter all over him.

"I did not enjoy the sensation, but I believe it worked." Gryphon shivered and tugged his vest down. "Splendid. Shall we go? I would prefer to move on with this shopping."

Emmeline plodded down the hall, waiting for the alarms to sound. She tried to brush away the worry of discovery and concentrate on the magick. But she was a scientist. Magick didn't exist. Yet she walked down the hall with Gryphon dressed in strange clothing and no one stopped them. The spell had worked. Holy crap. She had done magick.

CHAPTER 12

Harrisburg, PA 2017

Emmeline left the ASSD Christmas party before midnight. The weather had taken a nasty turn with frigid wind blowing snow across the parking lot. She had never done well in a crowd. She expressed a lungful of air, making little clouds as she walked. Warm jammies and a heated Winter Jack lay at the forefront of her mind, followed by Brad arriving to warm her toes.

Emmeline climbed into her Ranger, turned over the engine, and flipped the defroster to high. She let the truck run while she scraped snow and ice from the windshield. The scrapper got stuck on a twig under the wiper. Emmeline broke the wiper free and grabbed the little bit of plant material. Sage?

Shrugging her shoulders, Emmeline rubbed her hands together and blew on her fingertips. She tossed the twig in the cab with the scraper and climbed into the driver's seat. Some drunk probably thought it was mistletoe. Although, to her they didn't look anything alike.

Applauding herself for throwing 300 pounds of salt in the back, she put the truck in gear and pulled out on Old Jonestown Road. Even with the extra weight, the light truck seemed incapable of keeping its ass-end on the road.

Heat blasted Emmeline's face, so she glanced down to adjust the blower. The second she lifted her head, her eyes widened, and she slammed on the brakes. A black cat sat in the middle of the road. The little truck spun three times before coming to rest buried in a deep snowbank.

"Fuuuuck!" She pounded on the steering wheel.

It took a shoulder butt against the door to get it open. She climbed out to assess the damage. No way would the four-wheel drive have enough power to back out of the pile. Pulling her cell out of a pocket, she tried to call Brad, but with no answer, she scanned both directions for a porch light, music—anything to indicate life. Even the stupid cat had disappeared.

"Why do I always end up screwed? I didn't drink enough to deal with this shit." Emmeline squeezed her hands into fists as she talked to her truck. The Ranger sat silent, half-buried in snow.

The cold sliced through Emmeline's crappy winter coat. It had looked warm hanging on the rack at Goodwill, but the storm surpassed its insulating ability. Shopping there was a habit left over from her foster home days. New clothing was a luxury and took money away from booze and cigarettes for the foster parents.

"I have paychecks coming in. I'm going to buy a brand-new coat. A warm one." She nodded at the truck as if it could hear. A loud cracking sound penetrated the storm, and she glanced toward the tree in front of the snow pile.

The tree snapped above the snow pile and toppled across the cab.

Emmeline ran to avoid being swiped by the massive ever-green. The half-dead branches had the tell-tale signs of a wooly adelgid infestation. Emmeline stared at the mangled remains of the well-loved little pickup and she realized how close she had come to dying. What if she had been inside trying to spin her way out of the pile?

"Why does my life suck?" Emmeline shouted into the sky.

Large fluffy flakes fell in disregard to her plight. She snapped the ends from several branches of the old hemlock and threw them on the ground. "Stupid, fucking, invasive species."

Emmeline took a moment to calm down and tried Brad one more time before the inevitable long, cold walk to find help. She pushed the unanswered cell into her pocket and jumped up and down to create heat. The road toward her apartment was sparsely populated, so she turned and headed back to the bar.

"So much for a new coat. Damn." Emmeline trudged down the center line and wondered if God would send help if she sent up a prayer. She shook her head side to side. Some all-powerful entity living in the clouds didn't make her spin off the road, buy crap coats at Goodwill, or curse her life. She snuffled her runny nose and set off toward the Lighthouse Bar. The one truth she'd learned in foster care was that she had to take care of herself.

A vehicle's headlights broke through the blowing snow. Blinding lights hurt her eyes before they dimmed. Betsy's VDub slid to a halt, and Minerva jumped out and ran to hug her.

"Oh my goodness. Emmeline. You okay?" Minerva shouted into her ear.

"I'm fine. Can I have a ride to a phone?" Emmeline asked.

"Jump in. We'll take you home, and you can call from the safety of your apartment."

Emmeline climbed into the back seat as the older woman brushed the snow from her back. Minerva was an excitable old lady with a pleasant personality and a love for everything ASSD. Emmeline took everything she did in stride and remained grateful.

"Thanks, M." Settling into the seat, Emmeline asked, "Why does the bug smell like coffee?"

"Oh gosh. How coinky-dink." Betsy giggled over her shoulder. "It's your gift from the Christmas party. You didn't wait for the exchange. It does smell yummy. Magical even. I intended to bring it over tomorrow. Did you have too much punch?"

Betsy was constant in her intervention over Emmeline's alcohol consumption. Overall, it was nice to have someone concerned for her. Until she had joined ASSD, no one had ever demonstrated the inclination.

"No punch. I did shoot a couple of bourbons."

"Did you call Brad?" Minerva asked.

"He didn't pick up." Emmeline's hands and feet remained cold while she pondered the location of her missing boyfriend and whether the women would want to stay and visit. Rude as it was, all she wanted to do was go home, warm up, cry about the truck, and not play host to two half-intoxicated gabs. She loved these two women, but they could try one's patience at times.

Minerva peered over the headrest. "Now tell us what happened to your poor little truck."

Emmeline explained what had happened on the rest of the drive, hoping Betsy could handle the storm. She related the encounter with the black cat and the tree crushing the cab as they passed the accident site. She drifted into thoughts of how close to death she had come.

"Emmeline?" Minerva said.

A dull prod on her sleeve brought Emmeline back to the present. "What?"

"Maybe the cat saved your life, or perhaps it was magick," Minerva said.

"Sure, magick." Emmeline coughed out a stilted laugh. "If it existed, I would use it to repair my truck."

A long fifteen minutes later, Betsy pulled into Emmeline's driveway.

"Thanks for the ride. Do you want to break open this coffee?" Emmeline asked, holding up the bow-topped package.

"Heavens no. It would ruin my buzz." Betsy waved out the

window. "Brad owes me one for the rescue. Kept him from dragging his lazy ass out of the bar tonight."

"Harsh, Bets. You've never liked Brad," Emmeline said. "Night, girls."

* * *

The first day of the winter break, Megaera threw her cell phone at Thomas after receiving a report on the druid. "Those damn familiars! Dead. I want them all dead."

She stomped across the scrying room at Haven House, spinning on her heel and pointing one of her crooked fingers at Thomas. "When I take over, I'll cast a worldwide spell causing all familiars to disappear. You will search all tomes and find a spell."

"Yes, High Priestess." Thomas returned to his phone.

"I need more coffee." Megaera stormed off, a black puff of smoke rising from each foot stomp. On the seventh step of the stairs, her business-appropriate shoes hit the damp shale. She slipped, twisted, and grabbed for the rail. Missing the hand grip, Megaera went several feet airborne, landed on her ass, and slid step-by-step toward the bottom of the staircase.

She ended the descent in an ungraceful position, with her legs spread and one foot bare. The other shoe rested several feet away. Megaera attempted to rise several times and met with a painful defeat on each try. A small sign on the wall near her head read: Stairs will be slippery—Hold rail for safety. Megaera gawked at the sign. Verne had placed it there after some inspector went through the building and required it for the insurance company.

Norman and Thomas stood speechless ten feet away.

"Are you two going to stare or help me?" Megaera asked.

"Where does it hurt, High Priestess?" Norman strolled to Megaera's feet and knelt.

"Would you like us to call for an ambulance, High Priestess?" Thomas asked as he leaned over with his hands on his knees.

"You incompetent fools. You should have rushed to catch me." After an attempt to rise, she dropped back to the step and tried to whisk. "Sssssss. It hurts. I can't concentrate. The pain distracts me. Use your magick and whisk me to the healer."

Norman and Thomas each lifted an arm and whisked Megaera to the healer.

Each magical movement jarred the fractures, sending shooting pain through her body. "If you jar me again, you will both remain toads for a year," Megaera said.

"The Returns of Three struck hard this time," Thomas said.

The healer arrived, preventing Megaera from shooting a strike of lightning at Thomas. Once she was better, she would take her revenge. In private.

The healer tried several spells. None had any effect. Puzzled, the healer said, "I would prefer to consult my leaves, High Priestess. Prepare yourself to stay awhile. The injuries may be from a Return of Three. If so, my magick cannot heal you. Only time can."

"Thomas," Megaera said. "Before you leave. Why didn't you tell me the spell missed our little witch the second you found out? You work for the boyfriend, don't you?"

"I don't work for Brad. We build cars together in my spare time, and the shop's closed for the holidays."

Thomas whisked away before she could order him to do anything. The apprentice annoyed her at every turn. She would have to ask a scrying bowl about his purpose. He was from the Dewlight line, after all. He could be a spy. She grimaced as the pain in her hip reminded her to stay still.

Over the next several weeks, Megaera found directing the coven and school from bed problematic. Her pain interfered with concentration, and her magick set small fires in and around the healing house. The fires she could see were controllable, but a time came when Haven House paid the price.

The healer arrived, tears still falling from her cheeks.

"What happened?" Megaera asked.

"The wind took up the bonfire for St. Brigid and lit the roof and timbers on fire," the healer said. "Nothing's left of Haven House but a smoldering foundation. Witnesses swore they smelled brimstone."

Megaera watched the black smoke lift into the sky from the window of her room as the healer prodded her hip and pain shot down her leg. She narrowed her eyes. "Why have I not healed?"

"My tea leaves said the injury is the result of a Return of Three. I can't heal a punishment from the fates." The healer made to leave but turned back at the door. "You should learn to make offerings to the Grand Master."

"Fire Witches do not make offerings to the earth. Leave, you useless witch."

Two days later, Megaera summoned Mirielda.

Mirielda whisked into the room. "I'm busy trying to find homes for the coven members who lived at Haven House. What do you want?"

"To speak on the exact subject. I have found a new home for MichAudah." Megaera levitated a folder across the room into Mirielda's hands. "I hold you responsible for our tragedy. You did not control the fire during Brigid."

"It's a Return of Three for casting dark spells and destroying our cauldron, as is your broken hip. Don't blame me for this. Have you wondered why it doesn't heal?" Mirielda snapped and showed no regret for her outburst.

"Forget the blame. The property will suit our needs. See it done by the end of the week." Megaera floated her teacup to the nightstand. Her hands fisted the sheets as she waited for Mirielda to read the material in the folder. The girl took too long.

Megaera said, "The house is perfect for us. Ten thousand square feet, ten bedrooms with baths and forty-four acres of land. There are features the coven would love, especially those outdoors like the fireplace, kitchen/BBQ, patio, swimming pool with spa, and formal gardens."

Mirielda narrowed her eyes at Megaera. "How is this available, and how can we afford it?"

Megaera smiled. "The house needs a little work after the police raid. I'm sure the coven can spare some magick. And we do have insurance money coming from Haven House. It's in Fishing Creek. We'll call it the Ivory Tower because of the massive marble supports on the front porch."

"As you wish, High Priestess," Mirielda said.

"Norman and Thomas will use magick to convert the southern part of the basement into my personal quarters. The rest of the house and grounds belong to the coven."

A week later, Megaera climbed out of the healer's car and limped with a cane into the Ivory Tower. An elevator took her to the basement to inspect her new quarters. Norman waited by the door with his head down, shuffling his feet.

"What's wrong, Norman?" Megaera asked.

"We moved the cauldron as ordered. I believe the crack grew bigger."

"Bigger?" Megaera stormed across the floor to the vessel.

"You seat the cauldron and altar inside?" Mirielda asked as she stepped from the last stair.

"What better way to protect it. Besides, I detest the cold," Megaera said. "We have this huge basement. Why not fill it with witches?"

"Flames and smoke—"

"Vents and fans were installed." Megaera tilted her head and tapped a finger on her chin. She pointed at the cauldron. "It doesn't go here. Move it to the new altar."

The movers exerted magick, levitated the heavy cauldron, and floated it across the floor thirty feet. The iron pot clunked on the slate floor and echoed against the stone walls. It remained covered in ice and snow from sitting outside. The acrid odor of burning hair and sulfur seeped into the room. Another witch floated in behind the cauldron, saturating the air with burning sage and sandalwood.

"I don't see any damage except for the previous fracture." Megaera walked around the vessel. Her cane made a click-thump with each step.

"A new crack exists by the handle." Thomas pointed out a spot. "How will we ever suspend it over a fire?"

"Using this cauldron could end us," Mirielda said.

"What shall we do?" Norman asked.

"I will take care of it. Have faith in my ability. Fire magick will fix the issue." Megaera tapped yellowed nails against the damaged vessel.

Days later, a semi-truck pulled into the driveway. The handlers unloaded a huge wooden box and left. Megaera whisked into the waiting crowd. They parted to give her room to approach the crate.

Megaera called the wind. The weak breeze had difficulty lifting her robe and failed to give her the appearance of power she wished to present. Shaking off her weakness, which she blamed on the injury, she called her fire. The boards of the crate burst into flames and burned fast to reveal a bright copper-colored vessel.

"I present to you our new cauldron," Megaera said. She raised her hands in the air and called lightning to strike behind the crowd and then threw balls of chemical magick at the coven's feet. Little snaps followed by rising smoke added the illusion of power she wanted.

Murmurs and gasps reached her ears. It was not the response Megaera expected.

Mirielda shook her head. "Cauldrons come from a magical place. They are created with the hands of druids during the time of Beltane and passed down through a coven. You cannot make a new cauldron."

"I know we can't make a druid's cauldron. But we need a

vessel to hold a brew and reveal a vision. This one is made of tantalum and hafnium carbides. It will never crack, melt, or fail to boil under a hot fire."

"Our cauldron was made of iron from the earth, not those modern ceramics," Betsy said. "I will never believe a vision cast in this monstrosity. Prepare for the consequences when MichAudah refuses to follow your lead."

"I know what's best for our coven. Do as I say or pay the price for insolence. Take the vessel downstairs and prepare it for a blessing ceremony." Megaera whisked away.

Harrisburg, PA 2019

Once in the East Mall, Emmeline was absorbed by Gryphon's child-like enthusiasm for the different stores. He was pointing in windows and touching the items for sale in the center aisle kiosks. People were laughing or staring at his outbursts and questions. Either the spell had worn off or it only worked on ASSD property.

Most of the voyeurs were female, of course. Emmeline had to punch back an unexpected spike of jealousy. Dredging up excitement for his questions, she made honest attempts to answer them. Some questions bordered on insane while others were inappropriate regarding some of the novelty shops.

"Gryphon," Emmeline said. "Keep your voice down. You're attracting too much attention."

He did a one-eighty. "What draws their attention?"

"You. People can see and hear you."

Gryphon's smile faded. "The spell didn't last?"

"Apparently not." Emmeline gestured to the group of students who made a point to follow them and take videos. "I wonder how many hits you'll get tonight."

"I do not understand...hits?" Gryphon whispered in her ear.

The damn salty sea breeze made all of her girl parts tingle, and the wisp of his breath brushed her ear, making her wet. Glancing down, she noted he was also affected. However, she didn't know if it was her or the mall getting him excited. Emmeline frowned at the thought.

He lifted his hand, and Emmeline took it as they strolled toward the DXL shop. She tried to figure out why it felt so natural to hold his hand. She'd only known him just over twenty-four hours, and she'd never held hands with Brad or any other boyfriend.

Her mind traveled to the upcoming clothes shopping. While thinking about fitting those broad shoulders into a modern shirt, she lost track of her charge. Looking at her empty hand, she lifted her head to find Gryphon in front of a lingerie shop.

"Let's go, big guy. Unless you're a crossdresser, I doubt anything in there would fit you."

"I believe I favor this ensemble."

The display mannequin wore a red lace corset and matching thong.

"No way. Thongs ride up your ass."

Their eyes locked. Gryphon leaned toward her face. Were they the only souls in the world at this moment? His scent pulled her into the depths of those sexy lavender eyes. Would he kiss her like he had in the kitchen this morning? She waited.

"Perhaps later this evening, we can investigate this moment further." He stood up and walked away. His baritone chuckle brushed her ears.

Emmeline stopped breathing. Had he just released his mojo, made her all bothered, and left? Pulling her libido back into place, she followed him into DXL, contemplating revenge. It came in the form of the clerk, Jeffrey.

The store clerk plastered a huge smile across his face as he gave Gryphon a once-over. "I'm Jeffrey, and I identify as genderqueer. May I assist in your shopping?"

"You sure can, Jeffrey." Emmeline pulled Gryphon between

them. She smiled so much her mouth hurt. "This poor guy lost all of his clothing in a fire. He came home from play practice and found nothing but ash."

"How terrible." Jeffrey rubbed Gryphon's arm and moved closer. With a hip twist and outstretched arms moving in a half circle to encompass the store, he said, "Do you want formal, business, or casual? Lots of sales today."

"Go with casual until the insurance kicks in. Jeans, a couple Henleys, flannel, and a button-down. Keep it basic," Emmeline said.

"I'll need to take some measurements." Jeffrey pulled a measuring tape from a pocket and let it unroll in the air.

Emmeline watched Gryphon's expressions as Jeffrey went about measuring his shoulders and inseam. The sexy witch's jaw remained tight, but like a little trooper, he stood his ground.

"No worries, sweet Emmeline. I have been measured before," Gryphon said.

Emmeline felt a breeze fluff her ponytail. She raised her eyebrows at Gryphon and had to bite her tongue to keep from laughing. Hoping he didn't shoot any magick at Jeffrey, she grabbed a shirt from one of the displays and sauntered over to him.

Gryphon stared into her eyes. "Your freckles make me want to play connect the dots with my tongue."

The clerk cleared his throat, rolled his eyes, and smiled. "You'll find the Henleys on a BOGO sale today."

"What is a BOGO?" Gryphon asked the clerk.

Emmeline swallowed. How could Gryphon say something so outrageous and return to a previous conversation without a stutter? She let her eyes fall toward the floor and paused half-way. She quirked a smile. He wasn't quite as unaffected as she'd thought.

"What do you think, slim, regular, or relaxed fit?" Jeffrey

held up a pair of designer jeans from the other side of the store. "All of the pants are BOGO as well."

Emmeline coughed. "Make them relaxed fit, and we'll take Lee jeans with buttons and a pair of lightweight cargo-style pants if you have them. Mix it up."

She flashed a glance at Gryphon before she said, "Zippers could be a hazard."

Gryphon's cheeks blushed as Jeffrey handed him several pairs of pants and took him to the fitting rooms.

When he emerged, there were no words. The jeans hugged his muscular thighs while the dark maroon Henley fit with perfection, clinging to his muscular frame. Gryphon was drop-dead gorgeous. He had to be the sexiest man she had ever seen, and from Jeffrey's expression, it was ditto for him as well.

"Did I put something on wrong?" Gryphon asked. He patted his legs and chest and glanced down at his bare feet.

"No. It's great. Go try on the other stuff," Emmeline said. She shook her head and handed Jeffrey a multi-pack of Gildan boxer briefs, socks, and a debit card.

"You're a rare kind of friend," Jeffrey said. "I would make him work off the bill, if you understand my meaning."

Emmeline nodded but found it difficult to speak. Gryphon kept the last outfit on after changing. The dark red and purple flannel complemented his eyes and his long black hair, highlighted the color contrasts.

As they worked their way out of the mall, she also purchased a pair of sneakers and manly boots before stopping at Auntie Ann's pretzels. She ordered several—cheese and mustard, butter and cinnamon, and one plain with several toppings on the side.

He consumed every crumb. A tiny smear of mustard drew her attention to the corner of his mouth, and she reached up with a napkin to wipe it off. Their eyes locked with each other, the moment intimate.

"Which one did you like the most?" Emmeline asked.

"If I had to choose, the cinnamon and butter," Gryphon said. He wiped his mouth on the napkin while chewing the last bite. "Can you tell me how the merchants receive reimbursement for their products? I did not see you exchange any currency."

She held out the debit card. "I'm too tired to explain it right now. Consider it today's version of cash." Their fingers touched when he took it from her. It might have become another moment, but then he opened his mouth and became the ass she'd met on the mountain.

"When will I have this form of currency? I am embarrassed to have a female provide for me." He stood, holding out a hand. "Shall we return to Betsy and your home?"

Emmeline didn't take his hand. Tucking the card back into her wallet, she tossed the trash and left him standing with his hand extended, heading for the exit.

The ride home, including a stop at KFC, was silent. Her mind whirled with questions. Why would a man like Gryphon want her? He was out of her league in looks alone, carried a fancy title, and was fated to become a coven leader. Who was she? His Key. What would happen when he got his coven back? What would happen if he didn't? Her mind swam with more questions than answers as she pulled into her driveway.

Betsy's VDub was parked in the driveway when Emmeline pulled in. Betsy jumped out of the old bug, ran up to the truck, and opened Gryphon's door. Even old women fawned over him. Wait until some no-waist fashion diva put her hooks in him. She couldn't possibly be his type.

"Geez, Bets. I believe he can open his own door." She looked at Gryphon. "Don't forget to bring in the packages. Let's go. I picked up KFC."

"Did something happen at the mall?" Betsy asked.

Emmeline remained quiet and headed into the house.

After setting up the table for a grab-and-go with paper plates, the three sat down to eat. Gryphon filled his plate multiple times, and the 20-piece family meal, extra potatoes, coleslaw, and biscuits didn't last long. A chicken thigh levitated out of the bucket. All eyes followed it to the floor.

Emmeline dove to grab the meat. "Luna, no. Leave it."

"Come on. I haven't had chicken since our first days together."

"Oh honey, I'm sorry, but no." Taking the leg away and replacing it with Kangaroo jerky, Emmeline said, "Here you go, baby. It's better than some ole chicken bones."

"I'm not a dog, remember?"

"Luna's correct, Emmeline." Gryphon wiped his mouth and finished his last bite before speaking. "To educate you, familiars look like animals but are, in reality, Fae. And although quite patient, Luna has never liked being treated like a dog. Her revenge was, at times, unpleasant."

"Fae, as in fairies?" Emmeline asked. "Never mind. Besides, chicken gives her gas, and she sleeps with me. So no chicken. If the fairy has chicken, she will sleep with you."

"What if I sleep with you?" Gryphon asked.

A knock sounded at the back door. *Saved by the nosy neighbor,* Emmeline thought.

Edemay stepped into the kitchen, followed by a black cat. It went immediately to the living room, where they heard a bark and a deep alto cat yowl.

"I guess I'm not surprised you ended up living next to me." Emmeline stared at Edemay.

"We cast a spell," Betsy said. "We wanted you to have some protection nearby. Edemay belongs to the Dewlight side of the family. She's Gryphon's aunt."

"I told the old Crones to tell you." Edemay waved a hand and cleared everything from the table but the coffee and Betsy's salted caramel bars. She added a plate of cookies, pulled out a chair, and sat down. "We have much to discuss."

Emmeline stared. Nope. She wasn't going to question what she had just seen.

They sat around the table, the quiet broken only by the

slurp of coffee and an occasional umm. Gryphon went to referee the two familiars, and Emmeline fixated on his snug jeans. The cat jumped into Gryphon's arms, and he carried Ben back to the table.

"How are you, Ben? It has been years," Gryphon said.

Emmeline watched his lavender eyes glow as he stroked the cat's fur in long, sensuous sweeps. He glanced at her as he filtered its tail through his fingers. She swallowed, and her core tightened. She grabbed another salted caramel bar and wished she were the cat.

CHAPTER 13

Harrisburg, PA 2018

"You take too long, Norman." Megaera paced the scrying chamber in the Ivory Tower. "The eclipse will occur tomorrow during the snowstorm. The new year brings us the perfect opportunity to prevent the prophecy."

"Don't strike me with fire, but—" Norman said.

"But what? You try my patience." Megaera sneered and tapped the ball of a foot.

"Why don't you release Gryphon yourself? Perhaps he will side with you and help."

"I've tried on several occasions. But each time I try to raise the box, the earth holds tight and the wind whispers to wait for the Key," Megaera said. "I think there was more to the spell than I realized after it was cast."

"Perhaps you need a raising spell."

"I think I can raise him if the Key is gone from this world. I will hear no more of your prattle." Megaera checked the calendar. "The eclipse will happen in two days. We must cast the spell tonight."

"The news already predicts a blizzard for the second,"

Norman said. "I wonder if there is significance in the date. It will be Groundhog Day, after all."

"Why humans think a woodchuck can predict anything I will never know." Megaera watched the snow fall at a steady rate outside the small basement window. "But in this storm, even Phil won't find his shadow."

Remaining silent, Norman worked the pestle into the herbs.

"Are you finished?" Megaera pushed him out of the way. As she waved a hand, pages flipped in the Book of Fire. She tossed in a pinch more crushed arum lily and a zap of fire. The mixture melted in the ancient alabaster bowl as the elements converged. Megaera worked her sore, arthritic fingers to weave symbols of fire magick in the air over the vessel.

"If the spell works as I believe it will, a freak weather incident will cause a flash freeze to strike a designated place without warning." Megaera wore a deep smile and rubbed her hands together. "Any living entity at the location will die in an instant. Oh, glorious."

"It's a complicated spell. How will you guarantee Emmeline's in the spot when this happens?" Norman asked. "And what of other unexpected beings? They too will die."

"I have a plan. You need to trust I know what I'm doing." Megaera twirled an errant hair on her chin that continued to sprout regardless of how many times she pulled it out. "You don't need the details. You'll see the results. Now, where's Thomas?"

Megaera searched the casting room. Unable to locate her Second Level, she gave Norman no time to answer. "You'll have to do it. Set the fire. Our new cauldron will cast its first spell."

Norman lit the fire beneath the copper-colored vessel. Green whispers of gas escaped the ore, undulated across the altar, and escaped out of the vent installed for fumes. The witch's brew, made from elements of the earth only the seer knew, started boiling.

Megaera carried the casting bowl to the new cauldron and emptied the mixture into the brew. The herbs were swallowed like quicksand. The ensuing odor drifted from its center. It was maleficent.

Hands in the air, Megaera's nasal voice emerged. "Sister Brigid, hear my call, this night of bloody moon. Sacrifice I honor thee and ask you for a boon. Wind blowing cold, a freeze unique. I ask your breath to seek the prophetic Key. Emmeline Callen is named. End the life that shouldn't be. So mote it."

* * *

"Guess the weatherman was right about this one." Emmeline stood outside, looking up at the roof and the three-foot icicles hanging from the gutters and dripping down toward the snow-covered ground. Winter continued its oppressive grip on South-Central Pennsylvania. Snowfalls and blustery winds bombarded the area in a deep freeze.

"I have serious doubts Punxsutawney Phil will even try to come out of the hole tomorrow," Emmeline said. The puppy at her feet remained on her boot. Several feet of snow were piled on the roof, and an unusual two-day warming spell followed by below-freezing nights caused the gutters to fill and freeze. According to Google, the roof could become damaged if they weren't cleaned out.

"Buy a house, Betsy said. Put down roots, Minerva said. The damn lateral roots from the maples grew right through my sewer line. It's a money pit. How do guys know how to fix all this shit?"

The puppy jumped off the stoop into a two-foot snow drift.

"Well, little Griffin. What do you think? Should I find the ladder and knock down the icicles?" Emmeline blew out a deep breath and tried to remember where she'd left the ladder after cleaning the leaves out of her gutters during the fall.

The pup blew a puff of snow into the air. Emmeline

couldn't help but laugh. Named after a mythological griffin, the fur behind the puppy's head resembled a lion's mane, and he had razor-sharp baby teeth. The name fit the pup in attitude and good looks. His long, silky black fur covered most of his body and gave him an exotic appearance.

The expected snow would cancel school and most likely extend her weekend by at least two days. Emmeline decided to forget about the ice until tomorrow and play a little more with the dog. She tossed a snowball across the yard. The pup tore off after it. The snow was so deep, she could only make out his position when his head or ears made an appearance.

"Come on, Griffin." Emmeline decided her frozen hands and toes had had enough of the cold. She walked up the steps and opened the door. The boisterous puppy ran through the door, slid on the kitchen floor with snowball-packed toes, and slammed into the refrigerator. She busted a gut laughing. "Oh, baby. Come here. You're fine."

The phone on the kitchen wall rang. In most cases, she ignored it. No one she knew would use the old landline anyways. Caller ID read as a local number and not spam. Shrugging her shoulders, Emmeline answered.

"Hello."

"Ms. Callen," the raspy voice said.

Her stomach churned at the sound of the voice on the other end. Emmeline pushed the record button on the answering machine. "Yes, Dr. Caroline. What can I do for you on a Sunday?"

"I need you to come into school," Megaera said. "A break-in occurred, and we need people to inventory supplies and make a list of the missing items for the police."

"Today?" Emmeline's jaw dropped open. "It's Sunday."

"I am capable of reading a calendar," Megaera said. "Since you're the department chair, it's your responsibility."

"It's impossible. The roads are closed," Emmeline said. The panic ramped up her heartbeat. "Assuming school's canceled tomorrow, I can drive in after they open. Besides, I wouldn't know about missing equipment from the Chemistry and Physics rooms. I don't use their equipment."

"Why do you choose to defy me every time I ask you to do something for the district? I don't think you care at all. I will have to make a note of this on your record."

"With all due respect, Principal Caroline..." Emmeline didn't want to give the wrinkled bitch the satisfaction of the title of Doctor. The slight would go by most people without note, but the arrogant woman would notice. "I'm sure you know you can't order me to do work outside of school hours. I will have to make a note of this and inform our association."

Emmeline had learned fast to show a little backbone in dealing with Caroline. "I will go tomorrow if school gets canceled."

"Fine. I will expect you at the back door at ten. The superintendent has already closed the school. Don't you watch the news?" Megaera hung up before Emmeline could respond.

"What a horrible witch."

Griffin sat cockeyed and lifted a hind paw to chew out a snowball. "Now I do have to pull down the ice."

"I wish the ladder could set itself up," Emmeline said. Pulling her coat closed, she tried to remember where she'd left the ladder. A quick gust of freezing wind had her pulling on a knitted hat. With her eyesight half blocked by the hat, she stepped outside. "Fuck me. It's cold."

Emmeline found the ladder leaning against the back side of the house. "Crap. Did I leave it up this whole time? It could have caused some damage if it fell the wrong way. Shit."

With the roof tool in hand, she climbed the ladder and started pulling the snow and ice off. The internet said to make sure as much of the roof was exposed as she could manage so the shingles would warm up and melt the snow faster. She cocked her head after ten minutes.

"If I had a handsome knight on a white horse instead of

Brad, I'd be warming my toes on the couch right now." But Brad was all she had, so she sucked it up and did it herself. She moved the ladder to the back of the house and tried to level it. The slant of the property meant there was no flat spot, and the ladder wobbled with every step up.

Losing the winter light and her fingers frozen, Emmeline pushed to finish. On the highest end of the house, a gust of wind blew at the same moment Griffin decided to chase Ben under the ladder. She jerked, the ladder wobbled, and the wind pushed her over.

The roof rake flew out of Emmeline's hand as she grabbed for and missed the gutter. She landed ass down in a big pile of snow, ice, and bushes. Her leg was wrapped around the rungs, and her head was throbbing as a result of its collision with the ladder on landing. With the wind knocked out of her, she remained determined not to black out.

It took a minute to assess the damage. Her leg and ribs fired off riots of pain and her head throbbed, but at least she was breathing again. Patting herself for her cell phone, she found nothing but empty pockets. She pounded her untangled hand into the snow.

"Fuck!"

Regardless of the effort, the ladder wasn't going to move on its own. On the bright side, she hadn't broken her neck or back, and her toes could wiggle in both boots. Tilting her head up, she found Ben, the neighbor's cat, grooming itself on the back stoop and Griffin posed on the bottom step ready to pounce.

Emmeline loosened one leg from around a rung and breathed through the pain. Sucking in deep breaths of cold air, she tried to figure out what to do. If she could get out of the ladder, she could crawl into the house and call for help. Some of the roads had to be open.

"Ben, where have you gone?" Mrs. Caststone's voice sounded from around the corner.

Emmeline's neighbor was looking for her cat. How the heck

the old lady was walking through two feet of snow crossed her mind, but since she was in need, she yelled, "Mrs. Caststone. Help. Please."

Edemay popped her head around the corner of the house, Ben shot off the porch, and Griffin chased the cat up the tree. He was making quite a racket for a puppy.

"Oh, Ben. What are you up to now?" Edemay said. She emerged from behind the house.

Emmeline raised her eyebrows. Who knew the woman was in good enough shape to snowshoe?

"Did I hear you—by the stars and moon, girl, you'll catch your death down there." Edemay strode through the gate and leaned over Emmeline. "Goodness. Did you fall off the ladder?"

Emmeline nodded. "I can't get my other foot through the ladder. I think my leg's broken."

"I hire people for such work. Perhaps you should ask your Brad to do it next time."

Emmeline pushed while Edemay pulled, and they were able to free the broken leg. Emmeline lay back in the snow as she rubbed the leg and sucked breaths through her clenched teeth. "Fucking hell."

"Such language. Do you suppose the neighborhood heard? Let's take you to the emergency room." Edemay helped Emmeline to the stoop. "Can we take your truck? My little car will go nowhere in this snow."

"My keys are hanging right inside the door. Could you put Griffin inside as well? The crate's in the dining room. I'm sorry for my expletives, but everything hurts."

Mrs. Caststone grabbed the keys, put the dog in the crate, and helped Emmeline up and supported her the whole way to the truck.

"You're stronger than you appear, Mrs. Caststone."

"Perhaps I used a little bit of magick." Edemay snickered as she walked around the truck to the driver's side. Once they were both in the cab, she said, "You should try it sometime."

"If only." Emmeline snorted. "I would snap my fingers and not have a broken leg."

The old Chevy grumbled as Edemay shifted into low gear. "Will your bucket of bolts manage in the snow?" Edemay asked.

Emmeline had replaced the crushed Ranger last year with her dream truck, a '54 Chevy and its sexy front end. She was working on restoring it bit by bit at Brad's garage. She wondered if she was using him. She was not truly in love with the man, but he proved useful for his mechanical skills, pretty good sex, and excellent gift giving. The sex relieved stress, so she'd live with it, but it didn't equal deep, soul-wrenching love. Brad was not her "one."

"Brad put the four-wheel drive in this fall. We should be fine," Emmeline said. "You ah…can drive stick?"

"Of course. And there's the township snowplow. I'll follow it to the main road." Never one for extended silence, Edemay asked, "When did you adopt a puppy and what did you call him?"

"Griff was a Christmas present from Brad." Emmeline grimaced in pain when the bump of the truck through icy plow piles jarred her leg. With a deep breath in through her nose, clenched teeth, and a long hiss, she let out another expletive. "Fuck."

"Miss Callen. I need to find a tea to cure your foul mouth."

"Sorry. I grew up in a tough world. Mean and nasty worked." Emmeline gripped the armrest on the door to keep from jarring her leg. "What was your question?"

"The dog. What's his name?"

"Griffin. I thought the little fur feathers behind his ears and legs reminded me of one of those Greek figures, part lion and part eagle. He has sharp teeth too."

"Brad bought you a German Shepherd and you named it

Griffin?" Edemay laughed so loud it vibrated the vents on the dashboard. "The name, it fits splendidly."

Emmeline took a quick peek at her neighbor but couldn't figure out why she was laughing. "Mrs. Caststone, did you take too much CBD oil this morning?"

"No, dear. Someday, the irony of Brad's gift will occur. Enjoy the pup." Her laughter continued to the hospital.

The next morning Emmeline sipped coffee and watched the morning news from her hospital bed. There was a report about a strange weather phenomenon called a "deep freeze" striking a small area of West Hanover Township. Several deer and rabbits were found frozen on the spot. A shiver ran through her shoulders. It could have been her.

Harrisburg, PA 2019

Emmeline stood watching the two women interact when Gryphon came from behind and pulled her into his arms. He nuzzled the sensitive skin below her ear. Shivers of excitement ran along her neck and down to her toes.

She swatted his arm. "Quit doing that."

"Doing what, Emmeline?" Gryphon asked. His smirk lit his eyes.

The innocent plea and cute one-sided curl of his lip made her want to hit and kiss him at the same time. "Sniffing me. Add sneaking up behind me to your crimes."

"Enough." Edemay jumped directly to the point. "We have a purpose here."

"Helping Emmeline find and control her magick becomes the first step," Gryphon said.

He had retreated to the kitchen archway and leaned against the wall with his arms crossed. Emmeline thought the position suited him. Supervisory, as if he were watching over his coven. The whole package appealed to her in spite of his occasional slip into a "man's world" persona. She would never admit it, but she liked when a man took charge.

"May the Grand Master save me from young witches," Edemay said. "I think the first action should be to retrieve the Book of Shadows and the Wiseman family quilt."

"I don't think it's possible until both Emmeline and Gryphon have their full powers," Betsy said. "Gryphon needs to be freed from the Witchbox, and Emmeline must find and practice druid magick. What little we've seen was out of control."

"Thanks, Bets," Emmeline said. She toyed with some of Edemay's cookies.

"Megaera has your book." Edemay flashed a glance at Gryphon. "No one has seen the quilt since the fires."

"Luna told me the Fire Witch took my tome and quilt," Gryphon said.

"Megaera took it when Cold Springs burned," Betsy said. "Everyone panicked and ran to the springs without possessions. They were unprotected. Flames and witches do not go together well, as you know."

"Thomas remarked about a beautiful quilt in her private rooms. He thought it looked familiar but could never get close enough to verify," Edemay said.

"Wait," Emmeline said. "Thomas, as in Brad's and my friend Thomas?"

"Who is this Brad you mention?" Gryphon asked.

"Never mind Brad," Edemay said to Gryphon. "Thomas was your apprentice and family. He spies at great risk to himself. He is, after all, a witch of the earth."

"Thomas is a witch?" Emmeline asked. "Why—"

Betsy cut her off. "None of this matters. The questions still remains. What's our plan?"

"I should have ended the fires. I think my wind gave the embers power." Gryphon paced the length of the dining room. "I was foolish not to listen to my advisors and their warnings."

"I don't think you could have prevented the fires," Emmeline said. "According to the history, the drought was severe. The worst on record for Pennsylvania. Lightning could have sparked the flames."

"Magick lit the fires," Gryphon said. "If not, the other settlements would have burned as well."

"Verne suspected Megaera, but we had no proof," Betsy said.

"You didn't have time to call for rain from what Wilmott said." Edemay patted his shoulder. "You were a young witch without guidance. Kenter should have taken more care."

"Excuse me," Emmeline said. "Who are Wilmott and Kenter?"

"Kenter was our High Priest and my father," Gryphon said. "Wilmott is a warlock and Kenter and Edemay's brother. My uncle, I suppose."

Emmeline closed one eye and tried to wrap her mind around the family tree he'd outlined. "Okay. Got it. Why don't you say 'my father' instead of using his first name?"

"Witches don't claim fathers, only mothers," Gryphon said. "We take our mother's lineage, so I am a Wiseman. We are witches of wind, but my mother controlled all the elements and was powerful. I was working on the same legacy."

"And I am of the Dewlights. My line is of the four elements." Edemay pulled Emmeline to sit beside her. "On the night of your birth, I tried to reach your mother, but for some reason she shielded herself against witches' magick. The Fae are known to do so at times. I suppose she meant to protect you and your sister, but I couldn't find you after the car accident."

"Sister?" Emmeline asked.

"A twin," Edemay whispered, her eyes watering. "Dark magick killed the lamb at birth."

Emmeline pulled out of Edemay's grip. Gryphon took the old witch's place, and his thumb trailed over the sensitive flesh on the underside of her wrist. She melted under his heat and compassion. His finger wiped her tears away.

"How do we take down this bitch?" Emmeline shook her head, eyes flared wide, and she pushed away Gryphon's grasp. "Principal my ass."

"And now our Emmeline's back," Betsy said. "Good. We're going to need her."

"We have to find a way to open your mind to the druid's path," Edemay said, dusting cookie crumbs from her hands. "We need to test what you can and can't do and go from there. Betsy, what's the first magick you teach the neophytes?"

"Levitation. It's a base magick all witches have, even from birth," Betsy said. "We teach them to control it by moving stones around."

Edemay took a cookie from the tray and set it on the table. "Emmeline. Levitate this cookie. Move it across the table and set it in Gryphon's hand."

Emmeline stepped to the edge of the table and checked out the cookie. One finger slid it across the top, proving it could move. She rubbed both hands together, lifted and set down each foot a couple of times to steady her stance, reached out with her hands, and blew out a deep breath.

"Work equals force times distance." Emmeline nodded, mumbled something incoherent to herself, and stared at the cookie. Through clenched teeth, she said, "Move."

"Why does she grimace?" Edemay asked.

"Oh dear." Betsy put her hand on Emmeline's arm. "Dear girl, your magick equals the force in the equation. Tell it to move the cookie in a calm manner. Don't bust a blood vessel."

Gryphon stepped behind Emmeline. She could smell him and sense furnace-quality warmth before the contact with her skin. A sweet-scented breath tinged with hazelnut caressed under her ponytail, making the broken stubs of hair move and tickle.

"Quit doing that."

The cookie flew off the table, hit the wall, and ricocheted. Turning to Gryphon, Emmeline saw cookie bits stuck in his hair.

"We now know two facts," Edemay said.

All eyes focused on the old witch.

"Emmeline has all her powers, and Gryphon's the switch to turn them on." Edemay burst out laughing. "I say our problem is solved. Now they need to practice together until she has control and has released Gryphon from the box."

"Add the coven cauldron as well," Betsy said.

"What do you mean, the cauldron as well?" Gryphon's eyes widened. Wind magick swirled around the dining room. Cookies, napkins, and silverware became airborne.

"You will stop this nonsense, young man. Control your magick." Edemay waved a hand in the air. The wind disappeared. Airborne items dropped to the floor. "A witch your age should not let their magick go haywire. Have some sense. How will you become High Priest and lead a coven when you act like a neophyte?"

Gryphon and Edemay locked eyes. "You have a bit of power yourself, old witch. Explain the cauldron."

Unsure what they were talking about, Emmeline watched Gryphon have an eyeball fight with Edemay. He puffed up, a cock in the hen yard, setting his back and shoulders straight. Did poor Edemay have a chance? Emmeline needed to learn a whole lot more about witches, covens, and the hierarchy of power as soon as possible.

"Does physical strength make any difference in a magical bitch fight?" Emmeline asked Betsy.

"Not always. Older witches have far more power. Bet on Edemay. I watched him grow up; he was slow to learn," Betsy said.

"Dang, Bets, we will need to have a girls' night with lots of bourbon. I have so many questions," Emmeline said.

"What do you do on a girls' night?" Gryphon asked. He stood up and broke his contest with Edemay.

Emmeline and Betsy fell into a round of laughter.

Once back under control, Betsy admonished Gryphon. "Edemay did not reside with us at the time. Don't become snide." She pushed between the two, and a handful of cookies appeared in Gryphon's hand and a fresh cup of coffee in Edemay's.

"The Grand Master told us to find sanctuary after the fires." Betsy held up a hand to keep Gryphon from replying. "We were directed to Dauphin, where we founded Haven House. We traveled to the altar site for festivals, but Megaera hated the long commutes. So for her convenience, she had the cauldron moved."

Gryphon swallowed the cookie he was chewing on. "We go to this Haven House and put the cauldron back on the High Altar."

"Verne tried to stop Megaera. An eclipse happened, the cauldron cracked, and fire once again took our home. Haven House burned." Betsy played with her coffee mug. "During the second move, the cauldron cracked again. Everyone fears to use it, even Megaera."

"Moved twice! Cracked?" Gryphon stirred up the wind once again. The cookie plate flew across the table and onto the floor. "It needs to sit on sacred ground. Megaera never seemed a stupid woman or a horrible witch. Impetuous and disillusioned perhaps, but not horrible. Why would she challenge the fates and move the cauldron twice?"

"The Crone practices only dark fire magick," Betsy said. "It corrupts everything. No one will challenge her. She grows stronger each year. But we have one advantage. When Megaera gets frustrated, she loses control of the fire and power escapes. Keep this in mind in the battle."

"Battle?" Emmeline asked.

She was ignored.

"If a witch could capture the lost power and add it to their own well, it would increase their magical strength," Edemay said. "You have the skills to do so, Gryphon."

"How does the coven conduct vision quests without a cauldron?" Gryphon asked.

"Megaera had a new cauldron made." Betsy shook her head. "A shiny abomination of modern materials. I never go to the celebrations anymore if I can help it. The brew doesn't smell right. Mirielda does the best she can."

Gryphon pushed for more information. "What of the sacred vessel?"

"Our cauldron sits protected in a corner of the Ivory Tower, our new coven home," Betsy said. "We believe the quilt shelters the Book of Shadows near the cauldron in Megaera's private chambers."

"Many of the old ones believe once the cauldron goes back to the High Altar, druid magick can heal it." Edemay chewed on a cookie and took a sip of coffee. She gave a nod to Emmeline.

"The issue is solved." Gryphon reached for another cookie. "We will go to this Ivory Tower and steal the cauldron, book, and quilt."

Edemay gave a witch's warning. "Betsy was correct. You can do nothing until you're free from the box. Work with Emmeline, practice your magick, and teach her to use hers."

CHAPTER 14

Harrisburg, PA 2018

"How does the girl manage to evade every spell I cast?" Pacing across the chamber, Megaera emitted sparks of energy with each forceful step. The freed energy caught the wall hangings on fire.

"I smell—" Megaera found the tapestries on fire and both of her advisors ignoring them.

Norman and Thomas sat at the workbench playing with their phones, even with smoke filling the chamber and the curtains aflame. They didn't budge. Taking heavy, deliberate steps, Megaera came to rest behind the pair.

"Why aren't you putting out the fire?" Megaera yelled in Norman's ear.

"I assumed you would take care of your own fire magick, High Priestess." Norman looked up from the phone.

"I'll put it out." Thomas grabbed the fire extinguisher from under the bench and sprayed the tapestries until the flames went out. He smiled at Megaera. "Will you repair them, or should I order another set?"

"Lazy witches. You should have used your magick, Thomas."

"I thought the Returns too great a price." Thomas went back to his phone.

"You will never advance in the coven." With a wave of her hand, the tapestries returned to their previous state. "Shouldn't both of you be working on inventory and spring cleaning?"

"We finished yesterday, High Priestess." Norman glanced up. "I sent you a text. We wait for your next directive."

"Put down those stupid phones." Megaera slammed a hand onto the bench. A blush of fire shot through the chamber and ruffled pages in the Book of Fire. "I swear, cell phones will become the witches' demise. You see what they did to the students of ASSD. They think all the answers lie in their phones and now can't function in the world. Stupid humans."

"Indeed." Thomas handed Megaera an electronic tablet. "This is a list of the herbs and chemicals needed to complete your stocks."

"You should take care with your tone, Thomas." Megaera examined the list and tossed the tablet across the table. It slid toward the edge, and Thomas scrambled to catch it before it hit the hard floor. "Use your magick, Thomas. What would you do if it smashed on the floor?"

"I took caution and stored everything in the cloud." He leaned back in the chair and crossed his arms. "Will you collect the items yourself or order from the internet as you did last time?"

Megaera's expression hardened, and a vein popped on her forehead. "Order them from the internet. When they arrive, label them with the proper symbols and stock the shelves."

"Right away, High Priestess. I'm honored you have selected me for this task," Thomas said. He took the tablet and raised a hand to whisk.

"Wait." Megaera held her finger in the air. "What vial sits on the casting bench?"

"I forgot," Thomas said. "I found the vial on the top shelf of your apothecary. You need to decide if it's spoiled or not."

Megaera lifted the vial of Dragon's Blood from the table, removed the cork, and sniffed. Her head jerked back as the acrid odor of rot burned the inside of her nose. She set the vial on the table and wiped her hands on her skirt. "It can't spoil, you idiot. I will take care of it. Leave me now."

Thomas whisked away.

Megaera trailed a finger over the Book of Fire, admiring the sparks of power. It had less power now than before the fires. Perhaps she'd harvested too much in the rush to take over the coven. Her arm passed over the pages and tipped the open vial of Dragon's Blood.

"High Priestess." Norman tried to grab the vial.

The viscous black solution oozed across the table and struck the edge of the heavy cover of the book. Acting as a sponge, the centuries-old leather and parchment drank the ooze. Shadows covered page after page, occluding the words. The top page burst into flames.Norman waved a hand in the air, directing his earth magick to smother the fire. "I don't understand. Why didn't the book protect itself?"

"No pages burned. The blurry words should heal in time." Megaera thrummed long, sharp fingernails on the tabletop. The *click-tap* sound echoed against the stone walls of the chamber. "The book will reward you for your attempt. I, however, will withhold a boon until we have readied the spell I wish to cast."

"High Priestess. What preparations do you wish?" Norman asked. "I need to finish soon. We have a school board meeting tonight."

"Tonight?" Megaera stared at Norman. "I don't have time for such nonsense."

"Appearances remain crucial, High Priestess." Norman put his phone in his pocket.

"Very well." Megaera handed over a list. "I have written a spell and need these herbs prepared. Take note. It's on paper."

"You wrote a spell?" Norman asked.

"I can write spells. Your insolence has cost you the boon I owe." Before Megaera whisked, she added, "Have the herbs ready before we leave for the board meeting. After which you will not be needed.

As the clock struck midnight, Megaera whisked back to her private chamber and called for fire. Her power needed an outlet, as the irritating humans had prattled most of the night about the budget and fixing the roof on the high school. She had plans for the funds slated for the roof. It's not like it would collapse. She ignited the dried ingredients in the bowl and recited her spell.

"Found by the power of flame, Griffin is named. Long fur, dark eyes, his death takes its toll. Destroy the Key's power, destroy her role. Sneak past protections, power restrained. Strike from this world with a heart's pain, the power of fire will make a gain. So mote it be."

Chartreuse smoke rose in the air, swirled about, and left through a vent near the window. Now it was released into the world, Megaera would wait for the malevolent magick to find its target. It could take weeks. She would be patient.

* * *

Emmeline parked her '54 on the outside truck rack at Brad's auto repair shop. Today the guys would replace the suspension while she worked on the body. Griffin sat anxiously on the bench seat with his tongue dripping saliva down the open window. School was out for summer. Emmeline was relieved.

She walked in to find Tom leaning against Brad's '65 Nova and chatting with a recognizable pair of boots sticking out from under the chassis.

"Thanks for helping today," Emmeline said. She handed Thomas the part she'd brought. "I could never afford to pay someone for this work."

"No problem. I would work all day for one of your home-cooked meals." Thomas gave a little bow. "By the way, I think you could do much better than Brad."

"Anyone in mind?" Emmeline chuckled and flashed a smile at Brad's feet.

Griffin picked that moment to chase Brad's dogs through the shop. The canines exited for a few minutes and ran back through. Griffin carried the leg of a deer. Gunner and Sarge were hot on his trail.

"You never know when the right guy will pop up. If you're getting busy with Brad, you might ignore Mr. Right," Thomas said. He grabbed the part and left.

Brad rolled out from under the car, and Emmeline sauntered over, taking his extended hand and helping him up from the creeper. He pulled her into a bear hug and initiated a kiss. She allowed the play for a few minutes more before she pushed off his chest.

"Bet Thomas has the first spring off while we're in here messing around. I better hit the sandpaper and filler."

"Baby, he can wait. I need taken care of," Brad said.

"Gonna have to wait, babe. Can't drive home without a suspension." Emmeline blew him a big smooch and headed outside. Dropping a bucket of water on the ground, she ran a hand across the rear quarter panel. Thomas peeked out from under the chassis.

"I really do appreciate you helping, Thomas."

"It's nothing. I want you to have a dependable vehicle to drive around in," Thomas said. He lifted the spring into place. "Could you start the screws for me?"

"Sure." She grabbed a long screwdriver and turned the tool until the spring attached to the bracket.

Brad showed up and took over. Emmeline went back to sanding.

The day droned on with the sounds of dogs barking, locusts singing in the trees, and the hollow metallic bang as the new suspension found its home. A loud clap of thunder accompanied by a darkening sky distracted everyone from the job.

"Hey guys, I think we might get rained out," Emmeline said.

Brad climbed out from under the lift and took in the changing weather. "News didn't say anything about thunderstorms. We need to finish, rain or not, or this beast isn't driving away from here."

A cold wind blew against them as they watched the clouds roll to a stop overhead. "This storm's freaky. The sky's clear on top of Blue Mountain." Emmeline shivered. "It feels like it's targeting us."

"Sure, hon." Brad brushed a curl from Emmeline's cheek. "Like a storm decides where to hit. Let's move on or you're walking home."

"Nice." Thomas punched Brad on the arm.

"Damn. I was joking," Brad said.

"You don't deserve her," Thomas said.

"Boys, settle down." Emmeline put a hand on Brad's shoulder.

The unexpected storm brought torrential rain, bolts of lightning, and rumbles of thunder so loud the windows in the shop vibrated. It lasted only five minutes. Little spirals of water vapor rose from the blacktop and dissipated into the air.

Brad's dog ran up to Emmeline and sat, lifting a paw. "What's the matter, Gun-boy? Did you hurt your paw?"

The dog stood up. He moved away and came back to sit in front of her. He repeated the motion and whined until Brad walked over.

"Gun wants to show you something," Brad said.

Emmeline dropped the wet sandpaper into the bucket and followed the dog around the back of the house. Ahead on the ground lay Griffin, motionless.

"Griffin, oh my God." She dropped to the ground. The dog

panted, unable to move. Emmeline became hysterical. "We have to take him to the vet."

An hour later, Emmeline paced across the waiting room, chewing on her fingernails, hugging herself, and avoiding Brad's comfort. Another fifteen agonizing minutes passed before the vet walked out with one of those hate-to-give-you-the-bad-news looks and shook his head.

"I'm sorry. We took an X-ray. A tumor ruptured the stomach. Strange illness for such a young dog, but it happens. You need to decide how you wish to handle the remains."

Brad took over and pulled Emmeline into an embrace. "Whatever's cheapest, Doc."

Emmeline stilled. Tears tumbled down her cheeks. Pushing Brad away with both hands, she said, "I want Griffin cremated and the ashes back. I don't care how much it costs."

"Babe. Be reasonable," Brad said.

"Thomas. Will you take me home?" Emmeline asked.

Harrisburg, PA 2019

The morning sun warmed Emmeline as she sat on the back stoop watching Gryphon and Luna play Frisbee. Forty-eight hours ago, she'd found a witch in a box and learned the principal was an actual witch and that her dog wasn't a dog and could talk. Of course, she needed to include her own magical powers in the total shit show now deemed her life. It seemed too much to comprehend.

"Luna loves to chase these round discs." Gryphon sat down and grabbed a mug of coffee. He tossed the frisbee again and leaned back on an elbow, sipping the brew.

"You threw it too hard and it's going over the fence." Emmeline pointed at the frisbee in mid-air. It froze in place. Messing around, not thinking anything of it, she lowered it to a height appropriate for Luna to catch. "Well, okay then. Shit."

"You cast magick and don't even know it." Gryphon

stroked a finger over her calf and chuckled. "You may have more power than me."

The touch fired off every neuron in her leg. Whether from magick or the man, the electrical signals traveled straight to her already active core. She'd dreamed about Gryphon all night. Sexy, toe-curling dreams that kept her restless. She'd woken up tired, as if she had been up the whole night having mind-blowing sex.

"How could I have magick and not know it?" She wrapped both arms around her legs and settled her chin between her knees.

"You sound sad, my dear Emmeline. Magick's wonderful. You'll learn." A finger drifted around the side of her breast, where it tickled her nipple into a peak.

Emmeline shivered and gasped when he repeated the motion. She arched her back. Gazing down at the caressing appendage, she realized she wanted this man more than anyone she'd ever met. But her mind resisted. This whole witch situation required caution. It was unfortunate her traitorous body seemed to want the attention regardless of what was on her mind.

"You don't understand. My whole life's been planned out for me by these fates you and Betsy keep describing. People have died because of me. I thought I decided my path. Knowing I don't makes me feel out of control."

"I too follow a path designed by the fates. I do not know if they planned my imprisonment. Perhaps they improvised after Megaera stole me from the coven." Gryphon paused a moment, sat up, and wrapped her in his arms.

Emmeline savored the heady feeling of...love? Passion? Pity? Laying her head on his chest, she listened to his heart thump a quiet rhythm like a sexy love song. The pulsing beat drove her libido a hundred miles an hour.

Clever fingers tickled along her chin as his mouth lowered for a kiss. The brush of his soft lips silenced everything in the world except for the steady music of his heart. Those pliant lips insisted she allow entrance, and their tongues danced a blissful waltz of need. The earth trembled.

"Did you feel the earth move?" Emmeline asked. Ragged breaths gave a staccato beat to the words.

"I do feel something." Gryphon chuckled and continued the seduction.

One hand made its way under her shirt and along her spine in long, sensual caresses. He pulled her on top of his hard, muscular body as he leaned back along the steps of the stoop. Emmeline had no will to resist. She surrendered. She threw her head back as a masculine thumb drew circles around one nipple. The other hand pushed the barrier of shirt and bra out of the way while warm lips nipped and sucked at the other breast.

Emmeline was ready to drag his fine ass into the bedroom to reenact last night's dream. His hard cock pulsed heat through her jeans. She thrust her hips closer to the fire and reached for the waistband button on Gryphon's cargo pants. Expectations were dashed when a wet, cold nose found her cheek.

"Betsy's here. Man, did you feel those tremors?" Luna sat beside the pair. *"I bet the Richter scale will ring in an eight when you two consummate the partnership."*

"You, my friend, have terrible timing," Gryphon said. "What possessed you to interrupt this moment?"

"We have company." Luna's nose directed them to the gate.

"Children. When you're done warming up, we need to move on with our magick lessons." Betsy stood with her chin on the gate. "You didn't hear me pull in or shout hello a few moments ago? It's time to work."

"Jeez, Bets. You could have called or texted." Emmeline's neck and face flushed hot.

"Last night we arranged to meet this morning. Why the surprise?" Betsy readjusted the strap on her herb bag. "I do think your selection of the back stoop a rather public place to… It's impolite. Time for magick practice. I think it best completed in the basement."

Betsy whisked away. Emmeline stared at where the old Crone stood a second ago. "Wow. Can I poof?"

"I suspect you can poof, as you call it. We call it whisking." Gryphon moaned as he stood and readjusted his crotch. He pulled up the zipper and fastened the waistband button. His eyes were a dark, stormy purple. "You, my dear, have many delightful talents."

Emmeline blushed on the way to the basement. Disgruntled she'd missed the opportunity to explore his heated cock, she wasn't paying attention when a flying end wrench soared inches past her head. Now aware of her surroundings, she followed the heavy tool with her eyes as it circled the room and hooked itself on a pegboard. Other tools flew about and seated themselves on the hooks while a broom swept the floors and the trash disappeared.

"Uh, thanks, Betsy."

"Have you ever tried putting something away after you use it?" Betsy asked.

"I live alone. Why bother?" Emmeline shrugged and leaned against the dryer.

Betsy raised a finger and drew a circle in the air. A rectangular table materialized in the middle of the room. She unpacked a bag of chemicals, bowls, candles, and herbs on the work bench. "Now we're ready. We'll start with Emmeline."

Betsy waved Emmeline to the long table and rubbed her fingers together. A small pile of rocks appeared.

"I've consulted some of the old texts," Betsy said. "Druids don't need a spell to invoke magick. They find it within themselves. You did magick yesterday when you saw the Gaelic words in the air and put them into the beaker."

Betsy lined up three rocks on the end of the table. "Roll the middle rock to the other end of the table."

"So all I have to do is think"—Emmeline used both index fingers raised in the air to put quotes around the next word—"'roll' and the rock will roll?"

"Remember the cookie last night?" Gryphon asked. "But don't push too much magick at it. I would prefer it not end up in my hair."

Emmeline rolled her eyes. She planted her feet and stuck both hands out in front of her body. Staring at the rock, she said, "Rock, I wish you would roll to the end of the table."

She stared so hard without blinking, her eyeballs hurt. Nothing happened.

"Gryphon, go to her. Perhaps a small push of your magick will kickstart hers," Betsy said.

Gryphon stood behind Emmeline. His chest kissed her back while his hands squeezed her shoulders. Erotic waves of lust pinballed through her body. Her flesh tingled and her clit throbbed. Shifting her feet, Emmeline tried to concentrate. The rock started to bounce like an underinflated basketball. She gulped air as it rolled across the table. Instead of stopping at the edge, it became airborne and circled the room, gaining speed with each trip.

As excitement tangled with the magick, the stone gained altitude and velocity. Betsy ducked to avoid it, and Luna took refuge under the stairs. The rock jetted across the basement and busted through the window above the dryer. The crash broke the tension in the room.

"Holy shit," Emmeline said.

"Edemay said something last night about Gryphon unlocking your magick." Betsy gave Gryphon a knowing smile. "I believe he catalyzes your magick. It's imperative you remain together."

"*She has fathoms of power,*" Luna said. She whisked from under the stairs. "*But without control—*"

Betsy waved a hand to stave off the rest of Luna's speech. She used magick to fix the window and pointed to one of the remaining rocks at the end of the table. "Try again, but this time, rein in your excitement and feed it emotion slowly and with purpose."

Emmeline took deep breaths and paced through the garage, shaking out her hands. She went back to the table. The morning passed, and she repeated the process. Even with Gryphon's help, the magick went haywire at different stages and damage was done. Stones flew through windows, pipes burst, and an unsuspecting can of soda exploded.

"I'm sorry," Emmeline said. Soda dripped off Betsy's chin. As she mopped up the majority of the mess, she shook her head. No way was she ever going to be able to do magick like they wanted. A glance across the room found Betsy, Gryphon, and Luna with their heads together. She'd bet money they were going to take away her magick card if she had one.

"Can't you wave your hands and clean this up like you did in the lab?" Emmeline asked.

"You made the mess. You clean it up. I tire of repairing windows and pipes." Betsy wiped her hands on an apron. "Gryphon, it's your turn."

Gryphon straightened. "I will have to cast spells by memory without my grimoire."

Betsy nodded in agreement. "Let's start small. I have some paint here in this cup. I want you to paint this box." A small wood box of nuts and bolts rested on the table. Betsy took three steps to the far side of the basement. "A Second-Level witch with your talents should find this child's play."

"Should we use paint?" Emmeline tilted her head, raising her eyebrows. She tossed the ruptured soda can into the trash and moved to stand beside Betsy. "Maybe something less...messy."

Luna padded over to stand near the two women. *"No worries. Gryphon can do this blindfolded."*

"Emmeline, pay attention." Betsy grabbed her arm. "He'll have to disassemble the paint, move it through the air, and lay it back down on the box. He will visualize each molecule. Don't interrupt once the spell begins. Try to understand his words."

Emmeline watched every move. Gryphon cleared his throat, tossed a pinch of powder into the air, and encircled the open can of paint with his hands.

"He offered the Three Sisters," Betsy said. "I'll explain later."

Gryphon lifted a hand into the air and chanted in Gaelic.

His mesmerizing voice wafted into Emmeline's center and became part of her. On automatic, she translated what he said in her head and spoke the words out loud in English. "Powers mine I call on thee. Paint the vessel before me. Pigment blue and water fresh, make my mind the painter's brush. So mote it be."

Within seconds a breeze picked up in the room. Tiny drops of paint lifted from the cup and dissipated into a fine mist suspended in the air. Emmeline watched Gryphon guide the blue cloud with an extended hand as he lowered the mist toward the box.

"Holy shit!" Emmeline shouted.

Emmeline's voice became a magnet, and the blue mist changed direction and headed toward her and Betsy. "Betsy. What's happening?"

They had to duck to avoid the cloud as it wove its way around the room. Like the rock before it, it moved without purpose, seeking a place to go.

Betsy shouted to Gryphon, "Control your magick."

"It's not my magick," Gryphon said.

The blue cloud missed the women a second time. On the third trip around the room, the women ducked, and the cloud disappeared. A loud snarl and growl sounded behind them. They turned to face Luna.

"I warned you the girl has power."

Now covered in thick blue latex, Luna walked over to

Gryphon and shook. The paint splattered across the basement, covering Gryphon, the table, and the walls. Luna ran out the open door.

"Oops," Gryphon mumbled.

They followed the familiar outside to find her rolling in the grass.

"Fates save me, Luna. Use your magick," Gryphon said.

"*I tried. It won't come off.*" Luna sat up and stared. "*I think a druid did this, and by ownership a druid must remove it.*"

All eyes stared at Emmeline.

"Me? I didn't— Did I?" Emmeline frowned. "How did I do this?"

"I heard you translate the words to English as Gryphon recited the spell," Betsy said. "I believe your magick's so strong you overpowered his. We will have to take more care next time and make sure you each practice without the influence of the other."

"*Perhaps with something less...sticky,*" Luna said.

"I said the same thing." Emmeline nodded her chin and crossed her arms. "I wish the paint was gone from Luna. And the basement."

Most of the paint disappeared from Luna's white coat at Emmeline's request, although blue shadows remained. They found a similar situation upon returning to the basement. A few spots of blue remained here or there, on the dryer, the wall, and the workbench.

"You have more power than we could have hoped." Betsy grasped Emmeline's hands. "Perhaps we should wait for Edemay. She may have better ideas for managing this than I do. We wouldn't want to burn down the house after we start practicing fire."

"Fire?" Emmeline's eyes widened.

CHAPTER 15

Harrisburg, PA 2018

"Emmeline. We came for a visit." Betsy opened the back door of Emmeline's house and stepped into the kitchen. Minerva and Mirielda followed behind carrying several containers of cookies. They waited for an answer.

"In the living room." Emmeline made a weak attempt to sit up and nodded as the three women entered the living room. She greeted them with a weak, "Hey."

"Oh my," Betsy said. She took in the room and blew out a deep breath.

Dog toys were strewn among unopened boxes of flowers and salted caramel chocolates, and two empty fifths of Jack sat on the floor beside her chair. The television played with no sound, and a plate with an uneaten sandwich sat on the ottoman. Unable to generate enough energy to facilitate embarrassment over the state of her living room, Emmeline curled back into the blanket and sank into the recliner.

"Oh dear," Minerva said.

"It's freezing in here," Mirielda said. She went to the control panel and turned down the air conditioning.

"Leave it on. I want to stay wrapped in my weighted blanket," Emmeline said.

"It appears Brad has put in several appearances." Betsy surveyed the mess. "We let you wallow in your sorrow all summer. Life has moved on, and school starts next week. You need to snap out of it."

"I can't. My heart hurts. Everything hurts," Emmeline said. "I can't do anything without crying."

"Which boy do you mourn, Brad or Griffin?" Minerva asked. She picked up a box of flowers. "I didn't care for Brad, but it appears he has tried to apologize for his misdirected statement."

Emmeline lifted her head. "How do you know what he said?"

"Thomas told us," Betsy said.

Emmeline frowned. How would they know Thomas? It didn't matter. She curled into a tighter ball and pulled the blanket up to her chin.

"Have you considered another to take care of?" Mirielda asked. She started picking up the dog toys and putting them in the basket under the window.

Emmeline raised her head. The foot of the recliner lowered to the floor. Silent, she rose and walked into the kitchen. The aftereffects of too much Jack, including the fuzzy tongue, dehydration, and killer headache, announced their presence. Closing her eyes in pain, she downed four aspirin and a glass of water.

"What a mess." Betsy began loading dishes into the dishwasher. "Sadness is no excuse for sloth."

"Don't waste your time," Emmeline said. "The dishwasher broke last week. Water leaked all over the garage. And before you ask, I did mop it up. Sorta."

"A handyman could fix the dishwasher," Mirielda said. "Call Thomas. I know he would come if you called."

Thomas again? They acted like he was an old friend of

theirs. Emmeline shook her head to clear the fog. "How do you know Thomas?"

"He's part of our wicca," Betsy said. "You've been invited to join for years."

"You should come to school with us today," Minerva said. "We can set up our classrooms for opening day. I have a wonderful idea for a new bulletin board I'll share with you."

"I don't have the energy," Emmeline said. She waved her hands in the air and returned to the living room and her recliner. The Jack continued to beat on her brain, and she felt nauseous. She needed to eat. "Maybe tomorrow."

"The opening game's on Saturday afternoon in State College. You can ride up with us and watch the Little Lions hand our boys their asses on the old Blue and White platter," Betsy said.

"Okay. I'll go to the game with you. What time do you want to leave?"

"We'll pick you up Saturday at ten. We need to leave early because of the traffic," Betsy said. "By the way, I left you some of your favorite cookies on the counter."

Emmeline watched the women file out the back door. She sighed at the mess. Needing a shower and missing the dishwasher, she wondered if perhaps Thomas could help. With a deep sigh, she focused on the cookies. Not nutritious, but Betsy's cookies were the bomb. And perfect for her hangover. She opened the tin and stuffed a cookie into her mouth. Salted caramel with a crunch and crystals of sugar on the top. They were like magick. After the third cookie, she felt seventy percent better.

She picked up the phone and pushed Thomas's number.

After making arrangements for Thomas to help with the dishwasher, Emmeline started the cleanup. She picked up a box of chocolates. Brad never understood. Chocolate with nougat was not her feel-good choice, and nor were flowers that died in a vase as they littered discarded biomass across the floor.

With her fuzzy brain clearing, she saw the whole house for the first time in months. It took three trash bags, three hours, and three cups of coffee to clean up her three-month mess. She stood back with her hands on her hips and blew out a deep breath.

"Wow, three must be my lucky number." She smiled and looked toward Griffin's dog bed to tell him. A single final tear ran down her cheek. "Life moves on."

Saturday arrived with all the pomp and circumstance of a season-opening game.

The cramped ride to State College in Betsy's four-door Volkswagen did nothing to lighten Emmeline's mood. Although she appreciated the classic car, four seats or not, it was not meant to carry four people. She sat in the back shoulder to shoulder with Mirielda.

Minerva looked over her shoulder and clapped her hands in excitement. "Shall we make a wager? Winner gets to pick the restaurant when we return. I'm in the mood for Thai."

"You always pick Thai," Betsy said. "Besides, I thought we'd eat at the game."

"You'll want to eat again," Minerva said. "Game food is not filling."

"Are you in the mood for a wager?" Mirielda asked Emmeline.

"It doesn't matter to me. Whatever you guys want," Emmeline said.

All at once, the three older women were arguing, and the noise echoing in the little car's small interior had Emmeline holding her breath. She asked, "Does anyone think the Stags can win?"

Silence.

"Nice support for the Stags. So the bet falls into a win-by situation," Emmeline said.

"I think the Stags lose by seven." Betsy tossed her score in first.

"You're kidding," Mirielda said. "The Lions will rip us a new one. We lose by twenty-one."

"Twenty-one to zero. Right?" Minerva asked. "I say Stags lose by twenty-one, but we do score. I call Lions twenty-one to seven."

"Fine, I wanted us to score, but I'll take twenty-one to zero," Mirielda said. She took ahold of Emmeline's arm. "What do you bet?"

"I say the Stags win. The score doesn't matter." She snapped her fingers. The women's sudden silence translated as odd. "Oh, come on, ladies. It's possible."

"I never expected you to use the snap in such a precise manner," Betsy said.

"What?" Emmeline asked.

"Never mind, dear," Minerva said. "Perhaps your little snap will send a little magick to our boys and they'll win."

"Sometimes I wonder if you girls drink more than me," Emmeline said. "Magick. Right. What do the Stags need besides skill and better coaching? Why a genie in a lamp?"

"Your sarcasm doesn't play well with me, young lady." Betsy met Emmeline's eyes in the rearview mirror.

Emmeline shrugged.

At the game, the Stags ran across the field grunting like rutting elks. The cheerleaders gyrated body parts like they were at a rave instead of leading cheers. It was all too much for Emmeline. She didn't want to be there. Her melancholy remained an oppressive cloud over her head.

Both teams scored once. With a minute to go and the Stags in possession, a big storm blew in from the north. The quarterback made a "Hail Mary" throw toward the end zone. It seemed like the wind blew the ball those eighty yards and lifted the receiver to intercept. He carried the ball across the line. The Stags won, fourteen to seven.

It took forever to get out of State College, and the storm stayed with them the entire time. Torrents of rain beat on the roof, blowing the little Bug askew in the lanes while they navigated the Seven Mountains section of the ride. Betsy fought to keep the little car on the road, and a collective sigh of relief filled the interior as they finished their descent through the sharp turns.

"Five fatalities have occurred on this section of the road this year," Minerva said.

"Why do you know this, Minerva?" Mirielda asked.

"We're here. I thought it prudent." Minerva gave a single nod. "Since we could face a Return of—"

Betsy cut Minerva off. "Emmeline, you won the bet. Where are we dining at tonight?"

"I don't want to eat. The hotdogs and popcorn filled me up. Drop me at home, and you can go anywhere you want," Emmeline said.

"As you wish," Betsy said.

"I think this storm's getting worse," Mirielda said. She leaned forward to watch the long bolts of lightning strike somewhere in the distance.

They made the exit to Fishing Creek Valley Road without any mishaps. But once past the housing developments, leaves and limbs blew across the asphalt, playing dodgeball with the car. A huge tree came down thirty yards ahead, and Betsy had to slam on the brakes. Once stopped, Betsy tried to exit, but her door was wedged against the trunk.

"I'll check it out," Emmeline said.

The wind knocked Emmeline back into the door opening. As she pushed against the branch, it seemed to levitate and spin. She decided the log must be lying on a broken branch stub acting like a fulcrum. She gave a push, and the tree moved enough to get the car by.

"Excellent job," Mirielda said.

Emmeline started to climb back in when a flash of something white caught her eye.

"Wait, something—" Emmeline walked toward the side of the road and peered through the pelting rain. A white piece of garbage wiggled under some bushes. Her instincts kicked in when the bag moved against the wind.

Minerva shouted out the window, "A flying branch could hit you. Get back in here right now."

Emmeline ignored her with a wave of her hand. The draw to open the bag pulled her like gravity to the ghostly object. As she untied the handles, a pair of pointy ears, a white head, and two imploring black eyes popped up.

"Oh my God. You poor baby."

Reaching down, Emmeline lifted a soaking wet puppy from the bag. Shivering and skinny, the dog had a streak of blood along its muzzle and shoulder. Emmeline hugged it to her sopping sweatshirt and ran to the car. As she climbed inside, the storm stopped.

"Emmeline, what in the world?" Mirielda focused on Luna's pitiful stare.

"Whatcha got there?" Betsy asked.

"Some asswipe disposed of this beautiful girl in a garbage bag. May a thousand toads fill their car, and may they contract projectile diarrhea," Emmeline said.

"Oh no," Mirielda said.

"It's fine," Betsy said. "They deserve every toad for this act of cruelty."

"I plan to watch the news over the next few days," Minerva said.

"What?" Emmeline asked.

"To identify who in the community had a toad incident and shit themselves," Minerva said.

"Make sure to let me know." Emmeline rolled her eyes and went back to the dog. The dog shook, flinging water everywhere.

"Oh, for the love of the Fairy Queen," Mirielda said.

"It's about damn time," Luna said.

"Who said that?" Emmeline asked.

"I said it," Betsy said. "I think we need to move before something else happens."

"I agree. This girl needs to warm up. She's so skinny. I can feel every bone." Emmeline hugged the pup tight as they finished the drive. "Strange the storm let up so fast."

"Strange indeed," Betsy said.

"Can you girls come in and help me for a couple of minutes?" Emmeline asked.

Emmeline walked into the living room and sat down with the pup on her lap. "Betsy. Grab several towels from the bathroom. Perhaps one of you can find something in the kitchen for her to eat. Lunchmeat or something. I think there's tuna in the pantry. And a bowl of water."

"We can." Mirielda pushed Minerva into the kitchen.

Mirielda handed a paper plate to Emmeline. "Here's some lunchmeat. I think you need a trip to the grocery."

"And the pet store. I gave everything of Griffin's to the Humane Society," Emmeline said. They fussed over the dog until she fell asleep in Emmeline's lap. "I think I'll call her Luna."

"She glows like a bright moon. Splendid choice," Betsy said. "I'll call you tomorrow and go to the pet store with you."

Noting Emmeline's nod of agreement, they all left.

* * *

"It was a Return of Three for Emmeline's magick," Minerva said as they drove away. "I'm sure of it. You wait. The toads will find the perpetrator with a shitty ass."

"She's a druid," Betsy added. "Does druid magick follow the same rules as ours?"

"I don't know," Minerva said. "We should consult Edemay."

"A bit of power caused the storm. Do you think Emmeline cast it with the finger snap? Poor Luna looked like she was in the bag for some time," Mirielda said. "Or it could be part of the magick that took her Griffin. The spell of sickness had Megaera written all over it. She hates familiars."

"Griffin wasn't a familiar," Minerva added. "But maybe it's time to tell Emmeline the truth."

"With Luna here, we should expect Gryphon anytime," Betsy said. "Emmeline heard Luna speak. The girl's magick has power, but I'm not sure she's ready. A talking dog could send her over the edge."

"She needs to find the box first. We should wait," Mirielda said. "Someone will have to tell Luna and Edemay."

"I'll take care of Luna and then stop to visit Edemay before I leave tomorrow," Betsy said. "I bet Ben will be excited Luna's back."

Harrisburg, PA 2019

"Fire?" Emmeline's eyes widened.

"Yes, dear. You need to practice in all four forms of magick: wind, water, earth, and fire. Every well-rounded witch should have some command over all of them. Although it can take hundreds of years. But water before fire." Betsy chuckled and set a cup of water on the table. They spent the rest of the day practicing.

Edemay arrived. "The earth trembled this morning. Did you make pro—" A blue spotted version of Luna ran through the garage. Emmeline followed waving a towel and brush. "I guess not."

"I set Gryphon to task so Emmeline could...rest," Betsy said. "In a strange turn of events we discovered Emmeline's power can circumvent Gryphon's. Hence the reason Luna's now blue."

"Those little rumbles from this morning. What were Emmeline and Gryphon doing when they happened?" Edemay asked.

"Kissing on the back stoop for all the world to see. Why, they were both undone, if you know what I mean," Betsy said.

"I'm a grown woman and do as I please in my own home." Emmeline crossed her arms and took a stiff stance. She cast a sultry glance at Gryphon. "We were interrupted and didn't get far."

"Witches, please." Edemay interrupted the side conversation and picked up a spilled cup of water. She raised an eyebrow. "Megaera will have sensed the magick release. I await a call from Thomas to hear what the Crone thinks."

"Emmeline's magick, whether cast or sewn, awakens the earth," Betsy said. "We should expect more rumbling and prepare for the consequences."

"What does 'cast or sewn' mean?" Emmeline asked.

"The rumbling didn't come from the magick practice," Betsy said. "It happened when Gryphon kissed you. You influence each other's magick when you touch and intertwine both kinds of magick. We call this sewn magick."

"But when a spell is recited, it is said to be cast," Edemay said.

Edemay tapped her cheek with an index finger. "Although it will happen again, we'll have to take care in combining their magick in the future. Every witch in the area would feel the release of such powerful magick."

"What does all of that mean?" Emmeline asked.

"This morning. When you and Gryphon kissed. You caused a little earthquake." Betsy smiled, holding an index finger and thumb about a half-inch apart.

Edemay waved off the discussion. "Try the stone again, Emmeline."

"Earth's the easiest element to learn." Gryphon nodded and placed a stone on the table.

"Sure, why not." Emmeline stared at the rock and wished it to move. Nothing. Putting effort into the idea, she squeezed her eyes shut and scrunched up her nose.

"Do you need to use the privy?" Gryphon asked Emmeline. He put a hand on her shoulder blade.

Warmth and need shot right to her toes. His scent made her core clench. The rock lifted and moved to the end of the table, where it plopped into the cup of water. Silence alerted her to a possible problem. "What did I break this time?"

"Now we know how to make her magick work, but I'm not quite sure of the logistics," Edemay said. Changing tactics, she waved Gryphon to the table. She placed a candle in the middle. "Since Megaera's a Fire Witch, you'll have to counter her power. Light this candle so we can see what skills you've retained."

"Wait." Betsy laid her palm on Emmeline's arm. "Don't repeat his words like you did when he was moving the paint."

Emmeline nodded and bit her lower lip.

Gryphon concentrated on the candle. He sprinkled a bit of dust into the air and recited an ancient spell in Gaelic.

Emmeline listened and translated the words to English as he spoke. She didn't comprehend until he spoke the last word.

"Power of light, Power of flame. Light this candle bright to flame. So mote it be."

With a wave of his hand, a small flame jumped to life on the wick. Gryphon smiled as all three women applauded his success. During the bow and acceptance of his accolades, the paper towels in the trash smoked and caught fire.

The fire alarm went off.

"Do you have a fire extinguisher?" Betsy asked Emmeline.

"Behind the door." Emmeline pointed. She rushed to push the off button on the fire alarm. "Glad I'm not the only fuck-up."

"Gryphon. Your magick continued to grow while you were in the box. Now you need lots of practice with control." Edemay extinguished the flames with a wave of her hand. "For shame. You're all witches. Use your magick."

They continued to practice until after sunset. Despite her effort, Emmeline failed more than she succeeded. Her stomach rumbled so loud she brought silence to the room.

"Perhaps we should take a break and have a meal," Edemay suggested. "Who's cooking?"

"Cook! Why not whip up some magical food?" Emmeline asked.

"Oh my. You have much to learn." Betsy waved an index finger in Emmeline's face. "You should never use magick to benefit yourself."

"You've said that several times. Yet you never explain." She frowned at Betsy before leaving to climb

the stairs, mumbling a litany of examples. "Magick was used several times today. The broken windows and splattered soda, for example. Gryphon zapped the blue paint. The fire. They need to make up their blasted minds."

After a heated discussion about indigestion and flavor profiles, Emmeline ordered Chinese for delivery. While they waited, Betsy returned to the subject of magical rules.

"We only restored the damage to its original condition," Betsy said. "It's not a better window, so the cost will remain small."

"Cost?" Emmeline lifted both hands in question. "What cost, and who do you pay?"

"Magick of the light costs the caster, whether good or bad," Gryphon said. "The Returns of Three will fall upon you, so always remember there will be a cost before you use magick for yourself."

"It can benefit someone else's welfare," Edemay said. "But the cost for making someone richer, killing someone, or making someone fall in love with an unwilling participant will be brutal."

"You pay the fates for the magick," Betsy said. "What energy you take, you must replace. A witch's magick is not infinite. If the spell doesn't harm another, the Returns are inconsequential. A broken nail, a cold, or little mishaps such as a sprained ankle."

Edemay pulled a small pouch from inside a sleeve and showed it to Emmeline. "You must pay for the use of magick. We offer the Three Sisters. I carry a bit with me for all occasions."

"What is the currency of magick?" Emmeline asked.

"Energy," three voices responded together.

Edemay gave Emmeline the pouch. "My gift to you. It's a mixture of ground corn, squash, and beans. The Three Sisters. The explanation goes back thousands of years and is better left for another time. An offering of the three will return bits of energy. It helps to pay the debt, but it also dissuades witches from using it for daily tasks."

"You should always be sure you need the magick. Using it for daily chores and tasks is a waste of the energy," Gryphon said.

"Did you research druid magick?" Betsy asked Edemay. "Does a druid need the Three Sisters for the use of magick?"

"I have Thomas digging in the library now," Edemay said. "Megaera keeps every legitimate book on magick she can get her hands on. He said it sits and rots on the shelves, but his suggestion she share with the coven was met with a painful burn."

"Thomas. Brad's friend Thomas?" Emmeline said. She frowned. "Oh right. You did say he was a member of your wiccan."

"He's Second Level advisor to Megaera Caroline. But he's your friend and loyal to the bone," Edemay said. "He works there at great risk to himself, so he has full access to her private quarters at the Ivory Tower. Also, he's my nephew and Gryphon's apprentice. You can trust him."

"Sure." Emmeline went into the kitchen and stared at the bottle of Jack. There was so much to think about. All this time she'd lived with witches and no one had revealed themselves. Their auras should have warned her somehow. Even if she disbelieved them at the time, all the shit piling on her plate over the last two days would make more sense. Maybe would even be easier to accept.

In her heart she knew they were telling the truth, but her head still had this little niggling ache. Would she wake up and none of the last several days had happened? No magick practice. No Gryphon. No kissing. She could almost hear the imaginary brakes squealing with the last thought.

The Jack on the counter seemed to dare her. With a quick glance over her shoulder to verify everyone's location, Emmeline twisted the lid on the bourbon and guzzled a two-finger shot straight from the bottle. She set it on the counter and whispered, "Shh. Don't tell Betsy."

The food arrived. They filled their bellies, laughed at Gryphon's attempts at using chopsticks, and gave Emmeline a crash course in Magick Manners 101. When everyone was full and the fortune cookies broken, they returned to the previous night's discussion. They still needed a plan.

"Megaera will need a distraction when we take the cauldron out of the basement," Betsy said. "It took seven witches to bring it from Cold Springs and the same to move it to the Ivory Tower. Will Gryphon have enough power to move it by himself?"

"I think my power combined with Emmeline's should suffice. She's exceptional." Gryphon squeezed her hand. "We will need a convincing distraction."

"How much time would we need to retrieve those items?" Emmeline asked.

"It took several hours to empty, load, and transport the

cauldron. It's now empty, so the task becomes a matter of moving it," Betsy said. "If we knew the location of the book and quilt, we could grab all three at the same time. I would say twenty minutes."

"There's two school board meetings every month. They last three or four hours if you count the executive session." Emmeline seemed pleased with herself.

"Brilliant," Betsy continued. "We can pick the time to take the treasures back."

"We don't have much time. She would have felt the release of ancient magick," Edemay said. "But I think we need to wait until the prophecy reveals the time and place of the battle."

"I will have to follow Emmeline to work every day until I am released," Gryphon said. "I think it becomes problematic to wait. Can we scry for the time and place?"

"Emmeline will have to take a leave of absence," Betsy said. "We can try to scry. But bowls don't produce good visions."

"Wait," Emmeline said. "I don't want to quit my job."

"We all sacrifice for the coven," Betsy said. "Besides, I said a leave of absence. Not quit."

Edemay stood. "Gryphon and Emmeline will keep practicing their magick. Mirielda will help when she can. We need to wait and hear from Thomas. For now, this is all we can do."

CHAPTER 16

Harrisburg, PA 2018

Megaera paced her office. Once again, her spell had backfired. Instead of sending the girl into a gully of depression and mourning, she'd ended up with another level of protection. How had Gryphon's familiar found her way to this time and place?

"Norman, we need to find a spell that identifies traitors and make an example of them at a coven meeting. Yule would provide a proper platform."

"High Priestess, I do not think—" The buzzer on Megaera's' desk interrupted him.

"Dr. Caroline." The secretary's voice filtered through the phone intercom.

"What do you want?" Megaera snapped at the secretary.

"Marie Alley wishes to meet with you," the secretary said.

"Send her back," Megaera said. She leaned across the desk toward Norman. "I need you to do something other than carry my coat. Find a traitor spell in the Book of Fire."

Norman whisked away as the pudgy-faced female entered the office and sat in front of the desk.

"What do you have to report?" Megaera asked.

"Emmeline, Betsy, Minerva, and Mirielda plan on going to New York City for New Year's Eve. They want to watch the ball drop." Marie Alley dropped her head, pouty lips downturned and quivering. "I tried to invite myself, but Betsy said I couldn't go."

"Not making friends like you were supposed to?" Megaera's words were drenched in sarcasm. "You have months to figure out a way to go with them."

"After Callen's gone, you'll allow me to join the coven?" Marie asked.

"Of course. You will have earned a reward." Megaera's eyebrows lifted as a crooked smile appeared. She handed the twit a strip of paper with a phone number on it. "Call this number when Callen's in a big crowd. You're dismissed."

Megaera rolled her eyes as Marie Alley exited the office. "Stupid human. Boo-hoo. Nobody likes me." She couldn't stand the little snitch, but at the moment, Miss whatever her name was still had her part to play.

She picked up the cell phone and paused. Taking this step would produce consequences she didn't want to think about. Her toes tapped the floor. She pinched her lips between her teeth, swallowed, and pushed the quick dial.

"What do you want?" Wilmott said.

"I have a job for you."

"I don't do business over the phone. I'll meet you in Cold Springs at the start of the Witching Hour. Tonight."

"There are better—"

"It's there and then or never." Wilmott hung up.

"The warlock still treats me like a child." Megaera tapped her long nails on the desktop. Her thoughts drifted back to her childhood lessons. Wilmott was a hard teacher. Nothing was ever good enough. The bell rang, dismissing the school for the day. Megaera whisked to her scrying room in the Ivory Tower.

"Did you find what I asked for Norman?" Megaera asked.

"As far as I can tell, no traitor reveal spell exists in the Book of Fire." Norman handed over the tome. "You'll have to write one yourself."

"Can you read Gaelic?"

"No, High Priestess, but Thomas can."

"Set him to the task of searching the Book of Shadows." Megaera checked the clock hanging on the wall. She handed him the key to open the chest where the tome was stored. "I have a meeting. You're not needed this evening."

At the designated time, Megaera whisked to the old altar site above the Cold Springs ruins. As she stepped up, her poorly healed hip argued with the cold. Nothing she'd tried alleviated the pain. She'd exchanged business shoes for sandals to stay on her feet at school. Megaera had convinced herself someone had cast a spell. She'd never considered the pain as a Return of Three.

Moving out of the shadows, Wilmott emerged. His black form stood out darker than the night. The robe he parted was decorated with glowing Gaelic symbols. She could feel the dark magick pulsing from his being.

"What do you want?" Wilmott asked.

"I need you to kill someone for me."

Wilmott reached up and bit into a cheroot. "Does this one little witch give you so much trouble? For someone with your power, I'd have thought her gone by now."

Megaera stepped toward the man. "The girl has more protection than she should. It fights my magick."

"I know your plan. I told you to call me when you were ready and I would help." Wilmott leaned against a boulder. "Instead, you tried to destroy her on your own. I could have told you, you don't have the power."

"I offer you a position in the coven," Megaera said. "High Priest. You can take your brother's place."

"It's kind of you to offer what should already be mine. And what of Gryphon?"

"Released from the box, he holds rank at Second Level." Megaera laughed. "The Viscount will do whatever he's told."

"You stole the High Seat from me when you murdered your mother. I was fond of her, as you know." Wilmott floated to the ring of stone that marked the old coven fire. "I thought burning the whole town a bit of an overkill, by the way."

"Mother would never have seated you as High Priest. She feared your power." Megaera stomped across the old altar. "Will you take the job or not?"

"My price will include the Book of Shadows and the Wiseman quilt," Wilmott said.

Megaera's eyes widened. "I thought you wanted the High Priest seat."

"I want nothing of the sort. You suggested the position. I'm too much of a free spirit to remain long in one place or to run a coven with you."

"Outrageous!" Megaera shoved her hands into her coat pockets. The cold now soaked into her bones, and every joint hurt. "The book and quilt burned with everything else in Cold Springs. I don't have them."

"I'm not stupid, Witch." Wilmott waved the cheroot in the air. A tiny trail of white smoke rose and danced on the light wind. "I have recognized the winds carrying the dust of Earth Magick across the valley over the last century. The book resists your use, doesn't it? Who knows, maybe the Book of Shadows causes your spells to fail. It has a magick of its own. You should show wisdom and part with it."

"I don't have the quilt, but you may have the Book of Shadows." Megaera crossed her arms and turned her back on the warlock.

"I know you have both. My price remains fixed. And if you try to argue again, I will also want the old cauldron."

His mention of the cauldron inhibited her breath. It took a minute to clear thoughts of losing something she considered necessary in the fight for coven control. "I will find someone else. You've wasted my time."

"No one else will take the job." Wilmott smiled and narrowed his eyes. "Even some of your Fire Witches wish for the little druid to succeed. You have driven the coven mad with your self-absorbed actions."

Dropping her arms to her sides, she faced her father. "I'll text you the details."

As Wilmott dissolved into the dark, Megaera fisted her hands. She whisked home, still furious about his price and threats. Who had provided information to him on the location of the Book of Shadows and the Wiseman quilt?

Back in her private chambers, the Book of Shadows lay two feet from the Book of Fire. Both belonged to her. How dare he want them. She moved to stand over the Wiseman tome, her hand several inches away. As she moved toward the cover, an invisible force pushed against her palm to warn her off, and it slammed shut. Even the Book of Fire had enough sense to keep its distance from the book of light.

Winter struck in early December with a vengeance. Snow accumulated over the next two weeks, and the year ended with another deep storm. Megaera sat in her office, staring out the window. Another foot of snow had fallen over the last two hours.

The school was supposed to have an early dismissal, as it was the day before winter break. But here they sat, waiting for the plows to clear the roads so they could dismiss at the normal time. The kids were complaining, the parents were calling, and the teachers were bitching. Under Norman's advice, she'd altered the schedule to longer class periods and announced the winter pep rally had been moved to the end of the day. Under the circumstances, it was the best she could do.

Norman whisked into the office. "Afternoon, High Priestess. We have much to do today since the schedule was changed. The children are on their way to the gym, so you must start judging the door-wrapping contest. Then you can announce it before dismissal."

"You assume we will dismiss. I've yet to see a district plow sweep the road so the buses can park."

"Have faith, High Priestess. You can command it done, you know."

"And so I shall." Megaera cast a spell and sent it out an open window. It would still take the plows time to get there and plow a path wide enough for the buses. "You go judge the door-wrapping contest. I'm up to my neck in this holiday cheer. Why don't humans celebrate Yule in a less festive manner?"

"I'm not sure I would call our ceremonial activities less festive," Normal said.

"I need to be coming up with another plan to keep the druid's power from growing, not judging how well a teacher's homeroom can wrap a door in Christmas paper." Megaera pushed back the chair and swung in a circle. "I thought sorrow would work on her. Miss Callen is so emotional. But those damn Crones somehow managed to find her another damn dog. Gryphon's familiar. Damn it! I can never catch a break."

"I've always believed one makes one's own history, High Priestess," Norman said.

"Yes. You need not remind me." Megaera tapped sharpened nails on the desk.

One of the school secretaries burst into the office, out of breath. "Dr. Caroline, you need to come to the gym. The roof collapsed!"

"Collapsed? How horrible." Megaera eyed the secretary. "Have you called 911 yet?"

"Yes, of course," the secretary said. Every phone in the office started to ring. "The students in the gym have already called their parents, and they're already storming the school to remove their children. The roads must be open."

"Tell the rest of the secretaries to quit answering the phones and go to the gym to assist," Norman said, pulling the blinds down. "Keep the doors locked and tell the staff in the class-room sections to go into lockdown. Call it an outside intruder drill."

"Everyone's in the gym for the pep rally," the secretary said. "But I'll put out an all-call."

Norman crossed his arms and stared at Megaera. "Did you—"

"I didn't ask for this." Megaera held a hand up before Norman could finish. "Unless it's residual from the spring when I sent the dog to hell. I never heard of magick taking so long to settle."

"You should attend the incident. The staff and students will look to you for direction."

"I need to find a spin to put on this before we go." What explanation could justify the missing funds when the school board, press, and parents asked? She'd thought she had the money trail covered after pilfering the roof funds for other purposes.

Megaera waved Norman to her side.

"Dr. Caroline. What's so important at this moment that you keep me from aiding children?"

"I will receive the blame for this mess." Megaera grasped his arm and pulled Norman close. "Remember the funds I had you transfer?"

"I do." Norman's eyes widened. "Was it the money to repair the roof?"

"How was I to know a larger than normal amount of snow would fall this year or the roof was so weak it would collapse?" Megaera smoothed down the jacket of the woolen business suit. "I assumed the inspector exaggerated about the roof's deficiencies."

"I find it difficult to serve you more and more these days," Norman said. "You need to express sympathy and sorrow now. I don't know how to explain the missing funds."

"Start thinking while we attend this…tragedy."

Megaera followed Norman to the gym. He was unusually upset with her. The apprentice should fear her, not threaten to leave his position. He was the only witch she trusted, and most of the time her trust was marginal. What if he was her traitor? He set the herbs for her spells. He would know what she cast and when she cast it.

The gym was in chaos. Snow fell into the gaping hole, and the wounded made their way out of the tangle of iron beams and roofing. Megaera searched the destruction. Where would the little druid and the Crones lie?

Megaera stepped over the debris until her shadow loomed over Minerva. The old witch was trapped under a green I-beam, and blood ran across the polished gym floor, creating whirls around bits and pieces of concrete.

Megaera squatted and whispered, "It's unfortunate the collapse happened during a pep rally."

Grimacing, Minerva attempted to sit up. With her last few breaths, she gasped, "You have no respect for the old ways. This tragedy is your second Return of Three. The first already delivered, as Gryphon's familiar now resides with Emmeline. The third will cost you more than you know. In the meantime, the fates make us all pay for your evil nature. Like the night Cold Springs burned."

"Returns? This furthers my plans," Megaera said.

"Your mother told me she feared your use of dark magick would end you." Minerva gasped for breath. "Joan Caroline was correct."

Megaera saw the light leave the old Crone. A glance across a pile identified the location of the Key and Betsy. They pulled students from under debris and comforted others with their hugs. Megaera shivered at the thought of touching one of the students.

Her hands clenched into tight fists in an attempt to control the anger rolling off her in waves. She'd wasted her time and power trying to do away with the girl herself. Now more than ever, hiring the warlock made sense.

From her office, Megaera saw the last ambulance pull out. School buses left half full, and parents walked their children through the snow to their cars haphazardly parked along the highway.

"We need to prepare a spell for the school board. I must remain in this position or, better yet, be promoted to superintendent. We'll put out the word that I argued for more funding to fix the decrepit roof."

"I'm afraid your spin won't work this time." Norman remained calm, but his heart raced. He said in a restrained voice, "Twenty-five students died here today. Forget the job. They will want your blood."

Harrisburg, PA 2019

After Edemay and Betsy left, Emmeline and Gryphon sat beside each other on the couch. The toe of his new boot rubbed up and down her ankle with soft touches while she demonstrated how to search for different programs using the voice remote control.

Emmeline lifted the remote to her mouth. "BBC World News."

They watched in silence for some time.

"War has changed its tactics, but anger between different people will always occur." Gryphon shook his head. "What the Europeans did to the natives here in Pennsylvania is unforgivable. I grew up around religious zealots like the Moravians. They tried to impose their religion on our coven, and we feared a repeat of Salem."

"I've never known a world without war," Emmeline said.

Gryphon took the remote and stumbled across *Supernatural*.

"These two demon fighters have many skills. Perhaps if

you watched, you would find more magick within yourself. They do a fair job of casting spells."

"It's make-believe. A show for entertainment," Emmeline said.

"Magick's not make-believe." Gryphon lifted her hand to his lips.

Those gorgeous lavender eyes darkened. Since this morning, Emmeline had noted they tended to do so when he became aroused. She laid a hand on his thigh to test the theory. A deep amethyst flashed through the normal, paler color.

Gryphon's arm went around her shoulders and pulled their bodies close together. Emmeline smiled and wondered if pioneer cabins had couches so guys could practice the move. Or was Darwin onto something with his theories of inheritance? Were men, witch or human, born with the make-out gene?

Soft lips found the back of her hand and whispered a sweet caress across her knuckles. Emmeline quickly forgot about the couch and Darwin. Her head fell back to the cushion, and she blew out a deep, relaxing breath. "I wish I could go back to the beginning."

The wind blew around the room. The drapery flapped. The air turned bitterly cold as the pressure dropped so fast their ears popped. Darkness enfolded them into a whirlwind, spinning and spinning. Emmeline became dizzy.

Her feet grew cold, and when she opened her eyes, she was sprawled across Gryphon. They lay on the ground in the woods. She lifted her head to look around. The leafless trees rattled their branches like they were possessed by spirits. A cloud blocking the moon floated away, illuminating the surrounding area in silver light.

"Holy shit!" Emmeline said in a strained voice, still lying on Gryphon. He was warm and comfortable, like an old couch. Squishy in some spots, firm in others. She sat up saddle style across his hips. Firm was a definite description. The moonlight was so bright, Emmeline could see every detail of his face. Of course, he wore his cocky smirk, and his eyes twinkled with little sparks.

"As much as I enjoy our position, sweet Emmeline, unless you intend to fix my current condition, I suggest you stand up."

Using his chest for support, she pushed up and stepped to the side. Even in the moonlight, she could see the huge boner tenting his pajama pants. "Man, it doesn't take much for you, does it?"

"I have never been so affected by a female before," Gryphon said. "I blame you and your druid magick."

Emmeline felt the heat brush her cheeks as she reached down to take his hand and help him up. "Why did you bring us here? It's cold."

"This was not of my doing. Your magick has whisked us back to the beginning, like you asked. Perhaps refrain from 'wishing' again." Gryphon shifted his stance. "You have immense power, Emmeline."

Emmeline started pacing. "Why did it work now? I can't do this magick shit."

"Your magick is within you, and now it's been released, you can't put it back." Shaking his head, Gryphon stilled her pacing. "I must use spells and herbs to summon my magick. You possess the kind of magick most witches would cherish."

"Take us home," Emmeline said.

"Your magick brought us, so it must take us home." Gryphon encouraged her to take action. "Perhaps if you concentrated on sending your magick through something. Call it magick training wheels."

"Like what?" Emmeline started shivering. She clapped her hands over her arms to try and warm up.

"A talisman you treasure. Something you would not leave home without."

Patting down the front of her clothing, Emmeline held up

her hands. "Object. Well, maestro. I have nothing. I'm in pajamas." Her voice echoed across Stony Creek.

Gryphon smiled. "But Emmeline, you have your fingers.
These are keepsakes from my mother and Kenter." Gryphon
held up his left hand to flash the rings seated on his middle
and pinky fingers. He pulled his mother's ring from the little
finger and grabbed Emmeline's left hand.

"What? No." Emmeline tried to pull the hand back.

Gryphon chanted a short spell, and the stones on the ring
glowed as he transferred it to her left ring finger. The metal
warmed against her flesh. Emmeline examined the beautiful
ring as it glittered in the moonlight.

"It belonged to my mother. She passed it down to me as her
seventh son. Willa would want you to take it. I believe you're a
seventh as well."

"You lost me on the seventh whatsit. I can't take this. It's
beautiful, but—" She broke off as he wrapped her in his arms
and kissed her. The conversation forgotten, he enveloped her
in his warmth.

Emmeline drank in his scent. The heady feeling traveled
straight to her sensitive core. As her clit throbbed, she wrapped
a leg around his thigh in an attempt to satiate the need. She
wanted to crawl inside and become one with him. As he deep-
ened the kiss, Emmeline needed air but remained connected,
so afraid letting go would destroy the moment, whether illusion or reality.

Gryphon broke off the kiss and lifted her hand.

"It is a witch's ring." His deep voice sank into her brain like
a sedative. As he moved her hand back and forth in the moonlight, he nuzzled her neck. He whispered into her ear, "If you
tilt it in the light, a star winks in each stone of the outer circle.
They are black star sapphires."

"The seven surround and protect the three in the center. In
the daylight, you will see they are red. Made of a rare emerald
called red beryl, they represent the Three Sisters, the Returns of

Three, and the Three Fates. They provide light and guidance to the coven."

"Three is important." Emmeline nodded, lost in his presence. Gryphon kissed along the arch of her neck and nibbled on her earlobe. Her whole body shivered.

"All of life. Magick, the coven, and the elements," he lifted her hand once again, "rest on the strength of these nine bars down each side, cut from Irish Connemara marble. I have given it to you, and it accepted you. Did you notice how well it fits?"

Emmeline was so far gone from the ring, the only thoughts she had swirled around her arousal. Gryphon continued to assault her senses. The gold warmed her finger as she lifted her eyes to meet his intense stare. It fit so well she would have sworn it was made for her.

"Use the ring as a conduit for your magick until you don't need it anymore," Gryphon said. "Then use it to seek wisdom. It will guide you well."

"You talk as if it were alive."

"The ring has a sentient nature. It chose to accept you."

Gryphon traced his fingers down her arm. In the same moment, his other hand found its way under her nightshirt. Little strokes across her nipple with his thumb had her shifting from one foot to the other. She gasped at the pleasure as it built.

Swirls of lavender filled Emmeline's mind while she rode the explosion of passion so charged she climaxed. The release packed a punch, and the petite explosion made her clit throb for attention. She didn't even know you could orgasm from nipple play while standing up.

"Next time, I shall like to be deep within you, and we will ride the euphoria together." Gryphon chuckled and held her up. "You shiver. You need to take us home before you catch your death."

"Not cold now." Unwilling to lose the warm embrace, she

closed her eyes and tapped her heels together. She giggled into his chest. "There's no place like home."

"I agree. Now take us there," Gryphon said.

"It's hard when you don't understand a movie reference. Put *The Wizard of Oz* on your watch list." The hoot of an owl in the distance followed by the shuffling of leaves sent them spiraling back into darkness.

Emmeline's feet were on warm, solid ground. She opened her eyes, still in Gryphon's arms. Luna sat in the recliner.

"Where have you been?" Luna asked.

"I had an accident," Emmeline said. "On the other hand, I can poof now."

The phone rang. Gryphon answered.

"We are fine. No. No need to come. We were practicing. Emmeline can whisk now." Gryphon hung up and tossed the phone on the ottoman. "Edemay thinks we should stop for this evening. The earthquakes are more noticeable now."

"Earthquakes?" Emmeline questioned.

"You didn't feel the earth shake when you—" Gryphon asked. "No matter. It did when you did. Edemay worries others will trace the magick."

"I'm going to bed." Emmeline stopped in the kitchen and grabbed the bottle of Jack on the way to her bedroom.

As she walked down the hall, Gryphon asked, "Would you like some company other than your distilled spirits?"

Swallowing hard and wanting to indulge him, Emmeline took a deep gulp of air. She listened to the logical portion of her brain rather than the soft tissue throbbing between her legs. Her heart did a double beat. Slapping her thigh, she said, "Luna baby. Come with me."

"Sorry, Gryphon," Luna said. *"Habits and all."*

"You know you're not a dog," Gryphon said.

* * *

Gryphon went to the kitchen for a snack and spotted the cookies left over from supper. Grabbing them and some beer, he remained in front of the TV for the rest of the night. His interest remained on the football playing on ESPN.

He fell asleep, and the cookies worked their magick. He had erotic dreams of Emmeline. Naked and impaled on his hardened cock, riding him hard and fast. Emmeline, biting his nipples. Emmeline, taking his entire length into her mouth. Emmeline—

Knocking sounds brought Gryphon back to reality. He wiped the sweat from his brow and recognized his cock straining against the lounge pants. He swallowed the pain while he tried to soften the hardest morning wood he'd had in his life.

Gryphon forced himself to walk to the back door and found Betsy and Mirielda on the stoop. Damn those old hens. If they wanted Emmeline and him to fornicate, why did they keep interrupting?

CHAPTER 17

New York City, NY to Harrisburg, PA 2018-19

Emmeline watched the buildings flash by as the train pulled into Grand Central Station. She was still reeling from the tragedy at ASSD not even two weeks ago and had wanted to postpone the trip for another year.

"Minerva would insist we celebrate as planned," Betsy said. "The old girl loved a party."

Emmeline remained melancholy as she checked her phone for directions. "Our hotel's up ten blocks and on the left."

She remained quiet as Betsy and Mirielda gushed over the stores as they walked past. Ten minutes later, they found their hotel and checked in. The room was dingy and malodorous.

"I think the last occupants still live here." Mirielda sniffed, her lips pulled back across her teeth in a grimace and her nose wrinkled.

"Let's make the best of it. We're here now. I'm glad we kept the reservations. The ball drop was on my bucket list too." Emmeline sat on the bed and winced at the sagging mattress.

"You're too young to have a bucket list," Betsy said.

"Not since joining ASSD. Every time I turn around,

someone on the staff dies. I intend to do as much as I can before my association kills me as well," Emmeline said.

"How…preemptive," Betsy said.

Mirielda shrugged her shoulders. "Emmeline has a point."

"We have reservations at Buca di Beppo at seven," Emmeline said. "It's on Broadway, two blocks from the ball drop. We can go to the bathroom before we find our assigned stall in the crowd."

Betsy laughed and clapped her hands like an excited child. "I don't need to worry about the bathroom. I googled this. Many people suggested we wear adult diapers so you can go when you want."

"You mean you plan to pee all night long in a diaper?" Mirielda glared at the old woman. "You want to walk around with a cold, squishy ball between your legs?"

Betsy tossed a package on the bed and crossed her arms. "I brought one for each of us."

"I'll do a little wiccan spell," Mirielda said. "We won't have to pee all night."

Emmeline followed the conversation. These women were friends for life, but at times they were hard to take in big doses. Nevertheless, she loved them so much. She settled the argument. "Ladies, why don't we do both. Diapers and your little spell, Mirielda."

Mirielda lit a candle and rubbed some powder between her fingers. She recited a little poem. "Witches' bowl, grant me your grace. Three witches seek your assistance in this far-from-home place. For the night till three, we wish to not pee. In the future we will gift you your due. So mote it be."

"Holy crow, how funny. Not peeing till three." Emmeline tried to contain the laughter but couldn't hold it in. "I don't mean to disrespect your beliefs, but man—"

Betsy nodded. "It did sound a bit juvenile, Mirielda."

"It was the best I could come up with on the train." Mirielda shrugged her shoulders and grabbed her coat. "We need to leave. We have a thirty-minute walk to the restaurant."

The trio were less than half a block from the hotel when Marie Alley popped out from behind a newspaper machine.

"Hey, you three. I can't wait to spend the night with you girls. What a great suggestion for a girls' weekend. Where to first?" Marie Alley asked.

"What the hell do you think you're doing?" Mirielda asked.

Marie Alley shrugged. "I made a reservation when we discussed coming here. Remember our planning meeting in the break room?"

"You weren't at our planning meeting," Emmeline said.

"I guess I misunderstood." Marie Alley pouted. She lowered her eyes and sighed. "I'll try to find a place to eat. Alone. I'm sure somewhere in the city on New Year's Eve a restaurant exists that doesn't require reservations."

"You have your little poor-me scenario down to a science, don't you?" Mirielda crossed her arms and tapped a boot on the sidewalk.

"It's the only science she knows," Betsy said. She allowed her pent-up frustration with Marie to flow. "You need to find your own friends. Ones who don't care when you run off to tell Dr. Caroline everything."

"Marie. If you promise to refrain from your usual annoying behavior, you can go to dinner with us." Emmeline acted as the referee and, noting the crestfallen expressions plastered on Betsy and Mirielda's faces, added, "We had reservations for four anyways, and the last couple of weeks have been rough on everyone. Perhaps a little charity, ladies?"

"Fine. But if you backstab us this time, you'll never have the chance again. Understand, you little nit?" Betsy leaned into Marie's face.

"I do." Marie Alley stepped back.

After an amazing and expensive dinner, the quartet strolled toward the cattle pens set up for the occasion. Time flew by, and soon the clock struck midnight. The ball dropped, and everyone sang 'Auld Lang Syne' and hugged and kissed. The police moved them out of the square in slow waves of people.

The temperature had dropped, and snow fell at a steady rate. A shout from behind them caught Emmeline's attention. She stopped as other pedestrians pushed past, knocking her shoulder and slamming her into Betsy. A shiver ran down her spine.

Marie ran through the crowd, trying to catch up with them. Out of breath, she pulled up next to Betsy. "Wow. You girls can move when you want. I thought I'd never catch up to you."

Emmeline noted a thin black aura over Marie's head. Strange. It had never looked black before. The color defined deceit and betrayal. Her stomach hurt, and she got a little dizzy. Her face paled as she searched the flow of people. The feeling was ominous.

Motion from along the buildings caught Emmeline's attention. A man in dark clothing and a face mask came running through the crowd brandishing a knife. The crowd parted to avoid the slashing blade, and he lunged at Betsy and Minerva. Emmeline pushed them out of the way with enough force to knock them down into the slush on the sidewalk.

The man didn't slow and plowed into Marie Alley. He knocked her off the sidewalk and into the path of a bus.

Tires slid in the slush as the bus tried to slow. A splat sounded from the impact and was followed by a horrific sucking sound as Marie Alley's body slid down the windshield and dropped to the street. The bus expelled a vapor cloud as the air brakes released pressure.

A dark red stream of blood illuminated by the streetlights ran toward a drain. From the misshapen corpse, Emmeline knew the ambulance would arrive too late. Several people screamed while others recorded the gruesome scene with their phones.

"Holy shit," Betsy said.

"Another member of ASSD bites the dust." Emmeline covered her mouth and widened her eyes. "OMG. I'm an awful person."

"Interesting take on the situation," Mirielda said.

"Maybe we should all find a new place to work." Mirielda wrinkled her nose at the mess.

"We need to give the police a statement. It's strange, but I can't remember anything about the man with the knife," Emmeline said.

———

Megaera stormed into the cauldron room at the Ivory Tower. The power in the room, an oppressive resonance, pounded against her. Hearing a throat clear from the far corner, she clenched her jaw.

"Wilmott. What do you want? I'm busy."

"I have come to claim my book and quilt," Wilmott said.

"Yours?" Megaera approached. "You failed to kill the girl. You get nothing."

"I didn't fail." Wilmott stepped from the shadows, an evil grin accompanying a crooked smile. The warlock's hood shadowed his facial features, and the long sides folded back over his shoulders revealed an expanse of emptiness.

"I killed the stupid little human. A necessary task under the circumstances." Wilmott picked some lint from the cape and dropped it on the floor. "She was a complication you didn't need."

"You killed the wrong girl." Megaera laid a palm on the Book of Fire. The pages always comforted her. The thrum of power in the room increased its tempo. She could feel it pulsing and pushing against Wilmott's energy.

"Did I?" Wilmott's baritone chuckle echoed in the chamber. He removed his hood and angled toward the casting table. "You have known for a long time you would have to face the

Key in battle. You should not try to circumvent prophecies. I cannot kill her any more than you can."

Megaera cocked her head. Was he right? Had she wasted her time and energy these last two years trying to kill her? It would explain why every spell she cast failed in its purpose. She looked up at Wilmott, now only three feet from her. He moved without sound, his beard shifting with the rhythm of the power filling the chamber. He emanated a lethal power.

"You have only the power of fire to fight the Key. Had you heeded the warning of your youth, the balance of power would not be slanted toward the light," Wilmott said. "You continue to underestimate the ancient power of the druids. I have heard rumors of several attempts now returned to punish you. How's your hip these days?"

"The girl has help," Megaera said. She tried to erase the whine from her voice and considered her position in the room. Wilmott had the scent of betrayal riding his presence. "Traitors sit close to the seat of power in MichAudha."

"Perhaps the current seat remains occupied by a pretender. There's more than witch magick protecting the girl." Wilmott leaned toward Megaera, waving his index finger in the air. "You refuse to realize the true problem. Druid magick gave rise to witches' magick. Neither your power nor mine can destroy it."

Megaera called flames and sent long shards to strike the warlock.

Wilmott deflected the flame back at the impetuous witch with a crooked smile. "I still hold a great deal of power. I could have given you everything, but you remain a disappointment, daughter."

Magick escaped Megaera's control. Her anger drove more flames to reach for anything that would burn. "I'm the High Priestess of the MichAudha. You have no stake here."

"Humph. You cannot truly control the magick you wield. How would you handle more?" The warlock pulled a ball of fire from the air, stirred up currents of wind, and drew the smoke to him. "The High Priest robe was mine by birthright. I wanted you to serve as High Priestess by my side. But no longer."

Megaera summoned the Book of Fire. She blew a stream of air through the smoke, hit the fireball, and extinguished Wilmott's flame. "I want no part in your history. Gryphon will become my second."

Opening the Book of Fire to a well-used page, Megaera placed a hand on the page and chanted a spell. A loud rumble of thunder sounded, and a strike of lightning shattered the glass in a tiny window. Wind swept through the chamber, strong enough to toss the chairs. Bowls and packets of herbs took to the wind.

With her hands glowing white-hot, Megaera took a menacing step toward the warlock.

Wilmott jumped out of the way as one glowing hand swung in an arc through the air and released a beam of white-hot fire. Megaera smirked as the beam landed on his booted feet. His cloak ignited along the floor, and the flames climbed with haste toward his shoulders.

Wilmott raised his hands in the air and chanted. The flames burned through his clothes, heat searing flesh from bones. The rancid smell of burnt flesh filled the chamber. Wilmott reached for the Book of Fire. He commanded it. "Come."

Megaera fired more flames. A bright flash of light flared as the book took on the same glow as Megaera's hands. "You die tonight, Wilmott, brother of Kenter. Your family line dies this night."

The light was so bright, it blinded Wilmott. He backed away, but the flames followed, and a seething orange-red glowing fissure opened in the floor. Hot sulfur smoke rose in feather-shaped tendrils, and flames reached from beyond.

Flames crept like ivy growing up a building. The stench of scorched flesh filled the room along with a musty sweet perfume with a dash of copper from boiled blood. The room shuddered as the fissure widened. Steaming hot waves of heat and noxious gas shot out, burning both witch and warlock.

"I may not win, but I'll take you with me," Wilmott shouted as his feet melted, adding to the overwhelming odor of frying fat.

His bones softened and flesh dripped into puddles on the floor as Wilmott's final words dissipated into a cacophony of moans and groans. A final effort to dislodge the Book of Fire from Megaera's glowing hands ended in failure.

Realizing she had the upper magical hand, Megaera ignited the rest of his cape and sent Wilmott across the room on a current of air.

Aloft over the molten fissure, Wilmott's remaining physical form combusted, charred, and fell. The fissure closed as fast as it had opened.

The High Priestess's horse-laughs were absorbed by the smoldering remains of the tapestry on the wall and mingled with the scent of brimstone long embedded in the fabric.

"I'm ready to fight even the fates." Megaera sniffed the air. "Who hides in the shadows of my sanctuary?"

"I came to check and make sure you have everything you need, High Priestess." Thomas stepped out. "But the warlock arrived, so I hid myself."

"And now you have seen my power. Who will you tell?" Megaera rubbed her fingers together in a slow circular pattern. "It matters no longer. When do you think the battle will take place?"

"Since the fates decide, the battle will take place with the rise of a full moon. It ends where it began, I think."

"You're smarter than I thought, Thomas." She stretched her neck and shoulders and glanced at the calendar hanging on the wall. A full moon would soon rise.

. . .

Harrisburg, PA 2019

"Why do young people forever waste the day in bed?" Betsy asked. She walked into the back door of the house with a box of donuts. "There was a small quake last night. What on earth were you two doing?"

"Emmeline whisked us to Cold Springs." Gryphon picked up the empty coffee pot and waved it in the air. "By accident, of course. But I think I fixed the control issue."

"Whisked? Fixed? How?" Betsy asked.

"Not in the way any of you old Crones think, although I did try, you know." Gryphon chuckled and sniffed the treats Betsy had brought. "I gave Emmeline my mother's ring to focus her energy. We returned unharmed. I do not understand your concern."

"Willa's ring? It accepted her?" Betsy asked.

"Yes. It took to her without pause—and on the proper finger, I might add."

"Emmeline carries great power." Betsy paced the kitchen. "It's dangerous for her to throw out magick without knowing everything about it. What would have happened if you were not there?"

"She's resilient. I do not think—"

"I need to find Edemay and Mirielda. Practice your magick, not hers. I will return. And don't burn the house down."

Betsy whisked away.

"Did I hear Betsy?" Emmeline stumbled into the kitchen and grabbed the coffee from Gryphon's hands.

"Betsy told me to practice my magick. She will return," Gryphon said.

"I'm glad you mastered the coffee pot."

"Indeed." Gryphon changed the subject. "I need to cast a memory spell on myself." He grabbed her hand and pulled her toward the basement. "I need to remember what I learned about druids. Kenter taught me. Maybe I can stimulate your magick."

"A double entendre if I ever heard one." Emmeline giggled but jerked her hand away. She reached for a donut. "Not before breakfast."

Gryphon handed her a donut. He followed her finger as it swiped some of the powdered sugar and licked it. Taking possession of the errant finger, he pulled it between his plush lips and licked off the remaining crystals. He could feel her shiver as he tasted the sweetness that was Emmeline.

"We should, um, wait for Betsy. Your last spell left poor Luna blue all day." She smiled and took another bite.

Gryphon pushed out a little rush of breath. He lifted her hand to stick her finger back into his mouth and pressed his teeth down for a pretend bite. Her pupils shrunk into pinpoints, and little sparks fired in her eyes.

"Stop that." Emmeline pulled her hand away.

"We need to unlock your powers." Gryphon drew his thumb along the line of her jaw. "Sitting around eating sweets does us no favors. Our little trip last night could have ended in tragedy."

"Stick and mud." Emmeline stuck her tongue out at Gryphon before she refilled her coffee, grabbed another donut, and sauntered off to the basement.

"Fates save me. Sometimes I have no idea what she's talking about."

Gryphon worked to prepare the spell and cast a quick glance at Emmeline. She remained quiet and observant, drinking coffee and eating another donut. An errant lock of hair lay across her cheek. He fought the urge to tuck it behind her ear and touch her soft neck. He wanted to play connect the dots with her freckles.

"Need something?" she asked.

Gryphon shook his head as he came out of his trance. How embarrassing to be caught fixating on her freckles. Although she wouldn't know, would she? He looked back to find her making a show of shoving a bite into her mouth and sucking her finger. She knew something.

Gryphon stroked the stone mortar like one would pet a small kitten. He chanted to the bowl in words so quiet Emmeline wouldn't be able to hear them. He wanted to make sure her magick didn't send the spell off kilter.

His finger continued its sensual strokes, rounding along the graceful curve of the bottom.

"Fuck me." Emmeline blew out a deep breath.

"Did you need something, Emmeline?"

"Huh? I wondered why you were touching the bowl so—?"

"Our casting bowls are alive, or at least sentient in nature," Gryphon said. "They must like you, for lack of a better explanation, or they will not help cast a spell."

She stepped closer, and he placed her hands around the bowl.

"It's warm. And heavy." Emmeline's eyes widened.

"The bowl takes to you. Perhaps Edemay will gift it." Gryphon returned the bowl to the table. He raised his hands and chanted. "Years of past, remember me. A witch of earth, began with thee. Bring to mind, the witches' rhyme. To free my memory. So mote it be."

A cool puff of wind blew through the garage, and goosebumps rose. The power moving around the room wrapped him in a warm embrace, and the air pressure felt like it dropped for an instant, as if he had dived into deep, warm water. And then it left him.

A muffled alarm from behind him set him spinning to face Emmeline The candle sitting next to the casting bowl went out with a loud pop. A thrumming pounded their ears as magick danced around the room unfettered by a direction. It landed on Emmeline.

"I see a parchment with druid symbols on it. It is modern yet yellowed and wrinkled," Emmeline said. She pointed to a vision wavering in front of her.

The earth rumbled, shelves rattled, and cans fell to the floor accompanied by the sound of breaking glass. Outside the house, several muffled car alarms went off then were drowned out by the siren of the nearby firehouse.

Edemay whisked into the basement, eyes narrowed and her lips pinched in stern disapproval. "What did you do? For Samhain's sake, you have spewed magic all over the place."

"I called magick to remember," Gryphon said. "But —"

"Emmeline repeated your words." Edemay crossed her arms and tapped a foot on the floor. "Didn't Betsy relay my message this morning? Emmeline was not to practice."

"I remember." Emmeline spoke, but her eyes remained focused in the air, and her hands started writing with an imaginary pencil.

Gryphon captured her hand. He could feel her warmth and smell of her caramel scent. It remained in his mind as she dropped his hand and finished. Words written with Emmeline's magick hung in the air for seconds before a breeze dispersed them into nothing.

"I've seen this before." Emmeline spoke in a robotic manner. "An old man gave it to me at Bill's funeral. He was kind, but his aura was gray with black specks."

Her head swiveled toward Edemay and back to Gryphon.

"Betsy was talking about going out for a drink." Emmeline looked down at her hands and continued in a monotone speech. "It was written in Gaelic. I couldn't read it at the time. Betsy remarked about the sprigs of sage and rowan."

"Where's this paper now?" Edemay asked.

"I was going to throw it away but decided to wait. It came home in my purse. I don't know—"

Gryphon took her hand. He sent energy into her fingers, and she lifted her head to meet his eyes. "What do you keep close to the heart that could hold a note?"

"My mother's box. It's upstairs in my cedar chest."

CHAPTER 18

Harrisburg, PA 2019

Everyone whisked to Emmeline's bedroom. She pulled a colorful quilt from the cedar chest on the far side, and dropped it on the bed.

Edemay laid her hand flat over her heart. "How long have you had the quilt?"

Emmeline bent over to open the cedar chest and paused before lifting the lid. She turned her head to glance at the quilt on the bed before opening the chest and grabbing her wooden box. "I found it at a yard sale while I was in college. I couldn't afford it. An old woman pushed it into my hands. She told me the quilt wanted to go with me."

"It's an ancient witch's quilt, hundreds of years old." Edemay spoke in a whisper, as if a voice to loud would disturb it. "It channels power. The old woman who placed it in your hands must have known you were the Key in the prophecy."

Emmeline straightened with a small wood box in her hand, and flashed Edemay a questioning glance. "How is that even possible?"

"You've been the Key since the vision first showed in the brew in 1742," Gryphon said.

"I must say, I've never felt its magick the whole time I was with Emmeline," Luna said. *"I've wondered where your strong protection came from."*

"The Grand Master works in mysterious ways." Gryphon pointed to the box in Emmeline's hand. "Let's move on. The note?"

She tried to hand the box to Gryphon, but he refused to take it.

"This is a Witchbox. I am not of its line. I cannot open it."

"It doesn't bite." Emmeline rolled her eyes and sat on the bed to examine the box. Her fingers caressed the wooden rectangle with caution. The last time she opened a wooden box, she ended up bringing home Gryphon. "I never thought of these carvings as witches before. But now, I think this is a battle scene."

"It is." Edemay maintained her distance. "An ash box with magical powers in itself. And the battle scene you see is from the Isle McGee. It tells the history of the ancient line of druids that gave birth to the MichAudah."

"It was my mother's. I had to hide it in my foster homes or the other kids would have stolen it," Emmeline said.

Edemay pointed out several features. "The High Priestess pictured on the top was one of the most powerful druids of all time. She ruled for seven hundred years before falling to the dark magick that attacked the Isle McGee. Maeve was loved and respected. You wouldn't have this unless it was your family line."

"My middle name is Maeve," Emmeline said. "I always thought it was pretentious. When I was seventeen, I went to live with my last foster mother. She told me to keep it safe, and one day it would become the—Oh. My. God."

"The what?" Luna asked.

Tears ran down Emmeline's cheeks. Her core warmed as Gryphon put his arm around her and gave her a reassuring hug. "This is crazy. She said it would become the key to my future."

After a brief respite, she wiped her cheek. Gryphon played with a curl of her hair, and it tickled the back of her neck. She shrugged away from his touch, until she realized she was happy he was there, keeping her safe and warm. Her new reality set in. Magick was real.

Both her heart and head, now in agreement, told her Gryphon would remain a part of her life. She shivered as he nuzzled her neck and pressed a soft kiss on her temple. With acceptance came relief. For better or worse, this man—witch—was now a part of her life.

"*Emmeline. Open the box,*" Luna said.

Emmeline held her breath as she lifted the lid. A puff of bright green dust rose on beams of late afternoon light, and danced across the room. At the bottom sat a piece of notebook paper yellowed with age.

"Why didn't I remember this earlier?" Emmeline asked.

"I think my memory spell fell upon you, when you repeated my words." Gryphon gave her a reassuring squeeze. "We will need to have a discussion about your need to disobey me."

Emmeline snorted. "Like 'obey' is in my dictionary."

Gryphon frowned.

"A fortuitous error," Edemay said. "Quit fondling the girl so she can read the note."

Emmeline blushed as Gryphon's lips pulled from her ear. Bereft of his comfort, she unfolded the paper. A drawing of a heptagram woven with vines sitting on the palm of a hand lay at the top, symbols of ancient Gaelic spread across the page, and the dried sprigs of sage and rowan were pressed into the page at the bottom.

"A seven-pointed star?" Emmeline asked.

"It's a mark of seven," Gryphon said. "The seven-pointed star adorns the Book of Shadows, my family's spell book."

"Seven means strength and wisdom and remains a sacred number to our coven. Gryphon is the seventh son of a seventh son and seventh daughter," Luna said.

"And Emmeline. I believe you're the seventh daughter of a seventh daughter," Edemay said. "Maeve had seven daughters, as did her seventh daughter and her seventh daughter."

"Seven? That's a lot of daughters." Emmeline pursed her lips. "And drama."

She remembered the foster homes with multiple females trying to dress for school or work in the morning. Everyone wanted the bathroom at the same time. She shuddered. "As far as I know, I don't have any sisters."

"If your mother was from the line of Maeve, you did or do." Edemay tapped the paper. "Read the poem, dear. We can sort out family trees later."

"So who was the old man who gave this to me? An ancient ghost?" Emmeline asked.

"No," Gryphon said. "See the small hand beneath the star? It is my uncle's mark."

"Betsy never mentioned Willmott's presence," Edemay said. "I haven't seen my brother for years. Why would he give Emmeline a spell?"

"Unless he hoped to gain something from it," Luna said.

The strange tangents of players was giving Emmeline a headache. She tuned them out and read the spell. "Ancient beings hear my call, release the Key from ancient stone." Emmeline shook her head. "These spells never rhyme well, do they?"

"Don't be flippant," Edemay said. "You don't want to piss off the fates."

Emmeline took a deep breath and continued. "Fire, wind, earth, and water, combine the power of the seventh daughter with power of the seventh son. The battle may soon be won for in the world you join as one. Magick strong, magick bold, to combine the power seven-fold. So, mote it be."

Something was happening to her. She could feel it from inside, like a climax. But instead of starting at the center and flowing outward, the electrical sensation ran along her limbs to form a pool in the center of her torso. Emmeline grasped the quilt in her fists. Her fingers whitened, and she gasped for air.

The earthquake struck without warning. Gryphon leaned over her and shielded her body as plaster fell from the ceiling. Windows rattled, cracks appeared in the plaster, and knick-knacks fell from decorative wall shelves. The temperature dropped, and the candles sitting on the dresser burst into flames. The whole house shook as the electricity went out, and car alarms sounded throughout the neighborhood.

As the shock waves stilled, Gryphon remained on top of her. She recognized a certain part of his anatomy burning along her thigh. There was something to be said about going commando. Holy mother of a big one. As her clit began to throb, she realized how absurd her thought was. In the middle of an earthquake and finding out she was a witch with lots of relatives, she was thinking about sex.

"Do you think you could calm the big guy down a little? We have company," Emmeline said. She tried hard not to laugh, and the suppression came out as a snort.

"Indeed." Gryphon stood up and pulled Emmeline to her feet with him.

Emmeline snickered as he adjusted his stance and blushed. She'd never seem a man blush before. It was endearing.

"Perhaps we should have waited to figure out the warlock connection before she released her power."

"What warlock connection?" Emmeline felt like she'd skipped several chapters in a book and now regretted it.

"We can discuss it later. How do you feel?" Gryphon asked. He brushed the plaster dust from her shoulders and wiped a smear from one of her cheeks with his thumb.

"Feel about what? Feel about the wreck I used to call a house? Feel about the fact you make me so...fucking horny I want to jump you right now?" Emmeline waved her hands around, shaking more dust from a sleeve. "I can't fix this. I don't have the plaster gene."

"*She's deflecting again.*"

"I know not of this gene. I refer to your magical center," Gryphon said.

Emmeline shrugged. "I guess I have one now. It feels like my gallbladder has a stone."

Gryphon tilted his head. "I know not your meaning."

It was obvious he was trying to figure out her last statement. He could Google it. But then he lifted a hand, brushed a stray lock of hair from her face, and took a moment to play with one of the reddish curls along her neck. The gallbladder was forgotten. Her original problem had returned.

He leaned toward her ear and whispered, "I will fix your horny problem when we are alone."

Her eyes widened as she slapped his hand away from her hair. She drew a close mouthed inhale in an attempt to calm her need. She looked at Gryphon. "Are you real? Will you still be here when I wake up?"

She was now afraid of losing him. The idea stole her breath. Fated or not, her head and heart were now attached. It would wreck her if he poofed away. "I dreamed of you the night before we met. Will you disappear like you did when I woke up?"

"*Is that the dream where he was naked and you kicked me off the bed?*" Luna asked.

Gryphon frowned at the familiar. Ignoring her, he picked up Emmeline's hand and kissed the back. "I promise I'll remain, my sweet Emmeline."

She stared at his hand, gasped, and her head snapped up. "Holy shit! I know who I am. I had a mother and a father. They were both witches."

"Oh my. She is the seventh daughter of a seventh father. Grand Master, be praised," Edemay said.

"I'm so tired now, I could fall asleep." Darkness descended.

When Emmeline's eyes popped open, the sun must have set because the room was dark with the exception of a few lit candles. Gryphon's lavender eyes stared down, little sparks of mischief danced in the paler outer rings.

The sensation of a finger stroking her shoulder in little circles brought her all the way back to reality. She was curled around Gryphon like a kitten with her palm flat against his chest. They were both under the quilt, and she could feel his heart thumping against her palm.

Her eyes widened. She was naked. Her heart was beating so fast, she thought it would rupture her rib-cage. Her hand caressed warm flesh. He too, was naked. She withdrew her hand and lifted up on her elbow.

"Um. What happened?" Emmeline asked.

Gryphon's intense lavender eyes were fixed on her. They glittered like gemstones. His purple aura was doing some kind of disco dance over their heads. It was strange when the puffy ring grew to encircle them both. An overwhelming feeling of happiness overtook her as his scent of sea breezes and salty spray calmed her heartbeat. The cloud of purple settled in what one might describe as a pastel police outline around them on the bed.

"You fainted, my beautiful little witch."

"I don't faint."

"Okay, you passed out." His lips quirked at the corner as his hand played with one of her curls. "Finding one's magick can be exhausting. You took in a lifetime's amount at one time. I cannot even imagine."

Gryphon dropped the curl and slid his hand over the surface of her arm, moving the fine hairs and sending shivers of anticipation to her core. A wave of excitement rolled through her shoulders straight to her toes which curled in need.

"Why are we naked?" Emmeline asked.

"I undressed you after you fainted. I used magick, of

course." The corner of his mouth curled into a little smirk. "I remained a gentleman the entire time."

Emmeline frowned. Yesterday morning she'd accidentally undressed him the kitchen. So it was possible to "remain a gentleman" and undress someone with magick. Now she had to decide if she was offended or grateful. She returned her hand to his chest. Silk over iron. Was he this way everywhere?

"I took it upon myself to make you comfortable. Edemay and Luna left us alone, so I took advantage of their absence."

Emmeline lifted her eyebrows. "Advantage?"

"Perhaps advantage was a poor choice of word." Gryphon's lips quirked at one corner.

She sat up and pulled the blanket across her breasts. The move pulled most of it off his chest, and it now lay seductively covering one leg and his package. She held her breath as his obliques formed the famous sexy as hell "V" and left her imagination to what lay below. His pose was straight out of a magazine, one hand playing in her hair, again, and the other tucked under his head.

Erotic images popped into her mind, erasing all sanity as she followed the trail of dark hair from his abs to where it disappeared under the blanket. If she pulled the quilt a bit more— His fingers distracted her. He made little circles up her arm and along the top of her shoulder. One finger followed the edge of the quilt across her breast and slipped under the fabric to continue the caress.

Emmeline remained silent while her mind rushed through a litany of thoughts. What would having sex with him mean to her? To him? She ignored her body and heart and used her brain. No doubt about it, she was attracted to him in some deep, visceral way. And the thought of losing him made her heart skip a beat.

"I thought your magick would be better received from the quilt if you had no barriers. Hence, you're naked." Gryphon put his hand around her neck and pulled her across his chest to kiss her.

Emmeline melted into his lips. His other hand came from behind his head to frame her face. They were warm and strong. And protective. Her core, her mind, her heart were all on the same page. He was her one. The dream she'd had ran through her mind. The sex was hard, fast, and so intense, her clit throbbed its own cadence along with her contracting womb at the memory. And, it was only a dream. She took a breath as he broke the kiss.

"A condition I find rather enticing."

His seduction was working. She tossed the quilt from both of their bodies, threw her leg over his thighs, and pulled herself into a sitting position. Driven by sex appeal, scent, and magical need, she leaned forward and licked along his chest to find his nipples. His hands stroked along her sides to find and cup her breasts. He kneaded and squeezed as she continued to nip and lick her way to his lips.

Her clit clenched as she rubbed along his cock, already hard and waiting. She lifted her head and moistened her swollen lips with her tongue. Her whole world narrowed to the essence of Gryphon.

Gryphon let her hair spiral around his long fingers. "Did you know arousal lights golden flecks in your eyes?"

Emmeline found it impossible to speak. His hard-as-steel erection pressed heat against her sensitive flesh. Her hands traced the broad expanse of his chest, as she pushed herself into a sitting position. The unblemished skin stretched for miles along the hills and valleys of his muscular frame.

"Your skin. Soft and yet so strong." Emmeline said. She arched her back, sliding his cock along her slick feminine lips. Her own liquid honey coated his shaft. The slick surface generated enough friction to make them both moan with pleasure.

Gryphon lifted his shoulders, and attended to her sensitized breasts. He sucked on one nipple, and pinched the other with his free hand. The juxtaposition of pleasure and pain shot through her belly, and was captured by her already sensitive clit. Her hands curled into his hair and she fisted the long, silky locks as he built up the pressure in her womb.

She lifted her hips settling his granite shaft at her entrance.

"Emmeline…you test…my control." Gryphon had a difficult time speaking. A deep vibrato moan filled his chest as he arched on the mattress to meet her. He fought for breath. "I must—"

As a pair, they levitated into the air and rolled, putting Gryphon on top. It was heady and somewhat disorienting for her. The only thing she could find to hang on to was his shoulders as they floated back to the mattress. His weight pressed his cock into her hot, slick folds.

"I want to reach euphoria together our first time. I want to be buried deep inside to feel you squeeze and pulse around me when we both find enlightenment," Gryphon said. His hips arched, and his steel drilled into her in one smooth move.

He stole her breath. Lights flashed in her mind as he slowly withdrew and pushed back in. A brief pause allowed her vision to clear, and her muscles to adjust for the exotic touch. Moments of time passed until there was nothing but Gryphon. She arched into him, wrapping her ankles around his thighs. Gryphon's heat sent shivers along her arms and into her core.

Emmeline caught the subtle change of his scent. The soft sea breeze changed to a storm of salty waves slapping against the beach and releasing echoes of the ocean. He met her eyes as his body mimicked the tempest. The lavender of his eyes was now a deep royal purple.

Gryphon set the pace. Faster and faster as the heat and pressure pounded into her core as she arched her hips upward to meet his strokes. Her muscles clenched, grabbing his cock so tight they melded into one unique being. Movement behind his head caught her attention. Knickknacks and pieces of clothing were floating in a circular pattern along with his purple aura. The faster his pace, the faster they circled.

Green vines rose from the floor and intertwined with the purple aura still circling them.

"Do you see—," Emmeline asked.

His pace quickened as he reached down with his mouth and bit her nipple before sucking her breast. She arched her back as they levitated once again. Heady. Erotic. She imagined it like a canoe floating down a river with rapids and long stretches of calm water: hard and fast fading to slow and sultry. His fingers found her clit, and she swore she could feel the ridges of his fingerprints dragging across the surface.

Emmeline rocked her hips and adjusted her legs so he could sink deeper, if it was even possible. She lifted as he pushed, seating his cock so deep that his balls slapped against her heated flesh. The sound alone sent more of her liquid over his cock.

"By the fates, you are exquisite," Gryphon said.

His heart beat against her chest and into her soul. His lips kissed along her neck, lifting her up to a higher level of sensation.

The euphoria came over her as she moaned, unable to find words. Every muscle tightened as wave after wave of sparkling purple glitter exploded in her mind. He pushed and dragged against her inner folds, hitting the perfect spot again and again. Purple and green waves of light danced in her eyes. Her clit echoed his cock's heartbeat while they rode the sensation.

Gasping for breath, Emmeline grasped his firm ass as the earthquake started. The bed shook as Gryphon released, pulse after pulse, in rhythm with the earth. Her vessel filled with his hot seed and it trickled over her sensitized clit and they sank back into the mattress. With her eyes fully open, she saw in shades of green and purple, the colors forming beautiful whirls in the room.

Emmeline's vision cleared and she regained the ability to

think. She lay on the quilt breathing heavily, her fingers still in the air, trying to grasp the glitter of purple and green making its way back to the earth.

Gryphon lay semi-hard still impaled inside her. Gasping for air, she could feel his heat as she rode the orgasm's wave to satiation. A light pressure nudged against her still sensitive walls, and she released another coating of her own honey. He hardened.

Emmeline was so high on euphoric pleasure, there were no words. His salty sea scent filled her senses with wind-swept beaches and burning sun. She could feel the pulse of his cock and decided she would prefer to remain in this position forever.

He moved. She growled her protest.

"Easy little witch. I am far from done."

Gryphon rolled over to his back, taking Emmeline with him. She remembered floating in the air when she came. The whole floating thing during sex was quick becoming a favorite of hers. However it happened, she wanted to do it again.

"You're very good at floating us around. I like it," Emmeline said.

"I did not levitate us, it was all you. But I must agree, it should be repeated. Often."

Emmeline lifted her eyebrows. "I can float. Good to know."

She laid her elbows across his expansive abs and played with a nipple. She pushed her hips down along his torso, and slid his cock from her channel. She worked her way down his body to linger over the semi-rigid rod. Her tongue reached out to lick the head, and it darkened to a deep red, like a light beckoning for attention. A second glancing blow across the head made him suck air, and brought weeping drops of pearlescence across the surface. Gryphon fisted the sheets as she returned to slide both lips around the burning hot shaft. The flavors of sea salt and her own caramel mixed on the taste-buds, and quickly became an obsession. She wanted more.

She wanted to eat him up. Licking the stem from root to tip she sucked the length of him into her mouth. Her tongue lavished praise on its length as Gryphon moaned. As the head hit the back of her throat, she glanced over his ridges and valleys of muscles to meet his eyes.

Muscles in Gryphon's jaw flexed and his irises darkened to black. Little bursts of light erupted in his eyes as his chest grabbed for air. The salty ambrosia rolled across her tongue and entered her blood stream, pulsing throughout her entire body. She could taste her own caramel flavor as she treated the shaft to a slow, pressing lick. Pushing the head deep in her mouth, his taste of mineral salt overrode her ability to think. Her tongue danced with the shaft, stroking along the back vein from root to blossom. One hand to cupped his balls and a tiny squeeze drew more moans from her sexy witch.

Gryphon's entire body stiffened. Her hot tongue lathed across each sensitive place as she licked and sucked making his cock grow. Salty and musky, the liquid drops dribbling down her throat flared with heat, both in temperature and spicy tang. Nothing could compare to the taste of Gryphon.

Gryphon hissed and murmured, "By the blessed fates."

Emmeline could feel Gryphon tense. His abs were rock hard and his thighs gripped along her shoulders. She anticipated how an entire hot shot would taste as the tip of his cock hit the back of her throat. She wanted to feel his muscles tighten.

Emmeline moaned as the blood rushed through her ears. He released. Shots of hot streams of salty essence flowed down her throat. Gryphon spewed a poetic string of Gaelic. Her brain translated but failed to recognize specific words, only their intent. He thanked the Grand Master for all that was given to him including his blessed Key. It made her smile around him.

Their magical energy mingled, and power surged. There was nothing in the whole world but her and Gryphon. As she approached the summit, a need filled every pocket of space in her mind. It took her only seconds to realize, the need was called Gryphon.

His fingers kept up an onslaught of light touches over every inch of her body. She could have gotten off on those alone. The floodgates opened, and indescribable pure energy escaped. The second earthquake struck in tandem with her epiphany. Gryphon's eyes glowed a brilliant deep purple as they rode out the storm of pleasure together.

A fissure the length of the bed opened in the floor. It illuminated the room with light so bright she was blinded. Magical essence danced on currents of air in swirls of purple and green aura. The colors didn't blend but remained pure yet entwined. After shocks rattled the house on its foundation as the fissure closed. The room vibrated with power as lavender and green dust settled, showering sparkling glitter over their sweat slick bodies.

Emmeline fell to his side, with an arm over her head. "Will this happen every time?"

"I have never made the earth move for any lover. Perhaps one of the Crones will know." Gryphon kissed the palm of her hand and continued kissing until his lips found a sensitive spot at the top of her hip.

Emmeline cupped his face in her hands. "Your eyes are glowing."

"As are yours," Gryphon said. "They are the deepest emerald green. Deeper than the finest emerald stone a jeweler could shape. I am overwhelmed and complete. But the shaking earth could bring trouble. We should take care."

"What if I'm not finished yet?" Emmeline asked. She waggled her eyebrows, waved her ring hand, and smirked.

Gryphon growled.

A loud, attention-grabbing crash emanated from the open closet.

Still licking her lips and holding his cock, Emmeline glanced over her shoulder to find all of her clothes laying in a pile on the floor and flowing out of the closet. The hanger rod sat cockeyed along the back wall.

"You might be right about the earthquake." She frowned.

"Your magick was uncontrolled during our lovemaking. You need to take care with the hand wearing the ring." Gryphon played with an errant curl, plastered to the side of her face.

His magick reached out to cling to her like a weighted blanket keeping her panic to a minimum. Emmeline straightened to lock eyes with him. Gryphon gave her strength. She closed her eyes, swallowed, and opened them, knowing she would see eternity.

Betsy burst into the room. "Have you lost your minds? I sensed the magick release all the way on the other side of town. What were you doing?"

Emmeline squeaked and grabbed for the quilt to cover them.

Gryphon sat up and pressed a heavy kiss to Emmeline's lips. "Emmeline found the rest of her magick."

"So loudly?" Betsy asked. She observed the damage in the room.

The room was a mess. Knickknacks were tossed about, clothes spilled out of the closet, and lavender sparkles danced on the air. Gryphon grabbed the hand with the ring and pulled it down to his chest.

Two pictures fell off the walls. Emmeline frowned.

"We weren't sure what would happen after you read the spell," Betsy said. "But the blending of your magick caused a shift in the earths ley lines and notified the world of the arrival of an old power once lost."

"Gryphon, do you feel any different?" Luna asked.

"Different?" Emmeline still lay against his chest as he continued to trace swirls on her skin with his finger. Stilling for a moment, Gryphon tilted his head, and smiled. "By all the fates. My tether to the box has disappeared."

CHAPTER 19

Harrisburg, PA 2019

Megaera stared at the surface of the new cauldron. The bubbles rose higher than usual. They broke, splattering the brew out when the earthquake hit. Her chair vibrated across the floor, jumping several inches at a time. She was unable to stop the movement, and her fingers paled as she tried to remain seated. One chair leg snapped. Arms flailing, Megaera fell to land hard on the stone floor.

"For fates' sake." Megaera rubbed her hip and wiggled into a sitting position.

Plaster fell from the ceiling as the foundation of the Ivory Tower shook. Elemental magick swirled around the new cauldron. Green and blue flames jumped up toward the ceiling as the room filled with the noxious odors of sulfur and burning oil. The mixture in the new cauldron bubbled and beckoned with a loud hiss.

"No. Not yet," Megaera shouted and used the nearby table to hoist herself up. She limped to the cauldron and stared at the surface of the brew. A gasp echoed against the stone walls as an image came into focus.

The prophecy had come true. The girl had found her

magick and released a whirlwind of long-hidden energy into the world. Old, powerful energy from the light had shifted the ley lines of the world. The Book of Fire jumped on the table, its pages shivering in fear.

Wilmott had told her she couldn't avoid a prophecy. She had wasted her time and power. Uncontrolled sparks of fire magick jumped from her hand to set the wall tapestries on fire. She sought to control the release and found it difficult. The oppressive waves of light energy made her nauseous.

Norman whisked in behind her. "What have you done this time?"

"It was the earthquake, imbecile. The druid has discovered her powers."

"What would you—"

The second quake prevented Norman from finishing his question. Mirielda and Thomas whisked into the room. The fissure reopened in the floor. The cauldron sat precariously on the edge of the abyss. Stones embedded around the cauldron lifted from the floor, and within seconds, the floor collapsed into a fiery void, taking the monstrosity to the same fiery pit that had swallowed Wilmott.

Flames shot from the depths, and the long tendrils reached for Megaera. The old Crone stepped back to avoid contact. Megaera called the Book of Fire to her arms, where it glowed with power. Even the casting table collapsed into the hell hole. The sacred casting bowl slipped along the surface, heading for the fire.

Norman grabbed for the bowl and tossed it to Thomas as the flames rose up and tangled around his ankles. Like an anaconda with a new meal, the fire pulled him into the fissure, where he melted into a glowing orange mass. Norman's screams were snuffed out within seconds.

Without notice, the earth quit shaking and the fissure closed.

"Norman." Tom sat up, still holding the bowl. "Help him, High Priestess."

"I cannot. The fates decided," Megaera said, hugging the Book of Fire. "You're promoted to Third Level, Thomas. Put my bowl away in my chamber." The High Priestess focused her attention on Mirielda.

"Your little druid found her power. But she still won't know how to wield it. The battle is upon us," Megaera said. She raised a flaming hand. "Before you run off to give the news to your little bevy of witches, I want you to know I will no longer tolerate your insolence and betrayal."

Mirielda's eyes widened. "High Priestess, I remain loyal to the coven."

"The coven?" Megaera floated across the room, power thrumming a bass resonance. "I am the coven. I should have killed you sooner, perhaps at the same time I took your sister. Poor Verne."

"High Priestess, you can't," Thomas said.

The corner of Megaera's mouth twitched, and she threw a flame, setting Mirielda on fire. Her high-pitched cackle rose as Mirielda screamed. The flames consumed the seer within seconds. Blackened ash fell to the floor in a macabre rain, bits still burning as they hit the damp stone floor and sizzled out.

"Mirielda." Thomas lifted tearful eyes to the High Priestess. "Our seer. How will we discover the future?"

A huge smile arose on Megaera's face. "I will find another seer. They're not irreplaceable." Her eyes scrunched to narrow strips as she gazed at Thomas. "You have a cousin called Edemay. Does she still live?"

Thomas swallowed. "Yes, High Priestess. In the old country."

"She's a seer?"

"Yes, High Priestess," Thomas said.

"Bring her here." Megaera whisked away.

* * *

As morning light beat through the windows, Emmeline found Betsy and Edemay asleep on the couch.

Their eyes popped open to stare. Betsy stretched and gave Emmeline a once over. "Well, don't you appear well fu—"

"No need for crass language," Edemay said, standing up, arching her back, and wincing. "I'm too old to sleep on a couch."

Emmeline blushed and left to search the kitchen for coffee. Betsy shuffled into the kitchen, twisted a wrist in the air, and whipped up some cinnamon rolls. Emmeline reached for one, and Betsy grabbed her arm and held it back.

"I offer the Three Sisters in sacrifice." She yawned and tossed a small pinch of powder in the air. "Now you can have one. Edemay, breakfast's ready."

"Thanks." Emmeline snagged a sweet roll.

Gryphon whisked into the kitchen behind Emmeline and wrapped her in his embrace, nibbling on her neck. She ducked her head and giggled. Rolling her eyes, she said, "I keep telling him to stop, but he never listens."

He was shirtless, jeans half zipped, and the top button undone. His hard abs flexed, and one of her hands snaked toward the opening while she stuffed the sweet roll into her mouth with the other. Her loyalties were momentarily tested when Gryphon leaned forward to bite the sweet.

Emmeline raised the preoccupied hand, spun, and pushed against his chest while jerking the treat out of the way. "Mine."

Edemay's phone rang.

"Children, quit playing around," Betsy said.

Luna whisked in. *"You've wasted half the morning frolicking about in bed. A hundred years later and you continue the same behavior that landed you here."*

"Emmeline and I had a few concerns to work out between us," Gryphon said. "Now it's fixed."

"Indeed."

Emmeline sipped her coffee and leaned against Gryphon while he consumed two cinnamon rolls. At one point, he slid a bite into her mouth. Her tongue curled around and drew his finger into her mouth, removing the remaining icing. Emmeline's only plan for the day was to return to bed. There were many acres of salty male skin left to explore, and she still needed to return for her hot shot.

"I understand. No, come to Emmeline's." Fury rode Edemay's expression as she hung up. "Norman and Mirielda no longer exist on this plane. Norman by the will of the Grand Master. Mirielda by Megaera's hand. I'm summoned to take over as coven seer. She expects me to whisk in from the old country and take orders from her, the insolent witch."

"How dare Megaera take another life from the coven." Betsy's tears flowed free across her cheeks. "With Mirielda gone—"

Gryphon caught Emmeline as her legs collapsed. Hyperventilating, she clung to his hand and avoided the floor. She quaked in his embrace. "They all died because of me."

Putting Emmeline on both feet, Gryphon gave her a small shake. "They died because Megaera is a selfish witch who thinks power gains respect and cooperation."

"Mirielda, Norman, and all the others will have their revenge," Edemay said.

Tears filled Emmeline's eyes. The room started shaking. Glasses vibrated across the shelves, clinking into each other. The silverware drawer opened, and cutlery rose and danced on the counter. The coffee pot floated across the room and crashed into the sink. The pot lay broken in hundreds of pieces in the drain.

"Emmeline. Control yourself," Betsy said. "There's more at stake here than the lives of a few friends. Cold as it may seem, the fate of all MichAudah balances on the outcome of this battle, whether it happened to be you or a different Key."

Gryphon embraced her and gently kissed her neck. "Calm yourself."

"I think perhaps the Grand Master tests our resolve," Edemay said.

"Excuse me for taking a moment to mourn." Emmeline pushed out of Gryphon's hold and walked into the living room, continuing to rant and wave her hands. "What a shame my friends got in the way of some magical battle. We can mourn later. I understand."

"Emmeline. Stop." Gryphon followed, stomping out little bits of fire as they fell from her waving arms.

Gryphon's voice penetrated the haze in her head. Her anger folded into a slow simmer.

She sat on the couch. One last blossom of fire settled on the rug at her feet. As she sat staring at the little flame, a large tear fell. Emmeline directed it to fall on the flame. Her head could no longer argue about the existence of magick. She now had total acceptance of her ability to do magick. So many had died. Because of Megaera Caroline. She was pissed.

"Amazing." Gryphon sat down beside her and took her hands with his. "Your magick exists on a different plane from mine. The wonder of it. I cannot find the right words."

Thomas whisked into the room, holding the alabaster bowl.

"Welcome, Thomas," Edemay said. "Do my eyes deceive, or do you hold the coven's sacred casting bowl?"

"Megaera stole it while Cold Springs burned." Thomas handed the bowl to Edemay and stepped in front of Gryphon. He leaned in and grabbed him by the shoulders. "Viscount, my eyes heal from sorrow to see you."

Gryphon stood and pulled Thomas in for a bear hug. "My heart fills with joy that you remain alive."

"For real. You two should rent a room." Emmeline shook her head and fell back against the couch cushions. Making eye contact with Thomas, she said, "Even you held back all of this. I thought you were my friend."

"I'm still your friend, Emmeline. Remember, I told you Brad was not the one for you," Thomas reminded her.

"I would make inquiry to know more about this Brad." Gryphon raised an eyebrow. The lavender in his eyes darkened.

Edemay took over the conversation. "The earthquakes have shortened our timeline. Now Megaera knows. Will she force the issue of the battle in hopes of catching us off guard?"

"We need to acquire our corie, Gryphon's book and quilt," Betsy said. "We will need a distraction when we take the cauldron out of the basement."

"It took five witches' power to move the cauldron," Thomas said. "Both times."

"We have Emmeline," Gryphon said. "Her power has no end."

"The old witch has requested my presence," Edemay said. "Emmeline and Gryphon could create a distraction, as I'm sure she will want to confront them. Betsy and Thomas will move the cauldron outside so Gryphon and Emmeline can whisk it away."

"And the Book of Shadows?" Besty asked.

"I will acquire the book and quilt from Megaera's private scrying rooms. Thomas will provide the locations. He will not return to Megaera's employ unless I'm there to protect him. She'll notice the bowl gone."

"When will we make our attempt?" Gryphon asked.

"On the rise of the blood moon, as dictated in the prophecy. Back where it all began," Edemay said. "Until you have word from me, Betsy will continue with magick training for Gryphon and Emmeline. Thomas, you stay to help."

"Take care with Megaera. She has become unpredictable of late," Betsy said. "Unbalanced, at least, if not outright mad. No one's safe."

Edemay pulled a small book from a pocket and tossed it to Emmeline. "It's my personal grimoire, and it has served me well all my years. You may find some of the spells more druid in nature. Practice with Gryphon. Synchronize your magick so it complements each other. If Gryphon calls fire, you call water. Balance will remain important."

"Shall we head to the basement, young witches?" Betsy asked.

Gryphon pulled Emmeline into his arms and kissed her. While they remained connected, eyes closed, they moved. Whether from the kiss, the magick, or both, she couldn't decide. When she opened her eyes, they were in the basement.

Gryphon stepped back, breaking their contact. "I must say, I rather enjoyed moving through space and time with you. From now on, we will use your magick to whisk. Tis warmer."

"You need practice yourself, young Gryphon," Betsy said.

"Bosch, you act as if I cast as a neophyte." Gryphon faced Betsy. "Shall we move on with our practice?"

Emmeline glanced at Thomas, trying not to snicker. While Betsy and Gryphon argued, she leaned over and whispered, "Will this go on for long?"

"After Gryphon's mother died, they were famous for their arguments. Gryphon went as far one day as to whisk Betsy into the creek."

Trying to contain an outburst of laughter, Emmeline focused back on the squabble.

"Gryphon, face it." Betsy gave him a magical push backwards. "When you were training, every time you tried new magick, it went wrong. You set barns on fire, rained on fresh-hung clothes, and remember when you came close to drowning Ben? Kenter was beside himself."

Emmeline laughed out loud. Everyone turned to stare. "Sorry. I know it's inappropriate, but how old were you, Gryphon?"

Gryphon shook his head. "I believe eleven, still a neophyte. Mother tried to advance my training, but each new skill came with unintended consequences. She offered the Three Sisters every time I practiced to no avail."

A bucket of dirt upended on the table. Betsy nodded. "We practice with soil first."

"I will go first, since I mastered earth and wind as a child," Gryphon said.

He pointed to the pile of dirt on the table. Eyes closed, hands in the air, he chanted a spell from memory. He called for wind. Currents swirled the room, picked up the pile of soil, and carried it to the bucket. To finish the spell, he reached into a small bowl on the table, grabbed a pinch of powder, and tossed the Three Sisters to the wind.

"Holy shit." Emmeline walked over and looked into the bucket. "I can't do this."

"Emmeline, my love. You are a druid. Druids do not need spells to make magick happen. Channel your thoughts through the ring or keep a hand on me. Either will help you with control."

"If they were all-powerful, why don't they exist today?" Emmeline lifted her chin, arms crossed over her chest.

"Who?" Gryphon asked.

"Druids. If they're all-powerful, why don't they show themselves and help me?" Emmeline asked.

"I'm sure others such as yourself wait for their power. After the battle's over, we will search for more."

Taking a deep breath, Emmeline looked into the bucket. Gryphon pressed against her back, warm and enveloping. She emptied her lungs and closed her eyes while she whispered, "I wish the dirt would move out of the bucket."

A timid warm breeze began to circulate the room. A spider web trembled, and the dryer sheet lying on the floor ruffled. The breeze swirled around her legs. Grain by grain, the pile began to move. The breeze picked up strength, swirled around the pile, and carried the billions of grains into the air. Soon the entire pile circled the room faster and faster.

"Emmeline, open your eyes," Betsy said. "Direct your magick."

Luna dove under the stairs as the cloud of soil began to disperse and move throughout the space, out of control. *"I suggest you take cover, Thomas."*

Thomas remained sitting in his chair but called up a protective bubble around himself. "I have faith in Emmeline."

As the wind died back, Gryphon and Betsy stood covered in soil from head to toe. Clenched lips and set jaws suggested their displeasure. Thomas remained inside a magical bubble free of dirt and eating a cinnamon roll. Luna climbed from under the stairs, dirt falling from her white coat.

"Oops," Emmeline said.

She shifted her stance, because a tingling in all her girly parts became overwhelming. Doing magick made her horny. How could she explain this to the others without making herself into some freak show?

Trying to relieve the insistent need, she shifted from foot to foot. She grimaced. "What did I do wrong this time?"

"I believe you lost control. We made one small mistake," Gryphon said. "You need to have a beginning, middle, and end to your magick."

"I think a small amount of preplanning becomes necessary," Betsy said. "Direct your magick to a task. Don't leave it out there without purpose."

"You've got this, Em. Give it a try," Thomas said.

Emmeline tightened her jaw and blew out a fortifying breath. "Well, if I can make a mess, I can clean up the mess." She willed the sexual sensation to redirect its energy toward the task. She whispered to herself, "I wish the dirt would come together."

Emmeline lifted the hand with the ring in an unconscious move and pointed at the cloud now forming. A controlled breeze touched every drop of soil in the room: the bits in the cracks of the dryer lid, the small amount caught in the little holes of the pegboard, as well as the dirt from the surface of the tools. Even the grains settled in Gryphon's hair were picked up and circled the room. Power surged through her body to the point that she levitated.

"Hold the feeling you have right now," Gryphon shouted over the blowing wind and soil. "This is your middle. Now, focus on the end. Where will the magick return to?"

Emmeline touched back to the floor, changed her stance, and swallowed an imagined gulp of water. She focused on the cloud. "Into the bucket."

The particles of soil hovered over the bucket and fell like fine snow. A loud metallic thunk sounded. She glanced into the bucket to find a large rock sitting in the dent it had made when it fell. Looking at Gryphon, she exclaimed, "Holy crap."

"Exceptional." Gryphon kissed her. "But next time pull back a little."

Emmeline wrapped her leg around his hip and kissed him back. She shivered with expectation. All of a sudden, her hormones surged, and she climbed his body, kissing and licking.

"Emmeline, we don't have time for this," Betsy said. She frowned at the display. "Let's try something harder."

Betsy grabbed a bucket of water and set it on the table next to a pile of dirt and stones. "I want Emmeline to use the water to make mud and Gryphon to make tiny bricks and stack them. Then Emmeline will meld the bricks together, forming a mortar."

Emmeline remained wrapped around Gryphon, kissing.

"Emmeline." Betsy pushed a small breeze at them to catch their attention.

"What?" Emmeline asked. Somewhat annoyed at the interruption, she sent Betsy a dark glare as her libido continued to blow neural pathways.

"You're not sixteen, young lady. Attend the magick," Betsy said.

Brows furrowed and lips pouty, Emmeline released Gryphon, sliding to the floor. She stared at the intended project, her heart beating at twice its normal rate. She gathered her wits and began the task.

Gryphon's strong hand grasped her arm and gave a little squeeze. It seemed safer remaining connected to him when she did magick. Like the kiss-whisk, contact made the ring warm on her finger and boosted her confidence.

Emmeline weaved her fingers through Gryphon's.

"Wait. I don't intend to get muddy. I'll join Ben at Edemay's." Luna whisked.

"Think about what you want to do," Gryphon whispered into Emmeline's ear.

Tiny puffs of air tickled the side of her neck as she shivered with excitement. Using the libido boost, Emmeline stared at the dirt pile. She added the water and stirred. Once it was at a brownie batter consistency, Gryphon chanted a short Gaelic spell, and little bricks the length and width of a finger formed. He levitated them from the bucket and set them on the table.

Emmeline pointed at the little blocks lined up to fit on top of each other, and as they touched, a mud formed between them and sealed them into a wall. She chewed on her bottom lip as Gryphon's fingers flexed around hers.

Emmeline took a second to remove her hand from Gryphon's, shook out both to expel the stress building, and wiggled her fingers in the air. Eyes closed, she saw flashes of Gryphon pounding his cock in and out of her, and her back arched to take on all of him. She moaned, and purple and green dust appeared and swirled around the room. Her head spun.

Emmeline pulled Gryphon's head down for a lip-smacking, tongue-twisting kiss. Releasing him, she cha-chaed around the room, singing and swinging her arms back and forth in beat with her moving hips. "I did it. I did it. I made mud. I did it, cha cha cha."

"Superb happy dance, Em," Thomas said. "Now, it's Gryphon's turn. I'm on pins and needles waiting for this."

"I believe 'shut it' is an expression of today," Gryphon said. "Something's not quite right."

Extreme excitement rushed through Emmeline. Wind pushed through the space, as if someone had opened a door. Their little brick wall exploded.

Emmeline used magick to pull Gryphon into an embrace and strip him of his clothes. With the wave of one hand, Gryphon lay flat on his back. She sat saddle style over his hips.

"Emmeline." Grabbing her hands to still her, he said, "What do you intend? I don't mind, but we do have company."

"What?" Emmeline's eyes widened. Straddled across Gryphon's naked hips, she identified the hard cock sending heat through the thick denim of her jeans. Glancing across the room at Betsy and Thomas, she could feel the heat rise up her neck and across her face. She jumped off and scooted several feet across the floor on her ass.

Gryphon dressed himself with the wave of a hand.

"Holy fuck me tomorrow. What the heck's going on? I'm so horny right now." She curled up, arms wrapped around folded legs and her head parked between her knees. She shivered.

"What troubles you, Emmeline?" Worry marked Gryphon's face.

"Well. I'm horny as hell right now." Emmeline stood up and paced the room. "I want to fuck you so bad, I can't think of anything else. It increased after I absorbed your magick. I can't turn it off."

Betsy burst into hysterical laughter.

"Betsy, none of this is a laughing matter. I can't go into battle if every time I use my magick, I have to stop and get laid," Emmeline said.

"The old stories told tales about druids and sex. They had a tendency to fall into orgy after casting group spells," Betsy said. "I guess your ancestors were free thinkers. Even Kenter encouraged us to release our sexual energy in our celebrations."

"Holy hell. You mean every time I create magick, I'll want to roll around and have sex?" Emmeline put her hands on her hips. Spinning around, she started talking to herself again, "Well, won't this present an inconvenience during a battle. I know. I'll hold up my hand and summon the first dick that walks by."

Gryphon issued a low, rumbling growl. It echoed off the walls of the basement. Emmeline's body took the rumble as foreplay and tingled. She squeezed her legs together and slapped at Gryphon's arms. "Stop."

Gryphon flashed her a predatory glare, the lavender of his eyes darkening to amethyst crystals and drilling into her mind as if he belonged there. It both scared her and made her shiver in already sensitive places.

His predatory walk and fixed stare had Emmeline stepping backwards as he approached.

"Oh no, my little druid," Gryphon said. He pulled her up against his obvious erection. "You will not have sex with any dick who walks by. You are mine. You will use only my dick."

Betsy and Thomas burst into laughter. Emmeline tried hard to contain it, but after several snorts, she joined her friends. Gryphon's heart was in the right place, but he needed a few more lessons to pick up the nuance of twenty-first-century language.

Covering her mouth to stifle the last few guffaws, she nodded. "Okay."

Could Gryphon become any sexier than right now? Intense, passionate, and so darn cute she couldn't stand it. The glare held everything she'd ever wanted. If they lived past this battle, she would want to remain with Gryphon in whatever capacity worked for both of them. Which did she want? Friends with bennies, fuck buddies, or the whole package: married with children?

"Emmeline, did you hear what I said?" Gryphon asked.

A slow smile formed on Emmeline's face. "Sure, as long as you can change the diapers."

Gryphon tilted his head at her comment. "Again, I cannot figure out your meaning."

Betsy giggled. "Believe me, Viscount, it's best left for another discussion. I do suggest, however, you need to proceed with your practice. We don't have time for a quickie. Work with water and fire next. Thomas, I have a task for you."

CHAPTER 20

Harrisburg, PA 2019

Megaera leaned over the new casting table, talking to the Book of Shadows. A small current of air stirred, blowing the burnt tapestry and spider webs about. Footfalls on the slate stairs drew her attention.

"What took you so long to arrive?" Megaera asked.

Edemay finished the last several steps, holding the handrail. "You should post a sign warning of slippery steps."

Megaera's pupils flared as she studied the old woman. She could feel old-world power seeping from the woman, although they'd never met before. How was she to make sure the Crone wasn't a pretender?

"I had to whisk to Greenland and Canada. I'm not familiar with this country, so I made smaller jumps. Greenland is lovely this time of year." Edemay dropped her shawl on a chair.

"I have need of a new seer. The last one betrayed me."

"Thomas told me the story when he called. I did take some offense. To receive an order instead of an invitation is quite rude. I thought Joan Caroline would have taught you better."

"You knew my mother?"

"Joan and I learned magick at the knees of the same elders."

"I will not offer apologies, as time is crucial to my plans. I need your specific skills to read the Book of Shadows." Megaera waved, and the tome appeared on the table. "You can still read the old dialect, can't you?"

"Of course, I can read Gaelic." Edemay glanced at the book. "You're old enough to have learned. I'd assumed it burned with Cold Springs. We heard rumors that few MichAudha survived. It's why I stayed in the old country once the news reached Ireland."

Megaera studied Edemay, trying to read deceit. "I need to find a spell to remove a protection guarding a druid who threatens the coven. I will pay you with the Book of Shadows after you complete the task."

"Why not scry for the spell in the cauldron?" Edemay waved a hand toward the vessel sitting idle in the corner.

"The cauldron's useless. It fractured in the move from the High Altar. No one dares use it."

"Broken?" A hand landed across her heart, and her face paled. Her fake surprise was well played. "You follow the ways of Fire Witches and failed to make a proper offering, didn't you?"

"Take care how you address me. It's not your job to question my choices. As High Priestess, I decide what's best for the coven." Shifting two steps toward Edemay, she hissed, "Find a spell. You will use a casting bowl and then the book's yours."

Edemay raised a hand and twisted the wrist. The ancient casting bowl appeared on the table. "We will need something stronger than your stone bowl to cast such a spell."

Megaera narrowed her eyes at the bowl. Strange. The bowl was identical to the one that had fallen into the abyss with Norman. Could duplicates exist? The first was carved out of a piece of rare Connemara marble, found only in the mountains of County Galway, Ireland, and was sacred to the MichAudah.

"You have a marble bowl?" Megaera reached a finger to touch the marble. On contact, the earth rumbled, shaking the

Ivory Tower on its foundation. The fissure snapped several stones in the floor but went no farther. She withdrew her hand. Her bowl was not afraid of her.

"I brought mine own. Other witches' bowls are...dirty." Edemay walked over to the old cauldron. Running a finger along the rim, she glanced back to Megaera. "What magick causes the earth to shake? It does not bode well for casting powerful magick."

"Forget the earthquakes," Megaera said. "Do we have an agreement?"

"Yes, High Priestess." Edemay gave a quick bow. "I could use Thomas's help. He knows where the herb storage sits."

"You will have to call him. The stupid witch refuses to answer my calls."

"I'm not surprised. He said you threatened to set him ablaze." Edemay removed a cell phone from her pocket and searched for the number. Tapping the screen, she waited. "Thomas. I have arrived and need you here to assist me."

"I didn't realize you two were close," Megaera said.

"He's my eldest sister's only surviving grandson. She died in the witch trials in Boston. Since Kenter and Wilmott have departed, Thomas remains my last surviving relative. I think," Edemay said. "I remain fond of him."

Thomas whisked into the chamber. "Aunt Edemay. You appear well. How was the trip?"

The two hugged like long lost relatives. Megaera watched for any signs of deceit, but the old woman carried her own sphere of protection. She was old, like Wilmott, and with age came power. She would need to be careful around this witch.

"Thomas, after you show Edemay the herb collection, I have need of you for a minute. I will wait in my private chamber."

A half-hour later, Thomas whisked into her private chamber. He trembled. She liked her coven showing her their fear of her.

"Does Edemay have you busy at this moment?" Megaera asked.

"I presented the herb pantry. She takes inventory and searches the Book of Shadows for the requested spell," Thomas said. "I'm unoccupied for the moment."

"I need you to go to Stony Valley and find these herbs." She handed him a list.

"We have these in the pantry, High Priestess."

"They must come from the soils of Cold Springs," Megaera said. "Go do as you're asked."

Edemay walked into Megaera's chambers holding the marble bowl. She set it on a small table, waved her hands over the opening, and whispered several words. The materials flared with flame and melted into a smooth liquid. After several more chants, the old witch lifted her head.

"High Priestess. What do you wish to know?"

"I want the day and time of the battle identified in the prophecy," Megaera said.

Edemay nodded. She looked at the surface. "The battle takes place where a Fire Witch's spell cost the coven two great leaders. It must end where it began, at the height of a blood moon during the Witching Hour."

"Of course it does," Megaera said. "I suppose it—"

A loud commotion down the hall diverted her last words. The loud screech and hiss of a cat was followed by a black streak zipping by. Thomas followed as Megaera jumped onto a stool.

Megaera sneered. "What purpose does a familiar have here?"

"Apologies, Priestess. It's not a familiar. He travels with me and kills rats."

"How stereotypic." Megaera eyed Edemay. She sneezed. "Don't leave it here when you leave, and I don't want it in the cauldron room or my private chambers."

"Yes, High Priestess," Edemay said.

"I wonder if you betray me," Megaera said.

Thomas ran back through the chamber, chasing the cat.

Megaera directed a flame at the cat. It shot across the room and bounced against the walls like an uncontrolled racquetball. She had to duck to avoid a strike from her own magick. One strike hit the casting bowl. It hissed, boiled, and shattered. The sound was deafening as it echoed off the empty stone walls.

"You dare take something of mine," Edemay said. "I surprised you with my power. My longevity affords me more power than you can imagine. Your mother told me you would amass great power but would not gain the ability to control it. Your impetuous and self-centered nature will destroy all you seek."

"When would you have spoken to my mother? You lie!"

"Joan wrote to me when you began to learn magick from Wilmott." Edemay pierced her with an angry gaze. "She asked me to come help contain your magick. I've lived here for years watching you destroy the coven. I wanted to act, but the elders asked me to wait for the prophecy."

For a moment, Megaera traveled back to the little girl getting scolded for doing something the elders or her mother did not approve of. Uncontrolled magick set fire to all the candles in the room. "I'm not a child. I'm the High Priestess, and you will show me respect."

"Humph. You must earn respect. You forced it on others using fear. Now you beg me to help you. You're impulsive, entitled, and cruel. Your mother would die of shame if only you hadn't killed her."

Edemay flew to the casting table and scooped up the Book of Shadows. She waved it like a victory flag. "The Book of Shadows belongs to Earth Witches."

Edemay whisked away before Megaera could react.

* * *

Emmeline and Gryphon continued to alternate rounds of magick with sex. Each time they cast magick, they could feel the bond between them grow. They discovered they could enhance the strength of each other's magick, making it faster and stronger than when they cast alone. Their last attempt got a little out of control on Emmeline's part. The papers in the small trashcan continued to burn, filling the basement with smoke.

"Let me put out your fire," Gryphon said.

"At least we were smart enough to disengage the smoke alarm this time." Emmeline chuckled as Gryphon manipulated the water hose. His clever fingers danced on the magick in the air. At first, she thought it the smoke from the fire, but then she discovered lavender and green swirls of magick playing on the air currents.

"Can you see how our magick intertwines?" Gryphon rolled over and kissed her exposed neck. Earlier, they'd conjured a pallet to lie on while Emmeline found release for the pent-up energy she made during magick casting.

She wiggled her fingers at the water hose, and it rose to quench the fire in its entirety. Gryphon nibbled on her ear and kissed trails along her breasts before taking one ripe nipple into his mouth.

"Gryphon, stop." When she batted his hand away, the hose remained aloft, so Emmeline willed it to the ground. The enchanted hose snaked away from the trash can. At the same time, Gryphon moved his talented mouth across her belly toward her sensitive mound.

His lips found purchase between her legs. She burned with pleasure and by accident sent magick toward the hose. Snaking its way across the floor, it rose like a cobra ready to strike and shot freezing water at the couple.

"Emmeline," Gryphon pleaded, trying to contain the hose. "Shut your magick down before the bloody hose drowns us both."

"You were in charge of water." Her hysterical laughter continued as the water drenched them. "Why do you think it's my magick?"

"My magick requires—never mind." As he chanted a spell and waved a hand through the air, Emmeline watched swirls of purple and green dust dance on the weak rays of light beaming through the small windows. The hose shut off but hovered in the air, the nozzle aimed at her.

"Don't you dare," Emmeline squealed. Raising a hand, she motioned for the animated hose to return to the floor. The dispirited hose fell with a thump. "Awesome!"

Emmeline climbed on top, straddling Gryphon's hips. Little sizzles of water evaporated as she poured her own heat over his wet, firm body. Steam joined the purple dust in the air. She licked the final drops of water off one nipple at a time.

In a circus-like move, he rolled them over so he was on top, but they were floating in the air. His hot, hard cock lay sandwiched between them, and cool air against her ass stimulated her libido so much, it felt like they were in heaven. Did heaven allow hot, kinky sex?

Their heartbeats synced as he hardened. He was ready every time she got a little excited. At this pace, they would never get any work done. She wrapped her legs around his thighs to pull him closer. She started to wiggle her butt past his thighs, a certain target for her tongue in mind.

After several more successful rounds of sex and play, Emmeline fell to the blankets, completely satiated. "I have so many plans for the whole sex and levitation thing we got going on."

He rolled to his side and nuzzled her neck and ear.

"Gryphon."

"Yes, my sweet witch."

"What's on the ceiling?" Emmeline pointed.

"A message from the Grand Master, perhaps. It has his flair, appearing in the air as it does. We should read it together."

In unison, they read, "The witch and key have found each other. They join their magick to defeat another. In an ancient language, power earned, the tables can be turned. Faith and commitment must accompany the magick leveled on this eve. On the rise of a blood moon where restless spirts abound, Cold Springs rises from the ground. The seventh son and the seventh daughter can triumph over Fire Witch power. So mote it be."

The house shook at the recitation of the last word. The shocks were more powerful than any before. Emmeline's basement windows ruptured, spraying glass everywhere. Nothing remained untouched as the quaking quieted. Alarms from the entire neighborhood could be heard, and the Three Mile Island warning alarm rang across the countryside. Fire house whistles blew from multiple firehouses.

"Holy shit," Emmeline said.

"I would tell you two to get a room, but it would defeat the purpose of my interruption." Luna appeared like a cold, wet blanket smothering their fire.

"What can we do for you, Luna?" Gryphon asked, his voice raspy as he lowered them to the ground.

"Something's happening in the world. You should come." Luna whisked.

"I guess we're out of time to practice," Emmeline said.

They whisked to the living room.

"What in bloody hell took you so long? Turn on the television." Luna sat.

As they flipped on the TV, the newscaster was reporting the magnitude of the earthquake at 4.7 and giving a damage report.

"Biggest in Pennsylvania history. Congratulations," Luna said.

"Crap. We can't keep doing this if every time we do, the earth shatters. Talk about cosmic birth control," Emmeline said.

"In two thousand years, I have never heard of such a reaction occurring after fornication," Luna said.

"Actually, this one was caused because we read a message from…" Emmeline looked at Gryphon. "The ceiling. He said it was the Grand Master. Wait. You're two thousand years old?"

"Stop deflecting. Please dress before they arrive. I would not want to hear those old witches giggle at Gryphon's exposure."

Emmeline flashed a glance at Gryphon and then cast her eyes down her own body. They were stark naked. His muscles flexed. Hard again. The guy was insatiable. She wanted to drag him back to bed and feel his huge cock, hard and demanding, pound into her.

"Shit. What is wrong with me?"

"Emmeline." Gryphon broke the fantasy. "You need to stop projecting your fantasies into my head."

The slide of clothing over her body drew her attention. "Thanks, babe."

Edemay whisked in and lifted her brows. A small smile tipped her lips. "Gryphon. What on Earth have you two been doing?"

Emmeline burst out laughing.

"My apologies, Crone. Emmeline and I were practicing." His eyes widened. "My book. How can I thank you? May the Grand Master reward you for your efforts."

"We don't have time for sex games. I don't know how Betsy put up with it all these years." Edemay handed over the grimoire. "I couldn't find the quilt, and we still need the cauldron."

"How do we retrieve it?" Luna asked.

Betsy whisked in. "Did you feel the last quake? What a doozy. What were you two doing?"

Emmeline and Gryphon answered together. "Practicing."

"Is that what you're calling it?" Betsy raised one eyebrow and winked at Emmeline.

"I say we walk in and take it." Edemay caught everyone's attention.

"I definitely missed something," Betsy said inquiringly.

"I'm trying to finish our plan for getting the cauldron," Edemay said. "We shall walk in and take it."

"Walking into the lair of a Fire Witch, casting druid magick, and getting out alive seems a suicide mission, yet insane enough to work," Gryphon said.

"We're without options. The earthquakes have announced your power. Megaera prepares for the battle with jealousy raging in her mind. She has discovered the time and location of the battle."

"Cold Springs on the rise of a blood moon," Gryphon and Emmeline chimed together.

Betsy lifted another eyebrow. "I can tell the practice has fortified your magick."

"Where's the cauldron?" Emmeline asked.

"The coven bought an estate in Fishing Creek Valley. Megaera calls it the Ivory Tower," Edemay said. "The cauldron sits in the basement."

"We will need a distraction," Gryphon added.

"She would come out of hiding if she thought you the prize, Gryphon." Edemay placed a hand on his arm. "But a few moments ago, her worries centered on the location of the battle and less on acquiring you. Can you wiggle, wiggle?"

"First, you're quoting a Jason Derulo song, and that's just wrong." Emmeline shook her head. "Second, you want to use Gryphon as bait to draw her out into the open? Absolutely not."

"Would someone tell me what has happened," Gryphon interrupted. "Why does Emmeline care if Edemay wiggles, as obscene as it seems?"

"None of it's important," Emmeline said. "Gryphon is not a worm."

"I think it's an appropriate choice, dear. Megaera has trotted after the boy since she could walk. She won't be able to resist," Betsy said.

"Oh, hell," Emmeline said.

"Don't worry, Emmeline." Gryphon took Emmeline's hand. The contact doused her magick, and the wind stopped. "If Megaera wanted me dead, I would have burned at Cold Springs. She protected me by putting me in the box."

"You're all insane." Emmeline stared at the two witches. "How can we protect him?"

"His protection, my dear, remains your responsibility," Edemay said. "You'll figure it out. Use and trust in your magick. Our fate, your fate, and the coven's fate rest in your hands."

"We will try for the cauldron before sundown," Betsy announced. "The red moon rises this eve. The battle's upon us at the Witching Hour."

They spent the next two hours going through the Book of Shadows, searching for any spell that could give them an advantage. Several times, they cast a spell but found it ineffective against fire. After the last round, Emmeline whisked Gryphon to the bedroom, slamming and locking the door.

"You do know they can whisk right in?" Gryphon said.

CHAPTER 21

Cold Springs, PA 2019

Footsteps and whispers forced Emmeline's eyes to open. A glance at the end of the bed revealed one set of furry ears and two old women standing with arms crossed and a dour look on their faces. She moaned with an expelled breath.

"I swear, Emmeline will wear Gryphon out," Edemay said.

"When Kenter and Willa were involved, it took hours," Ben interjected.

Emmeline's eyes widened. The voice was not Luna's. She lifted her head to discover Edemay's black cat grooming himself on top of her dresser.

"You all know this is inappropriate. Right?" Emmeline asked. She pulled the quilt up to her chin and gasped when Gryphon's hand squeezed her breast. She elbowed him.

Gryphon wiggled to a sitting position, wedged against the headboard. "I suppose you're all here to tell us we must move on with our plan."

"If you can walk, yes," Ben said.

The witches snorted a short laugh and whisked out of the room.

"Do I have enough magick to keep them all out of here?

There has to be a spell or something." Emmeline dropped her feet to the floor and stood. With a wave of her hand, she was dressed. "This magick shit has its advantages."

Gryphon leaned away.

"What are you doing?"

"I'm waiting to see what Return punishes you for using magick for your own benefit. I could swear we taught you about the Returns of Three."

"Edemay said she didn't know if—"

A dresser drawer burst open and spewed underwear across the bed.

"Never mind." Emmeline walked to the bathroom.

Half an hour later, Emmeline hid behind a bush in the Ivory Tower's backyard and prepared to use magick to protect Gryphon. Would she find the strength to call her magick when needed?

Even before Emmeline knew Megaera was a witch, the woman always knew how to play on her insecurities. Now, knowing the bitch could combust people with the lift of a finger, her heart sped up as she heard Gryphon call into the house.

"Megaera Caroline, come face your crimes," Gryphon said.

Megaera appeared on the lawn, twenty feet from him. "Gryphon. You don't appear a day older than when I saw you last."

"I do apologize, as I am unable to return the compliment," Gryphon said. "What have you done to yourself? I've seen self-care advertisements. You should make a call."

"You've picked up the new ways faster than I would have guessed. Your little druid continues to excel as an educator." Megaera brought flame to her fingers. They danced as her fingers traced dark magick symbols in the sky. "I'm High Priestess. You should drop to your knees, not insult me."

Emmeline cringed as the oily black slick of power locked on to her position.

"You might as well come out, druid. I can sense your presence." Megaera faced the bush hiding Emmeline.

Emmeline stirred the wind, emerged from the hiding spot, and drew dark clouds over the sun. Betsy had told her it would provide cover for their little caper. She sent a quick brush of air across the space between them. Megaera's hair flicked away from her face.

"Taking a few days off from school, are we?" Megaera chuckled as she took several steps closer. "I see you enjoy playing with the wind."

Finding no need to hide, Emmeline sauntered up to Gryphon and took possession by looping her arm around his. Megaera's smirk fell, and she pinched her lips and flexed her jaw. Emmeline knew it was time to put on big girl panties and find the courage Megaera had taken over two years ago. She swallowed and squeezed Gryphon's arm.

"Gryphon's mine, you fucking old hag." Emmeline stepped in front of Gryphon and cast a burst of air at Megaera. Satisfaction built up her bravado when it pushed the skaggy witch off balance. She planted her feet and set her hands on her hips.

"I'm trying to decide if I'm impressed or not." Megaera levitated and brought flames to her hands. She hovered several feet in the air and scratched her chin. "I'm not."

Gryphon leaned over Emmeline's shoulder and whispered, "Do not let her know your full strength."

"You're foolish to challenge me out here in the open." Megaera moved closer. "I feel your earth magick, little druid. It's weak and ineffectual." She fired a strike of flame toward them. It landed near their feet.

"Did you miss or come up short?" Emmeline taunted Megaera so Gryphon could feed magick to Betsy, Edemay, and Thomas. The three witches whisked into the basement as Gryphon's magick sped over the lawn and found an open window to the basement.

While Megaera postured, drawing flame and dropping shards with precision at their feet, Emmeline caught a glimpse of a large dark object forming near the back of the house. The image wavered before forming a large black cauldron. Emmeline was a bit disappointed the cauldron had the same shape as a Halloween decoration. In retrospect, the idea did have to come from somewhere. Maybe Hallmark was owned by a witch.

"What did you hope to accomplish, arriving here before our prophesized battle? Even I wouldn't test the fates and try before the Witching Hour," Megaera said.

"It didn't stop you from trying to kill me several times over the last two years," Emmeline said. She took several steps forward. "I find it hard to believe you destroy your coven because of an unrequited childhood crush. But lack of sex can make a person—er, a witch—cranky."

Megaera narrowed her eyes and formed fists. Her pinched lips suggested Emmeline's last statement had hit home.

"I agree. I wasted my time. Had I waited, I would have killed only you." Megaera moved lightning fast, shooting flames at the pair.

"I'd hoped to talk you out of this fight." Gryphon pulled Emmeline back against his body. "You already stole a hundred years of my life. Why? You know we were never destined to serve the Grand Master together."

"If you had cooperated, we would have ruled together these last hundred years." Megaera checked beside and behind her, looking for something. "I told you as a child I would sit in the High Seat."

"It was not your destiny," Gryphon said. He pulled Emmeline behind him and continued to prod her. "Emmeline's my destiny. It came with every vision quest the cauldron showed for almost three hundred years. Why would you think different?"

"I will—" Megaera turned her face into the magical breeze.

She sniffed the air. Her eyes widened. "Brimstone? You're trying to distract me."

The cauldron wavered twenty feet above the ground as Betsy, Edemay, and Thomas materialized beneath it, arms raised to keep the vessel aloft. Emmeline smirked as she and Gryphon joined hands and sent a huge push of entwined magick toward the cauldron. In a flash of purple and green sparks, they were gone.

Megaera fired a wild blast of fire at Emmeline. Having little time to think of a way to ward off the incoming attack, Emmeline closed her eyes, waved a hand with the ring in the air and said, "Shower."

A rectangular structure popped up and captured her and Gryphon. As the flames struck, the water spewed over them and doused the outside flames. They remained dry.

"Unconventional, I admit, but effective," Gryphon said. He gave Emmeline a small nod and tried not to laugh. "I think in the future, you should be more descriptive when you call your magick."

Megaera floated to the shower and alighted on the ground. She tapped on the glass. "You think you gained an advantage in stealing the cauldron. But the cauldron's broken. You can't use it anyway."

Megaera's high-pitched cackles cracked the glass, and the shower disintegrated around them.

Emmeline stepped forward and pushed a finger into Megaera's shoulder. "You can't steal something that isn't yours, Megaera. It belongs to the coven," Emmeline said.

"What would you know about the coven?" Megaera asked. "You're nothing but a poor orphan girl who lost everything to my dark magick. Your parents, your twin sister. Everyone you cared about died by my hand. Their druid powers didn't help them at the time, and yours won't help you now."

Emmeline's jaw trembled. She tried to rein in the sadness and anger, but she drifted back to feeling like the new teacher sitting in front of an uncaring, vicious principal. Warmth and comfort spread up through her hand from the ring. Was it strange to think her possible future mother-in-law looked out for her from the grave?

As she lifted her hand in the air, the ring glowed as it warmed her flesh and gave her strength to push away the ugliness. A force of air blew Megaera back several feet. The skaggy witch's eyes widened.

"I will cut my ring from your finger before I send you to the netherworld," Megaera said. She regained her balance and tried to take a step back toward Emmeline.

The ring pumped power into her hand. Emmeline lifted her head and smiled. "I orgasmed the second he slipped the ring on my finger. The stones glowed and the world turned. Later, we reset the ley lines as we fucked each other's brains out."

Megaera narrowed her eyes. "It matters not. The battle's set. The blood moon rises tonight. We'll meet where it all began, and I will destroy you and take what I want. What I deserve." In a blink, she whisked away.

"Well said." Gryphon pulled her to nestle against his chest. His soft lips brushed their way along her neck, and he pressed a kiss on her temple.

Emmeline shivered with excitement. She chided, "Stop that. Now what do we do?"

"I suppose we go to the High Altar and make sure the cauldron arrived." Gryphon held out his hand, palm up. "We shall whisk. I enjoy traveling by your magick."

"I suppose we should." Placing her fingers in his offered palm, she whisked them to the High Altar on the mountain behind Cold Springs. The September air was tinged with cold, but the sun beamed warming rays onto the huge stones covering the summit. Her feet were on a large flat rock bearing ancient symbols. She looked out over the whole valley. "Holy shit."

"Beautiful, isn't it?" Luna asked.

"Only in autumn when the leaves fall can you take in the whole valley," Betsy said.

Thomas arrived with an armload of wood. He set the wood in a pile and smiled. "Welcome to the High Altar, Em."

"Emmeline, come. You should learn about these herbs." Edemay sat with a mortar and pestle in hand. Several dried plants were scattered near her hip as she worked the tools. "We begin with copper for strength and flexibility, spicebush sap for purification, and blackthorn sprouts for warding off dark spirits."

Emmeline looked around for something to do. "Um, should I do something?"

Betsy shrugged her shoulders and deferred to Edemay while Thomas whisked away for more wood.

"No, dear. But stay close. You will have purpose later," Edemay said.

"Great. I think Gryphon owes me a tour of the area." Taking his hand, Emmeline led him down a well-worn trail. Her libido had fired up from the confrontation with Megaera, and she sought a bit of privacy.

"Can I do something for you, my sweet witch?" Gryphon asked.

Emmeline shrugged and offered a shy smile. "You're the closest dick that walked by."

"Indeed." He waved his hand toward an old hemlock with low-swinging branches. "The graceful limbs of this old hemlock hang like a curtain and form a blanket of privacy from the world. I am pleased to know it's still here. It was a favorite of my mother's."

"It smells wonderful. Wait, your mom had sex in the woods with your dad in this exact spot?" Emmeline's smile caught his attention, and she pulled him into the bower. "Shall we visit too?"

Gryphon leaned on a low-hanging limb while Emmeline spread her quilt conjured from home. Sitting down on the blanket, she patted the space beside her, a little twinkle of mischief in her emerald eyes.

Before he had a chance to utter a word, a draft of cool wind blew across his skin, and his clothes disappeared. One particular appendage appeared immune to the cold. He smirked and crossed his arms.

"All the magick we used to confront Megaera plus whisking around has settled in a certain part of my anatomy." Instead of waiting for his reply, she waved her hand.

Without warning, Gryphon ended up flat on his back.

He raised his hand and waved it in the air. Her clothes disappeared. "Two can play the same game."

Emmeline mounted him and trailed hands warmed by the ring across his chest. She traced each muscular ridge, circled around each nipple, and tickled down below his belly button. Gryphon's staccato breathing encouraged her to continue. She felt him harden between her feminine lips.

Emmeline gave a little wiggle and worked her way down his ripped abs until her mouth sat poised at the tip of his engorged cock. The dark red head was already weeping, and her tongue darted out to wipe the head clean.

"Emmeline, I—"

He didn't get to finish as his abs contracted into steel when her tongue lapped the pulsing organ. It seemed sucking him off would become her new favorite way to initiate sex. Maybe it was her druid side, but man-oh-man, he had a spectacular cock. She craved his flavor. His taste of fresh, unrefined mineral salt livened up every tastebud it touched.

One of her hands wrapped around the hot shaft as she sucked it into her mouth. The other free hand reached for his sac. As she rubbed, the lambskin slid over his hard balls, and the rubies in the ring lit up. The red light reflected on his pale flesh and gave his entire package a glow. Wow, talk about family jewels.

Gryphon moaned and tried to sit up. His hands stroked her breasts, and his fingers pinched and twisted her nipples.

"No way. I didn't get my hot shot last time." Emmeline used magick to hold him in place while she worked him into a frenzy. He moaned and threw his head from side to side as he arched his hips. She took him deeper and deeper until his head hit the back of her throat, and he released a stream of hot, salty cream. She swallowed the entire treat.

Neither noticed the rumble beneath them as she swallowed. When she pulled his spent cock from her mouth, licking her lips, a smile formed as he hardened again. Emmeline's eyes flared.

"I must say, I rather enjoy being tied by your magick. Shall we go again?" He lay back with his arms over his head, exposing his entire body to her.

"Just like the energizer bunny, you keep going and going," she said.

Gryphon frowned and tilted his head to question her remark.

Emmeline didn't want to waste time explaining fuzzy battery-operated rabbits. She leaned into him and pressed a kiss to his lips. "I think I'll have another turn."

Emmeline floated over Gryphon's waist and seated herself on his shaft. Inch by tantalizing inch, arching her back, she accommodated his entire length.

Gryphon seemed to forget how to talk. His moan turned into a rumble as she changed positions. She decided she liked his noises and continued moving. "I could stay here forever."

Her eyes widened when he flipped them so he was on top and made his way to her private curls. He threaded his fingers through the fine hair as his lips and tongue found their home. She surrendered to his attention as she came with the insistence of his tongue.

He lifted his weight from her, and they both fell against the tree trunk to catch their breath.

"How many earthquakes did we cause?" Emmeline asked. She played with the fine line of hair trailing over his washboard abs while his finger drew little circles on her shoulder.

"I would imagine one for each time we reached perfection together." Gryphon tilted his head. "Why?"

"I'm still having a hard time imagining doing this during a battle. I think we should keep going right now, to last us the rest of the night."

Gryphon's hands slid along her thighs, and with each wiggle she made, he squeezed harder. She looked forward to finding his fingerprints as bruise marks decorating her thighs tomorrow. If they were alive tomorrow.

At one point, he waved his hand and levitated them from the blanket.

"Softer than the ground," Gryphon said. "I find it difficult to think my mother—"

"You should not go there." Emmeline chuckled.

Gryphon took over control of their activities. He rolled them over, falling between her legs, still embedded in her warm embrace. She enjoyed the increase in rhythm as they approached another climax. In one final thrust, he released.

The earth rumbled, shaking the hemlocks and raining evergreen leaves and several small pinecones on them. He brushed the pine needles and cones from her skin and lowered them to the quilt.

"I hope we didn't do too much damage this time," Emmeline said. She curled under Gryphon's strong arm and laid her head on his chest. A finger circled his nipple in slow, lazy circles while they basked in the aftershock of the ground-shaking lovemaking.

Gryphon stretched a leg, and his foot knocked into the pile of wood pieces from the Witchbox. "Emmeline, why did you bring the box? We no longer need to have it with us."

Sitting up to examine the box, Emmeline levitated it while she rested her chin between her knees. It hung in the air, a macabre three-dimensional puzzle. "I know. But I recognize the pull of magick from it. Maybe we could use it as a distraction in the battle if we could put it back together again."

"Brilliant idea, my little druid." He tried to sit up. "You will have to do it. I fear I am drained of all my strength. Tis all your fault."

"Gryphon."

"Yes, Emmeline."

"Use your magick. You need to practice too." She chuckled.

"Remind me," Gryphon sat up, "to keep you well away from Betsy and Edemay from now on."

Holding a palm up, he levitated the individual pieces, spinning them in the air like a computer graphic. Using his other hand to grab a fistful of pine needles, he brought them to his nose, sniffed them, and sifted them through his fingers over the floating pieces. He chanted a little spell he knew from childhood, and the box began to reassemble in the air.

"Wait," Emmeline said. The pieces quit moving, so she poked at them. "What's the pine for?"

"Something from the earth as an offering. I don't seem to have my pouch of powder with me." Gryphon chuckled, grabbed her hand, and kissed her fingers. "You froze my magick. I much enjoy being at your mercy."

"I'll keep that in mind for another time," Emmeline said. She cocked her head. "I have no idea if it would help, but I think it should go back together differently than before. Could a different configuration affect her magick?"

"Rearranging it is an excellent idea."

"*Children, the old ladies wait for you. There's no more time for play.*" Luna padded into the bower and sat at their feet.

"We'll come along in a few minutes," Gryphon said.

Emmeline followed each piece as Gryphon reassembled the box. He had managed to scramble the top shapes to form a different sentence. She closed one eye and tilted her head as she tried to read the symbols.

"I'm pretty sure the inscription reads, 'To open return what was taken.'"

"Perfect. Now, whisk us back to the cauldron," Gryphon said.

Cold greeted her feet as they whisked back to the altar stone. She glanced down to find herself and Gryphon naked again. "Oops."

Gryphon chuckled, and with the wave of his hand, they were both clothed.

"You could have told me to add the clothes," Emmeline said.

"Emmeline, it's time," Edemay said.

Setting the quilt and Witchbox on a boulder, Emmeline stared at the cauldron. It sat on its little peg-legs beside the fire. Flames reached out and touched the vessel with a sense of urgency; it was as if they needed to touch it. She paced back and forth, her hands together with fingers intertwined. "What if I can't?"

"Emmeline. You can." Gryphon smiled. "I believe in you. I love you."

"I love you too." She felt a rush of relief flowing in her veins. They loved each other. The pacing ended. She locked on to those beautiful lavender eyes, and acceptance and belonging reached out to her like a hand offering help. Emmeline had always wanted the feeling but never thought she'd have it. Needing something real to hang on to in case this dream fell apart, Emmeline conjured a bottle of Jack. "I'm ready."

Gryphon crossed his arms, flashing disapproval. He moved to take the bottle away. She snatched it up before he could take it.

"Let's keep it for later," Emmeline said.

Gryphon walked in a circle around the vessel. His large hand gripped the rim as he ran his hand around the thick cast iron. "Emmeline, come here."

Emmeline circled the extraordinary vessel. She wanted to

touch it but remained an armlength away. At the location of a large crack, she followed the damage as it ran from the rim to a leg. The fissure, now an inch wide, penetrated all the way through the inch-thick iron. A closer examination showed another defect running around the bottom edge and stopping at one of its stubby legs. Any farther and the entire kettle might crack in half.

"It's the spitting image of a Halloween decoration, but bigger than I thought." Emmeline stepped back to take in the huge pot. She glanced over the rim of the chest-high vessel and rubbed her nose. Her voice had a metallic echo as she spoke into its vast internal space. "What's the horrible smell?"

"You smell brimstone," Edemay said. "It comes from the brew to warn witches of evil magick."

"Halloween decorations? Am I missing some information here?" Gryphon asked.

From somewhere deep in the cauldron, a weak, faraway voice shouted, "Save me. Save us."

Checking to see if the others had heard the plea, all she found was four pairs of eyes staring at her. She frowned and tried to encompass the entire vessel in a big hug, the metal warm against her body on the cool fall night. Even adding two more people, the whole cauldron couldn't be encircled. Emmeline closed her eyes to connect to the sentient being living in the iron. She whispered, "I'll try."

The round bottom stood above the ground on four large peg-legs. The base was burned a dull black at the bottom from years in coven fires, and the rest of the bowl felt bumpy as she moved her hands over the cast-iron surface. The cauldron vibrated with pleasure at her touch, as if it found comfort. It was alive, like her ring.

When Emmeline looked up from the cauldron, she said, "I know it sounds like I tipped the Jack, but it asked me for help. I was unable to resist."

"Our cauldron has consciousness," Gryphon said. He

seated his hands over her shoulders and gave her a reassuring squeeze. "It holds the story of our past and the potential of our future. Our cauldron's as old as Stonehenge. The coven brought it to America when we first came to the New World. We cherish our coire as humans would a holy relic."

"It must like you," Betsy said.

"Emmeline, ask your druid magick to heal the vessel. Make it whole again." Edemay pointed to the crack.

"Okay, I will try. How do you heal a cauldron?" Tapping a finger against her lips, she shrugged and whispered, "Heal the cauldron."

Opening one eye, she peeked at the crack. "It didn't work."

"Oh, Emmeline," Betsy said. "You need to tell the elements what to do. Remember, you have to command something from the earth: include it in your magick."

"Right. Let's try again." Emmeline walked over and grabbed a handful of reddish soil. "Red means iron in the soil. Guess we're lucky I studied science."

"Iron in my palm, I wish for you to heal the broken cauldron."

The wind picked up and swirled around the altar. Every grain of earth from her palm lifted on the gentle currents. Particles traveled to the cauldron and swirled around it, waiting but not entering the crack. The wind died, and the material fell to earth in a circle around the vessel.

"What went wrong this time?" Emmeline asked.

"I believe you will need to add fire to forge the metal," Betsy said.

Emmeline redirected her focus to the pile of tinder sitting next to the cauldron. With a quick thought, it caught fire. The wind rose again, and the red earth circled the vessel. Concentrating, she directed the fire into the circle of red earth and changed it into a molten flow of metal. The flow of soil circled the cauldron, and with a wave of her hand, it filled the open wound.

The molten metal glowed red in contrast to the black of the cauldron. It appeared as a bolt of lightning emblazed on the surface. It made her think of lava cooling to its dark crust. Emmeline levitated a bucket of water and splashed the red areas. The hot surface hissed, steam escaped, and the bright red faded to black. Finished, she slapped her hands together to brush off the dirt and then set them on her hips.

"What?" Emmeline noticed the frozen expressions. "I figured it out, okay?"

"How did you know to use all four forms of magick?" Betsy asked.

"Easy. I realized I needed the elements to make my magick work. I remembered to make iron, I needed both fire and water. I added a little breeze to carry the ingredients and water to make it work. And voila." Pointing at the repaired cauldron, she plastered a smile on her face. "Easier than I thought. Now, if you don't mind, I require Gryphon for a moment."

CHAPTER 22

Cold Springs, PA 2019

Megaera whisked to the church ruins at Cold Springs. Even without the walls, the oppressive presence of the Moravians remained. Their stilted religion still drummed in her ears as the craggy old preacher tried to convert the natives and the Mich-Audah, as if his mortal words could keep the coven from giving tribute to the Grand Master.

The cool September air caused Megaera to pull the Priestess cloak tighter. After the earthquakes and Norman, even the neophytes refused to serve her. Now alone, the quiet of the early fall woodlands exemplified her lack of followers. The thought of crushing the herbs herself caused her lip to curl.

Darkness enveloped the old church foundation. The blood moon illuminated the tomb in crimson. The druid stone lay back in place, but signs of a disturbance showed in the leaves. She sniffed the air. "I smell a druid and Earth Witches here."

"High Priestess." A young witch with white-blond hair whisked in beside the stone tomb.

Startled, Megaera jumped several feet across the ground and put a hand over the rapid beat of her black heart. Widened eyes gave away her surprise. Why was there no sign of incoming magick? Staring down her nose at the offensive party, she gave the tiny witch a once-over for any signs of treachery.

From the pointy ears to the booted feet, the girl had a familiar essence about her that she couldn't place. Her tiny stature might confuse some into believing the witch was a child. But in spite of her short stature, just over three feet tall, age showed in her eyes. Not so much with wrinkles or moles, but with the wisdom that poured from the unusual pewter eyes and the gray hidden among the white hair. This witch might exceed five hundred years of age and have Fae blood.

"What do you want?" Megaera asked.

"The blood moon rises," the girl said, pointing at the setting sun on the western side of the valley. The early curve of a large red moon peeked over the ridge.

"Who are you?" Megaera stepped back, unsure of the witch.

"I'm your new apprentice, High Priestess," the girl said. "The Grand Master sent me."

"Why would the Grand Master send you?" Megaera sensed only a small amount of magick in the girl.

"I do not pretend to know the Grand Master's mind." The girl removed a decorated herb satchel from her shoulder and offered it to Megaera. "He told me to give you this."

Megaera took the pouch. Her mother had one similar, before the fires. She opened it. Leather-wrapped packets of herbs filled the center pocket. Unfastening one, she found a whole stem of valerian. The crushed roots would produce a sedative property. The skins surrounding the herbs were old, made perhaps centuries ago.

"If I let you stay and give you work, will you do so without complaint?" Megaera asked. "I prefer my assistants quiet, useful, and already versed in basic chores."

The girl nodded. "I'm exactly what you need. I will stay,

but I'm not from this century. Modern electronics are beyond my skill. I do well with mortar and pestle."

"Do you have a name, what level have you achieved, and can you whisk?" Megaera crossed her arms and tapped a foot with an impatient tempo.

"I'm called Luna and have reached the Second Level." The girl produced a slow smile. "I whisked in, so—"

"Don't sass at me, little witch," Megaera said. "My last advisors were burned to a crisp for insubordination."

"I shall not make the mistake again, High Priestess. What shall I help with first?"

Megaera raised a hand and whisked in a six-foot plastic folding table. Another flick and the Book of Fire, a tablet and pencil, and a broken casting bowl appeared on its surface. Opening to a page in the book, she wrote a list of herbs from a spell and handed them to Luna.

"Prepare these and have them ready in the next hour."

Luna read the list, conjured a mortar and pestle, and pulled several packets from the pouch. Worn and aged, the unusual green granite tools were several hundred years old, maybe even a thousand. The girl moved the broken casting bowl away from the workspace with the flick of a wrist.

A whirling breeze collected an acrid odor of fire and brimstone from the vanishing bowl and blew through the ruins. Megaera heard a whisper. It sounded like multiple people chanting, "Daughter." The blood moon cast red shadows of leafless trees across the ground, and a cold wind settled in the treetops. Shaking her head, Megaera tried to quiet the voices.

"The warlock still haunts me," Megaera whispered.

"Did you need something, Priestess?" Luna asked.

"Nothing. I had a remembrance. Go back to work." Megaera called the Book of Fire to her lap and sat on a chair reviewing the spell for tonight.

Confusion marred Megaera's face. Unable to remember last night, she worried the pages with her fingers. Something was on the edge of her memory. She furrowed her brows and observed the new helper crushing herbs. Her actions were normal for herb crushing, except for the occasional toss of a bit of powder into the air.

"What herb do you—" The earth rumbled, refocusing Megaera's attention on the cause. The druid bitch and Gryphon were practicing magick together. Previous thoughts obliterated, she curled her hands into fists and stomped a foot where she stood. "No spell they cast can save the cauldron. They're fools."

Luna laid out ground packets of the requested herbs in neat rows, arranged by name. As she stood back to examine her work, she offered, "Perhaps the quakes rise from love-making and not magick."

"Do you know where nothing goes? They should align in the order the spell asks for them." Megaera rearranged the herbs.

Luna's pointy ears flickered as if a fly were bothering them.

Megaera wiggled her nose at the strange behavior. Something about the witch didn't fit. Perhaps it came from the large nose on such a small head. She appeared unbalanced and quite ugly. Dismissing her gut feeling, Megaera's attention went back to the tasks at hand.

"In what vessel will you mix the herbs, High Priestess?"

"We will use the—" Megaera realized the casting bowl was broken. "Whisk back to my chambers and bring another bowl."

"I believe the broken bowl I disposed of was your last, High Priestess," the girl said. "I could go find another, but it would take a moon tock or so."

"Moon tock?" What century spit out this being, Megaera wondered. A glance at the helper's strange color returned her memories, including the altercation where the bowl had shattered. As she pulled out of the memory, her eyes came to rest on the druid stone topping the tomb in the ground. She levitated the cap to the table and stared into the stone-encased hole.

"We will combine the herbs in the stone tomb." Megaera crossed her arms, as if the obvious was a genius idea only she could have thought of.

"As you wish, High Priestess." Luna rearranged the table and herbs for the casting of the spell and lit a long black candle.

Studying the spell, Megaera went over each line and the required herbs. She mouthed the last line and pointed to the mineral springs. "Bring water."

Luna whisked in short order and returned with a stainless-steel dog bowl full of water.

Megaera scowled at the vessel but decided to move on. "I will weave a resurrection spell to bring back the town, since the prophecy needs to take place where it began."

"Wise choice, Priestess."

As Megaera read the ingredients, Luna checked each and nodded.

"Wait." Megaera made the assistant stop. "We need the essence of the town. How do I put the essence of a long-gone town into the bowl?" She tapped her chin and played with the errant hair sprouting from a mole on the side of her jaw. "Go find a small stone from the foundation of one of the old buildings."

The young witch whisked and returned seconds later.

"You're sure this rock comes from a foundation?" Megaera took the stone, rolled it around in her hand, and threw it on the ground. "It's not a foundation stone. Can you not tell sand-stone from shale?"

"I'm sorry, High Priestess. I will try again."

"I don't have time for incompetence." Megaera called the flame to her and fired. The strike missed, and as the smoke cleared, a white dog sat where the girl stood. "Beast! I knew there was something wrong about you."

Megaera lifted a hand to strike the dog down. It vanished. Had the familiar even existed, or was it an aberration? A cold wind blew, causing her to shiver even under the weight of the cloak. First traitors, now ghosts.

Megaera pounded her feet on the ground through the forest. Now painted blood-red by the rising moon, the shadows cast from leafless trees rose across the hillside. For the spell, she would need to picture the buildings as they had existed before the fires. She thought about the mercantile, hotels, and post office where coven members greeted human residents in idle chatter about crops and the weather. Megaera had always hated mixing with the humans, and for that matter, most of the coven as well.

Startled by a noise, Megaera raised fire. "What manner of ghosts still haunt these ruins? I have no patience for the foolishness." She spoke in a loud, shaky voice as she walked where the main street of Cold Springs had once been.

Megaera smelled lavender as the earth rumbled. Her jaw tightened as she pictured Gryphon and the slut fornicating somewhere on the mountain. Perhaps if they were preoccupied with sex, they wouldn't be ready when she came.

Continuing to search for the remaining essence of Cold Springs, she heard noises behind her. Bending to pick up a stone, she threw it down. The little wisps of unidentified sounds drew her attention. Haunting by way of the trees, ghosts of long past residents wandered aimlessly through the ruins. Where did they live when at rest?

"Trees hold memories. I need a piece of old hemlock, not a stone."

She lifted her chin to follow the steep slope. The path toward the High Altar remained a faint game trail through the blueberries and laurel. Old hemlock stumps sat below the ridge near the old altar site, so Megaera whisked there. Rubbing her unhealed hip, her attention focused on the sounds seeping out from a hemlock bower. Were the sounds also from the ghosts?

Another earthquake caused her foot to slip, sending Megaera to the ground. The veins in her neck stood out as she stared at the offending place. Rising anger accompanied a replay of the day she'd planned to take over the coven. Kenter and Willa were still alive, fucking in the bower. Her fingertips burst into flames. "I will stand for this no more."

She rubbed her fingers together, and uncontrolled drips of flame fell to the ground and ignited the detritus. Stomping out the little fires, she sneered and searched the area for any witnesses to her lack of control. How, after all these years, could this place still make her feel the fool?

The flames retreated as her breathing slowed, and a cold wind blew down the slope, throwing her off balance. She slipped on frost-tipped leaves and skied down the rather steep slope on her feet. Her arms flailed about in the air, trying to grab something to stop the upcoming crash. Tossing out a magical rope, she ended up face-first in the dirt beside an old hemlock stump.

As she regained her feet, her shoe knocked into something hard. "How fortuitous."

Massaging her hip, she reached for the hemlock stump. Over three feet across, it had short spikes six inches long sticking from the saw cut; it was the only remaining sign of the ancient giant. In another ten years, all signs would disappear, back to the Great Mother where they came from. She grabbed a small vertical piece and pulled, dislodging a splinter. Sticking it into her pocket, she whisked back to the church.

As she materialized, Ben walked the length of the table, his long black tail knocking over candles and sweeping herbs from the table. Without a word, she fired a streak of fire at the beast. It missed and set the pouch of herbs on fire. The cat disappeared without note as she rushed to put out the flames before they crawled to the Book of Fire.

A new object caught her attention, the cat forgotten. The Witchbox, without invitation, sat on top of the Book of Fire. A faint smell of burnt paper rose from where the bottom made contact with a page in the tome.

"Where did you come from?"

If everything was needed back at the beginning, the appearance of the Witchbox made sense. She had used it to trap Gryphon. Little wisps of smoke struggled to leave the book where the box touched. Megaera grabbed it and noticed that a shadow of the shape remained burned into the pages.

"What have you done to my book? Your earth magick can't prevent me from casting spells. You fail. I can still read the words through your burnt shadows."

She examined the box and saw the druid writing. Unable to read the script, she opened the box lid and peered inside. "Ugh, my mother and the need to conform to the coven." She dumped the corn, bean, and squash seeds into the tomb and threw in the box after them. "I do not need silly earth magick to complete my spell."

The blood moon reached its apex above the horizon as Megaera cast the spell. Using the herbs remaining on the table, she sifted them into the tomb. The last additions were a pinch of ground bloodroot and the splinter of hemlock. She sent her fire, and the small tomb burst into flames.

Megaera read the spell. "Taken by fire, by the fire return. The town once here, has since burned. Raise the buildings, raise the coven of brick and wood, and mortal cousins. Return it to its full power, at the time called the Witching Hour."

She tossed the final ingredients into the open tomb, dripped in more fire, and stirred the ingredients. Nothing happened. When she glanced down at the spell, she saw a small arrow at the end pointing to the next page. Strange. She had read the spell several times and never seen the arrow before. Flipping the parchment, she saw the rest of the spell remained unspoken. Calling back her fire, she read the words without thought or tribute to the Three Sisters.

"Awake the souls of those who burned, to reclaim what was never earned. To join the fight for those to lead, the coven strength reclaimed by need. Grand Master's choice, the strongest witch, to lead again, in proper niche. So mote it be."

As she finished chanting the words, her eyes grew large as she realized what the spell did besides bringing back the town. The winds gained strength, trees shook, and the earth trembled as buildings rose. Lightning strikes illuminated sagging roofs and peeling paint on the walls of buildings long past repair. The church bell rang over her head in the wind, chasing Megaera into the streets.

The screams of murdered witches echoed against the leafless trees and bounced back into the main square. Cries for help beat on Megaera's eardrums. She rushed to the town square. The ethereal forms of witches from the past floated in the air. Some moved toward the spring, some lingered on the sidewalks. Too late, she realized her mistake. Not only had she raised the town, but also the spirits of all those who had died in the fires.

"Murderer. Kill her," echoed against the decrepit buildings.

* * *

As the earth rumbled and pushed the old town from its sedimentary grip, Emmeline and the others stood shoulder to shoulder, reading the vision in the cauldron's brew. The earth gave birth to the town in a burst of blood-moon color. Spirits, now free, called for revenge.

Betsy gasped when a vision emerged of Gryphon on his knees in front of Megaera. She grabbed his hand and squeezed. "Take care when she has you on your knees."

"Thank you, seer." Gryphon returned her squeeze.

Emmeline shook her head from side to side and stepped

back when Gryphon reached for her. "How can you be so calm? Where am I in this freaky horror show?"

"We don't know the whole story," Betsy said.

"The cauldron seldom shows us everything. You are not meant to see your own future." Edemay stirred the vision from the brew. "Believe in your magick."

"Where did the vision take place?" Gryphon frowned at the surface of the cauldron.

"Go to the town center. Megaera will come to you," Edemay said.

"You are the dream I never had." Gryphon moved closer to Emmeline and took her hand. Pressing his lips to the back, he vowed, "If I lose, my spirit will always thank the fates for our time together. I love you. I always will."

Gryphon whisked to play his part in the final battle.

Emmeline tried to follow, but Betsy grabbed her hand. "No, my dear. We need Gryphon to show the Grand Master he has what's needed to lead. He needs to face Megaera on his own."

"I know you think you know best. But I'm the Key. I have a part to play as well."

"Go to where it all began," Thomas said. He stepped to Emmeline's side. "It all began at the church. Megaera cast her spell there. You found Gryphon there."

Emmeline leaned forward and pressed a kiss to Thomas's cheek. "You are a good friend."

"Wait." Betsy grabbed her arm. "Do you love him? I mean, love of your life, love him?"

"Yes. I love him." Emmeline pulled out the bottle of bourbon, took a long swallow, put the cap on, and tucked it under her arm. "And I'm going to go stomp some Caroline ass, right now."

Emmeline whisked herself to the church building. It was a bit creepy with four walls, a door, and windows. She pushed open the door and walked down the center aisle. The tomb was exposed, and the Witchbox sat in the bottom. A modern table sat cockeyed over a pulpit. It had a large book lying open next to a series of leather envelopes. A gust of wind rattled the old windows, and the bell sounded from above. She reached for the book.

"Stop," a voice said from a darkened corner.

"What the hell?" Emmeline's heartbeat thumped so loud she could hear it. Calling her magick, she pulled a ball of energy from the air. It glowed blue as it bounced in her palm. "Who's there?"

"I'm impressed, young witch." A shadowy figure floated into view. "Your power is as prophesized."

Emmeline stepped back as she took in the aberration. Dressed in a long skirt and woven shawl, the woman seemed as if she had stepped out of a TV Western. The bonnet was the only piece missing.

"Witches did not wear bonnets."

The ghost, for lack of a better word, stepped into the aisle and floated toward Emmeline.

"Holy shit. You can read my mind?" Emmeline increased the size of her glowing orb and searched the building for another escape. She backed away from the table.

"I cannot read your mind. But I've stayed updated as the years passed. Your time is exciting and wonderful." The figure floated closer to Emmeline. "I'm sorry I missed the wonders of it."

"Who are you?" Emmeline asked. "What do you want?"

"So many questions." Laughter echoed around the church. "I am Joan Caroline."

"Caroline?" Emmeline stepped back again. "You're a Fire Witch!"

"I'm Megaera's mother." Joan floated toward the table. "After all, she was born. Someone needed to have the misfortune."

"You're dead," Emmeline said. "Damn, now ghosts exist. What's next, Bigfoot?"

"Yes," Joan replied. She held up a hand to stave off more questions. "I am dead and a ghost, if it maintains your understanding. The other, I cannot say."

"What do you want?" Emmeline tilted her head. Chipped and peeling paint was visible through the translucent figure. She really was a ghost.

"My daughter cast a spell to bring back the town. In doing, so she also succeeded in releasing ghosts. Ghosts who died the night the town burned. I pay for those evil deeds in my eternity."

The ghost didn't have an aura, so Emmeline was at a loss in determining if she was friend or foe. If talking to Megaera's mother was her job, she'd follow through. She allowed the magick ball to fade. Picking up the bourbon bottle to use as a club, she planted her feet and prepared for a fight.

"No need to waste quality bourbon, child. I do not wish to fight with you." Joan focused on Emmeline's hand. "Gryphon gave you Willa's ring. The fates have picked well."

"I will ask again. What do you want?"

"I wanted to prevent you from a huge mistake. The Book of Fire belongs in the ashes of what Cold Springs became. Its power will corrupt you as it did my daughter."

"Why would you help me?"

"Because I've resided with the Grand Master these last hundred years, and we both agree, Gryphon needs to become the new High Priest and you the High Priestess. Together you will lead the coven in a balanced way and save everyone from my daughter."

Joan floated around to the other side of the open tomb.

"Megaera's corrupted by dark magick and is a little bit, what's the term from today—psycho. Yes. She's psycho."

"Your right about the psycho part. I've dealt with the horrible bitch for the last couple of years now. No offense. She's fucking nuts." Emmeline recovered and reignited her ball of energy, tossing it in the air and holding it there.

Joan ignored her magical threat. "Put your toy away, dear. It has no effect on ghosts, and Gryphon needs you to help him defeat Megaera, navigate your time, and find his full magical potential. He will make terrible mistakes without you."

"Okay. I better go do that." Emmeline turned to leave but found her feet unable to move.

"Not yet. First, you must read from a page of the Book of Fire this one time. When you touch it, ignore the feeling of power it gives you or you'll become like my daughter. After you read it, drop the grimoire into the tomb and go to the town square." Joan Caroline's visage began to waver in and out of sight.

Emmeline approached the book. Its pages flipped open and settled. The ancient druid language stood out like a beacon. She made a point to meet Joan's eyes. "How can I trust you?"

"You only have your own magick. I cannot convince you of my intent." Joan drifted closer. "Trust in yourself. If the book lets you read, you're safe."

Emmeline skimmed her fingers across the page and frowned. She discovered something cold, wet, and sticky. "Eww."

"I should have warned you. Dark magick has a slimy, cold, and wet feeling. Push on. Use the strength Gryphon has awakened in you."

The ghost disappeared, and Emmeline focused her attention on the book, reading the old Gaelic as the words translated in her brain. The earth rumbled, and the old building shook. Dust and pieces of the roof fell on top of the old pews. Loud cracks of lightning skewered the steeple on the old church, and it wavered in the wind. The ringing bell was ear shattering.

"I think that's a bad sign," Emmeline said.

"Quickly, before it's too late," the apparition whispered from the corner.

She read the spell out loud without practice and stumbled

on some of the words. Those damn personal pronouns were a bitch in ancient Gaelic.

"Place of shadows, place of wind, I summon you, my will to bend. We seek to save one of our own, interred by evil, powers grown. I offer you the Book of Fire and an evil witch who casts without Three Sisters in her pyre. The seventh son to find his way, will place her in a darkened grave. In the Witchbox the stone returned. So mote it be."

Emmeline tossed the book into the open tomb. The church continued to shake as she ran out the door. She spotted Gryphon standing in the town square as a bolt of lightning struck the ground and released the distinctive yeast-like aroma of ozone. She yelled so loud her throat hurt.

"Gryphon!"

CHAPTER 23

Cold Springs, PA 2019

Gryphon stood in front of the Grand Hotel. Each building appeared as he remembered. He was headed to the town center when Luna whisked to his side.

"I am happy to have you by my side, my friend."

"I feel the same way."

"I was foolish to ignore the warnings from my two best friends."

"I'm not sure if you could, even if you knew," Luna said. *"The Grand Master would have wanted you to wait for Emmeline. Perhaps it was his and not Megaera's plan."*

"You missed Emmeline healing the cauldron earlier. Where were you?" Gryphon asked. "She is spectacular."

"I'll tell you later. Something wicked and ugly moves in our direction."

A dark figure appeared at the end of the street, hidden by a long cape and hood.

"The hag comes for us."

A high-pitched screeching gained in volume as the dark figure floated into focus. Megaera raised her hand to remove the hood. The fabric of the cloak took on a sinister blood-red color in the moonlight.

"You make it too easy for me." Megaera hissed her words and pointed a crooked finger at Gryphon. "I see the beast remains by your side."

"The blood moon does your complexion no favors." Gryphon placed his hands on both hips. "Your dark magick exacts a great toll. You should have stayed with the light. Even your robe of power weighs you down."

"You know nothing. I have spent years perfecting my magick and gaining power." She raised a glowing hand, the fingertips igniting in flame. "I'm going to make you pay for your treachery. Then I'll enslave you to use as I wish."

"Treachery? You condemned me to a box for over a hundred years, not to mention killing Kenter, my mother, and countless others." Gryphon pulled a ball of light from the darkened night. It appeared purple as the red moonlight blended with blue earth magick.

"They stood in my way. Will you make the same mistake?" Megaera fired a spear of flame.

Gryphon jumped to his left as the fire landed where he had once stood. Megaera's power was evident, as flames continued to burn like a staff lit on fire. The fire illuminated a circle of light encompassing both of them.

He threw the light balls in her direction, only to find the witch had vanished. Within seconds, the crack of lightning broke behind him. The pain stole his breath as the searing hot strike hit his back, knocking him to his knees.

Gryphon doused the flames with water conjured from the atmosphere and assessed his injuries. They would heal, but they could encumber him in a physical fight. He tried to rise but remained in place, held by an oppressive hand of evil.

Megaera circled Gryphon with a lazy stroll. "You won't have the power to defeat me. I will give you the chance to join me."

Coming to rest in front of him, she knelt and lifted his chin. "Join me, Gryphon. Together we can rule both the coven and the world. These mundane humans want someone of power to lead them."

"Rule the world?" Gryphon's eyes widened. He fought to use his magick to pull himself upright. He now stared down at the ugly witch. An ominous presence continued to press down on him, as if gravity had suddenly doubled. His shoulders burned. "Rule the world? How self-absorbed are you?"

Gryphon called the wind. He generated a brisk ground-level force that blew Megaera off balance and left her tangled in the robe on the ground. He smiled as she struggled to dig herself out of the voluminous folds of the cloak as it burst into flames.

He was surprised at the flames. He had not sent them. Had the old witch set herself on fire? Gryphon found Luna behind Megaera. Leave it to her to turn Megaera's magick against her.

Megaera whisked out of the pile of burning fabric and reappeared several feet from Gryphon. Singed by the fire, she threw several more flaming spears toward Gryphon. "Your power grew while you were intombed. You wield fire quite well."

"I will never join you, Megaera." He would let her think he had thrown the fire.

Gryphon levitated and called a sheet of soil from the ground to act as a barrier to her flaming javelins. The sheet smothered two strikes, but a third pushed through, searing a hole in his upper thigh. He fell to the ground, writhing in pain. The heat shot through his body, burning him from the inside.

Luna barked. A bucket of water appeared and dumped over his head. Steam rose into the night, creating a foot-thick layer of fog.

Megaera screamed, "I should have killed you this afternoon." She shot more flames at Gryphon and ignored the familiar.

The strike of fire seared through the muscle and bone of Gryphon's right arm and caught his clothing on fire.

Gryphon mustered enough power to form a mud ball and splashed it over his head to drench the burning clothing and soothe his seared flesh. The relief was short-lived, as fire magick pinned his casting arm and hand to the ground.

Like a vulture circling a recent roadkill, Megaera stalked around Gryphon. A high-pitched screeching laugh proclaimed her victory. "Where's your little druid now? I guess the prophecy exaggerated her threat."

Gryphon grunted as he sat up, trying to evoke some protective magick. The short battle seemed lost. Weakness became his punishment as the Grand Master selected another to serve as High Priest. His eyes widened when he raised his head and Megaera's hand lifted for the final blow.

"It's a shame. We would have made a delightful couple," Megaera said.

A white flash flew across the square, struck Megaera in her midsection, and knocked her off her feet. Luna stood growling on her chest. *"I will not let you hurt my boy!"*

Megaera sent a force of magick at the familiar.

Luna flew across the square and landed in a heap next to the town well.

Gryphon crawled on his knees across the street, inch by inch, toward the familiar. He heard a cackle behind him. A glance over his shoulder confirmed Megaera followed. Step by step toward his doom.

* * *

Cold Springs town square greeted Emmeline like an unwanted nightmare. She followed the ash trail of the fire she'd shot at Megaera moments ago. The old buildings, painted red by the blood moon, were menacing in their silence. She could smell Gryphon's scent as the wind blew and hear

Luna's barking, but a dense fog blocked her from seeing the earth.

Emmeline walked around to the other side of the well. Gryphon was on his knees, leaning over a prone Luna. His shirt was burned away, skin seared, and rivulets of blood dripped down his strong back. His long, beautiful hair was singed shorter in some sections, and an acrid scent lingered in the air. A dark hole in one of his shoulders stole her breath.

Megaera stalked the pair, her steps pounding with purpose in the street charred with fire magick.

Emmeline whisked behind the old witch and said, "Get away from my family."

A gale-force gust carried Megaera to the other side of the square. It dropped her into an empty horse trough in front of the general store. The water was long gone under the pounding drought of 1900.

"You'll have to do better, little witch." Megaera whisked out of the trough and reappeared ten feet from Emmeline. She let out an ear-shattering screech, fire dripping from her fingertips instead of water. "I will take care of you and the abomination in a minute. I need to tuck my little trophy back into his box."

Megaera floated across the road toward Gryphon and levitated him to his feet. Gryphon was suspended in the air like a marionette, his head hung in defeat. She cupped his bruised and bleeding cheek and leaned in to kiss him.

The earth rumbled.

Megaera swung her gaze toward Emmeline.

Luna whisked to sit at Emmeline's feet.

Crossing her arms, Emmeline said, "Put. Him. Down. He's mine!" Her voice, amplified by her magick and anger, echoed against the aged buildings.

Megaera stepped forward to face her.

"When I tell you to, use your magick to move Gryphon out of the way," Emmeline whispered to Luna. She refocused on

Megaera. "I said, he's mine. Bitch. Also, you sucked as a principal.

"Now," Emmeline said to Luna. As Gryphon moved out of the way, she pushed another stream of wind at Megaera. The old witch fell backwards and slammed into the livery.

"Your power's weak. I'm still standing," Megaera said.

"Your roots are showing." Emmeline took a step toward the angry witch.

"You try to hurt me with words. Such a teacher thing to do. Poor little Miss Callen." Megaera raised her skeletal hands sporting long black fingernails now lit with flame. Bloodshot eyes added to her overall putrid facade.

Emmeline lifted her ring hand to throw more magick.

Megaera withdrew her magick. "The ring is mine."

Emmeline realized she had been handed another weapon. Megaera was unable to make her magick work when she was focused on something else. It provided an opening to strike a powerful blow.

"Gryphon gave me the ring, and it warmed as soon as he slid it on my finger." She held her hand up to show Megaera while sending magick into the stones. The rubies glowed. "It gets better. We fucked so hard we caused the biggest earthquake in Pennsylvania history."

Emmeline embellished the story and filled in more details. "I didn't tell you this afternoon, but when he chuckles, it twerks regardless of where it's at. Mmm. Feels so good."

Megaera's face scrunched up, and her pupils dilated.

"His cock's so big," Emmeline modeled it with her hands, "I thought I would die speared by his power. Did you know he has birthmark at the top of his hip in the shape of a crown? And his balls, oh-my-God. Handfuls of lambskin-covered iron. And his cum tastes like a salty sea breeze." Emmeline licked her lips and lowered her eyelids. "Best sex ever."

Megaera's face burned red with anger, and she threw fire from her closed fists. It was wild and out of control. Emmeline had to deflect only two bursts of flame. Using her hand as a shield, she deflected them like a superhero dismissing a beam of energy. The flames struck one of the buildings, igniting the old wood.

"You're burning the town again, Megaera. I thought you learned your lesson the first time."

"I will finish you." Megaera whisked away to the church and the Book of Fire.

"Emmeline," Gryphon yelled. "Release me from her hold."

Emmeline reached out to touch Gryphon and nodded toward the ring. "Release him."

Gryphon jumped to his feet, singed hair draping over his shoulders. The burns on his arms blistered and oozed. Unable to stand his injuries, Emmeline called for more of her magick and healed him on the spot.

Gryphon stared. "I am in awe of your mind as well as your power." He swung his fixed shoulder and flexed his fingers.

"Is that all you like me for?" Her slight smile made her eyes glisten.

Taking the opportunity, Gryphon pulled her into an embrace and kissed her. "We don't have time for me to list everything I love about you. We need to finish this, and perhaps when it's over, we will return to the bower."

Emmeline leaned into the kiss while he tweaked a nipple through her shirt. It was all she needed to fire up her libido to the level at which she could do more damage. Megaera had run, but she wasn't going to get away. She needed to pay for all the deaths she'd caused. Emmeline pulled back from Gryphon's grip.

Gryphon chuckled. "Best sex ever?"

"Truth," Emmeline said. "Now. Where is the old hag?"

"At the beginning," Emmeline and Gryphon said in tandem.

They whisked to the church to find the door unwilling to open.

Emmeline strutted past him, pushed with magick, and slammed open the door. With a bow, she waved him in. "Your majesty, you go first."

A scream sounded, and fire blasted the entrance. Emmeline and Gryphon jumped out of the way as the flames shot out of the church like a fire-breathing dragon warning visitors away.

"What happened to my book?" Megaera was pacing in front of the tomb, talking to herself. She faced the doorway, pointing at Emmeline. "You stupid little druid. You're ruining everything."

Megaera threw flame at Gryphon. He battled the flames with his own magick suspended in the air. They bounced off the shield he drew and returned energy to the earth. But eventually, the bombarding rays broke through and set him on fire.

Emmeline conjured a bucket of water and threw it at the flames bombarding Gryphon. As the water broke the magick, he fell to the earth. The smell of burnt flesh filled the air with a sticky, wax texture. He lay still on the ground.

Another earthquake shook the buildings. The bell rang.

Emmeline waved her hand, and everything was repaired again. "We need to find you some fireproof clothing."

Megaera fired a bolt of lightning at Emmeline. It knocked the druid off her feet and sent her flying twenty feet down the street. The hard landing caused her to gasp in pain. Leaping from the ground, she flew through the air like Superman, her ring hand leading the way.

Megaera continued to blast Emmeline with fire magick. "Why don't you burn?" Megaera shouted as the relentless shots of fire bombarded Emmeline and bounced off.

"Man, if I'd known you couldn't hurt me, I would have told you to go fuck yourself the first day you called me into your office." Emmeline set herself down in the doorway, following Megaera as she retreated into the church. She was bent over like her spine could no longer hold her mass upright.

A sudden quiet settled over the old town, causing everyone

to pause. The wind ceased howling, and a steady rain fell, attempting to douse the fires. Emmeline noticed Gryphon appearing several feet away from Megaera. He was unsteady on his feet.

"You old hag. I should have let you drown the day you fell in the river when we were kids," Gryphon said. He walked toward her with long, steady steps. His predatory pace pushed Megaera one step back toward the bell tower.

Megaera shot flames at Gryphon, who deflected the strikes with his hand. He chanted a powerful spell, generating blue balls of earth magick in his palm. He took Emmeline's ring hand, and the orbs of energy turned into white-hot flames. Together they sent them at Megaera on a gust of air. The impact caused her to stumble.

"Child's play." Megaera waved a hand, and the flames went out.

"Use air then wind magick," Emmeline said. Maintaining their clasped hands, they combined their magick to form an invisible, non-combustible wall of air. They pushed Megaera against the back wall of the steeple staircase. The building shook, and the bell rang again.

"Now!" Emmeline yelled. Together they called up a vicious cloud of soil. A funnel six feet high formed, increased its centrifugal force, and spun right into Megaera.

Megaera screamed in agony, her pleas weak and fading.

The abrasive force of the dirt and debris peeled the flesh from Megaera's hands as the twirling mass pushed the Crone against the ladder. Her face was now skeletal and devoid of flesh, her mouth still screaming as their magick increased its pounding assault.

The windstorm died as Megaera slumped against the ladder. Most of the building had collapsed around them, but the bell tower remained standing. The ladder to the belfry clung to support beams like a skeleton hanging from a tree. It rocked back and forth like a clock, each pass to the left whacking the witch's skull. The dull noise echoed each time against the remaining wall.

Megaera pulled her abraded form forward and she tried to walk. Chunks of flesh plopped with a splat to the disintegrating floorboards.

"You will no longer cast magick, Megaera," Gryphon said. "The coven rejects you as their leader. I, the seventh son of the seventh son, take my rightful place as the High Priest."

Gryphon put his hand in the air and pushed a wall of earth magick toward Megaera. He knocked her into the plastic table.

Emmeline waved her hand, and the table collapsed underneath Megaera's weight.

"Nice touch," Gryphon said.

Emmeline smiled.

Megaera lay on the ground, breathing heavily. Her tacky woven business suit was reduced to threads and clung to the joints of her now exposed skeleton.

Emmeline leaned over. "You're history. Witches and humans will celebrate your demise. You're a horrible being, and the Returns of Three have their revenge."

A new earthquake rumbled. Gryphon pulled Emmeline out of the way as the giant brass bell rang one last time before it fell, crushing Megaera under its weight. Like the wicked witch in the children's story, only her legs and feet stuck out from under the bell.

The final wisps of fire magick returned to the remaining timbers. The wood fragments acted like matches and caught fire. Everything burned, including Megaera.

Emmeline grabbed Gryphon by the hand, and together they whisked outside the foundation. As Emmeline turned to watch the last trace of the building fall to ash on the ground, a horrid odor filtered into her nose. "What's that smell?"

"Brimstone," Gryphon said. "It smells of sulfur, death, and malevolence."

"I'm not sure you can smell malevolence, but I agree it's sulfur," Emmeline said.

"We did it, Emmeline." Gryphon pulled her against his chest and kissed her.

As usual, it curled her toes and kindled a heavy need between her legs.

"One task left to do." Emmeline walked back into the ruins and waved her hand in the air. She levitated the bell and blew all the ash from the pile into the Witchbox sitting open in the tomb.

Emmeline used more magick to close the box and moved the old altar stone on top. She brushed the dirt from her hands. "Sealed inside, the evil witch will never arise again. No Key exists." As she walked away, the druid writing on top of the stone disappeared, and the bell fell to the ground and emitted a muffled dong.

"You wrote a spell?" Gryphon asked.

"I know. It didn't rhyme." Emmeline crossed her arms. "Does it matter?"

"I think not." Gryphon chuckled, lifted his hands, and buried the stone deep in the earth. It would take a miracle for someone to find it again.

In the dim morning light, the remains of the town sank into the earth. Leaves and soil blew over the site. Luna's barking drew their attention. Emmeline saw three ghosts waver in and out of view.

"I know the first one's Joan Caroline." Emmeline held up a hand and waved until Gryphon objected. "We met earlier, and she helped us. I don't know the other two."

"Mother." Gryphon reached out to the second female. Their hands passed through each other. "I have missed you so."

"And I you, my son. I'm proud this night," Willa said.

"Mother, Kenter. This is Emmeline Callen. My everything." Wearing the biggest smile, he pulled Emmeline under his shoulder and showed his mother the ring. "It took to her right away."

"I'm happy for you. She seems to fit with you," Willa said. Her expression seemed less than pleased. "Why does she dress like a man?"

"Holy shit." She leaned back to stroke Gryphon's chin. "Apple-tree."

"When will I understand your words?" Gryphon asked.

"Save us from mothers and daughters-in-law. Don't worry, my son. Even if they don't appear civil, a century and some separate them," Kenter said. "I would pat you on the back, except I am a ghost. Excellent job, by the way."

The ghosts flickered and disappeared. Emmeline and Gryphon dropped to the ground in exhaustion. Holding hands, they both roared with laughter.

Betsy, Edemay, and Thomas whisked into view.

"What a battle!" Luna appeared beside the women.

"It was spectacular." Betsy chuckled. "Emmeline, your power. It's unfathomable."

"What on Earth?" Edemay pointed at a blackened package sitting nearby.

Emmeline got up and walked up to the package. She pulled a clear bottle from the bag: the label read Jack Daniels and was dated 1899. Waving the bottle around with a big smile on her face, she exclaimed, "Joan did say not to waste good bourbon."

She cracked the lid, took a deep swallow, and handed it to Gryphon.

"Why not?" He tipped the bottle as well and handed it to Betsy.

"Oh my. Yes." The old witch grabbed the bottle and swallowed a long draw before passing it off to Edemay. "I think we need to go home. The magick will wash this place clean by the noon sun. You inherit a coven and all it encompasses, my High Priest."

* * *

Everyone whisked themselves to their respective homes.

Emmeline and Gryphon whisked into the backyard as the full morning sun beamed across the colorful fall leaves. His sultry sea breeze scent filtered into her nose, and she sighed as the familiar twitch of need continued between her legs.

"What do you think about?" Gryphon asked.

His deep timbre resonated in her clit as he nuzzled her ear and neck. The rumble sent shivers straight to her core. "Taking you to bed."

"I meant about our battle and victory." Gryphon chuckled. His hand caressed her cheek. "The coven is mine and all it encompasses. It's a big responsibility."

"So I've heard." Not knowing where they stood, Emmeline swished the ground with a foot. Trying to find the words and avoid being clingy, she ventured, "Now what?"

"Besides us ending up back in bed?" A smile curled up from the corners of his full lips. His lavender eyes twinkled. "I need a High Priestess to lead with me."

"Hmm," Emmeline said. "High Priestess. What's the pay? Maybe I'll apply."

"Pay?" Gryphon's head tilted as he flashed an irresistible smile. He pushed his hips against her back, the heat noticeable along with a growing part of his anatomy. "I will render funds right now, if you wish. We should make sure you're well rewarded before the children come along."

"Children?" Emmeline lifted her eyebrows.

"Yes, seven at least. We have to have a seventh. For the next transition of power." His smile grew bigger.

"Uh, seven boys or seven girls?" Her eyes twinkled in mischief.

"Girls? Oh, fates save me. No girls. I don't think I could live through daughters and the dating habits of this time. I cannot imagine the trouble they could drum up."

"Boys, huh? Well, I guess the fates will decide for us."

She lifted his hand, placing hers against his, matching each finger. A short time later, a small earthquake shook the neighborhood, and car alarms blared.

"Can we write an anti-car-alarm-during-sex spell?"

"We can try. I think we're going to need it."

ABOUT THE AUTHOR

From the time she learned to bait a fishing hook, build a childhood fort, and take down her first deer, **Sandra Ramsey** grew up loving the outdoors. She carried the love of musty forest debris and deep evergreen scent into a career as a Wildlife Biologist. After years of research, Sandra shared her love of everything outdoors with students in a thirty-two-year career, teaching Environmental Science and Biology to Pennsylvania youth. Her books reflect the love of the natural world, the mystery of myths and legends, and the power of love.

Please let me know what you did and did not like about the book in a review on:
Amazon, Good Reads, Sandra Ramsey on Facebook, or
Writingdogmom@gmail.com

www.ingramcontent.com/pod-product-compliance
Lightning Source LLC
Chambersburg PA
CBHW071527260626
47170CB00002B/541

* 9 7 9 8 9 8 7 4 2 9 3 0 3 *